THE TWIN

AMANDA BROOKFIELD

Boldwood

First published in Great Britain in 2025 by Boldwood Books Ltd.

Copyright © Amanda Brookfield, 2025

Cover Design by Becky Glibbery

Cover Images: iStock

A CIP catalogue record for this book is available from the British Library.

Paperback ISBN 978-1-83561-451-8

Large Print ISBN 978-1-83561-449-5

Hardback ISBN 978-1-83561-448-8

Ebook ISBN 978-1-83561-450-1

Kindle ISBN 978-1-83561-452-5

Audio CD ISBN 978-1-83561-443-3

MP3 CD ISBN 978-1-83561-444-0

Digital audio download ISBN 978-1-83561-447-1

This book is printed on certified sustainable paper. Boldwood Books is dedicated to putting sustainability at the heart of our business. For more information please visit https://www.boldwoodbooks.com/about-us/sustainability/

Boldwood Books Ltd, 23 Bowerdean Street, London, SW6 3TN

www.boldwoodbooks.com

For the other Amanda

Truly, we live with mysteries too marvelous to be understood.

— MARY OLIVER

NOTE FROM THE AUTHOR

I am lucky enough to have a twin brother, but he is nowhere within the pages of this novel.

BEFORE

1976

Through the bars of my cot, I see her across the room. She is brushing her long red hair. Her eyes are closed and she is turning her head this way and that, sweeping the brush down, again, again, again. When her eyes flick open, so blue and startled, seeing me, her face lights up. She presses a finger to her mouth and points with the hairbrush at the cot alongside mine. I do not look where she points. I keep my gaze on her. My mother, firing out love like a sunbeam.

* * *

Rob and I sit in a green bath, slapping the water with our palms to make the foam fly. On a stool beside us, the big towel over her knees, our mother leans back against the wall, watching with dreamy eyes, blinking slowly as she smiles. Her cheekbones are pebbles trying to push out of her face, and her skin is mottled white, like the ceiling. Gathered back off her face, her hair bursts out of a clip on the crown of her head, twisting and tumbling over her shoulders.

I splash harder and harder. I want her to laugh. I want her to move. I am better at it than Rob, who gets water in his eyes and starts to cry. She comes to life then, plucking first him, then me, out of the bath, folding us up in the towel, blowing funny noises into our necks until we giggle.

2022

1

CATHERINE

At the last moment, I kick off my flats and swap the staid, dark trouser suit for a short, black dress. Full of flattering Lycra, it hugs my bust and hips, showing I still have a waistline, unlike Joanne... I stop myself. To want to get one over on her on such a day – what sort of monster am I? I start to peel the dress off, but then let it fall. I am digging deep just to make it out of the house. And what are clothes anyway, but camouflage. Something to hide inside. I sway as Rob shimmers at the back of my mind, model-handsome, whether in tatty shorts and flip-flops, or the close-fitting, blue suit that, back in the day, I used to tease made him look like a wannabe film star, and he'd laugh in that easy way that showed me we still had our connection. Deep down, beneath all the other stuff.

The dress is for parties, not funerals. It needs proper shoes. I pluck out my smartest black heels from the pit of the wardrobe, spitting on them and rubbing with a tissue to heighten the shine. My bare feet, hot from sorrow and the day's mounting heat, fight the tight, black, patent leather. Squeezed inside, my pinched toes throb, but to be uncomfortable feels right, somehow. A reminder I should feel lucky to be alive. Or something. A wisp of eyeliner, a dab of colour on the mouth. Tissues. I pluck a fistful from the box on my dressing table and shove them into my handbag, and then gaze at my reflection in the full-length mirror pinned to the inside of the wardrobe door. I see a good-for-her-age forty-seven-year-old with long, wavy, auburn hair and big, scared, blue eyes, her slim legs looking unsteady in towering heels. I see a small person trying to look taller. A scared person trying to appear brave.

I can sense Al waiting downstairs, twiddling the car and house keys, checking his phone. I make it out onto the landing and then have to pause to breathe. Air in, air out. Things that should happen automatically. My ankles are jelly. Below me, at the bottom of the stairs, the front door is wide open, framing Al on the drive beside the car, a black hulk against the backdrop of fierce, blue, August sky. As I reach the hall, he steps back into the house.

'Okay?' He bends to brush his lips against my head, closing his hand round my elbow. Such mighty hands, big as garden forks, yet his schematics spiral from them like gossamer webs, filling the thick, white pages of his work pads.

'I'm fine.'

'Okay.' He releases my arm.

'The dogs?'

'Already in the kitchen.'

I nod, longing suddenly to feel the warm bodies of Belle and Bobby, our two big mutts, bouncing under my palms, celebrating every encounter as dogs do, as if they know without telling that each good moment needs cherishing, just in case it turns out to be the last. But Al will have settled them with treats and closed the door and it would be too cruel to raise and dash their doggy hopes. Left free to roam, they'd be upstairs in seconds, to sprawl and snore on our bed. 'She'll be asking for a cup of tea, next,' Al had laughed, catching Belle – a gift to me in a cardboard box when we made the move to Dorset ten years ago – with her huge head actually on one of our pillows, making sure to take a pic before booting her off.

'Is Tamsin coming?'

'She said she'd try.' I sound like I believe she might, when I have already steeled myself for the opposite. Tamsin is with Jules in Dublin, enjoying new love and a well-earned treat of two weeks off. Oldest friend as well as work partner, I know how much she deserves the break, the extent of the ask.

'And anything from the dreaded Oliver?'

'No, thank God. Jesus, Al, I don't know what I was even thinking, including him in the notification email.'

'Maybe you wanted to give him a jolt,' Al says mildly.

'Maybe.' A jolt – yes, that could be it. I half-relish the distraction of having to think about the sly, quiet half-sibling I haven't seen for thirty years, nowadays – according to the smug Christmas e-greetings that started arriving, out of the blue, a few years ago – running some sort of high-stakes investment company in New York, with a child in tow as well as a wife.

Oliver, Faith and Amelia wish you Happy Holidays!

If the paragraph of news is especially nauseating, I read it out so Al can share the laugh before I delete it.

Faith has found a new channel for her creative spirit through enrolment in an art class – Picasso watch out! Amelia is loving her violin and chess club. Oliver is heading up City-Tech's Global Outreach Program and has been learning how to make his own sourdough starter...

While Al locks up, I crouch down and watch a fat bee bobbing between the browning lavender in the tub by our front door. I snap off a few sprigs for myself. Lavender means something, doesn't it? Remembrance? Serenity? *Something.*

In the car, the seat burns the backs of my thighs through the thin black dress. I have been clasping the lavender sprigs too hard, turning them to dusty shreds. Their aroma, faint and sweet, drifts up from my lap. Al fiddles with the car satnav, though we know the way to Salisbury well enough. From there it is the ring road and then ten minutes north.

'It's saying an hour and ten.'

'Maybe Joanne will turn me away.'

'Come on now, Cath, not today. She's asked you to do a reading, for Goodness sake.'

John Donne. *Death, thou shalt die,* according to its last line. Really? The poem has been chosen by my sister-in-law like everything else. The task of standing in front of everyone, declaiming lines of preachy poetry I do not believe, sits in my head, an impossible mountain to climb. I try to reach for Rob in my mind, but only get him in pieces, as he used to be. His smile. The blue eyes, much more translucent than mine. The floppy, copper-gold hair. The mildness of his manner and a voice so gentle and low-timbred that you could only ascertain the shades in his moods by knowing him well and listening hard. During the rare get-togethers of the last decade, I have never seen Joanne doing that. She has her own agenda, my sister-in-law, and I am not part of it.

The road running beside our house is busy with traffic going to and from the Dorset coast. Al edges out of our narrow drive, hunching over the steering wheel to wait for a gap he can swing into. He is breathing heavily in the way large men do. His grey shirt is already damp and creased across his back, rucking badly where it is coming untucked from his dark, smart trousers.

Beside me, a doughty sparrow perches in the privet hedge bordering the drive, only just visible within the thicket, parched brittle brown like so much else after the recent late-summer heatwave.

'She'll be in the first seat in the front pew, no doubt. With her parents and the girls.'

'Of course she will, Cath – as shall we be, I'm sure, on the other side.' I can hear the exasperation in his voice. 'There will be two sets of pews, and he *was* her husband.'

'Yes, and he was my brother, and my...' I can't get my mouth round the next word, and Al, who knows it anyway and who has heard it all – and much more – before, a million times, sighs heavily, shaking his head.

As we join the road, I keep my gaze on my window, filling now with the blur of yellow-brown lawns and stubbly fields. I know I am talking nonsense about pews and so much else. All I can think is how many ways there are of losing someone; how being dead or alive can have nothing to do with it.

'It will be all right, okay?' Al pats my leg.

'Okay,' I say, because I love him, and in this one thing he is powerless and I don't want him to feel any worse about that than he does already. This day had been coming – I knew that much, despite the old, old battle of feeling I was being kept at bay – even towards the end. But I thought there would be more time. You always think there will be more time.

BEFORE

1977–79

Our father, gruff and business-like in his shiny two-piece suit, starts doing our breakfast: two bowls of Frosties, and toast – with golden syrup. Not enough butter and not enough syrup across the too-brittle, too-blackened squares. The hand working the knife is always full of haste, because he is late for his job at the bank, and it is our fault. Our mother appears in her dressing gown to give him a goodbye kiss at the door, then strokes our heads as she gently steers us back to the sofa where she will doze while we play and watch TV.

One day, she stays in bed instead of on the sofa and a friend we don't know called Diane comes by. She has a twangy accent because she is American, and red lipstick circling big teeth and an even bigger smile. But her large, slightly bulbous, green eyes make us wary, as do the thick, brightly coloured, elasticated headbands stapling her wispy, light-brown hair to her narrow head. She takes us to the swings by the supermarket and sits on the bench as we play, glancing occasionally over the top of the knitting that accompanies her everywhere in a faded, saggy, blue velvet bag. Scarves, jumpers, hats, she says, when we ask about the lumpy, growing chunks of wool dangling off fat needles, all destined for 'charidee', because doing good in this world is the Lord's command.

Indoors, Diane's favourite thing – apart from knitting – is for us to be quiet, even when we are playing tag, or decking ourselves in the big floppy hats, shoes and chunky necklaces from the dressing-up box. Because it is only without noise, or disturbance of any kind, she warns, over and over, her needles clacking like loose teeth, that our mother will get better from her operation. Aged four, this fills us with conflictions, because of how often we fail. For, even when we think we are quiet, it turns out we are not. Laughter is loud. Being happy is loud. Being sad is even louder.

Along the corridor, our mother shakes a small metal hand bell if she needs something – like a cup of tea, or a peeled orange, or us. At the first hint of its tinkle, Rob and I elbow and barrel our way into the room, for pirate games on the bed, or stories, or answering her questions about our day. We try to settle and attend. Most of all, we like to moan about Diane: how we hate her lumpy meat pies and the way she tells us what to do. But our mother says Diane is a good person from church who has had her own troubles, and who is a long way from home, just doing her best. Which is all anyone can do, she adds, kissing the tops of our heads. It won't be for long, she promises, because the doctors have taken the badness out and soon everything will go back to normal. Just the four of us. Like before.

* * *

Rob and I start proper school, a long walk from home, round the edge of the playground, through the shopping centre, and past the garage. Our father takes us on his way to work, his hands enveloping ours like too-big gloves, his long strides meaning we have to trot to keep up. We have a teacher called Miss Price, who says twins must be separated for their own good, but Rob cries when we are directed to tables in different rows, causing titters round the classroom. In the playground, beefy Brendon Slater, with his fleshy mouth and missing front teeth, starts following Rob everywhere, chanting 'Cry-baby Carrot-boy'. One day, I kick Brendon in the shins and he collapses with screams that turn into smirks once they grow loud enough to summon Miss Price. I am made to say sorry – to Brendon, to Miss Price, to the Head, and to my father, for my nastiness and the shame I have caused. He promises not to speak of it to our mother – because of how it would upset her – but he tells Diane.

'Sticks and stones will break your bones but names will never hurt you,' she declares, after cornering me alone to deliver her own long scolding. She is wrong, I explain, because being called Cry-baby Carrot-boy definitely did hurt Rob. From nowhere, her hand flies out and lands across my cheek. I am insolent, she hisses, the bulging eyes burning, and must learn not to answer back. My face throbs, but I do not cry. She wants me to, I can tell, and it makes me strong.

2

CATHERINE

The Salisbury ring road is solid. Al turns up the air con and drums his fingers impatiently on the steering wheel. He has an aversion to being late, from countless childhood mortifications generated by the poor time-keeping of his parents. I prefer punctuality too, but also have no desire to arrive at the funeral of my forty-seven-year-old twin brother. Getting stuck in traffic would offer a crude solution to that at least.

'The ring road needs a ring road,' I offer, because we have come to a halt again, and I can feel the tension pulsing out of Al's beautiful heart. He manages a dry chuckle. I close my eyes, feeling their grittiness from too much crying and not enough sleep. What was it like, Rob, to *die*? I wonder, biting my lip so hard that I taste a little blood.

'It clears by the roundabout,' Al reports. 'Twenty minutes, but at least that means we'll still be in time.'

'Right.'

'Got your words?'

'Yep.' I hug my bag in which the famous fourteen lines sit waiting for me, treble-spaced and font size sixteen, on a folded

A4 page. 'After we get back, I might do the afternoon walk alone. If that's okay.'

'Whatever you need, love, whatever you need.'

'Thanks, Al.' I want to cry because he is so kind. Even with the stress of the traffic. He has a wisdom about him, a stillness, which I picked up on the first time we met and which made me agree to a second date even though he was too old and not my type, with his lumbering body and almost bald head. His wife, Sandi, had been gone for over two years by then, taking their toddler son, Ryan, with her, in order to make a new life with a man called Mark, not only a fellow architect but Al's erstwhile best friend. It turned out the pair of them had had a thing for ages – even before the wedding, Al suspected, despite Sandi's denials. He had had to fight for a paternity test, and then for decent shared custody rights, even after the test had confirmed that Ryan was his.

But the net – *net* – result of all the pain, Al had told me, in his simple, steady way on our second date, was learning, properly, how to let the distress go; how to accept the currents of the universe, instead of fighting them. He was building a good relationship with Ryan, he said, whom he would have loved even if he hadn't been his own, because love was about more than gene pools, wasn't it. His big brown eyes had bored into mine across the sticky wine bar table, and I'd had to look away because of how my stomach was flipping. Before I knew it, some of my own twenty-six years of baggage came tumbling out, about the bad early days and still living with Rob – how we looked out for each other. I even told him about the thing with Jed Levy, the married university lecturer, which had only recently ended, five years on from my graduation. It had gone on so long precisely because of my *not* loving him, I explained – because that made it emotionally undemanding and ruled out the possibility of hurt – all of which Al had seemed, immediately, to understand.

'I'd certainly like to meet this twin brother of yours,' he said when we parted, 'if and when you are both ready.'

'Which might be never,' I had shot back, suddenly feeling the need to put the brakes on, because it was, after all, only an online dating site that had got us together and the man could be an axe-murderer for all I knew.

'That goes without saying.' Al had smiled his vast smile, unperturbed. 'I like you, Cath. Wherever this goes. It's all good.'

* * *

It could be a wedding, I think, when at last we've parked on a solid mud hump of a verge a good hundred yards beyond the small country church, and trekked back – me already bitterly regretting my show-off heels – to the wooden entrance gate decked with a garland of white roses. A narrow tarmac path leads up between the headstones towards the church entrance, where Joanne is waiting to greet arrivals, her face masked by a black, dotted gauze veil.

'You're supposed to say the hellos afterwards, aren't you?' I hiss to Al as we join the tail-end of the queue of mourners, not one of whom I recognise.

He shrugs, running a finger round the inside of his shirt collar in a vain bid to cool his neck.

I glance again at my sister-in-law, whose imposing, full-figured frame is elegantly covered by a loose black pyramid of a dress, behind which Laura and Stephanie, the eight and ten-year-old nieces whom I wish I knew better, peep like mice. They have the same dark hair as their mother and have grown leggier since I last saw them: two peas from the same pod, a fact which

Joanne likes to emphasise by dressing them in identical clothes. Today, it is tight, black, cotton dresses with lace trim round the necklines, and narrow, polished, black shoes, all of which I would tug off and fling into the shrubbery if I could. I deserve to suffer to look smart, but surely not these dear little girls, on this airless day, with the heat pumping down from above and up through the ground, and with their stricken hearts. Being young *and* sad, it can be complicated. Confusing. That Herculean shift from having a sick parent to a dead one.

As we shuffle nearer, the cluster of well-wishers ahead of us slowly thinning out, I manage to catch the eye of Laura, the eight-year-old. I see a flicker of hesitation pass through her expression before she gives me a tentative wave. I wave back, a little madly, my throat swelling both for her and because of the glimpse of Rob in the cupid's bow of her small, half-smiling mouth.

'Catherine?'

I turn at the voice, which comes from a tall, slim man in a light grey suit striding up the path, a yellow silk tie flapping against a crisp white shirt. The smart cut of the suit, the faint tan of his skin and the way his collar-length light-brown hair has been brushed back off his face suggest the chicness of serious wealth.

'Oliver.' I have to force the word from my throat, while my brain performs a swift, incredulous recalibration of the spoilt, tell-tale twelve-year-old shrimp of a half-sibling Rob and I waved out of our lives three decades ago. A steady job in our step-grandfather's real estate company in Seattle, free accommodation in the family home prior to finding their own place – it was too good an opportunity to pass up, our father had explained, by way of justification for the move. After all the years of his stop-start jobs in the backrooms of high-street

banks, the rows with our stepmother over money, it certainly
made sense. Just eighteen and having started courses at the
London Poly and Bedford College – Rob doing Business Studies,
and me History – my brother and I had quickly gathered that
there was no question of us getting on the plane with them.
There'd be visits soon enough, our father explained, along with
regular financial support. In the meantime, we had three
months' rent to run on the Wandsworth estate flat, plus our
university grants and bar jobs, to keep us afloat. It was Al, on
hearing this piece of my history, who first used the word *abandonment*. Although, all Rob and I had felt at the time was excitement. Freedom from castigating adults! Independence! Money!
Visits to America! We couldn't wait for the goodbyes, and would
probably have felt the same – for a while anyway – even had we
known they were to be our last. It took a few months – for the
aloneness – the difficulties – to set in.

'I am sorry for your loss, Catherine.'

The strength of the American accent is almost as much of a
shock as the fact of his presence. As I reach out – an automaton
– to accept the smooth, slender outstretched hand, it is Rob's
childhood voice – full of our shared loathing and mockery – that
erupts in my head. *Baby Oliver! Tell-tale! Wimp!* Because, yes,
words can hurt.

Oliver's hand encases my fingers. The pale-green eyes that
meet mine bulge a little, as they always did, just like his mother's. I jerk free with an involuntary gasp that's half a sob.

'It was good of you to come,' says Al, wading in. 'I am Alastair Boland, Cath's partner.'

'Nice to meet you, Alastair. I'm on a Europe trip – for work –
so I figured I could get here in order to offer my condolences in
person.' Oliver smiles as they shake hands, clasping Al's forearm
with his other hand, as if they are old pals, before returning his

attention to me. 'I was so sorry to hear Robert had passed, Catherine. Please accept my—'

'He hasn't *passed*,' I hiss, before I can stop myself, 'he has *died*.'

'Okay. Sure. I didn't mean to – look, I'm real sorry, okay? I had no notion he was sick...'

'No, you didn't,' I mutter, cursing again both my own moment of madness in copying the man into my Rob-has-died email and whatever online sleuth-work had got me onto his festive hit-list. *Lost the battle with cancer* was all I had said before the brief funeral details, not up to sharing the cruel facts: the small freckle, lurking on the underside of his left calf, a miniature time-bomb, ticking silent and unseen; the lockdowns contributing to the too-late diagnosis. 'So maybe get yours checked, okay, Sis?' Rob had advised in his light way, on one of the rare occasions my sister-in-law had sanctioned an actual visit. It had been just after a second round of chemo, when he was wiped out, but with hopes high. He had pulled his mask down to talk and made a comical to-do of hoicking up his left leg to show off the scarred pothole where the mole had been.

Oliver flaps his yellow, silk tie. 'I hope bringing some colour today was okay.'

'I don't know why you are here, Oliver,' I snap, a loose cannon now, despite knowing it is neither the place nor the time. 'I don't know why you've come. I wish you hadn't. The right to mourn someone has to be earned.'

'Cath, come on now,' Al growls, touching my elbow. I allow him to propel me away, because all at once, we are at the head of the greeting queue.

'Cath.' Joanne's expression behind the black dots is inscrutable. She doesn't hug me, keeping an arm round each of the girls, who squirm, dropping their gazes to their hateful footwear. Their mother's mouth, just visible below the hem of her veil, looks swollen and chewed.

'Joanne.' For all the awfulness – the awkwardness – of not being liked, compassion pierces me. Al was right to call me out. The woman has lost her husband. She has become a single mother to two young girls. She is devastated. The fact that I have endured a decade of being at the mercy of her gate-keeping – even, dear God, with only weeks to go – none of that *should* matter now, or ever again. 'I am sorry for your loss,' I splutter, fighting my own tears, aware that I have summoned Oliver's opening platitude to my aid.

'Thank you, Cath. And I for yours. I am so glad that you agreed to do the Donne reading. Rob would be too. It was on his shortlist.'

Shortlist? Why didn't I know about that?

Al's arm arrives across my shoulders. He bends towards Joanne to plant a half-kiss on the veil where it hangs over her cheek. 'We'll see you afterwards,' he says, gently steering me into the church like some carer dealing with a difficult charge.

BEFORE
1981

We are sent to the Isle of Wight to spend the summer with Granny Jean, who we've heard of but never met. Our father takes us on the ferry, where we cling to the railings, shrieking at the beat of the wind and the noisy heave of the sea, too lost to the adventure of the moment to worry that we are soon to be left.

'All right, Ian?' Granny Jean, waiting on the quayside beside a rusty, red bubble car, tightens the knot of the purple headscarf doing a poor job of reining in her straggly white hair. Despite the July warmth, she is dressed for winter, in a padded, mud-coloured coat that stops halfway down short, wide legs encased in thick beige tights. We have no idea that we are witnessing a seismic family rapprochement. Our mother's German personality – it had been marrying the enemy in Granny Jean's eyes, having had to raise her only son alone and in penury because of the war.

'Yes. You too, I hope, Mother.'

'Mustn't complain.'

'Thanks for this. We need a break. They can be a bit of a handful, and with Greta so under the weather...'

'I am truly sorry she's not well, Ian.'

Rob and I, hanging onto our father's arms now, exchange looks. There have been no pirate games in recent days, only summonings for holding and stories.

Rob starts to cry as our small, bulging, shared blue suitcase is stowed in the boot and we are herded onto the back seat of the little car.

'Be good now, you two,' our father instructs, having planted a kiss on each of our heads, and putting his face in the frame of the open front passenger window once Granny Jean is behind the wheel. His dark eyes are glassy. 'I'll see you soon.'

'In six weeks,' Granny Jean growls.

He stands erect on the pavement as we drive away, one arm held up in a farewell salute. In the distance behind him, the ferry that will carry him back across the water hoots its approach.

'There now,' says Granny Jean as Rob's tears become convulsions, while I swallow mine down, feeling the heat of his misery and the need to counter it. 'I've got someone I want you two chickadees to help me look after – small and away from his mum just like you.' She reaches into a basket in the footwell of the front passenger seat – causing the car to swerve so violently that Rob and I fall against each other – and holds up a small, squeaking, wiry-haired, brown dog. 'Say hello to Pip,' she cries, making the car rock again as she turns to deposit the animal into our laps.

We both gasp. Rob forgets to cry. We have never met a dog up close before, let alone a puppy.

'If he nips, give him a rap on the nose,' Granny Jean shouts as the puppy clambers and wriggles under our stroking. 'His teeth are sharp as tacks. And this is in case he piddles.' She reaches again into the basket and lobs a rag of a towel over her shoulder.

When the puppy suddenly falls asleep in the chink of space between us, Rob and I hardly dare breathe. The car roars on, careering round the bends of a winding road that hugs the ups and downs of the coast. Spread out alongside it, as far as we can see, is the sea, transformed from the choppy, grey stuff that the ferry ploughed through, into a vast, flat, glittering magic carpet, its glare blinding in the July afternoon sun.

Granny Jean points out her cottage long before we reach it, perched alone – a white stone dropped from the skies – on the green spread of its own clifftop.

* * *

'Hold hands,' barks Granny Jean as we stand on the station concourse six weeks later, surrounded by whistles and screeches and people. She is in charge of the blue suitcase, which has slowed our progress on and off the train. 'He said he'd be here.' She looks about her and we can sense her unease. Central London is closer to our world, but she is far away from hers. She looks tinier and more ancient among the crowds, with the towering ceiling overhead, pigeons swooping between its dirty panes. Rob and I pull on each other's hands, swinging and half-hopping on the spot, trying to stay in charge of our excited bodies, maddened already by Granny Jean's doubt and fluster.

'We stay right here,' she says, as if commanding herself for once, hoisting her big handbag higher onto her shoulder. 'Under the clock. That's what he said.' She gestures upwards, directing our attention to four clock faces pointing in different directions. 'Now stop fidgeting, the pair of you.'

We try. We know Granny Jean hates fidgeting, just as we now know that the blue worms in her skin, kept in check by the thick tights, are called varicose veins, and that a tin containing biscuits, with faded birds on it, can be reached by standing on the wobbly kitchen table – preferably with me leading operations, being bolder and a little bit taller. Indeed, after six weeks, we are brimming with insider knowledge about life in the little hill-top house: how our grandmother likes to fall asleep in the big chair by the fireplace, and then wake up and pretend it never happened; how she sips honey-coloured liquid from a big glass after her supper and snores so loudly in her bed that we can hear it from our bunk beds along the passageway, as we lie talking not sleeping. We have learnt too to lick our lips and rub our stomachs in anticipation of meals, especially if it is a Sunday roast, or shepherds' pie, or toad-in-the-hole, or apple crumble, or any of her homemade ice creams, breads, cakes and jams, asking for seconds – and thirds, if we dare. The effects are plain to see, in our fuller faces and the too-tight buttons and too-short sleeves and hems of our clothes. We have spent more time outside than in, always with Pip tumbling at our heels. We can swim, though Rob is still happier with arm-bands, and we have tanned, freckled faces and bodies, apart from the comically clear, protected white shapes of our swimming costumes. There is less orange in our hair and more gold. Our fringes are zigzags, and we have sticky-out clumps round our ears from Granny Jean's efforts with her big kitchen scissors. We have acquired toothless smiles like Brendon Slater and have two precious sixpences each to show for it. The entire wall of six weeks – all forty-two days of it – has crumbled with us barely noticing. We feel altered: older, full of tales to tell, our excitement about going home marred only by the wrench of having had to part from Pip. But we are going to ask our parents for a puppy, we have decided, encouraged by Granny Jean, who says a dog always improves a human.

Thanks to the station crowds – it is the afternoon rush hour,

Granny Jean grumbles – our father manages to arrive at our sides without any of us observing his approach. He has a moustache – a thick, black line flecked with grey – which scrapes my cheek as he kisses me, momentarily puncturing my joy because of not being part of the father I have known and kept safe inside my head.

'Children, Mother – how nice to see you all.' He pulls us to him, and for a moment, we bury our faces in his trousers, drinking in the forgotten but instantly familiar scent of home. But there is so much to tell, and soon we are jumping up at him, shouting over each other, about Pip chasing crabs, and being able to swim, and visiting a castle, and going out in a boat with a fisherman. When none of it seems to impress quite as we had imagined, we grow shriller. He tells us to calm down and to say a big thank you to Granny Jean who has to catch her train back home.

'Thank you, Mother,' he says, after we have chimed our 'thank you Granny Jean' in unison. He holds out his hand but she pushes past it, locking her stout arms round his waist and staying there even though she has knocked the blue suitcase flying. Her head only comes up to his ribs, but on she clings, pressing the side of her face against him, her eyes tight shut and leaking tears.

'They are good children, Ian. You can send them any time.'

Rob and I make pop-eyed faces at each other. To know we shall see Pip again is good. But for now, our focus is home.

'Thank you, Mother. That is kind. I shall almost certainly take you up on it.' Our father has to unhook her arms from around his waist.

'We had a fine time, didn't we, my lambs?' Granny Jean says, dabbing at the wet corners of her eyes with one of the big hankies that has AR stitched into the corner, while our father picks up the suitcase. The AR is another thing we know about, the letters standing for Alfred Reynolds, the grandfather whose airplane got shot down and crashed into the sea during the war. 'Come here, then, both of you. Be good and brave for your father, won't you, my chucks.'

We mumble assent, submitting somewhat warily to a bosomy embrace that bears no resemblance to the hair-ruffles and head-pats with which we are familiar. 'If your father says you can come again, you shall,' she declares in a thick voice, pushing us back towards him suddenly, before stomping off into the early-evening crowds.

On the outward journey, we had come by Tube and bus, but it is in a taxi that we set off for home. Waiting in the queue outside the station, our father gives us a packet of Refreshers to share, and listens better to our chatter, saying well done about swimming and for being good, but that our Ackland Court flat is much too small for a dog. 'Next summer, you can go again and see more of Pip,' he promises, 'if Granny Jean doesn't change her mind.'

He waits until we are sitting on either side of him in the black taxi, moving slowly past a towering brown wall of blocked-in arches, before clearing his throat and saying that while we were away, our mother got very ill indeed because the bad lump in her tummy came back. 'So ill that there was nothing more the doctors could do. She didn't want you to stop having your lovely holiday. She said she loved you both.'

'But when will we see her?' Rob asks, speaking first for once, but only because he is too dumb to understand.

Our father swivels his head to the taxi window, twisting his mouth into funny lines. 'I'm afraid you won't see her, Robby. Mummy got so sick that she died. It is very sad, but she is with

God in heaven now, where we shall see her again one day. For now, we must all be brave.'

'But when?' Rob repeats, swinging his legs so hard that his heels thump against the underneath of the taxi seat. 'I want to see Mummy now.'

Through my window, I keep my eyes fixed on the tall brown arches, which are bricked in and therefore stupid. Why have an arch you can't walk through? 'She is dead, Rob,' I shout through my terror. 'That means we won't see her again ever.'

Rob begins to howl, and our father pulls him onto his lap, and me into the crook of his arm. I don't cry. I stare up at my father's moustache – part of this new unbearable world – hating it, blaming it.

'I want Mummy,' Rob bellows. Over and over. For both of us.

Our father presses us so hard against him that it hurts. 'I do too, Robby. But we shall manage. With God's will. And with Diane, who has kindly agreed to carry on helping. She was a good friend to your mother and has come through her own difficulties.' His voice creaks. 'Mummy was very happy that you two were having such a nice time. Soon, we can visit where she has been buried and give her some flowers. Remember, she is in heaven and looking down on us all right this minute, not wanting you and Cath to be sad.'

From the crook of his arm, I stare up at the dingy brown ceiling of the cab, wondering how anyone could see through it, even from heaven.

When the taxi pulls up outside our block, our father gets out first, with the case, and then tells us to stand still while he pays the driver. He fumbles with his wallet and we stay near him, Rob still sobbing, streams of slime dangling from his nostrils. Out of the corner of my eye, I catch a glimpse of a shadow of a person behind the net curtains in our front room and my heart explodes. Mummy! She is not dead after all! Everything will be as it was! Just like she said! But when the door opens, it is Diane who emerges, in a purple dress and the faded yellow apron that lives on the hook on the back of our kitchen door. Her thin hair has been pinned off her forehead with a bright-green hairband and her narrow face is lit up with the reddened lips which she is eager to press against our cheeks. She kisses our father first, though, right on his mouth.

3

CATHERINE

'What exactly made you do it, Cath? I mean, it sounds like quite a...' Tamsin clears her throat. 'Quite a *thing* to have done.' We have hugged and talked – at length – about Rob and the service, and she is now peering over the rim of her laptop, her dark blue, thick-lashed eyes full of the kindness that comes as naturally to her as breathing. Not a hell-raiser, like me. Not a ranting, judgemental mourner who, at the wake following her twin brother's funeral and cremation, managed, somehow, to tip a glass of wine over his widow. White wine, just half a glass – a small glass – and leaving only an inky patch on the black dress – but still.

'I'm not sure how – or whether I actually meant to.' I have buried my face in my hands behind the shield of my own laptop. 'The glass, it just sort of slipped *forwards*.' I know Tam has been holding back on quizzing me, not wanting to pile pressure onto my still fragile state. Ten days on, and, at my insistence, we are in my kitchen, touching base as we always do, to go through upcoming events and take stock of our workload – a steady amount, what with the continuing post-pandemic bounce back and the recent spell of Mediterranean weather. Routine, rhythm, getting back to normal – I am certain it's the tonic I need.

Tamsin is properly returned from Ireland – and Jules – a two-week idyll broken only by the monumental feat of flying to and from England in order to attend the funeral, arriving late because of traffic, and having to leap straight back into her hire car after the committal at the crematorium, in order to perform the whole rigmarole of the journey in reverse. My first inkling of this heroic effort had been catching sight of her behind a pillar at the back of the small, already full church as I stepped down from the podium, the print-out of Donne's celebrated fourteen lines crumpled and damp in my hands, my throat still burning from the choking effort of having to read them aloud. To have such a friend – prepared to undertake such a journey, despite being on a precious break with the newly-discovered Love of Her Life – had made all the half-held-in tears flow. So much so that I froze, as everything – Tam's blue dress, the faces of the congregation, the small stained-glass windows, brilliant with sunshine – turned to porridge, until Al was there, leading me back to the pew.

'Oh God, Tam.' I part my fingers to meet her gaze over the screen of my laptop. 'I've written to say sorry, offered to pay for dry-cleaning, sent a pot-plant – an orchid, a beautiful pink one in full bloom. There's been nothing back, but then, for once, I can hardly blame the woman. Also, in between being kind, I think Al might be deep-down furious with me,' I confess hollowly. 'And of course he's right to be so. Al's always right. But honestly, Tam, I really don't remember *how* it happened. Except that I was trying to say something to the girls and she sort of yanked them back and I stepped forwards and... splat. Chaos. But there you go. It cannot be undone, and I have done my best to *atone*.' I sit up, sliding my hands off my face, endeavouring to blink the spreadsheet in front of me into focus. The best figures in the fifteen years since I founded the little event management company of which Tam is now co-partner, and I feel nothing.

Tamsin blows out her cheeks, her soft wide face creased with gentle concern. 'Well done for saying sorry and the pot-plant. Nothing says it like flowers.' She pulls a goofy face.

I want to tell her that it's too soon for being funny, but know this would be ungrateful, as well as heaping wrong on wrong. I nod instead, aware of the worsening grittiness under my eyelids from another bad night, and the drip-drip sense of having been cut loose from whatever invisible tether was responsible for keeping me on solid ground. 'It was something to do with the way she pulled the girls out of reach, like I was *infected*,' I burst out, needing for my own sake to go over it again. 'Outside the church – when we arrived – she did it then too.' I scroll up and down through the spreadsheet, not seeing it. 'To lose a parent – I *know* how that feels, Tam. I *know* some things to say that might help. I am their *aunt*, for God's sake, despite being treated like a pariah all these years,' I hurtle on, forgetting my private vow to avoid this territory altogether, 'never letting me *in*, not even right at the very end, when Rob was so close to...' For all my admonitions to Oliver about the right language for death, I find that I cannot, in this moment, make my mouth pronounce the word.

'But no one knew when the exact end was coming, did they?' Tam offers carefully. 'And you *had* visited – a lovely visit, you said, when he was full of hope about those new trials – not that long before. And, I'm sorry, darling, but at least Joanne was there when it happened. At least he wasn't alone.'

'Yup. At least there's that.' I've been forgetting to breathe again, I realise, flooding my lungs with air and releasing it slowly. 'I am glad too, that he wasn't alone. But you can't deny what a *gatekeeper* she was, Tam. How she *screened* his entire life, over-milking the bloody pandemic—'

'I know that it has always felt that way to you, dearest Cath.' She eyes me calmly, patiently – like Al, she has heard it all before. But, even more than Al, she remains the consummate diplomat, incapable of saying anything horrible to or about anyone, a quality that accounts not only for her friendship with me, but also – by her own admission – for the crap she has taken in relationships over the years, letting herself get trampled on and not making a fuss until her self-esteem is in shreds. For similar reasons, Tam has the perfect touch when it comes to dealing with the many close-to-meltdown clients who call on our services. Milestone events with big price tags, the stakes are always high. Birthdays and anniversaries tend to be more plain-sailing, but the planning for weddings and memorials often requires her patient expertise – soothing and cajoling where I would crash in with both feet.

'I don't think a Joanne conversation would be helpful to you right now, sweetie,' she says tactfully. 'She got her hooks into your brother a long time ago. End of. Whether he truly loved her for it, we shall never know. She certainly made him and the girls her entire life, and now she's somehow got to regroup. It will be hard for her too, that's the one thing you can be sure of.'

'I know, I know,' I wail, 'and I do not wish her ill, Tam. How could I?' I blink at her, managing a rueful smile.

'And as for Oliver showing up—'

'Can we not waste our breath on him. Tea?' I get up to fill the kettle, stepping across both dogs, who have a knack of lying exactly in whatever path I need to tread, preferring to be tripped over rather than ignored, which I sort of understand, even though it drives me nuts.

'No, thanks. I'd better make tracks.'

'Okay.' I put the kettle on its stand and turn it on anyway. 'Thanks for your amazingness, Tam.' I pluck a damp tissue from my jeans pocket and bury my nose in it.

'You are mad with grief,' Tamsin says solemnly, 'but it will get better, Cath. Somehow, it *will*.'

'Yup. Of course it will.' I ball the tissue in my palm and post it into the bin, riding a sudden glorious wave of feeling almost normal again. The zigzags, being okay and then not, coming and going of their own accord, are in themselves draining. 'I think I might write again to Joanne, beg even harder for her forgiveness. Or just call round. What do you think?'

Tamsin looks up from her screen, where she is closing down tabs. 'What I think, sweetheart, is that you must do whatever feels right for you. Though, maybe just leave Joanne alone for a little while. Let time perform its magic.'

'Yes. Good thinking, Batman.' The kettle has boiled but Tam is clearly going and I can't face the bother of tea without her. 'Hey, why not stay for a quick proper drink? It's gone five o'clock, after all.'

'Sorry, but Jules is arriving soon.' She throws me a sheepish smile, like she's guilty about her new happiness, so I cross the room to give her a hug, because she shouldn't be.

'Good luck with our Kent Bridezilla on Saturday,' I tease, wanting her to know that underneath everything, I am still alive and functioning. 'If she calls with more changes, just say a big fat no, despite any histrionics.' I release her and open the fridge to pull out a beer for myself.

'The September Kent nightmare shall remain totally under control,' she promises merrily, sliding her laptop into her rucksack and reaching for her bike helmet. 'Though I'm not sure she is back speaking to her mother yet.'

'All from a falling-out over table decorations. Jeez.' I swig the beer, which tastes fantastic.

'But nothing can touch the Great Vegetarian Canapés War of 2018, can it? Do you remember, the endless tastings, and the *actual* food-fight?'

'Indelibly etched on my heart.' I laugh at the same time as trying to take another swig of beer, choking a little – hysteria beckoning – as the bubbles fizz up the back of my nose.

'And on our bank balance,' Tam quips, pulling her crossed-eyes face and bending down to tighten the laces of what look like new cycling shoes – electric blue with yellow laces. Since Jules, she has been on a fresh fitness drive, dusting off the serious bicycle bought when she moved into her father's Ring-wood bungalow – instead of selling it – eight years before. Though the fitness plans had quickly fizzled out, the move had ensured the blossoming of our little business and our friendship – to the point where newcomers on either front haven't had a look-in.

'Love suits you, Tam.' I grin at her as she straightens, thinking of all the stop-starts until Jules – six months ago – offering a lift when Tam's car had broken down. I am blinking back tears as she crosses the room to give me and my beer bottle a bear hug.

'Have you thought about talking to anyone, sweetie? Grief counselling? It might help?'

'I've got Al, and he's given me a great grief book – all about the stages. Angry, denying, sad. *Acceptance*.' Inside, I can feel one of the tsunamis coming. A heat stirring deep in my bones and behind my eyes. But Tam has been stalwart enough and it must be fended off. 'Al really gets it. He loved Rob too, remember, from back in the days when we all actually spent proper time together, when Joanne was winning us round instead of pushing us away...' I plug the beer bottle into my mouth – giving my lips something to do other than repeat old complaints and tremble. 'And anyway,' I swallow a mouthful of beer, and the lump in my throat, 'the waiting lists for referrals are still miles long from all the people with legitimate reasons to fall apart.'

'Grief is legitimate, Cath.' On the doorstep, she fiddles with the zip of her rucksack, then with the chinstrap on her helmet. 'Jules is planning a small birthday lunch for me when she's over in October. It's the last Sunday of the month. We'd love you and Al to come. Bring the dogs and we can do a nice post-prandial walk. She's dying to meet you. And before you say it, I know I've been keeping her to myself – it's from not wanting to jinx things. Okay? But it's high time.'

'Super.' I am gripping the bottle so hard it is in danger of shooting out of my hand. 'We'll be there.' My throat is on fire. My voice sounds wrong – tight, not mine – but I am on the brink now, and losing the fight not to show it.

'You take care,' she cries, at last, scootering to check the road is clear, before settling herself properly into the saddle and pedalling off.

'You too,' I shriek, because it is only with violence that I can get the words out.

I stumble back into the house, along the hall, and fall onto the sofa, clutching my beer as my chest heaves. The dogs arrive on either side, puzzled, alarmed, trying to burrow their muzzles under my arms, but I am the animal, howling, with nothing left to give them, or anyone.

4

OLIVER

Oliver swallowed several times to counter the familiar tightening in his ears as the plane climbed steeply. Through his window, the grey sprawl of Frankfurt quickly receded to a blur, taking the triumphs and tensions of his most recent meetings with it. Lately, he had sometimes caught himself wondering why being successful – eventually – had to involve getting bigger. He was great at multi-tasking – thrived on it – but now there were occasional days when he felt stretched so taut, it was like he was one snap away from... what?

Oliver didn't know, and had been doing his best to ignore such moments, focusing on his manifold blessings instead. Like having his darling wife and daughter. Their tight, loving unit of a family felt more of a miracle with each passing day, for being so exactly what he had dreamed of within hours of meeting Faith, a few weeks after arriving in New York as a rookie corporate banker fourteen years before. Dazzled by her beauty and sweet nature, and the speed with which he was introduced to and embraced by her huge, warm, functioning family, Oliver knew at once that he had found the treasure he sought. The treasure he had never known.

The new European expansion programme of his venture capital fund was another cause for gratitude, despite the additional work it was bringing. Founded with a techy, hand-picked crew from his Harvard days, Oliver was happy to be the 'arts grad' of the group, leading on travel, because he was good with people and because – thankfully – personal interfacing still formed the bedrock of each deal. Faith, understandably, wasn't crazy about the role and he couldn't blame her. On this trip, what with the funeral diversion, he had already been away for two entire weeks. He missed her terribly, not to mention their home, a roomy, four-bedroomed apartment on the Upper East Side with a balcony overlooking the park, where Faith nurtured potted shrubs and herbs with her customary magical, home-maker touch. Most of all, Oliver missed Amelia, who, apart from making his heart explode with love every time he looked at her, had to be the smartest six-year-old the world had ever seen.

'Daddy,' she had asked, when he Face-Timed home from his hotel room the previous evening, pushing her pixie face right up close to the screen, so he could see the flecks of gold in the big brown eyes inherited from her mother, 'if the world is like a big ball, how come we don't fall off of it?'

And when Oliver explained about gravity, she had wrinkled up her little nose and said in her cute earnest way, 'But *gravity* means *serious*. So that's just dumb.'

Her mind was so sharp, so pure, so fresh – a blotter ready to soak up anything and everything – and still so utterly without the need to be afraid, that Oliver, remembering the unsafe world of his own childhood, choked just to think of it. And yet, here he was, choosing to add twenty-four more hours to an already long spell away, missing vital bits of the best thing that had ever happened to him.

But then, being away – being in the sky – there was definitely something calming about it, Oliver reflected, opening his eyes an hour later, astonished and delighted that he had slept. Perspective. Time out. A freedom of sorts. And here was the English coast already. He stared out of his small oval window, marvelling – for the second time in a week – at the tidy, crazy smallness of the country in which he had spent the first twelve and a half years of his life. The amount of green in its rural patchwork quilt of a landscape was astonishing, and kind of weird too, for being so totally at odds with his own, difficult memories of concrete and of conflict; with the drip-drip torment of the twins, and his mother, ready to blow at any moment – even if it was never at him.

'We live in your home town, honey,' he had pointed out gently, when breaking the news to Faith about wanting to make this second visit, since all three living generations of her clan were based within Manhattan, Maine and Connecticut, including a maternal grandmother who, at the age of ninety-one, still baked cookies, kept bees, and took offence if she wasn't allowed to host Thanksgiving. Oliver's parents couldn't have offered a greater contrast, holed up and sniping at each other in the Seattle Senior Assisted Living Facility that cost him twenty thousand dollars a month. The family real estate business had gone under when the sub-prime crisis blew and he had been supporting them ever since, doing his best by them because they were all he had. Now aged eighty-one and eighty-eight and in declining health, his mother's determination to pick holes in everything seemed to have spread to all their interactions, like rampant mould, Oliver often thought grimly. What was on the TV, the efficacy of the heating dial, the shortcomings of the home in general and of his father in particular – nothing escaped her crossfire. Sometimes, on his solo visits, Oliver put his headphones on, pretending to have to log into a meeting, just to get some peace.

At the front of the plane, the flight attendant bobbed into view from the galley with a tray of glasses. Champagne and orange juice. He would have one of each, Oliver decided, unbuckling his seat belt and settling his thin frame more comfortably in the wide seat. It was only a two-hour flight, and he wasn't in the mood for snacks. He tweaked his trousers to loosen them at the knees, wishing, as he always did on glimpsing the narrowness of his legs, that some of the gym labours he squeezed into his busy life could produce more obvious effects. At least to his thighs. Instead, no matter how heavy the weights he lifted, nor how many miles he accomplished on the home exercise bike or running round Central Park, his muscles hardened without getting bigger. Like they were compacting into themselves. Faith exercised to shake off weight – especially since having Amelia – and he to gain it. It had become one of the many little jokes between them over the years. Like her *needing* Hershey Kisses with her Sunday morning oat milk latte and his inability to occupy the same room as a spider without freaking out. Jokes that were about loving someone, Oliver had mused during the course of their most recent phone call, for every single foible in their being.

'Okay honey, seeing as it is just one more night and kind of makes sense,' she had said in her sweet way about the extra visit, which this time was to take a look at his old London home, 'you being so near and all. Though we're planning Europe for next summer, right? I mean, we could go then instead? Check out those London roots of yours together?'

'We could, but I just want to touch base on my own first,'

Oliver had countered, trying to explain something he hardly understood himself. Curiosity was part of it – wanting to *see*, literally, how far he had come, from a scrawny, shy, unhappy kid living in a concrete box of an apartment on the ground floor of a sprawling, South London block, to the owner of a piece of Manhattan real estate of which most people could only dream. But encountering Catherine again after so long had stirred something else – twenty-nine years older, with little dents at the corners of those sharp, cornflower-blue eyes, but otherwise utterly unchanged: the gold-red hair a glossy curtain, and all the bullying, angry energy still spitting inside.

The moment when she'd flung her wine over Robert's poor widow, Oliver had almost dropped his own glass. He had been standing in a corner with Joanne's father, a spry, eagle-eyed man in his late seventies, keen to tell Oliver how he had employed Robert in his Andover-based engineering company for fifteen years. They had both frozen mid-flow – as had the entire room, a near-comic tableau of disbelief – until Catherine's partner, Alastair, had moved in with apologies and wads of paper napkins, mopping up the damage in all regards.

'Bloody woman,' Joanne's father had muttered, leaving Oliver's side to join the fray, scooping up the smaller granddaughter and glaring at Catherine and Alastair's retreating backs. At which point, the mom had arrived too, the spit of her daughter, but larger, with fat pearls instead of a gold locket round her neck. She had clasped Joanne to her ample chest, even though Joanne herself – rigid and wide-eyed – looked like she neither needed nor wanted it.

Oliver had got the hell out. He felt bad for Robert's distraught and now wine-wetted widow, who had greeted him warmly, despite the weight in her heart, but it was Catherine who stuck like a stone in his mind. People did not change, that was the lesson. No matter how much your own memories of them might have mellowed, or the grown-up decency you had tried to show in establishing contact and reaching out. Two black sheep, his mother had liked to call the pair of them, back in the very early Seattle days when it had still been permissible for the offspring from his father's first marriage to come up in conversation. But even then, it was always clear to Oliver that Catherine was the bad one, pulling the hapless Robert along in her wake, leading the trouble-making.

Oliver had caught his evening flight back to Geneva and thrown himself into the Clean Energy Forum that had started the following day. Seventy-two whole hours mixing with potential investors in their favoured field – it was a gem of an opportunity and Oliver had networked and pitched every aspect of it tirelessly, posting progress reports back to New York each evening and using the tail-end of the week for some follow-up meetings. Then there had been other leads to chase in Milan and Brussels before Frankfurt. No one could ever accuse him of not working hard. And he slept well too, thanks to the pills he used when travelling.

It was only during his final 6 a.m. run on a treadmill in the hotel basement gym that morning, fighting grogginess and the absurd urge to compete with the much younger man pounding at higher speeds next to him, that the notion of what this second visit might entail crystallised into reality. It was Heathrow this time, a night at the Hilton. A rental car for the hour-or-so drive. He had fixed it all up, researched the route. South West London. Wandsworth. The street – the actual door behind which he was born. Google Maps, which he looked at before he showered, showed the place was still standing. He could maybe check out a

few other old haunts, like the big school near the railway line –
so generously paid for by his American grandfather – where
he'd learnt ball skills as well as the liberating power of his own
brain.

5

CATHERINE

'Are you sure you're up to it?' Al peers at me from behind the stand-up worktop – parked on the far side of his actual desk – where he likes to sketch. Beside him, in heaps across the floor, as well as in the normally pristine workspace surrounding his keyboard and computer, lies a swamp of papers from a much-moaned-about effort to see off his tax return. His autumn is already manic, I know, what with a Stockbridge barn conversion on its fourth revision and a big Southampton school extension project to be getting on with – a bid Al had won against impossible odds five months before. A little fish beating the big sharks, he had rejoiced afterwards, gleefully firing the cork of a celebratory bottle of champagne across the kitchen. We had drunk the whole lot very quickly, wolfing packets of crisps and peanuts, before slipping into making love, first on the sitting-room sofa, and then on the floor, much to the bemusement of the dogs – until they were banished to the kitchen.

'I've been *summoned*, remember?' I click my fingers. 'By *her* who must be obeyed.' I hang on the door, feigning lightness of heart, because being worried about is starting to feel like a burden amongst so much else, and because deep down, a part of me is rather relishing the prospect – at last – of a face-to-face with my sister-in-law. Al is chewing gum, a sure sign he is stressed, and I have no desire to add to his woes. 'I love you,' I say, partly because I do, and partly in concern at how his teeth are tearing at the gum. The memory of the celebratory sex is also with me, stirring a sort of nostalgia for pre-Rob-less days, not just before his diagnosis, but afterwards too, when there was at least still hope, because there always is.

'Come here, you.' He beckons me over and engulfs me in his hefty arms. I press myself against him, savouring – needing – his solidity and size. The closeness of our physical bond remains our cornerstone, Al having the capacity to make me feel as if he is as much inside my skin as his own, that every hum of my pleasure is his to create, control and relish equally. As I do him, he says.

'I could come with you, Cath. Moral support.'

'I shall be fine and you are going to have a lovely, quiet day, getting things done.' I make a playful to-do of having to bend my knees and wriggle downwards to escape his embrace. Making love, even a quickie, would have made Al so happy, I know. It has been weeks now, but he has been holding off, sensing my mindset, as he always does. 'I'll take the dogs with me – they're so good in the car – and then I can do their walk on the way back. I might stop near Everley, where there's a manor house by a river that I need to check out – the owners have asked if we'd be interested in having it on our books. When I get back, I'll fix us a nice spaghetti. I'll get the mince out of the freezer for it now.' At the mention of one of his favourite meals, Al's kind, round face lights up, so transformed that I feel almost guilty at how very easy life can be, when you know what to say to make someone happy.

In the car, with Belle and Bobby loaded into the roomy boot, I re-read Joanne's email.

Dear Cath, I hope you are well...

Well? How can I be *well*? Is she *well*? I moan out loud at the woman's unfailing capacity to provoke, which prompts the dogs to sit up and cock their heads, their soulful, questioning faces filling the rear-view mirror. I have done a heinous thing, I remind myself. It is a miracle my sister-in-law is writing to me at all. And saying she hopes I am well is because she is trying to be nice.

I would be very grateful if you had time to drop by tomorrow morning, any time between eleven and twelve.
    With apologies for the short notice – I am still struggling to get on top of things.
    Joanne

I too, am *struggling*, I wanted to – but of course didn't – write back, saying thank you instead, and how glad I was to hear from her, and yes, I would certainly be able to call round in her suggested window. I then made a list on my phone of all the things I would like to say during the encounter, complete with tactful turns of phrase.

As I set off however, it is the unhelpful, familiar sensation of being treated like some starving underling that surges – always being kept at bay, like a near-stranger expected to be grateful for any stale crumbs that happen to get scattered her way. Before long, the old seething is upon me. My brother's *gaoler*, that was what Joanne had morphed into. Early charm and then – boof! – she stole him away – to Wiltshire, to a desk-job with *Daddy*, and a family life spreading no wider than her own parents, and apparently so hectic that there was never any room in it for me, let alone Al. Not even after we, too, had removed ourselves from the London rat race to within an hour's drive of their front door. Al, peacemaker and sweetheart, liked to point out that there were no rules in families and that Rob could make his own choices, and Tam invariably said Joanne was Joanne and to let it be, but they didn't *know* my brother as I did. His own equally peace-loving soul. How he soaked everything up rather than fighting it; not so much a lamb to the slaughter as a lamb half-broken and yearning for a quiet life, even after he found out that his cough was not just a cough...

I am stuck behind a hay-baler, stalks of straw flying into my windscreen as it trundles. In the rear-view mirror, I note that a line of traffic has already formed. Vehicles are taking it in turns to pull out and accelerate past, shooting me looks of critical bafflement as they go, because the stretch of road ahead is straight and clear. But in the out-of-control aloneness of the car, my brain has bumped me on from Joanne to the other awfulness of what befell my beloved brother: all the months of not wanting to make a fuss, about headaches, swollen glands and a hacking cough; all the months of 'staying at home to save the NHS.' Eight worsening, wasted months.

I am grateful to the hay-baler, because for a couple of minutes, I can barely see to drive.

* * *

Parking nearby, I redo the big clasp losing the battle to keep hair off my face and rummage in my bag for the list on my phone. *Things To Say.* My eyes travel down the screen. Somehow, it had got quite long. More of an essay, in fact. My phone battery is blinking amber, so I turn it off. I know it all anyway.

I stride towards the house. Just Joanne's house now, I have to remind myself, managing a smile for the man on his knees chiselling at weeds in the front garden. My brother is dead and Joanne wants the garden nice. That's not a crime, even if it almost feels like one. At the front door, I take a breath, manifesting a calm which obligingly arrives, even when a glance to the window on my left summons a memory of Rob standing on the other side of the pane during one of my post-diagnosis visits; how we had both held our palms up against the glass, mirroring but not touching – playing it ultra safe: still a pair, but forced apart. Adolescence had seen him grow taller than me, and his hands much bigger than mine, but we still had the same slim fingers, the same slightly too-bent, double-jointed thumbs. How I had ached to take his pain. Or at least to share it. Not being able to – never having been able to – had always felt like failure.

'You will get better,' I had mouthed, stretching my lips in a slow, exaggerated way round each syllable, smiling brilliantly. And he had mouthed, 'Yes', firing his own laser-beam grin right back.

The bell hasn't finished its tinkling ditty when Joanne opens the door.

'Gosh, you're still wearing black,' she exclaims, tugging self-consciously at the floaty hem of the sunshine-yellow smock-top hanging over white, stretch cropped jeans.

'Yes... I... it just feels... right.' I tweak at my black shirt, tucking it more firmly into my dark trousers, aware of my summoned calm already evaporating. No one – not even Al or Tamsin – has remarked on my continuing choice of dark clothes. Sombre attire: it seems the smallest acknowledgement of what – who – has still, so recently, been lost. 'I've left the dogs in the car,' I stutter, 'but was wondering if perhaps they might have a run around in the back garden? I've got poo bags, of course, and will keep a weather eye.' I give my handbag a merry pat, despite the tightening of my sister-in-law's already tight face. They have never possessed so much as a gerbil, I remind myself grimly, let alone two loping, shaggy hounds.

'Round the side, if you don't mind.' She speaks stiffly, indicating a door in the high panelled fence to my left, and then going to have words with her employee while I hurry back to the car. Belle and Bobby pull on their leads like wild ponies, thrilled at release, eager to say hello. They are good animals, gentle and sweet, for all their exuberance and size, and not prone to jump up, even given their non-stop longing for human attention.

'Maybe the girls would like to throw a ball for them while we talk?' I pull a ragged tennis ball out of my coat pocket, full of hope, even though there has never once been an occasion when my nieces have played with Belle, let alone Bobby, our more recent acquisition. But we are in a new phase now. The rules might change. Or bend. The girls are the only family I have left, after all, as Joanne, surely, does not need telling. But my sister-in-law's expression darkens further, and I curse my dumbness in having dared to push at one of her precious unvoiced boundaries.

'Stephanie and Laura have Saturday clubs,' she says levelly. 'Chess and ballet.' She performs a quick, pointed consultation of her wristwatch. 'I need to leave to pick up Laura in forty minutes, though Stephanie gets a lift back. So, no, there will be no ball games, thank you, Cath.'

She waits by the front door, while I herd the dogs through the side entrance, stuffing their leads into my bag as I follow her into the house. A vast, ebulliently flowering white orchid that is most definitely not my much more modest apology-gift, holds centre stage on the hall table – a reminder message, it feels like, that my sister-in-law – despite the morning's invitation – does not *want* me in her home, or her life.

'Thank you very much for asking me over, Joanne, I really appreciate it. And can I reiterate my apologies for the accident with the wine.' Babbling and grovelling seems the only way forward. 'I honestly don't know how it happened – I just sort of tripped and—'

'You were upset,' Joanne says flatly, her bare feet slapping in her Birkenstocks as she leads the way into the sitting room. Through the window, I see that both dogs have flopped down, panting, in a patch of shade.

'I'll check for their mess before I leave,' I murmur, my skin goose-bumping as I begin to register all the images of my brother displayed around the room. Somehow, at the wake, with the throng of guests, they had been less obvious. But now Rob is everywhere I turn: in family collages, in individual frames – some with the girls, some with Joanne – and in solo portraits, including a painfully recent one in which his face is pinched and thin, but grinning determinedly from under the hood of a drenched cagoule, half-blurred by grey rods of falling rain.

'How are the girls?' I venture, while my brain scrambles to remember the carefully crafted sentences on my phone: *It would mean so much to me if I could see a bit more of Stephanie and Laura. From time to time. As and when it suits you all.*

Joanne buckles her plump arms across her chest. 'Not so bad. Enjoying being back at school – the routine, and so forth. Life goes on. Would you like a coffee or anything?'

'Just a glass of water, please.'

'Still or sparkling?'

'Tap is fine, thanks.' Grief is supposed to bond people, isn't it? I reflect wretchedly, staring after her as she heads off to the

kitchen. Across the hall, I catch sight of the half-open door into
the den where Rob had been encamped on what turned out to
be my final visit. I can see the corner of the big green sofa from
which he had greeted me. 'Welcome to my daybed,' he had
rasped in his jokey way, evoking a distant, hazy image of our
mother, propped among pillows, the flames of her hair bright
against their whiteness. She had died but Rob wasn't going to, I
had resolved in the same moment. His lymph nodes were long
gone, but there was still talk of clinical trials – new
immunotherapy drugs and something called BRAF-targeted
therapy, which he explained in detail when I probed, determined hope burning in his eyes.

Joanne, returning with my drink, blocks my eyeline, obliter-
ating my train of thought, and I am grateful. 'Thank you so
much for this.' I take a sip, wishing I had the courage to ask if the
dogs might have a bowl of water. 'You wrote that you were struggling,' I say instead. 'Of course, you and the girls must miss him
so. Me too.' I press the glass to my mouth in a bid to stop it
trembling.

'We are managing, I suppose. Coping. *Buggering* on. You
know.' She shrugs. 'Let's sit down.' She leads the way to the two
armchairs parked on either side of a low table in the bay
window overlooking the garden. She lowers herself into one, but
perches on the very edge of the seat, fiddling with the knick-
knacks on the table – which include the cagoule picture – while
I sit down opposite.

'There are some things I want to ask you,' I stammer, 'get
them off my chest, so to speak.'

'Really? What sort of things?'

'Just... like... with Rob... how it sometimes felt... as if you
were keeping me away.'

'Keeping you away? He had a seriously compromised

immune system. I was trying to protect him.' Her tone has hardened into one of defensive incredulity. She leans forward and picks up a small ornamental jar from the items on the table, running her fingers over the strip of tape keeping its lid secure. 'Any bug – the virus – he couldn't have taken it.'

'Yes, of course. Sorry, I didn't mean...' My tactful phrases are spaghetti. I had meant both *before* Rob getting sick, as well as *after*, but am already cursing my stupidity in imagining this could ever have been a moment for such a big conversation. Occasional attempts in the past to broach such territory with Rob had never got me anywhere. He would have no word said against his wife, and then, towards the end, it had simply felt too impossibly unkind. 'I suppose, not being there when he... when time was running out,' I plough on, 'that was the hardest thing. I just wish you had at least called me—'

'I am sorry, Cath. It came so fast. As I told you at the time.' She has gone very still and is blinking rapidly, like an animal scenting danger. 'No one can control these things, and you had at least seen him not long before...'

'Several days—'

'Actually, Cath, I'm sorry, but I do not have the... *energy*... for this right now.' She crumbles visibly, her posture collapsing, rocking herself. 'Whatever it is you're after... I cannot *deal* with it.' She fumbles to fish out a tissue from one of the sleeves of the big blousy yellow top and presses it over the lower half of her face like a shield. Her grey eyes meet mine over the top of it, glassy, but steely.

'I am not *after* anything,' I murmur, wretched at my own clumsiness, exacerbating her distress, making everything worse. Al was right, I was not ready for this. I should have cried off, asked for more time.

'Here. This is why I asked you over,' Joanne declares

suddenly, thrusting the little jar she has been fiddling with into my hands. 'Some of his ashes. The children and I will do our own private scattering in the garden – as Rob wanted – when we are ready.' Tears have started streaming down her face and she wipes and re-wipes them with her sodden tissue as she talks. 'I thought I could cope with seeing you, Cath, but I'm sorry, I just can't.' She gets up from the chair and moves to the window. 'You always make everything so hard – as if you see life as nothing but a battle. But what I want – what I need – is to be alone right now, if you don't mind. Please collect your dogs from the side gate. I honestly do not care what they have or haven't done in the garden.'

'But can I see the girls from time to time?' The question shoots out. I am already on my feet – as desperate to go as she is to be rid of me – and the room is whirling. Through the window, my hounds and the small tree where they have sought shade are a blur. 'It would mean a lot, Joanne, please?'

'Yes, I'm sure it would.' Her eyes also flick in the direction of Belle and Bobby, as if to say *because you chose to have dogs instead of children*. 'But for now, Cath, I think we all need a little space.'

In the hall, I stumble on the edge of the tasselled rug that leads to the front of the door.

A couple of minutes later, I am back out in the street, clasping the little pot with its precious contents in one hand, and dragging Belle and Bobby along with the other. Both are shuffling now, tails at half-mast, tongues lolling over their teeth as they pant. But there is no question of going back. The manor house is near a river, so they'll just have to wait for that to see off their thirst.

6

OLIVER

Oliver moved the teaspoon round and round the cup of thin, too-hot tea, swiping through notifications without taking any of them in. His seat, metal like the table and unsteady on its legs, was not designed for comfort. The overriding odour in the café was of cooking fat, but it had been the first place he had seen with any obvious space and he had badly needed somewhere to sit down, preferably out of the roasting, Saturday-afternoon London sun. Early September, and it felt like the Bahamas. A Coca-Cola had seen off his thirst, and he had moved onto tea because there was still a weird pins and needles thing going on with his legs and it had provided a pretext to continue sitting down. Around him, only a few other tables were occupied, each by weathered, weary-looking men on their own, like it was a place for loners. Losers.

What had he expected from this idiotic visit anyway, Oliver asked himself crossly, scrolling back to his photos and staring again at the ground-floor, concrete, terraced box – part of a towering complex of similar boxes – that had once been his family home. Its ugly greyness and smallness – so much more

extreme than the image he had held in his head for three decades
– had left him stunned, as had the wave of memories it
unleashed. Memories not so much of Catherine and Robert
themselves – his big, bad, loud half-siblings, fearless, in cahoots,
sniping, joshing, plotting, jumping out from round corners
waggling things he was afraid of, like cap guns or plastic spiders
– he remembered all that. No, it was the visceral sensation of not
being liked that had surged unexpectedly. The utter misery of it.
The loneliness.

One of his therapists had said that not remembering stuff
was a classic self-defence mechanism. And Oliver, unaware of
holding back on anything, had laughed out loud, saying what a
great system and wasn't the human subconscious the smartest
computer ever invented. It had never occurred to him that there
could be such a gulf between recalling things in a cerebral way
and actually *re-experiencing* them, as had been happening that
day. And it made no sense either, to let such emotions in, Oliver
scolded himself, given that it was Catherine and Robert, because
of their antics, who had always been the ones to get it in the
neck. He had been the 'lucky' kid, doted on, even if that doting
had thrown him into the firing line.

Getting on the plane to America, leaving his half-siblings
behind, had been the most thrilling thing ever, just as Catherine
and Robert's glee at being left had been plain to see. All grown-
up and attending university, the two of them had all but left
home anyway, his parents explained, when subsequent plans for
Seattle visits – talked up by his father – kept coming to nothing.
Since there were few subjects more guaranteed to provoke a
parental fight, Oliver hadn't minded much. And when his
mother pronounced a total moratorium on the subject, *because
the twins were evil and had almost ruined their lives* – he had felt
nothing but relief. The decision to see if he could track either of

them down two decades later had arisen mostly out of curiosity, along with the security derived from his own life having delivered spectacularly on everything he had ever dreamed of. Robert proved elusive, but he had got luckier with Catherine. Adding her to his and Faith's Christmas salutations had been partly to parade that security. Look, sucker! That annoying kid, whom you treated like crap, has done good! If he was honest, Oliver knew that a similar thread had played a part in the decision to attend Robert's funeral. Plus the coincidence of being in Europe that week. Seeing how dots in his schedule could be joined up. Oliver was a big fan of that.

But he hadn't reckoned with the discombobulation of seeing Catherine. And now, on this second visit, of that sensation growing deeper, worse. Like some filter had been removed, letting in colours too bright for him to see straight. Standing in front of the ugly block of his birthplace, the thin memories had thickened, until Oliver found himself swamped again by the atmosphere of poised hostility in which they had lived: every explosion a hair trigger away, yet somehow managing – always – to catch him off guard. The only certainty had been his own ensnarement in the middle – fodder for the twins' provocations and his mother's resulting fury, along with the fact of his father rarely being there for the worst times, and with his head down if he was. Not knowing. Or choosing not to. Oliver still wasn't sure. He had got out his phone to see off the swamping feelings by taking a photo. He was there purely as a tourist! Of his own past! A past talked through scores of times and every which way with health professionals. Instead of crushing the unwelcome feelings, however, a new memory had breached, of Catherine and Robert, aged around fourteen and in disgrace – again – for hiding one of Oliver's shoes in the kitchen trash. There had been the usual castigations, muffled thumps behind his parents' bedroom door, weeping from Robert, nothing from Catherine, because there never was. When the door finally opened, Catherine emerged first, being steered by his mother, her long auburn hair cut into thick, jagged clumps almost to her scalp, her gaze proud and unblinking.

'Look what the silly girl has gone and done to herself with my crimping scissors,' his mother cooed. 'Temper, temper, Catherine, but you won't learn, will you, dear? Now Robert's kindly going to sweep up, while I see what I can do to fix things with my good kitchen pair before your father gets home.'

The woman manning the hot drinks machine and snacks was hovering beside Oliver's table. 'Can I get you anything else?'

'No thanks, just the check, please.' Oliver whisked out his slim, tan leather card holder, conscious of a tremor in his hands. Catherine's wildness, he had forgotten the extent of it.

He would settle up and get back on the road, endure the log-jam London traffic back to the Heathrow Hilton. He shouldn't have come. He would eat like a king before the flight and then take a tablet. This time tomorrow, he'd be landing at JFK, back in the world where he belonged.

7

CATHERINE

I drive like an automaton, aware of the little pot beside me, wedged between the seat and my handbag. Rob. Bits of him. I need Al, but he has so much on, and will get it all soon enough, so I call Tam. It cuts immediately to her chirpy voicemail and I remember, with a tummy twist, that it is Saturday and she will be in the thick of the Kent wedding. To have forgotten is too unsettling to confess to, so I start a jolly message wishing her and our Bridezilla well, only to be cut off when my phone battery decides to expire.

I clutch at the steering wheel. Joanne – being in the house – all the pictures and memories of Rob – it has got to me. As I should have known it would. As Al tried to warn me. All I want is to get home, but I have set the car satnav for the manor house, which will make a nice breather, as well as giving the dogs a bit of exercise and the chance to slake their thirst. It is a small detour and one drive-by glance will tell me if the house is worth pursuing officially.

With a mile or so to go, I am directed off the main road and down a rapidly narrowing forest lane. Sensing the slow-down, the dogs grow restless. The little urn still sits in my peripheral vision. Such a tiny container. Smidges of Rob. But which *exact* smidges, I wonder wildly. The satnav screen displays an encouraging image of a river – and a bridge – but when the potholes in the road start to increase and the tunnel of foliage is close to burying us alive, I stop the car. I can't see what lies ahead because of a bend, and with the deterioration in the road surface, I don't fancy it. I look over my shoulder, reassuring myself that, with care, I shall – if necessary – be able to reverse all the way back to the main road.

When I finally turn the engine off, Bobby and Belle take it as permission to go bonkers.

'Okay, okay, you two.'

I clamber out and take a deep breath, relishing the fresh, woody scents and cool air. Just to be out of the car feels better. I am dazed and adrift. Rob-less. I retrieve my handbag from the passenger seat – wedging the urn carefully down one side among the clutter, because leaving it behind feels impossible – and then open the boot to release my now frantic hounds.

'Stay close,' I command feebly, as they hurl themselves with their customary, zingy joy at the world, quickly disappearing round the curve in the lane, while I break into a half-jog after them.

Rounding the curve myself, a gasp of relief escapes me. Everything makes sense; the crumbling lane abruptly opens out onto a large grassy clearing by a bend in the river. High-banked and some twenty feet wide, the water contains huge chunks of half-submerged rubble that clearly used to be – until fairly recently by the look of things – a bridge. Across the field on the far side, I can see what has to be the manor house, its tall chimneys and sloping roofs visible above a fenced, verdant oasis of a garden. Running through the middle of the field, there's a wide track lined with poplars, marking out what I guess must once have been the border of a long, elegant front drive. The postcode wasn't wrong – it's just the mode of access that is obsolete.

My mood rockets. To turn the car round in the clearing and head back to the main road will be a doddle. No need to reverse for a mile. No need to panic. I have found the manor house. The dogs are happy. Bobby is belting up and down the bank, finding places where he can slither close enough for a slurp of water, while Belle has slumped in a patch of shade under a willow tree, snapping idly at a horsefly bothering her head. The willow, half-toppling on the river bank, is a balletic miracle, with muscular flanks and shimmering, green limbs that trail gracefully over the glassy water. Dragonflies – velvet blue jets – dart in and out of the sun-glints between its branches. The air smells even sweeter here – cooler, creamier. The river itself is both moving and still, a living mosaic of reflected sky and trees. I stare till the colours merge, dizzy with elation. It is too much, I know – this see-sawing. I have lost my equilibrium. But oh, it feels so good, just for a wee while, not to be sad. Like a door has swung open, letting light pour in.

* * *

'So, you went swimming? In your clothes?'

'Well, I stripped off a bit obviously – but not totally. Though it did cross my mind.' I laugh, the exultation of my adventure still with me – the shock of the icy water – the sight of my black clothes strewn on the green bank of the clearing, like a shed skin. 'Bobby joined in, but Belle was having none of it – and actually, I was glad because the current was strong, and I can't tell you how cold the water was, even with the heat.'

'Actually, hon, it was pretty reckless.' Al is fighting with the spaghetti I have made, as usual preferring the hard option of trying to twirl it neatly into his spoon with his fork, rather than chopping it into a big scoopable mess like me.

'But it was sensational, Al, and afterwards, I felt—'

'I was getting worried, Cathy, I mean, *seriously* worried.' He pauses in his pasta twirling to give me a meaningful look. 'I'm glad to hear that it felt great afterwards, but on your own, with the current... and as for the dogs – remember that time Belle tried to "rescue" me at Lulworth, flaying me in the process? God, those scratches – tubes of antiseptic cream for days, remember? Christ, sweetheart, anything could have happened.' He has landed the spaghetti spiral and is chewing vigorously.

None of the conversation since my return has been going quite as I had envisaged. First because Al – after greeting me eagerly, albeit with a jibe about not remembering the charging cable for my phone – had to go back to a long Teams meeting; and now because of how he keeps managing to pick up on all the things that don't matter.

'It was so restorative, Al,' I try again. 'I mean, all this wild swimming stuff, I think I get it. You really do feel *at one* with things. Sort of super alive. It was such a beautiful spot, and even before I went in, I had this moment when... I don't know... I just felt that everything was going to be okay, if I can only...' Feeling the quaver in my voice, I snap my mouth shut.

Al holds my gaze, his expression softening. 'Which it will, hon. It will.' He reaches across the bowl containing a few remaining crumbs of grated cheese, and squeezes my fingers. 'And well done again, managing Joanne this morning. That sounds tough. But it seems like you held your cool, and actually, the woman is bang on: a little space – time – will do everyone good. We can all try to get on with our lives a bit now, right? Just like Rob would have wanted.'

He returns to his spaghetti, tipping the last of the cheese on top of it – without asking me if I want any – and I have to fight down a small surge of irritation at this, even though I would have said no. Al is speaking true things, I tell myself, and not simply finding pretexts for dismissing the subject of my grief altogether. *Space*, though. What an overused word. And for years now, as far as Rob and Joanne have been concerned, the damn stuff has hardly been lacking. 'Aren't you going to ask about the ashes?'

'Of course. I was just about to. I didn't want to rush you, love. I am guessing you might want to keep them close for a while. We can scatter them somewhere special whenever you are ready. If you want me there, which I'd like to be – just say the word. What about the Isle of Wight as an idea? We could perhaps go to Granny Jean's grave, or to the beach at the bottom of the cliff. Carve out a quiet time in our busy work schedules. Talking of which, I saw off the barn today, and will get on top of the tax nonsense tomorrow, then it will be all systems go on the school. Another serious mountain to climb. But at least Southampton would be ideal for an Isle of Wight visit – now there's a thought.'

His excitement at the Southampton school is pushing through. And quite right too. The biggest commission of his working life, it could be career-changing. And yet the heartiness with which he is eating while talking is really getting to me. I know this is unfair. On top of his excitement, Al is making loving, generous suggestions about what to do with the remains of my dead sibling and saying how he would like to support me through it all. And he has every right to consume his food with relish while doing so. He adores eating and manages to combine it with speaking in a manner that is entirely graceful. Many times during the course of the past twenty years, he has declared my version of spaghetti Bolognese to be almost as good as sex.

Which is saying something, because we are both very good at sex – or at least, very good at enjoying it with each other, which is entirely different and one of the myriad things I have learnt in two decades of being intimate with him. On top of which, the Isle of Wight is a sweet, inspired idea, and he is familiar both with the lumpy little graveyard containing Granny Jean's remains and with the beach below the little white cottage, because I took him to both places early on. But somehow, while acknowledging the sense of all these considerations, I cannot *feel* them. Instead, what I feel, is that the exquisite, much needed equilibrium so unexpectedly gifted by my off-grid adventure is being steadily whittled out of being.

'I did want to scatter Rob's ashes somewhere special, yes. Which is why I did it today. In the river.'

He puts down his spoon and fork. 'Gosh. I see. Okay. If that's what felt right.'

'Yes, Al, it is what felt right. I went in first with the dogs, and then on my own with the urn. I scattered the ashes as I swam. So that they were all around me. On me.' I watch him steadily, aware that I sound unhinged. Maybe I am unhinged. But Al is not allowed to think so. 'Then I filled the urn with earth so that it sank. Except for the lid. I couldn't make it stay on. So, in the end, it caught on the current and floated away.'

'Okay, Cathy, okay.' He has left his seat and come round the table to put his arms around me. Somewhere inside, I am grateful, but I find that I cannot hug him back, because the light of happiness that flowed into me at the riverside has utterly gone, and no kindness, no comfort in the world, can – in these moments – make up for the deadness of my brother.

'Let's take our wine and sit together on the sofa for a while, eh?' He gently levers me out of my chair and I do not resist. 'Telly and hounds. Come along, I'll clear up this lot later.'

Belle and Bob are not allowed on the sofa, which means it is their greatest wish, always, to occupy it. On this occasion, we let them, struggling to sit near each other in consequence, what with their sprawling, gangly limbs and us trying to sip from our wine glasses. Al finds a Netflix whodunnit we gave up on months ago, and we both keep half an eye on it between checking our phones and stroking the dogs. With each minute, I can feel my sadness subsiding, just as Al knew it would. Tam has sent me a string of thumbs-up and dancing people emojis by way of reportage on the Kent wedding, plus a quick reminder that she will miss our weekly kitchen meeting because of a Dublin visit to Jules. She has also confirmed the checklist schedule for the next big event – a Salisbury golden wedding party next Friday, which I shall be running on my own. I am making sure I have all the important numbers to hand, including a new marquee man Tam has sourced for the job, when Al's phone buzzes with a FaceTime call from Ryan.

'Hey, Dad, how's it going?'

'Hello, mate.'

Al shoves the dogs off the sofa and I freeze the telly, shifting closer to peer over his shoulder.

'Hey there, Ryan.'

'Hey, Cath. How are you doing? I was really sorry to hear about your brother.'

'Oh, thanks Ryan. That's kind.' I feel Al's hand arrive on my knee and clasp it gratefully. 'How's the music world?'

'Yeah, all good, thanks.' Ryan grins, with understandable relief perhaps, that the difficult thing has been said, and I think – for by no means the first time – what a polite, infectiously cheery, laid-back young man he is, and what a great job Al has made out of the seemingly impossible beginnings and grab-it-when-you-can parenting that followed. Through all Sandi's endless shenanigans, which for a spell involved living in southern Spain, until a second divorce brought her scuttling back home again, Al has stolidly and doggedly remained unchanged, unresentful, available, and the most loving father imaginable. I have done my best to support his efforts, while taking care never to try and assert myself as any sort of surrogate mother. Not wanting children was something I made clear to Al from the start, glad that Ryan's existence reduced the chance of any pressure on me to change that view.

'So, we've got this gig in a pub in Balham in November,' Ryan continues in his easy way, idly rummaging at the thicket of mousey, shoulder-length hair that Al claims to have enjoyed at a similar age. 'It's a Saturday in this really cool back-room space where loads of big bands have played, so I was thinking maybe you could share the link with all your rich London buddies. It's kind of a big deal, so Sadie and I want to push as hard as we can.'

'Of course – send it through and we'll share it around. Not that there are many London buddies these days, let alone rich ones,' Al laughs.

'Awesome. Thanks, Dad.'

'We'd love to be there too, but we're looking at a busy few months, so I can't make any promises...' Al glances at me. 'I've got a big school extension project starting and weekends can be tricky for Cath, so assume a no-show, unless you hear otherwise, okay?'

'No worries. I'll see you at Christmas anyway, maybe with Sadie – oh, hang on...' He half-disappears as his lead singer – and girlfriend of ten months – play-punches him out of the way to put her own face centre-screen.

'Hi, both.' She does jazz hands, blinking big, kohl-rimmed, brown eyes, which are full of shyness but immaculately and dramatically lashed as always. 'Can't wait to see you guys.'

'Busking, gigs in back bars, notching up a few likes here and there – how those two get by is a mystery to me,' Al says fondly once the call is done. He gathers up our empty glasses as he talks, retreating to the kitchen to keep his word about clearing up, it being one of Al's many virtues that he does what he says he's going to do.

Unlike, say, Jed Levy, I reflect sleepily, stretching out on the sofa in surrender to the exhaustion now rolling through me like a tide. Jed. Levy. A lover whom I didn't love but stuck with all those years. Grand Master at not delivering on promises, large and small – from arrival times, to getaway treats, to gifts, not to mention clearing up of any kind. A taker not a giver. Worst of all, a lover with a wife. As the years pass, mortification at my unwise, amoral younger self grows. Yet I can remember too – vividly – the version of contentment – of freedom – that Jed's and my no-strings deal allowed. Respite from Rob's ups and downs, which were in full swing by then, had been welcome too. Trying to keep my brother steady – safe – it was ever thus. Only the dangers altered... but I don't want to end the day with punishing thoughts. I close my eyes, smelling the faint scent of the river on my skin, still there even though I have showered. Muted clanks and clatters float in from the kitchen. The sink and worktops will be spotless when Al is done. He has a tidy, methodical approach to life. An architect's approach: plans and delivery. Dependable. No room for chaos.

My phone's ping jolts me awake. Blearily, I peer at the screen, wondering if Tam has put a new post on our work insta, but instead find myself looking at an image of a hefty block of grey-brick flats. A familiar block. Well over three decades, but it hasn't changed. There is a message with the photo:

> Visited Ackland Court today. First time in 35 yrs. Really took me back.

> Haven't told Mom or Dad about Robert yet. Figured it was your call because of the estrangement.

> They are still in Seattle, in a retirement home. Can give details if you want. Or I could pass on the news.

> Oliver

> (Got your cell from your sister-in-law's father – gave me his card at Robert's funeral)

I grip the phone, tempted simply to press delete. No one just hands out phone numbers these days. No one. Bloody Joanne and her father. Bloody Oliver. *Baby Oliver.*

Even so, I can't help being grimly fascinated by the picture. I stare at it, seeing not Rob, or me, or our father, but Diane, with her scarlet lips and big teeth, standing on the doorstep when Rob and I got back from our first stay with Granny Jean, minutes after we had learnt we were motherless. Within a year, there had been a wedding in a registry office, and then the swelling belly started. Baby Oliver. The bulge grew straight out from her pelvis, like a balloon you could pop – except you couldn't. I remember the tender gleam in her eyes as she cradled it – *her* baby, already as much a weapon as a child. Not that we had any idea then.

I wanted Diane not to have a baby and to go back to live in America, I explained to my father solemnly – having the wit to catch him alone one day, and never doubting his power to bring these requests into being. Rob and I would stop being naughty, I promised, and we didn't need a new mother because we had him and didn't want one. Lowering himself to his knees so that we were eye to eye, he said I was never to utter or think such things again. Even before Mummy got sick, he explained, she and Diane had been special friends because Diane had come from America with a broken heart and Mummy had helped her fix it. Nothing would make Mummy happier, he said, than Diane looking after us. He loved her very much and Rob and I should too. A *broken heart*. I had pictured a big red Valentine shape snapping in two. Glue. Only later did it dawn on me that there had been another man, who'd changed his mind – done a runner, probably, and good for him.

> No. Do not tell them.

My fingers fly, despite their tremble.

> Do not contact me again.

> Fyi it was never "estrangement" – Rob and I were abandoned.

I press Send and slide my phone under my leg, my heart pumping as more memories pour in: Rob and me muddling on as the money ran out, the drip-drip hurt of the early, sporadic letters, with talk of Seattle airplane tickets that fizzled into silence, the eviction from Ackland Court, the first bedsits, then the basement flat in Shepherds Bush, the extra bar jobs to make money, Rob quitting the poly and taking work on building sites. So no, *estrangement* really didn't cut it.

Al wanders in, a dishcloth still slung over one shoulder. I struggle upright, feigning a yawn, adrenalin having barged out all my sleepiness.

He looks at me tenderly. 'Time for bed?'

I fiddle with a tassel on one of the sofa cushions. 'It was upsetting seeing Joanne today.'

'I know, love, I know.'

'It's like she can't bear the sight of me. It always makes me worry how she treated Rob.'

'I get that – I really do. But I think your brother was all right. Or at least, happy in his way. He certainly adored those girls of his.'

'Yes, he did.'

'Next time, maybe we could go wild swimming together, eh?' He does a jig with the tea towel, pretending to dry himself.

'Yeah, right, Tarzan,' I murmur, eased by his sweetness, as he intends. Al's only version of getting wet – other than under a shower – is a quick dunk in a warm pool in a hot country between slotting on headphones and picking up his kindle.

A little later, in bed, he reaches for me and I tuck myself into him, wanting to be held, not fondled. 'Sorry, Al, I'm not...'

'It's okay, Cathy.' He strokes my hair. 'You must be whacked. But you know, don't you, that – as the saying goes – this too will pass. All of it.'

'Yes,' I say, thinking that Tamsin had said something similar and how it was just words, and wishing I could erase Oliver and his meddling message, still pulsing at the back of my mind. All I need do is block the number, I remind myself, pulling away from Al so that I can bunch up my legs, as I like to for sleep. He plants a peck of a kiss on my head and then gently rolls away too, a hulk in the dark. I think I can detect a shadow of rejection in his heart. Our lust expresses our love. The two drives are inter-linked, un-fakeable, inseparable. 'I love you,' I whisper.

'I love you too, Cathy.' He reaches behind him and squeezes my arm in the dark.

BEFORE

1998

Rob fixes us drinks while I sprawl on the lumpy, mustard sofa that sits below the window with its view of people's legs, striding or ambling past, oblivious to the gated iron staircase leading down to our peeling front door. I am reporting animatedly on my visit to Hendon – and Jed – doing my best to be cavalier and hilarious, in order to cheer my brother up, to inflate him.

'Mostly, I felt like an idiot. I mean, giving him the boot was something I was going to do, right? I just hadn't got around to it yet – mostly because I thought he'd be upset. When he said we were done, it was literally the dullest end to a relationship you have ever witnessed. I said something like, yeah, fine, and he started spewing clichés about how we had shared a good road and reached the end of it, while I looked around for my bag and coat. We had a sort of final awkward hug and that was it. Cue end of crap soap opera.'

I speak with relish, glad to observe Rob starting to shake his head and chuckling. I had felt the weight of his low spirits almost before I opened the door. To know someone so well is a weight as well as a joy. My brain is still humming. No more visits to North London – Tim, the friend who had been letting us use the flat from time to time, was putting it on the market, Jed had said, as if that made better sense of anything. We had needed an ending, he and I. But that hadn't stopped me feeling out-smarted, out-manoeuvred, winded.

'I am not even kidding,' I press on, forcing more merriment, and going to perch nearer Rob on the swivelling stool at the shelf we call our breakfast bar. 'At one point, we even discussed the weather, like we'd never even been particularly good friends, let alone ones with...'

'Benefits,' Rob finishes for me, standing back to check on the evenness of the quantities of gin he has splashed on top of the ice-cube clusters chiselled out of the tray from our too-frozen, mini North Pole of a freezer-drawer. He adds a couple more tots, one in each glass, then shakes the bottle which, despite my having bought it just the day before, appears to be empty. 'A bit like me and Gina.'

'Hmmm. Maybe.' I pull a faux thinking face, twisting on the stool so that it does the squeak we have tried and failed to see off by tightening screws and drip-feeding WD40 into its joints. 'Except that you and Gina – like most of your conquests, dearest brother – were together for about five minutes, as opposed to almost seven years.'

Rob laughs properly, picking a dirty knife out of the wash-ing-up bowl and using it to cut the scrap of lemon that's been browning in the bottom of the fridge into two miniscule, equal portions. 'Fair point, Sis. And by the way – as in, for the record – Gina found you daunting.'

'Daunting?'

'That's what she said.' He drops the lemon snippets into the glasses – our 'best' ones, survivors from a set bought by our father with things called Green Shield stamps – collected when you bought petrol, for sticking into flimsy books. Cloudy from use, they are debris from another world, like most of our scant household possessions.

'Daunting?' I blow a raspberry. 'Fucking cheek.'

'...she said, *dauntingly*.' Rob chortles at his own wit, handing me my drink and taking the dainty sip that always precedes his gulping. 'So, you're okay about this Jed business?'

'Truly okay. It had begun to feel like I was being summoned for sex – not that I didn't do a fair amount of my own summoning.' I roll my eyes gleefully, wanting to remind Rob that the emotionally undemanding terms of Jed's and my arrangement had once suited me well. 'Though lately, I've also had to sit and listen to him moaning, mostly about his workload and family.'

'What sort of moaning about his family?' Rob speaks absently and I sense I am losing him again. He has dropped into the springy jaws of the sofa and is blinking up at me, his sky-blue eyes glassy – confirmation that he is indeed full of gin, despite a recent heart-to-heart and another one of his promises to cut down. Through the dusty, high window, a beam of late-evening sun has found its way down the iron balustrade and into the room, casting him in its spotlight. His red-gold hair, freshly washed from the shower that he takes, with urgency, every evening, the minute he walks in the door, is on fire with light. He is wearing his old, faded-white shirt, open at the neck, and growing ever tighter across the shoulders from the labouring muscles that – to me – still sit oddly on his tall, but naturally slight frame.

'Oh, you know,' I go on gaily, having to work harder now as a secret rush of self-disgust assails me, for the whole Jed nonsense, for my manifold weaknesses in allowing it to start and then continue. Gina, who I only met a couple of times, got it wrong. Daunting would have been good. Better than being weak. Anything was preferable to that. 'Delectable subjects like the difficulty of getting projectile baby vomit off the walls—'

'Could you stop squeaking on that stool, do you think?'

'Sorry.' I clamber off and settle onto the sofa next to him. 'Horrible day?'

He makes a growling sound, like a suppressed roar. 'I feel this... tightness, Cath.'

'But you can't. You've got me.' I punch his arm playfully. 'More than ever now, right?'

'I tried to call him, Cath,' he mumbles, with the meekness of one who knows he is confessing to a crime. 'This time, someone picked up; I could hear breathing, I swear it – a man's breathing. Then the line went dead, like he'd put the phone down. How could he do that? How could he listen to me asking if he was there and then just put the phone down?'

'You don't know it was him. The number is years old now.'

'True. It was pointless to try.' He rests his head on my shoulder, rolling his already empty glass between his palms. 'Hope is what makes life so hard, don't you think? I mean, without it, there'd be so much less pain.'

'Hope is brilliant and I won't hear otherwise. Here, have some of this.' I tip the remains of my drink into his glass.

'I miss Gina a little, actually. She did stupid stuff and made me laugh.'

'I do stupid stuff and make you laugh.' I drop my head on top of his. I can feel the heat of him, the unhappiness. 'Also,' I blurt, sitting up when I can't bear another moment, 'drum roll and big news alert – I'm going to hand in my notice and set up on my own. I've been thinking about it for a while, but decided on the train this evening that I'm going to make it happen. A new post-Jed life. I've got a shed-load of contacts and there's this new fun girl at work called Tamsin who says she knows someone who'd design a website for me for mates' rates. What do you think?'

'I think that sounds bloody amazing.' He clinks his glass against mine and drains it. 'Here's to your new enterprise, Sis. So long as I can live with you when you make your first million and move into one of those mansions round the corner?'

'For sure,' I laugh. 'So long as you'll be my skivvy – booking jets and taxis, and taking my designer gowns to the dry cleaners.'

'Consider it done.'

'And you could do something different too, if you wanted, Rob,' I venture into the silence that follows. 'We're only twenty-six, for God's sake – we've got the world at our feet. You could go back to studying – I could pay – I've got some savings now and...'

He sits up, looking at me. 'What's wrong with what I do?'

'I didn't say it was wrong.'

'I like what I do. Being outside. It's healthy. Mindless. Life isn't all about passing effing exams and having sensible savings accounts. And thank God.'

'I never said—'

'I wouldn't want you to pay for me, anyway. I'll do what I want with my life.'

'Rob, you're upset.'

'Not correct. Not fair. I am just a realist who takes each day as it comes.' He shakes the ice shards in the glass and drains it again before thumping it down on the floor beside the sofa and folding his arms. 'And by the way, I'm bloody glad Jed's out of the frame. A man who clearly doesn't give an arse about his own family – his wife, his kids – I know you're not interested in any of that stuff for yourself, but the way he's behaved is pretty shite, however you look at it. In fact, you should have reported him when he made his first pervy move instead of getting on with teaching you whatever that course was supposed to teach you.'

I shift further along the sofa – away from him – folding my own arms. 'If this was your opinion, brother, then I would rather have heard it a little sooner.'

'It wouldn't have made any difference.'

'True.' I am running out of steam, quailing inside because Rob has found me out, as only he can. Free speaking is part of our deal, one of the luxuries of a bullet-proof bond. 'Whereas, if you found a wife, you'd never cheat on her, I suppose?'

'Never. And I'd be a bloody good dad too.'

'Aren't you the saint.'

'Yes, I bloody am. Except no one wants me – not for long, anyway.'

'Except me.'

'Except you.' He sighs heavily. 'Never mind about Jed, Sis. Water under the bridge, eh?' He reaches across the space and pats my leg. 'Like so much else. Sorry, I'm in a bummer of a mood, in case you hadn't noticed.' He shuffles nearer and pulls me close. 'Thanks for giving me your last slug.'

'Our last slug. And you said you'd cut down.'

'I did, and I shall. Soon. I promise. And actually – so you know – Gina dumped me, which isn't quite what I told you at the time. Her specific reason was that I am "dead inside", which I think is about right. I'd go after her, except she's moved back to Carlisle.'

'Long commute, that, for some nooky.'

'Almost as bad as Hendon.'

'Almost.' I nestle closer again, picturing Jed and every other worry, like an image in a rear-view mirror, already receding – water under the bridge indeed. 'Let's go down the road and grab a last one. It's Friday so there'll be a band.'

'Great. Except I'm skint.'

'I'm not.'

'It's really cool about your business scheme. Does it have a name?'

'I was thinking something with "party" in it.'

'Party-Party.'

'Party Package.'

We carry on talking as we leave the flat, linking arms once we are up the steps and onto the pavement.

'Perfect Parties.'

'Party Poopers.'

'Party Poppers.'

'I expect you will find someone, Cath.'

'I expect you will too.'

'At least I'm not daunting.'

'No, you're just a moody nutter – that's much more appealing.'

'We'll always have each other though, right?'

'Yes, Rob, we will. Through thick and through thin.'

'Thick and thin, Sis. And I'm never trying to call him again. I am done with that – with all of it. Our whole lives ahead, like you say.'

The band is a saxophonist, a drummer and an old man on an acoustic guitar. I buy the round and take it to our table.

'You are kind, Cath. Hellishly so.' He pulls a rascal face before taking a sip of his pint. 'Jed never deserved you.'

'I won't miss him. Or the Hendon sex commute.' I swig my wine, wishing I could as easily swallow the still lingering, peculiar hurt of being cut off from something I had long since stopped truly wanting.

8

CATHERINE

On Friday, I have such a clear run and so much time in hand for the Salisbury golden wedding that, on a whim, I swing off the ring road, head past the turning to Rob and Joanne's, and drive on towards the small girls' day school which I know my nieces attend. I have no plan except to look at the place, which is posh and private, paid for – as their house had been – by Joanne's parents. Not clear on exact starting and finishing schedules these days, I am half-expecting the place to have closed shop for the weekend.

Whims are good things, I tell myself, whizzing along the almost-empty country lanes, experiencing one of the little aftershocks of wellbeing that have been arriving since my impromptu and extraordinary river dip the previous weekend. A private – transcendent – farewell to my brother, it was too powerful to be ruined by Oliver's now deleted message or Al's failure to really 'get' it. Tamsin too, when I blurted it all out on the phone, had used a voice that suggested she was doing her best to sound understanding as opposed to a tiny bit horrified. It was a twin thing, I decide now, only to find the thought triggering one of my bloody tsunamis, arriving with such speed and force that I have to perform a last-minute swerve into a mini-layby, earning a horn-screech from the car behind. Don't panic, that's the key. I allow my body to heave and my nose to pour, pondering the utter loneliness of being sad.

Afterwards, I do what I can with the aid of my make-up bag and the rear-view mirror before continuing on my way, determined to see through the small indulgence of a fly-by of the girls' school. There won't be time for more, I know, since the evening event is big-scale – a hundred and fifty guests, a vast marquee attached to the back of the house, catering for cocktails as well as a sit-down dinner, a band, dancing; between us, Tam and I have teed everything up, but there is a lot to be managed.

The school – to which my aunt status has for some reason never qualified me for a single, measly invitation to anything – is only a couple of miles further on, set on the edge of a new housing development, surrounded by fields and with lots of space for cars along its front façade, between big yellow pedestrian crossings. Peering through its border railings as I start my loop, I can see that it is clearly still very much open. The staff car park, which I pass first, is full, and further on, there is an exercise class of some sort going on in a high-fenced netball court. It involves hula hoops and lots of shrieking – and Stephanie. I brake to get a proper look, pressing my hand to my heart at how my eldest niece stands out from her peers, so reedy and tall, her midi-length, bright-blue uniform kilt flaring like a parasol as she twirls, her dark hair – with the Rob-auburn hints that you can only see up close – bouncing in a thick ponytail across her back. The energy, the radiance in her movements, the laughter in her pale, freckled face – I am not sure I have ever seen anything so alive and beautiful. I wind down my window, enjoying the fresh, early-October chill on my face as I gaze. Until suddenly, a shrill whistle, blown by a woman in a purple windbreaker and black tracksuit bottoms, brings the fun to an abrupt end, and the children marshal themselves into ragged lines for filing back into the building.

More time than I intended has somehow slipped by. I do a quick three-point turn and head back the way I have come – in the nick of time, I note, cruising past the long line of cars arriving from the opposite direction. For school pick-up, obviously. And suddenly, there is Joanne, in their compact black family car, bang in the middle of the line. My stomach flips, but it takes only a couple of instants to pass her. Long enough, however, to observe that she is wearing dark glasses even though the day is overcast, and staring fixedly ahead, poker-straight, gripping the wheel with both hands. The contained tense determination in the pose, the solitariness, floods me with compassion as well as recognition. I would reach for her properly, if only she would let me. There was so much goodwill and friendship when the four of us began. It could have carried on. It could.

I accelerate, switching my focus to the task ahead, only to find myself joining a long, sluggish queue of traffic heading back into town. The Friday school rush hour. I am going to be late for the final setting up of the party. Very late. I am an idiot. As the line continues to edge forwards, the car clock ticking, I surreptitiously fire off messages of forewarning and apology to the party hosts, Mr and Mrs Lathbury, the caterers, the band, and Isaac, Tam's new marquee man. In return, I get just one – thankfully heartening – reply from the catering company, reporting that all is under control and not to worry.

The ring road is even worse – nose-to-tail and close to standstill, thanks to a sudden onslaught of torrential rain and also a broken-down lorry, as becomes clear, when my turn at last arrives to pull out past its flashing hazards. It is six thirty and still pouring when I finally reach the start of the high stone wall marking the roadside border of the Lathburys' handsome property, occupied for almost all of their many decades of wedded bliss, as they delighted in telling me when I met with them back in May. An elegant, articulate, fastidious couple in their late seventies, the meeting had included a site-tour of every flower and blade of grass in their grand garden, even after my suggestion – given the scale of their plans and the vagaries of early-October weather – to have a marquee attached to the back of the house. I had got that right at least, I console myself, squeezing my car behind the other vehicles in the drive, before putting my bag over my head by way of protection against the deluge, and scampering to the front door.

* * *

It is half-past midnight by the time I get home. Turning the engine off, I sit in the car, allowing the fatigue – kept at bay by the need to concentrate on driving – to settle over me. Apart from a leak in a corner of the marquee and a bit of feedback on a microphone during one of the speeches, the party had gone with a bang. I had stayed until the very end, to be absolutely certain it would, and to prove my commitment, earning a hug from Mr Lathbury – by then deeply in his cups and teary-eyed with sentimentality – for my pains.

I slide the key into the lock and open the front door in the quick way that avoids the creak, closing it with the same speed for the same reason. I hang up my smart coat – a camel wool-cashmere, a gift from Al – drape my handbag over the banister post, peel off my shoes, and tiptoe towards the kitchen, my mind set on herbal tea and a cuddle with the dogs before attempting to be just as soundless when I get upstairs.

'Hey, Cathy.'

'Al.' Happiness whooshes through me. Al needs his sleep and has the hang of it, unlike me. But here he is, in his boxers and a T-shirt, sitting at the kitchen table, nursing the treasured crystal tumbler that had belonged to his dad, who had hardening arteries no one knew about until he died when Al was in his final year of uni.

He smiles at me, blinking slowly, his eyelids heavy. 'I missed you.'

'Oh Al, what a lovely surprise.' I go to the back of his chair and slide my arms over his shoulders, placing a kiss on top of the smooth shaved dome of his head. The dogs have heaved themselves from their beds and arrive at my legs, thumping the table and chair legs with their tails. 'Hello, darlings.' I pet them a little before giving Al another kiss and peering at the remaining millilitre of what I know will be whisky in the bottom of his glass. 'Would you like a top-up?'

'No, I'm good, thanks. How did it go?'

'Great, apart from a little marquee-leak – not helped by me managing to arrive a bit late, when it had only just been discovered.' I concentrate on fixing my tea, blocking the memory of the stony expression on Mr Lathbury's face as he opened the door.

'Late? But you left so early.'

'Yes…' The kettle flicks off, and the water steams as I pour it. 'There was an accident on the ring road.' I squeeze out the teabag. 'A kaput lorry.'

'And no alternative routes?'

'No. I mean, the timing was just the worst – school pick-up, early weekend rush hour – and you know what it's like once you're on that blooming ring road. Everything was fine in the end. How was the rest of your day, anyway?'

'Okay, thanks. I got loads done, but then felt too wired to sleep, so decided to have a tot and wait up for you.' He pushes his chair away from the table and holds his arms open.

'I am so glad you did.' I put my mug on the table and flop onto his lap, putting my hands over his as they circle my waist.

'So, tell me more about this party.'

'Really?'

'Really. I want...' he nuzzles the back of my neck, '...a blow by blow.'

'Oh, do you now?' I laugh. 'Actually, I was kind of proud that I managed it—'

'Rightly so.'

'And it was pretty damn gorgeous. A real multigenerational *family* gathering. A great band. Sensational speeches, including some dear singing.'

'Singing? You mean from the band?' He kisses the back of my head.

'No, it was the grown-up kids, performing this song they'd written – no accompaniment, so obviously a family of musical geniuses. Such clever words and rhymes, about all the things their parents had done for them over the years. Then, after they'd finished, this baby starts squawking, and instead of it being a drama, everyone just passes it across the room, from table to table, like it was a parcel, until it gets handed to the daughter – who'd just been singing – and she just gets on with breastfeeding it, discreetly, no fuss... and it was all so... graceful, somehow and effortless and... I don't know, just *nice*.'

Al has gone very still. We were in a moment – a much-needed, too-long-absent moment – and I wonder suddenly whether I have managed to ruin it. 'I just mean, they seemed like such a big, functioning family,' I race on, 'but I bet they all tear each other to bits at other times. The father, Mr Lathbury, certainly showed a darker side over a few drops of water in the marquee...'

'Cathy.' Al's arms have loosened round my waist, and he is pressing his forehead between my shoulder blades, directing his voice downwards so that I have to keep very still to hear. 'I know you are still in the thick of feeling sad. About Rob. I can't pretend to understand exactly what you are going through. Grief is different for everyone.' He pauses. 'And I get that never seeing as much of him as you wanted, and not being there when he died, has made it much, much worse for you. And trust me, I also know from my mum, however many years ago it was—'

'Eight.'

'Eight, yes. I also know from that, how someone being terminally ill doesn't make actually losing them any less of a shock.'

My body wants to tense up and I am fighting it. There is a but coming, and I am afraid of it. Out of the corner of my eye, I watch the dogs doing the rare thing of settling down together on one of their big spongy beds, top to tail, Belle slumped with her jaw on Bobby's lower back, one paw on his belly, like they are old chums – which they are now, early jealousies long done with. I am aware of a momentary twinge of something like envy towards them, for their animal trust, with no danger of words getting in the way.

'But what I also want to say,' Al continues, the doggedness in his voice exacerbating my worry, 'and please believe that this has nothing to do with *my* needs or wants, Cathy, but... if, by any chance, what you are going through makes you regret not having had a shot yourself at being a mum, then we can still explore it. I mean, you are so fit, so in your prime, and these days, there *are* still options...'

'No, Al – darling man.' I could whoop with relief. I had braced myself for some riling platitudes about grief and Rob, but this is easy in comparison – as anything is when you *know* what you think. 'Nothing's changed Al. Yes, the menopause has yet to hit – thank God – but I don't want a baby. Rob was my family. And I miss him, that's all. A lot.' I swivel in his lap so we are face to face. A few tears have managed to find their way onto my cheeks and he wipes them away.

'Okay, Cathy, okay.' He brushes my hair back off my face, his eyes searching mine. 'Christ, I love you and need you, do you know that? Do you have any idea?'

'Yes, because I love you and need you too, Al.'

'And if you want to talk to someone about what you are going through—'

'I've got you to talk to.'

'Yes, Cathy, you have. Always.' He stands up as he speaks, easily lifting me with him. I wrap my legs round his waist, locking my ankles, clinging to him. My rock.

'Just stay open with me, okay?' His dark, beautiful eyes drill into mine. 'I'm not a mind-reader. Keep letting me in, promise?'

'Promise.'

'I would like to make love to you now, Catherine Reynolds.' He hoicks me higher, slamming the kitchen door shut with a back-kick before starting up the stairs, pausing to let me grab my handbag off the banister post. 'If you are amenable. To be more specific, I would like to take you to hitherto unknown heights of pleasure.'

'*Hitherto* unknown, eh? So, great heights of language too, then.' I nuzzle his nose as we continue our progress upstairs. This is not the conclusion to the evening I had envisaged, nor what my exhausted state really wants. Al cannot fix my hollow state, but I see suddenly how much it will help both of us if he believes, a little bit, that he can. We have been losing some of our precious equilibrium, and I want it back. I have indeed been too inside myself, shutting him out, and must do better – for my own sake, let alone his. There are things I have not yet shared that I probably should – Oliver sending the picture, my impromptu fly-by of the girls' school that afternoon – but things not told are hardly lies, I reason, and Al would only worry more than he is already. What couple on the planet shares everything anyway?

'Could you manage the door handle, do you think?'

'I could.' I reach out and open the bedroom door.

'And the light switch.'

'Lights on, then?'

'Yes, please. And I would like to undress you, if that's okay? I mean, it saves you the bother, right?'

'So thoughtful.' I giggle, dropping my handbag onto the chair by the door.

'So, all you have to do is lie back and relax.'

'And think of England?'

'Oh, now there's a good idea. Make sure to let me know how that goes.' He carefully places me on my back on top of the covers, and lifts up my dress to peel off my tights. I am pedalling my legs by way of assistance when there is a phone ping inside my handbag.

'I'll put that on silent, shall I?' he offers dryly.

'Good idea.' I lie still as he sees to the task, suppressing a wild, daft shiver of apprehension that Oliver might have chosen that moment – of all moments – to ignore my request to be left in peace, because though I keep meaning to block his number, I still haven't got round to it.

'You can get back to your other lover after I've finished with you,' Al jokes, strolling back towards the bed, keeping his eyes on mine as he starts pulling off his T-shirt.

9

OLIVER

Oliver had been clapping his hands so hard and for so long that his palms stung. Amelia was in the exact middle of the row of kids on stage, her mini violin and bow dangling carelessly from her hands as she joined in with the bow-taking, checking with her neighbours to time it exactly and grinning broadly enough to display the gummy gaps of her recently – and proudly – lost front teeth.

This is happiness, Oliver told himself, as he and every other parent clapped on, Faith, sitting on the edge of her seat beside him, pausing only to dab at her tears with the cuffs of her sleeves. Love, pride, joy. Here it was. Something to treasure – to bottle, if only he could, along with his six-year-old daughter's unbridled self-belief and purity. Yet even thinking that somehow took the edge off the moment – like he was watching himself rather than being inside himself. It had been happening a lot lately, especially when he was trying to sleep.

'It would be nice just to go home,' he murmured, once they were outside in the blessed cool of the October evening air, Amelia having been held and hugged until she was squirming to go off for the treat of a sleepover with little Erica, the best of her many 'best' friends, who happened, with wonderful convenience, to live in the very next block to theirs.

'I thought you were hungry.'

'I am.'

'Especially for sushi, you said.'

'I did.' Oliver took Faith's hand and kissed the knuckles. 'I guess I'm just pooped.'

'Poor honey. But it's Friday, and without Amelia, we can sleep late. And Petra would be so disappointed if we pulled out. We arranged this weeks ago, and – thanks to Brad's contacts – she's gotten us one of the window tables. You know you'll love it when you get there.'

'Yes, I will.' Oliver slid his arm round her waist, having to shorten his stride a little to match hers, even though she was speed-walking in the trainers she took everywhere in a back pouch. He kissed the top of her head as they bobbed along the busy sidewalk, as a heavier mantle of fatigue threatened to descend, despite the refreshing crispness of the evening. Get over it, he scolded himself, focusing instead on the neon-lit bustle of the city he had fallen in love with over a decade and a half before. A melting pot of a place with a beating heart that would take you in and treat you well if you surrendered to it. Which Oliver had, with the unquantifiable help of Faith – who had been working in an art gallery when they met – and her extraordinary family, who had seemed to know everyone and everything that mattered.

Faith had no notion of the real torture of his new tiredness, and Oliver wanted to keep things that way. She thought he was still a little jet lagged from his Europe trip, and maybe he was. If she got a whiff of something deeper, she would worry – she was good at worrying – perhaps ask questions to which he had no answers, and then, almost certainly, suggest he return to therapy. And then they would have an argument, because Oliver would refuse. He had spent more thousands of dollars than he cared to count, not to mention hundreds of hours of his life, pouring out the contents of his head and heart to fee-charging strangers. Much of it had felt great, and boy, had he covered all bases: crazily unpleasant half-siblings; an exasperatingly passive father; a domineering mother, who ricocheted between cosseting love and a terrifying temper; fear of poverty; guilt about liking his parents less and less; the terror of not being a good enough husband or father himself. Yet, none of it had *cured* anything, as he had recently learnt from dealing with the confusing onrush of emotions at the sight of his first home.

'Oh my God, it is *so* good to see you both,' cried Petra in her customarily exuberant way, when they arrived at the table, which was in the best spot, with views in two directions over the glittering city. 'And you look *so* well. Don't they look well, honey? Just *glowing*.'

'With pride,' said Faith, starting to tell Petra, who was her much older cousin, about the school talent show even before they had all hugged or kissed and sat down.

He just wasn't in the right frame of mind, Oliver told himself an hour later, swallowing yawns at Brad's description of a nail-biting round of golf that morning. Brad and Petra did not have children and were in their late forties. Family money – on both sides – meant that neither of them had ever had to go into an office to earn an income, and over the years, Oliver had gone from envying this position to harbouring a slight contempt for it.

'Don't you just get bored with yourself, Brad?' he found himself saying, half-banking on his companion's obtuseness to get away with the remark. 'I mean, do you ever read a book?'

Somehow, both of the women, who had been deep in a

conversation that required lowered voices – about organising the usual Thanksgiving shenanigans, from what Oliver could gather – immediately stopped talking and spun their heads in his direction.

'Excuse me?' said Petra, releasing the words on a half-gasp and glancing at Faith to check that she shared her dismay.

'It's okay,' Brad began, only to be interrupted by Faith, who said it was not okay at all and could Oliver please explain himself and apologise.

'I was just joking,' Oliver protested, flinging his arms up and sitting back in his chair, which had a curve in it that had been making his back ache. 'I mean, most of us barely read now, right? Except stuff fed to us on screens. And I get bored with *myself* half the time – at least with the contents of my head. Sorry, Brad, if I offended you.'

'No, bud, you're fine. I know exactly what you mean.' Brad slapped him on the shoulder and signalled to the waiter for their bill, which he insisted on settling.

* * *

'What were you thinking?'

'I'm sorry Faith, I was just—'

'I mean, we both know that Brad is not the sparkiest conversationalist, but he has a good, big heart, and does not deserve to be talked down to like that. Petra was really upset, I could tell. And I am too, Oliver. What the hell has gotten into you?'

Faith was leaning back against the marble-topped counter in their kitchen, arms folded in a manner that was rare for being intimidatingly combative. They had taken a cab home – a sure sign of how pissed with him she was – and she had then, slowly and silently, fixed herself a mint tea with some of the leaves of which she was rightly proud, since they grew from one of her own verdant balcony tubs.

'Look, sweetheart, it wasn't that bad, surely,' Oliver pleaded, 'just one of those things that came out kind of wrong. Brad was totally cool with it.' He took a swig from the inch of Bourbon he had poured over some ice cubes in preference to making his own tea. Having been issuing apologies throughout the ride home, he was beginning to think he had eaten enough humble pie. It was time to get things back on track and concentrate on enjoying their weekend. Faith, however, remained stiff and self-enveloped in her stance against the counter, sticking her neat triangle of a jaw out in a way that was equally rare, and which made Oliver even more wary.

'Since Europe, you've been so cranky. And you know what? I am not surprised. All this travelling – and for so long – with those *two* extra trips to the UK.' Her tone rang with all the resentment she had clearly managed to mask at the time of giving her blessing to them. 'Absence takes a toll, you know – on me and Amelia, for sure, but also on you, Oliver. You work so much harder than the rest of them anyway, from what I can see. All they get to do is sit around on their backsides in front of screens, using the information *you* provide.' She briefly unfolded one of her crossed arms to jab an index finger at him. 'In my opinion, it's time they took a turn at getting on airplanes to pitch and close deals in Europe. And if you don't tell them so, then I will. In fact, I might just call Harrison myself this weekend – explain that you're not coping, that it is too much.'

She was lobbing out dummy grenades, Oliver assured himself. She would never call Harrison Greenberg. Not just because it would be a little absurd, but also because Harrison, co-founder of their business and friend of Oliver's since Harvard, worked his butt off, as she well knew. As did the entire team. 'I am good at what I do, Faith,' he said cautiously. 'The travel has an important purpose, and for the most part, I enjoy it.'

'Oh really? Is that because it allows you to get away from me? Because I am so *boring*?'

'Faith – honey – that is insane.' A laugh of sheer despair escaped him. The conversation was hopping and exploding, a rogue firework that, Oliver suddenly feared, could do untold damage. They seldom fought, because they both hated it so. It had to be a hormone thing, he decided wildly. But he wasn't sure where she was in her cycle, and didn't dare get his head bitten off by asking.

'So now I'm insane, am I? And funny, too, apparently.'

'Honey, please. My laugh was just from... desperation. I am so sorry you are upset. I am also really sorry if I seemed rude to Brad, but what I said had nothing to do with you. Or us.' Oliver put his glass down and ran his hands over his face and back through his sweep of hair. He blinked as he did so, feeling the sore dryness under his upper eyelids, constantly there now from lack of sleep. He thought in the same instant how fresh Faith looked – the whites of her eyes so sharp against her brilliant-green irises, her loose, cream, silk shirt and black, velvet pants hinting at the soft curves of the beautiful body inside. Because he had protected her well from all the recent wakefulness, he reflected with a surge of love and pride. No rustles. Stealthy as a cat, whether reaching for his AirPods, or sliding his entire body out from under the covers in order to go to the bathroom, or to swallow one of the tablets resorted to so often that they were steadily losing their efficacy. 'You are the most sensationally un-boring person I know, Faith, darling. I love you more than words can say. When I am away, I miss you and Amelia so much, it hurts. And if I have been cranky lately, then I am truly sorry for that too, but please understand, it is only because I am still a little sleep-deprived.'

Rather to his amazement, Faith was still not appeased. 'You asked Brad about being bored because you are bored yourself. It's like a form of mirroring – a negative one.'

Oliver, familiar with mirroring techniques from his own many hours in analysis, wasn't sure he agreed with her, but knew it was no moment to get side-tracked by an irrelevant debate. That they were having such a prolonged, unpleasant discussion was bad enough, and he wanted, with every tremble of his tired, over-sensitised body, to find a way of resolving it. 'The only mirroring going on was because of the way I feel about myself right now. The tedium of my own thought patterns – all the stuff in my head, going round in circles when I can't sleep.'

'What stuff?' she said at once, frowning.

Oliver drained the last drops of melted water from his glass, aware that they had arrived at precisely the sort of interrogation he had hoped to avoid and for which he felt so ill-equipped. 'Work, of course,' he began carefully. 'Like, how to manage the challenges of growth, which keep on coming, and how to spend more time with you and Amelia in the face of that... Also... the UK trips – they stoked a few memories, just like I already told you, remember? Seeing Catherine again, just as bat-crazy as she always was, and then the visit to London, remembering all the conflict... I guess some of it is still playing in the back of my mind a little, taking advantage of the jet lag...'

Faith had come to stand in front of him and taken both his hands in hers. 'Oh honey, but you do look exhausted.' Her exquisite eyes had gone glassy with compassion, lightening the green.

Oliver blinked at her, his heart swelling, mostly with relief.

She was such an extraordinary woman and she loved *him*. He felt a surge of gratitude even stronger than his own love for her.

'You did mention those things when you got back,' she went on soothingly. 'And now I feel bad, for maybe not paying them the attention I should have. My poor sweetheart, all that's been playing out in your head, please share it with me properly.' As she talked, she led him by the hand – as she might have Amelia – to the big, soft, white sofa that formed the centrepiece of their glass-walled, open-plan living room. The blinds on all sides were still up, allowing the night sky of the city to sparkle in the glass panels, exactly as their eye-wateringly pricey genius of an architect had promised.

'I'm fine, truly,' Oliver murmured. All he really wanted was to go to bed, ideally to make love, the best route to forgetting and relaxing that he knew. Having shared the fact of his whirring brain blocking the path to sleep, he genuinely had no idea what more he could say about it. For a moment, he couldn't even think what exactly did swirl round his dumb head in the small hours. It contained terror, but with no defining shape. He didn't want to taint Faith with any part of it.

She sat next to him on the sofa, tucking her legs under her and resting her hands on her knees like when she was about to start meditating. 'Okay.' She inhaled and exhaled slowly. 'It is only because you are the kindest man on this earth, Oliver Reynolds, that you even went to that darn funeral. And as for that horrible half-sister of yours, and what she put everyone through, and where you all had to live...' She shuddered visibly. 'Going back was truly brave, darling, but you can leave it all behind now. It is the past. Done with.' She clicked her fingers, smiling at him.

'I was lucky in some ways,' Oliver found himself protesting quietly, partly because he was, but also out of some dim reflex to defend his own beginnings, no matter how imperfect they might have been compared to hers. Big money, big family houses, whether they were at home or holidaying in Aspen or The Vineyard, Faith had enjoyed an idyll of an upbringing. 'We're certainly not talking trailer trash or some Dickensian poor house. I had a great start in life in so many ways – a brilliant education. Sure, Mom was... volatile... and the twins were a pain in the ass – Catherine especially – but it definitely eased as they got older and then of course there was the move to Seattle.'

Faith had widened her eyes. From the stories she had heard, most of them during her and Oliver's first years together, when sharing life histories had been part of falling in love, *pain in the ass* didn't really cover it. As far as she could make out, her husband's early childhood had taken place in a virtual war zone, the miracle being that a man of such sweetness had emerged in spite of it. That it was her own beloved country which had given Oliver a second start in life made her glad and proud, even if she wasn't crazy about Seattle, and even less crazy about her in-laws who, to put it mildly, were hard work, especially his mother. 'But, dear Lord,' she exclaimed, looking to encourage Oliver to start opening up in the manner she had been envisaging, 'that vile woman, throwing wine over the *wife* of her dead *brother* at his *funeral*.'

'Yeah, it was pretty bad.' Oliver shook his head ruefully, seeing again the swing of Catherine's flaming hair – a flash of movement across the room – the freeze-frame moment that followed as everyone absorbed what had taken place.

'You might also recall that I wasn't keen for you to attend in the first place,' Faith persisted. 'I mean, of course I am sorry that the man passed – no one deserves to die so young – but he hardly warranted you paying him such an honour. Don't get me wrong, honey,' she added quickly, uncoiling her legs and curling up against him, 'I am super-proud that you did. But at least now, you can draw a line. Right?'

'Right.' Oliver slipped an arm round her, breathing in the scent of her hair. This was all he wanted. *This*. Life was as simple as you chose to make it. Equally important, the bubble of something bad between them had gone, and they could draw a line under that too.

Ten minutes later, they were side by side at their respective bathroom basins, steering their electric toothbrushes round their foaming mouths. Oliver had cleared his lower face of night stubble, as Faith preferred – in the hope, still, of lovemaking – and her peachy skin gleamed from her nightly cosmetics.

'So, have you told your folks yet – about Robert passing? Because if not, you really should.' Faith held her hair out of the way as she bent over to rinse out her mouth at the tap with the cup of her other hand, as she liked to do.

'Actually, I asked Catherine about that and she said not to.'

'Really?' Faith straightened, staring at him in the wall mirror above their two basins. 'But, honey, your mom and dad have a right to know, surely? Your dad especially.'

'It's been so long for both sides.' Oliver's clicked his toothbrush back into its wall-slot. 'And frankly, it's not my call.'

'You could make it your call.' Faith was still staring at him. 'And when did you ask her about it, anyway? At the funeral?'

'Yes.'

'Before she attacked the widow?'

'That's right,' Oliver muttered, bristling slightly at the hint of relish in her words. 'We spoke outside the church.' He faltered, uncomfortable with how he was tweaking the truth about when – and how – he and Catherine had communicated on the matter. Why he had done the tweaking, he wasn't sure. Except, to keep things simple – avoid opening unhelpful avenues that were closed now anyway.

'Oliver, I think you ought to tell your folks that your half-brother has passed.'

'Yes, honey, I heard you.'

'Even with black sheep in families, everybody needs to know the big things,' Faith added stoutly, before disappearing into their bedroom.

By the time Oliver joined her, he noted – with some regret – that she was on her back under the duvet, with her silk eye-mask ready to pull down.

'Are you sleepy, sweetheart?' She gave his side of the bed an invitational pat.

'So-so.'

'You could take one of your travel pills, maybe?'

Oliver raised his hand to twirl the capsule he was already holding. 'Some back-up.'

'Good thinking, darling. So, you don't mind if we just crash? I mean, we have the morning to ourselves, right?'

'Of course, I don't mind,' Oliver murmured, clambering in beside her and getting a kiss in before the mask got tugged into place. Her lips tasted of her night-time salve, sweet as cherries. He felt a mad stab of envy as she then covered her eyes and wriggled further under their goose-down comforter. She was leaving him, it felt like, going to the place where he longed to follow, if only he could. 'Goodnight, my darling Faith. I love you so much. Never forget how much.'

'I love you too, honey.' She groped for his arm and squeezed it.

Oliver took the pill at once and then lay very still, tracking the familiar signs of its advance through his system: the faint tingling in his extremities, the creeping weight inside his bones.

The minutes ticked past and his heart sank at how his mind refused to play ball, pulsing with images and thoughts, like it was a separate, autonomous being, instead of something that was his to command. It could freak him out if he let it. The important thing was not to grow anxious. Not to think – for example – about how succumbing to the power of the pill could sometimes be like catching a train. Miss it, and you got no second chance.

Oliver only knew he had fallen asleep because he woke up. For a while, he lay there, marvelling at how, with chemical help, one could be as oblivious to the topple into oblivion as the oblivion itself. From the quietness and the dark, he knew it was still the middle of the night. He shouldn't move, he told himself, but just lie there, feeling floppy and grateful, and listening to Faith, who swore she never snored, but quite often did – like an old man with bronchial troubles sometimes. Not now, though. Now she was releasing soft, breathy puffs from the back of her throat, like she was blowing at a feather.

Oliver carefully rolled onto his side to reach for his AirPods, intending to treat himself to more of *Moby Dick* – his all-time favourite novel, from which he had recently been drawing solace in the small hours. Instead, he let the roll continue until he was on his feet beside the bed. According to his cell, it was 3 a.m. Gently, using three fingers, he shifted the side edge of the bedroom blinds to peer outside. The sky was inky black. Below it, the city had the faint gleam of a bulb on low wattage. Sliding his sweat pants and polar fleece out from the pile of gear on his bedroom chair, and picking up his trainers, still with socks in from his most recent workout, he tiptoed out of the room and along the hallway, waiting until he was by the front door before pulling the clothes on over his boxers. He had forgotten his cell, but didn't want to go back for fear of waking Faith, who had stopped the breathy puffs the moment he moved – a sure sign that she was already disturbed. Taking a door key from the pot of spares on the hallway shelf, he let himself out onto the landing, before gently shutting the door.

Down in the lobby, his rubber soles made little squeaks on the polished marble floor. The night concierge was nowhere to be seen – something that would make the residents' committee mad, Oliver reflected wryly, but which suited him just fine. The guy could talk and talk – one of those who had ten things to say to your one. Hearing footsteps, he hurriedly pressed the exit button and pushed open the heavy door into the street. The cold air was like a punch in the face – so different from the gym and exactly the distraction he needed. He started jogging at once, landing on the balls of his feet, and steadily increasing his speed. Empty, the city was another world, though, being Manhattan, it was never empty. There were a few vehicles, already going about their business, and people here and there, coming to and from work or nights out, or sheltering in doorways and shop entrances, bundled up in dirty sleeping bags like corpses.

He was one of the lucky ones, Oliver reminded himself, turning right along Fifth, so he was skirting the park, which was locked at night. Lucky, lucky, lucky. He lived in luxury in a city populated by eight-and-a-half million people, of whom nearly 1 per cent was reputed to be homeless. Lucky, lucky, lucky. He ran faster and faster, forcing himself to maintain each new speed. He would run the entire circumference of the park, he decided, all six or so miles of it. He would run until there was no room in his brain for anything but the battle between mounting physical discomfort and the resolve to keep going. Then he would shower in the spare ensuite and ease himself gratefully – noiselessly – back under the covers beside Faith. Maybe a couple more hours of sleep could be his – the proper kind that came of its own accord. Then he and Faith would have a lovely, loving, lazy Sunday morning.

Oliver had made the left turn along the top of the park when his parents came to mind, rather in the manner of a sledgehammer shattering a dream. Sunday was the day when he Zoomed or called every other week or so, usually in the early evening. It always felt like a chore, and now there was the new burden of the dilemma concerning Robert to contend with, stirred by Faith's sudden forthright take on the matter. Until then, Oliver had felt no real qualms about acceding to Catherine's adamant, hostile request not to mention her brother's passing. He had been having doubts anyway. After three decades of estrangement, with his half-siblings having long been a taboo subject, he shuddered to think of the stir it might cause. From his mother especially.

Abandoned. The word Catherine had used in her text fell into Oliver's head with such force that it broke his running rhythm. He slowed, stumbling a little as his knees faltered. He had never thought of it quite like that. Not just because of the twins' evident glee at being left, but because the departure for Seattle had taken place in January, several weeks after they had turned eighteen. Officially adults – how could they be 'abandoned'? Let alone when they were a wilful, nightmarish pair, hell-bent on defying the people who – for all their failings – had done their best to raise them. On top of which, everybody knew that back in those days, all kids had grown up faster and left home sooner...

Abandonment, for Christ's sake. Oliver pushed the notion away, re-finding his pace and balance. Catherine – surprise, surprise – had been yanking his chain. Faith was right. The woman was still just a wacky firework of a creature. Eight years of friendly festive efforts to reach out and she hadn't acknowledged a single one. Hundreds of miles covered – at great personal inconvenience – to attend her brother's funeral, and his reward had been insults. A friendly photo of their first shared home, and he'd been forbidden to contact her again. She was not, and never had been, worth his time. A total joke. And he would tell his folks about Robert tomorrow, Oliver vowed – no matter how they reacted – because Faith was right: family was family, even if it was in smithereens around the globe.

He had arrived at an intersection. The street looked clear, but the *Don't Walk* sign was flashing. Oliver bounced impatiently on the balls of his feet, managing in the process to miss his footing on the edge of the sidewalk. It tipped him forwards a little. Feeling his ankle turn, he fell further still, not seeing the racing cyclist – who clipped him as it swerved and sped on – and not hearing the shriek of car horns and braking rubber that followed.

10

CATHERINE

'So, are you making notes on all of us?'

'Absolutely. All the time. No one is safe.' Jules speaks in a faux devilish voice entirely contradicted by the warm smile that has illuminated her expression throughout our conversation across Tamsin's dining table. A year older than Tam at forty-three, she has cropped, thick, spiky, black hair and an easy, fearless manner that has been filling me with a certain wariness as well as admiration. She writes and stages plays that are emotional juggernauts, she has explained, exposing the extremes of every human hang-up and emotion that she has experienced herself and observed in others. Having learnt from Tam that she's been through a painful divorce and episodes of addiction, as well as failed efforts to conceive a child, I keep thinking both how much the poor thing must have to draw on for her stories, and how I would rather pull out my own fingernails than lay myself – and those nearest to me – so bare.

'Every time I go into the kitchen, I whip out my notebook and jot down observations,' she goes on gleefully, her piercing, hazel eyes dancing, 'or whisper thoughts into my phone. How else do you think we creatives get new material?'

I know she is joshing with me, but I still can't help glancing over her shoulder into the bungalow's small kitchen, where – refusing any help – she has indeed spent a lot of time, coming to and fro with the most spectacular birthday lunch. Crayfish and pomegranate salad, hunks of sourdough, duck breasts, pink and moist in the middle and ringed by spiced rice, asparagus spears and shining, dark-green kale – we have feasted in style and still have the birthday dessert – a pagoda of a chocolate and cream cake crammed with candles – to come.

'So, do you like her?' Tam whispers, grabbing a moment when Jules has left the table again, this time – as she cheerfully told us all – because she was dying for a pee.

'Jules?'

'No, dummy, the Duchess of York.'

'Oh Tam, of course, I do. She's wonderful.'

'And a brilliant, cook,' Al puts in.

'She's just so beautifully *open* about everything,' Tam gushes. 'Hey, you didn't bring the dogs,' she adds, only just registering the fact and looking around the room, as if Bobby and Belle might yet waddle into view from under the table.

'No, we decided not to.' I glance at Al, who is suddenly studying the label on the wine bottle. *Not* bringing them had been at his insistence, on the basis that the bungalow was tiny and the weather foul enough for Tamsin to go off her idea of an after-lunch walk. 'Because of the rain,' I clarify for Tam, hoping Al appreciates my loyalty over what had turned into a bad row – part of a new, dispiriting pattern of falling out that we can't seem to break. The recognition that it must be connected to my still yo-yoing state and Al being at full stretch on Southampton –

nobly doing a lot of train travel so as to leave me the car – has offered no resolution.

'Actually, people tend not to recognise themselves in stories,' Jules says breezily, picking up the thread of our conversation the moment she's back in her chair, 'especially not if the character happens to be vile. I mean, we all secretly think we're the most reasonable person in the room, don't we? My monster of an ex-husband certainly thought he was...' She hoots with laughter. 'But I always notice things about people; it's like a reflex.'

'What sort of things?'

'Ah.' She eyes me steadily. 'Are you asking what I've noticed about you, Cath?'

'Go on then – yes.' I lean closer, glad that Tam and Al are deep in conversation about his work on the school. This is a woman who doesn't just look, I realise, but who *attends* to people and things, with unstoppable energy and charm. It makes more sense of the small theatre in Dublin she has apparently run on her own for eight years, weathering the lockdowns, putting on plays she believes in – including her own – keeping her head above water through relentless applications for shrinking grants.

'I see a barn-storming high-achiever of a best friend to the woman I love,' Jules obliges at once, 'with hair and skin I would steal, if I could, but wearing a huge, flashing *keep-out* sign across her forehead... Sorry, that was presumptuous.'

'No, you're fine,' I counter with a gaiety I do not quite feel.

'Actually, Cath, what I've really been longing to say is how terribly sorry I am for your recent bereavement. Tam told me. Please accept my sincerest condolences.' The concern in her expression, coming straight after the keep-out-sign comment, is managing to trigger one of the less frequent – but invariably inconvenient – urges to sob till I burst. I grope in my lap for my napkin, not finding it.

'Grief is such a bummer,' she goes on softly. 'Lived with, but never gone – believe me, I know.'

I know too, and wish she'd shut the hell up and go back to script-writing chat, or recipe tips for orange sauce. But then my fingers find the napkin and the upset – to my huge relief – recedes anyway, as quickly as it had arrived.

'I'll adore Tamsin until her teeth fall out, by the way,' Jules declares merrily, when we're in the kitchen a few minutes later – my help having been sought for assistance in lighting the tiers of candles on her tour-de-force of a cake. 'Now all I've got to do is persuade her to move to Ireland. Although, who knows what the future holds, right?' she adds hastily, peering at me through the rows of tiny dancing flames, her gaze momentarily drained of its easy, playful certainty.

'Who indeed?' I flash her my best toothpaste advert of a smile and fling open the kitchen door for our grand re-entry into the dining room. Yes, I can be inscrutable all right – a silver lining of a skill learnt early in life.

Jules launches into 'Happy Birthday' as we process in with the cake, deploying a strong, pure voice that testifies to yet another talent in her titanic skill set. I walk behind her, joining in with my own shoutier version of singing. Soon, Al is throwing his booming bass into the fray, while Tam presses her hands to her mouth, shrieking that she loves us all, before blowing at the rapidly melting candles with such force that flecks of wax and whipped cream fly across the table.

* * *

'Today was fun,' Al says, throwing a stick for Bobby, who is too busy scouting for rabbits to notice.

'It was.'

'And Jules seems nice.'

'She does.'

'Thanks for being designated driver.'

'I didn't mind.'

'Apologies for nodding off on the way home, and also for being desk-bound all morning – and yesterday too, come to that. It's no way to spend a weekend. Or a life, come to that.'

'It's fine. I knew, with Southampton, that it would be like this.'

'And the dogs this morning... I hope I am forgiven.'

'You are.'

'So why the mood?'

'What mood?' I kick a stone, wondering if there is any single thing in the world more guaranteed to encourage bad temper than someone claiming to see signs of it. I track the stone as it skips over the edge of the path, which, for this section of the coast, is lined with exclamation-mark signs, warning about landslip. It is a route we haven't walked since an airless day back in June, when we puffed and sweated in spite of our shorts and T-shirts. The conversation we had then has been coming back to me, because it was about Rob – or rather about Joanne, still maintaining the harsh rationing of visitation rights, although the pandemic was in full retreat and my brother's condition worsening. Getting into Alcatraz would be easier, I had joked darkly, and Al had pulled me close, kissing my head.

Today, we are in our cagoules and walking boots and both dogs are bounding on ahead, exultant at the treat of a decent leg-stretch after their incarceration in the kitchen. I sneak a sideways glance at Al. I might have had my defences up for Jules, but being *known* by this man – read like a bloody book most of the time – is one of the things I value most, I remind myself. And yet lately, confusingly, it has been making me feel as if I have nowhere to go. Nowhere to hide.

'Sorry, Al. You're right. I guess I'm still a bit all over the place. Up and down. You know.' I fall into step beside him and reach for his hand, balling my cold fingers up inside his palm, which is twice the size of mine and warm despite the freezing wind chill.

'Of course you are, love.'

'And Jules said she wants Tam to move to Ireland,' I blurt.

'Does she?' Al says mildly. 'Well, that sounds a bit premature to me. Certainly nothing to worry about. Why not sound Tamsin out?'

'Yep. Thanks – of course I shall. It just rattled me, that's all. Though Jules is a bit *much,* don't you think?'

Al frowns. 'No, I'm not sure I do. She seemed great.'

'It's just that I *need* Tam, not only because of work, but—'

'I know, love, and she's not going anywhere.'

I fix my attention on the chalky path ahead, a ghostly line as it recedes up the grey-green incline of the coast. A couple of other hardy walkers are trekking up it, like shifting pixels on a screen. *Bugger off, worry*, I yell inside my head. Everything can be good. Everything *is* good. But Al, gripping my hand more tightly, has begun talking – again – about how grieving takes time, and it's inducing a sudden, unstoppable dread that he might be about to deploy the old *this too will pass* adage. Again.

'My manic working hours won't last forever,' Al goes on, 'and your feelings, they too, will ease and pass with time...'

My hand jerks free of its own accord, it feels like. I flex my hot fingers in the cold air. 'It's fine, Al, honestly. Like I told you, I knew this is how it would be if you won the bid. So how can I possibly mind?'

'Because minding about something isn't a question of choice, is it?' he points out, ramming his empty hand into his pocket – as if the tugging free has hurt it – hurt him – which I know it has. 'It just happens. And lately, with you, Cath, I feel like it's been happening a lot. For obvious reasons, I know,' he adds hastily. Too hastily.

'I'm not totally keen on the *obvious reasons* myself, Al.' I am shocked at the sneer in my voice, but unable to contain it. 'Losing a twin brother, it's just so damned *inconvenient*, isn't it? Though I seriously hope that if I went and died after two hellish years of succumbing to a stealthy, mutinous mole on the back of my leg, you might see your way to being somewhat at sixes and sevens for more than a couple of months. You could give me, say, three months? Maybe four? After that, by all means – with my blessing, delivered all the way from the afterlife, which I have no doubt will involve the flaming pit of hell because of me being such a vile, touchy, crappy person – do dive back into the dating game to find yourself a younger, less pain-in-the-arse model.'

We have both stopped and turned to face each other during the course of this heinous outburst, Al fixing me with eyes that are both despairing and enraged. The dogs too, have come to a halt, sitting patiently, bless them. I meet Al's gaze with my own best version of a defiant glare. I have become a runaway train, and somewhere deep inside, it feels fantastic. 'You could go for a blonde this time, with long legs and decent-sized boobs—'

'Enough, Cath. This is beneath you.' There is such weary disgust in his voice. 'I could not be more aware that you are going through something hideous, and I've been doing my best to be supportive. And apparently failing.' He flings his arms wide in a gesture of helplessness and strides on.

'Oh yes, let's make this about you,' I cry, chasing after him, half in awe of this new voice that isn't mine. 'If my state of upset over the death of my brother has been getting you down, please accept my sincere apologies. I'll try to do better. Sir!' I have to yell this final word, since Al – for understandable reasons – has already turned and headed off, with both dogs bounding at his heels. I stare after them, self-loathing pumping through me so powerfully that for a moment, I think I might throw up.

* * *

'Sorry. I am a cow. End of. Don't even try to forgive me. A lobotomy is the only answer.'

I yearn for a wry smile, but Al just nods. We are back at the car, having completed the walk in an icy silence far worse than the one driving to Tam's. Al has put our animals in the boot and is taking off his walking boots, preferring to drive in his regular shoes.

As I get into the car, my phone vibrates with a new notification. A text. From Oliver.

Hey Catherine. I won't communicate again – as you have requested – but wanted to wish you well. Oliver.

'All okay?' Al growls, his damned inbuilt antennae sensing something as he settles behind the wheel.

'All good.' I drop the mobile into my pocket. 'Sorry again, Al – for all the things I said, for how I am being.'

'Just don't ever think that I am not trying, okay?' he says, with a bitterness I know I deserve. 'And remember, there's professional help out there if you want it.'

'Yup. Thanks. For now, I think I'll stick with that book you gave me. It's just the fact of Rob not *being there* that hurts, you know?'

'Yeah, I know, Cathy.' He reaches out a hand and I make sure to squeeze it hard, more for his reassurance than mine.

The early-evening dark thickens rapidly as we drive home, a reminder that the bite of winter is just around the corner. With all the cloud, there's no light at all, other than the glisten of the black road unfurling under the headlights as we speed along. When Al removes his hand to change gear, I sit deeper into my seat, closing my eyes. Yes, all of this *will* bloody well pass one day. If I can just find some sort of peace for more than a minute at a time. If I can just hang on.

11

OLIVER

Oliver balanced his cell on his chest as he gingerly shifted his position on the big sofa, bracing himself against the stabbing pains caused by changing the angle of the orthopaedic boot containing the lower portion of his right leg. His cell started to slide – despite his care – and he caught it just in time, checking that his sign-off text to Catherine really had gone. Since she had made clear her lack of desire for any further contact, he had felt wholly justified in clarifying that he wasn't, and never would be, hanging on for her to change her mind. They were done. And it felt good, empowering even – a particularly welcome sensation given his thoroughly disempowered physical state.

The final Sunday of October, and they were spending the weekend with his sister-in-law, Sue Ellen, the eldest of Faith's three sisters, and her husband, Don. He was encamped in the sunroom, a warm, luxurious space with a glass-panelled roof and walls, offering panoramic views of the large, impressively landscaped garden which always got Faith talking about whether it was time to leave the city. An hour in to his spoiling encampment however, and Oliver's butt was numb, while his back and neck had grown tired of the supportive positions in which Faith had painstakingly arranged several cushions, before heading off with the others on that day's adventure. Saturday had been an antiques market. Today, it was Cranberry Lake Preserve – for hiking, and to admire the last glories of the fall, until November hit and turned everything black and brown.

It wasn't a great day for the expedition, as the drear skies through the sunroom windows testified, but the copper, gold and red colours of the mighty trees ranged round the lawn outside were still holding their own, and from time to time, Oliver had spotted a hint of lemony sunlight behind the thinner stretches of cloud. The excursion group, which included Petra and Brad – also staying the weekend – and his in-laws' three hardy young teenaged sons, had been unanimously fired up with excitement about trying new trails and packing snacks for a picnic. Over breakfast, Amelia's burly, affable Uncle Don had assured her she could catch a shoulder ride any time she got tired, while Sue Ellen had promised a copious supply of her family-famous walnut and maple syrup cookies among the snacks.

And they were to visit a bird tower. Amelia had rushed to Oliver, squealing with the news. Birds were a new passion, thanks to a school project and a book Oliver had bought her with huge, vibrant-coloured pictures of parakeets. With Amelia kneeling by the sofa, peering over his hands, he had googled birds reputed to hang out at the Lake Preserve. Great blue heron. Red-bellied woodpecker. Mourning dove. Eastern wood peewee. She had repeated each name after him in her innocent, concentrating way, scrutinising the pictures so she would know which was which when she encountered them.

'But birds are very shy, remember?' Oliver had warned, fearing the likelihood of disappointment, 'and also smart. Oftentimes, they like to watch folks without being seen. So don't be surprised if they do just that instead of flying into view.'

'I'll be so quiet,' she had whispered, pressing her index finger to her lips, her sweet brown eyes blinking her sincerity, until she suddenly decided to bolt off, back towards the main body of the house, making a game of skipping between the rugs spread around the sunroom's handsome, heated, stone-tiled floor.

'You'll need to put your trainers on, honey,' Oliver had called after her, miserable at not being able to help with even this small task. A badly sprained ankle, a fractured fibular and two broken ribs. Six weeks recovery at best, of which Oliver had done just over two, but he should count himself lucky to have escaped with his life, the doctor had declared gravely, as had Faith, and every other person subsequently invited to share in the knowledge of his dawn jogging mishap. More privately, and on top of her inexhaustible kindness and magnificent coping with his state of incapacity, Faith had made it clear how mad at him she was: for the foolhardiness of running in the city in the small hours without his cell and without telling her. Waking to find him gone, trying his phone only for it to bleep from his bedside table, fighting panic for a further fifty minutes, whilst ringing round her sisters, and then to receive a call from the hospital, had been the *worst experience* of her life, she said.

Just imagine if he had *died*, she had gasped, standing beside his hospital bed after the doctor had gone, kneading his hand in hers so hard, it hurt. Just imagine her desolation and – worst of all – the effect on Amelia. Their treasure of a daughter, *fatherless* at the age of six – it was unconscionable. And all because of his recklessness. What had he been thinking?

It had been to try and stop himself thinking – to make himself properly tired – Oliver had countered groggily, hating her remonstrances, but accepting that she had good grounds to make them. But then, who could have predicted a misjudged sidewalk edge could topple him into the path of a cyclist, just as a Hummer was swinging round the corner? And the subject on his mind at the time had been Catherine, Oliver had remembered suddenly, as Faith, still clutching his hand, settled back into the visitor chair. The recollection had landed in his mind like a brick through a window, along with a resolution never to apprise his wife of the fact because of the impossibility of explaining or defending it. Instead, he had lowered his gaze to Faith's clamped fingers, enduring a horrible, sudden shudder at the thought that his difficult half-sister was simply a maelstrom of ill fortune, best left well alone.

The whole near-calamity was simply a wake-up call, Oliver had subsequently decided, feeling much steadier a few days later, when he was back home and trying out the settings on the state-of-the-art recliner Faith had bought as a get-well-soon gift. Even with the discomfort of his injuries, he had at last been able to catch up on a little sleep, while bouquets from well-meaning family and friends had left their apartment looking like an overstocked florist. There had even been a card from the driver of the Hummer, posted to the hospital.

Glad you're doing good, kind regards, Bill

Oliver had been touched, although rather less so on opening an email from his insurers a couple of days later, notifying him of the eye-watering claim for the minor repairs to the man's fancy tank of a vehicle. He had decided at once to contest it. Although it was a small price to pay in the general scheme of things, Faith had pointed out brightly, still on a high from having him home and because worrying about money wasn't in her DNA.

Oliver let his eyes fall closed. Very few things in life mattered, that was the truth of it. Amelia. Faith. Looking forwards, not backwards. Not taking dumb risks. Because, as everyone knew – but too often forgot – life could pivot on a dime, scooting you from hopping on the balls of your feet one second, to rolling in agony on a hospital gurney the next – en route to having your brain checked, not to mention your bruised and broken body. Oliver quailed at the memory. Just a couple of small fractured bones. But Faith was right, it could have been so much worse.

* * *

'Mr Oliver?'

Oliver blinked his eyes open to see the beaming, round face of Don and Sue Ellen's housekeeper, Consuela, bending over him. She lived in her own ground-floor annex attached to the side of the house and was off duty at weekends, but Sue Ellen had mentioned asking her to check in from time to time, just in case he needed anything.

'Sorry to disturb, Mr Oliver, but I have to go out now. Can I fix you something before I leave?'

'No, that's thoughtful, Consuela, but I'm doing fine, thanks.' Oliver tried not to grimace as he levered himself more upright. His ankle was throbbing a lot less, but his sore ribs were something else. Another half-hour or so, and he could swallow more of the pain meds which Faith had left on the table beside him, by a glass of water.

Consuela's cell rang and she hurried away to take the call. Oliver recognised the words *felicitaciones* and *cumpleaños* in the high-pitched, exuberant Spanish that floated out from the direction of the kitchen.

'My little sister has had her baby,' she cried, returning a few minutes later. 'Many weeks early, but they say all is okay. And today is also my cousin's birthday, so now we're going to the hospital instead of a restaurant.'

'What fantastic news. Wow. I am very happy for you and your sister.'

'A little boy. Not yet one day old.' Her voice was soft with awe. 'And your beautiful Amelia, she is six years now, right? Which is still only...' She paused to think for a moment. 'About two thousand one hundred days of life. It doesn't sound so much like that, does it?' She laughed. 'Even when it is a much bigger number than six... which is kind of strange.'

'That's so true,' Oliver chuckled, thinking both how smart she was – far too smart to look after other people's houses for a living – and of his beloved child. Only six and a half years on the planet. Consuela was right, it was diddly squat. At Amelia's age, he had been running to his mother over every small thing – sometimes for very good reason, sometimes not. Catherine and Robert had been the only obstacles to his peace of mind and he had been robustly defended on that score... at times too robustly by today's standards. The toxic twins. They sure had asked for it, though. Oliver shook his head, marvelling at the new hold his past seemed to have on him, and wishing he could press a button and put a halt to it. Instead, he found himself reflecting on the move across the Atlantic and how little it had solved. At least in terms of his mother. Without Catherine and Robert to turn on, she had simply found other targets for her grievances, including her own parents, his father and – finally – Oliver himself, mostly because of enragement at his decision to accept a place at a university three thousand miles away from home, even if it was Harvard. Nothing made her happy, that was the sorry truth. And when – after his first student year and all the bolder for it – Oliver had dared to probe his father for reasons why this might be the case, all the old man had said was that his mother had endured some tough formative experiences. A fiancé who deserted her and a baby she had felt obliged to abort, Oliver had managed to ascertain, after pushing hard. It meant she found it difficult to trust people, his father had added – as if this explained everything – before forbidding Oliver ever to raise the matter again.

Consuela had begun a rapid tidy-up of the already tidy room, tweaking the vase of New England asters on the coffee table and straightening ornaments. Absently watching her, it occurred to Oliver that the worst-case scenario Faith had thrown at him in the hospital – Amelia losing a parent – was exactly what had happened to Catherine and Robert. For they had been just six years old themselves when their mother, Greta, his father's never-mentioned first wife, had died. Somehow, he had never quite thought of it in those terms before.

'*Hasta luego*, Mr Oliver.' Done with her tidying, Consuela grinned and waved as she strode out of the room, the full skirt of the blue-spotted dress she was wearing swirling round her knees.

'Congratulations to your sister and the baby,' Oliver called, before the front door thudded shut.

It was Sunday – Seattle Zoom day – he reminded himself glumly and a face-to-face talk with his parents was long overdue. Since his accident, he had been making do with quick phone calls, wanting to be properly on the mend before he explained what had happened. They would only worry otherwise, he had told Faith, whenever she pestered, especially given that he had the big news about Robert to impart too.

'Hey Mom, hey Dad, how are you both doing?'

'Hello, stranger.' A favourite opening gambit of his mother's, no matter how recently they had met or communicated; the greeting never failed to rankle – even when, as now, it was justified. 'Your father and I have been wondering when you'd find a moment for us, haven't we, dear?'

'Hello, son.' His father fluttered one of his liver-spotted hands and smiled wanly, showing a glimpse of the handsome implants which had replaced his bad British teeth during the good Seattle years, before the subprime crisis had thrown them back onto their knees.

'Yes, it's been a while. Sorry about that. Work and family commitments, you know how it is. But I'm here now.' Oliver grinned, tenderness flooding him, despite his mother's snipes. They were sitting side by side at their small dining table, sharing the tablet he had bought and trained them to use, looking like a pair of beaten-up old puppets, propped up and ill-fitting in their hardbacked dining chairs. Somehow, he always forgot how old they were, his mother skeletal and stooped, his father with a few wisps of head-hair left and a neck so craned, it looked as if he was presenting it to have a dog-collar fitted. Like he had been tugged around all his life on a leash, which he kind of had been, Oliver reflected dryly, given the way his Mom was. 'The fact is—'

'Where *are* you?' his mother interjected, screwing up her eyes. 'That's not your apartment.'

'No, we are spending a long weekend at Don and Sue Ellen's place in Armonk. Faith's eldest sister?' Oliver prompted, noting their blank expressions. He would make no mention of the news about Robert after all, he decided in the same instant, not just because – for all Faith's arguments – both his parents were so frail and would hate to hear it, but because of the sudden recollection of Catherine's specific request and a firm sense that it should be honoured. With his sign-off message to her that morning, he had drawn a line under the whole business anyway.

'And I'm convalescing,' he added cheerily, 'from a minor mishap a couple of weeks ago with a sidewalk and a cyclist – a sprained ankle, a couple of sore ribs. A fractured fibular, resulting in *this*.' He shifted the angle of his screen to show off the protective casing round his damaged lower leg. 'But don't worry, all is progressing very well now.'

'Dear Lord, did you have surgery?' His mother was pressing her face even closer to the screen, entirely blocking his father's view. Her large eyes had to work harder these days, and were glazed with the cataracts that Oliver kept saying he would pay to have removed, but which she preferred to deny existed.

'No need for that, Mom – ribs heal on their own and the fracture was minor enough to need only—'

'I cannot believe you failed to tell us about this, Oliver. Something so serious. And you really don't look good – does he, Ian? Kind of puffy-faced. And your skin so grey. Isn't he grey, Ian?' She sat back, throwing up her thin arms in a show of exasperation.

'Bad luck, son,' his father growled. 'I had no idea you cycled.'

'I don't cycle; I was—'

'It's crazy to cycle in Manhattan,' his mother chipped in shrilly. 'Look at the state of you. And there was I hoping we might get a visit over Thanksgiving.'

Oliver, having redirected the laptop screen to his face, set about trying, gently, to steer the conversation back on track, explaining more clearly that he had been running and that he didn't – and never would – cycle anywhere in New York except on a stationary bike in a gym, before going on to remind them – with even greater gentleness – that, with the long-agreed system of alternating years, he and Faith would be spending Thanksgiving with her family in Connecticut. In the dismayed silence that followed, he hastily promised to visit as soon as he was more mobile. When this, too, prompted harrumphing sounds rather than a positive response, he couldn't resist raising the old, somewhat thorny question of moving them nearer Manhattan. 'I know you're not entirely happy with Fairview – you've made that clear many times – and there are some great places in New York State which I could check out. In fact, I could do it now and send you some links, so you could take a look for yourselves. Wouldn't it be good to be able to see more of each other?'

While he was speaking, his father had let his head hang lower so that his eyes were focused on his chest, like a man bracing himself to walk through a blizzard.

'We are humble people, Oliver,' his mother snapped. 'We do not expect much from life. We let the Lord decide our fate. Seattle is our *home*, and was yours too, once upon a time. We don't need fancy food or feather mattresses, not like some I could mention...'

Oliver found himself hanging his head a little too, letting it all blow over. Blow through. Nothing would change. Whatever the psychological root causes, anger energised her. Kept her alive, probably. And she was right, he was in many ways a bad son, not always feeling the right things, and for that reason probably not making enough of an effort, though he did his best.

'I understand, Mom,' he interrupted at last, when she seemed to have got lost in her own sentences and was rubbing the sore patch above her eyebrow that she always rubbed, so it never healed. 'Please don't worry. All I want is for you both to be happy.'

* * *

'Oh, but we missed you, Oliver,' Sue Ellen declared later that night, expertly slicing her homemade Key lime pie into even triangles and holding out her hand for people to pass their plates. The meal, of pulled pork – left in the slow-cooker all day – spiralised zucchini and sweet potato fries – was sensational, as always, and had been accompanied by excellent wine and tales of adventure from the lakeside. The three boys were told they could take theirs into the den and Amelia, who had spent most of the meal on Oliver's lap, refusing her own food, but eating his, was now being settled upstairs by Faith – too tired to stay up for dessert, they had both agreed, allowing her to take a brownie with her by way of compensation.

'So long as she knows it is just a one-time treat,' Sue Ellen had purred, fetching the brownie, and stroking Amelia up and down her back as she sprawled in Faith's arms. 'We don't want to get into bad habits now, do we.' Oliver, knowing how the comment would cut – a classic example of Sue Ellen wielding her sisterly power – had tried to throw his wife a supportive glance, but Faith had merely pulled Amelia closer and left the room.

'Well, I missed you all too,' Oliver confessed, accepting the plate of pie being passed back to him by Petra, seated on his left, 'and felt pretty jealous, especially when you guys started sending pictures.' There had been a lot of photos, including several selfies of the group, the bright colours of their outdoor gear defying the gloom, and even more of the boys and Amelia, perching on rocks, crouching near a toad, climbing a fallen tree, and taking various snack breaks against a backdrop of the water, which looked as dark and choppy as a ploughed field. Something about examining the images, alone in the sunroom, the expedition running on much longer than anyone had planned, had indeed made Oliver feel envious, as well as lonesome. It was partly fear of missing out, he knew, but also arose from Amelia, looking so settled, so separate, without him. In existence for a mere 2,304 days – Oliver had worked it out exactly since the conversation with Consuela – and already moving on, when she had barely begun. When *they* had barely begun.

'So, Oliver, what did you do to pass the hours?' Sue Ellen carefully tipped a few drops of cream onto the minuscule sliver of pie she had served herself, before passing the pitcher to Don, who was next to her. 'I do hope you were okay and managed to have a good time.' She smiled at Oliver across the table, pushing the long sweep of her blonde hair off her face with the back of one hand, while using the other to chisel off a tiny fragment of the dessert with the edge of her spoon.

'Of course he did,' cried Don. 'He'll have watched the game – the Giants turning it around with four seconds on the clock. I kept checking my cell.'

'Actually, being a Seahawks fan, I didn't watch much of that,' Oliver laughed. 'I found a movie instead – about a comet hitting the earth.'

'Oh, I know. Brad and I saw that one.' Petra squeezed Oliver's forearm. 'They have to hide in caves and the sick are left outside to die.'

'Sounds like a blast,' chuckled Don, getting up to do a tour of the table, offering to fill wine glasses and meeting mostly with regretful head-shakes, it being Sunday night.

'And I called my parents,' Oliver went on, nodding when Don reached him, because the wine on top of the meds had been ensuring that he had no pain whatsoever, not even in his ribcage, and certainly not in his leg, which was balanced under the table on a small footstool that one of his nephews had been sent to fetch from an upstairs room.

'Oh, your dear parents. How *are* they both?' Sue Ellen's large, soft blue-grey eyes found and held Oliver's, her long, pale, elegant face etched with concern. She set her spoon down, leaning on her elbows and interlacing her fingers to make a shelf on which to rest her chin. 'It must be so very hard for them – for all of you.'

Oliver found himself putting down his own spoon too, despite not having finished his last mouthful of pie. 'Yes, Seattle isn't exactly convenient.'

'That's true, but actually, Oliver...' His sister-in-law lifted her chin off her fingers, glancing round the table and back to him. 'I was thinking of the recent tragic loss of your half-brother.'

Oliver picked his serviette off his lap and pressed it to the corners of his mouth. 'Oh, so Faith told you about that?'

'That your estranged half-brother, Robert, passed – yes, she did, Oliver.' Sue Ellen dropped her arms into her lap and straightened her position in her chair, her gaze now ablaze with resolve as well as compassion. 'And she also told me how you were good enough to make a detour to England for the funeral, and how today, you were undertaking the difficult duty of telling your folks about it, despite the very great rift that has existed between you all these years. Yes, she did tell me, Oliver, because we are family, and because you are family, and we care for you.' There were sympathetic murmurings of assent round the table.

Don put a hand over his wife's, his big crinkled face nodding solemnly.

Oliver could feel his cheeks burning. Yes, they were all family, and this was kindness, and of course Faith told them loads of things he didn't necessarily know about, but reactions he couldn't control were zipping through his system. 'Thank you, Sue Ellen – all of you.' He let his eyes skip across their expectant faces, noticing Faith in the same instant, hovering in the small rear doorway of the big room, as if she had been there a while and not yet quite made up her mind whether to enter.

Since the excursion, they had barely had a moment to say hi, let alone talk about the call to his parents.

'All of it is just too heartbreaking,' pitched in Petra heartily, 'especially the distance that has grown between you all. How families can tear themselves apart like that, I do *not* know. But then, terrible things happen to good people, that is for sure.'

Oliver slowly turned his head in a show of giving her respectful attention. His somewhat convoluted past – being born in England, moving to the US, having twin half-siblings who had been rebellious and who had chosen to lead separate lives, was ancient history and common knowledge. When he and Faith were dating, he had been grilled on it from many quarters, countless times. A proud, protective, established clan, they had scrutinised his credentials shamelessly, and Oliver had welcomed the opportunity, equally proud of how his less privileged, messier beginnings only cast his high achievements and wealth in an even more favourable light. There had been no dwelling on ugly details, except occasionally, with Faith.

But now, something felt different. Like he was under siege alone, facing a tribe that was not his. Oliver could feel the heat in his face spreading through his body, bringing dampness to his palms, making his bad leg pulse and his broken bones ache. An ambush, it felt like, enabled by his wife, talking freely of business that was not hers to share. Across the table, Faith was now back in her seat and breaking up her piece of pie rather than eating it, shooting him defensive looks. Of course she talked about him, he could take that, but the fact of her not having bothered to ensure that her relatives kept their views to themselves – showed a lack of discretion – of circumspection – that hurt, Oliver decided, nonetheless adjusting his face into appropriate expressions as Petra, fired up with compassion and tipsily loose-tongued, continued with questions about Robert's illness to which he had no answers.

'Oliver is the glue in the family,' Faith interjected, speaking in the manner of one summing up a subject in preparation for dismissing it. 'And well done, honey, for calling them today. That cannot have been easy.'

'It was fine,' Oliver told her and the rest of the room, resolving that the implicit assumption he had broken the news of Robert's death to his parents could sit right where it was. And when Faith grilled him later, he would close the matter right down by saying they hadn't been moved or interested – just as he had expected – and that they would definitely not appreciate any further interrogation on the matter.

Afterwards, when they were all settling in the sitting room with the TV, teas, coffees and a box of salted caramel candy he and Faith had brought as a thank-you-for-having-us gift, it was Brad who surprised him. 'Sorry for your loss, pal,' he murmured, bending over the back of the chair Oliver had chosen and patting his shoulder. 'And for the third degree in there. I could see it made you uncomfortable. They all mean well, you know?'

Yes, he did know, Oliver had assured him, taking another of the salted caramels, which were wafer thin and dissolved the moment they made contact with the tongue. Through the door into the passageway, he kept getting glimpses of Faith, coming and going with dishes from the table, helping Sue Ellen and Petra – the men having been shooed away, leaving the women to chat, as they loved to do, no doubt squeezing in some remarks about him, Oliver mused gloomily. He wished he could just skip upstairs to check on Amelia, tucked in the bed with the fairytale awning in the beautiful nursery-cum-bedroom on the second floor.

It dawned on Oliver that if something were ever to happen to him, Amelia would want for nothing. Others would take care of her. Possibly even – one day – another man. Which was healthy on all fronts, he told himself – and something he and Faith had at times even discussed and agreed about. Even so, marooned in the faultless warmth and conviviality of her beautiful family, it gave him a sensation akin to vertigo just to imagine it.

12

CATHERINE

I am woken by the gurgles of the bedroom radiator coming to life and the window rattling in protest at another blowy, early-November day. It takes a moment to remember that I am alone – because Al is overnighting in Southampton with Phil Evans, the site manager he keeps raving about – and even longer to register that I feel rested. *Happy,* even. Good God. And in November too, such an in-between misery of a month with its leaf sludge, the new hard-to-take, damp, winter chill and the resumption of tedious routines like having to wear extra layers and dry the dogs off after every sortie – even if it's just been a measly sniff round our muddy square of a garden.

Kicking off the duvet, opening the curtains to a view of gun-metal skies and swirling leaves, pulling on old clothes for the usual morning walk, I half-expect my spirits to plummet. Instead, my mind whirrs through all I have planned for the day with a sense of anticipation that I hardly dare acknowledge for fear it might dissolve. On the walk, I go almost as fast as the dogs, thinking only about what to wear and how to manage my timings: Salisbury first, for a final check-in at the garden centre-cum-café where a dear, elderly client with a small budget and a big heart is planning a memorial for a friend, then on to lunch in Shaftesbury with Tam, just back from her most recent whistlestop visit to Dublin. The lunch will be on her, she insisted – sounding exultant – because life is short, and we deserve it. After which, I am hoping for time to do some paperwork for our various pre-Christmas events, before preparing a nice meal and setting off to meet Al's train.

Quite a day. Even to think I can manage it feels like progress, because, on the face of it, nothing has changed. Rob is still *not* here; and Al's crazy work hours have become the new norm, ruling out opportunities for further deep conversations, difficult or otherwise. We have found a different rhythm instead, revolving mostly around practical exchanges of information, eating, sleeping and goodnight hugs. We are not where we once were – or where we need to be – but the boat is at least steady and neither of us has any desire to rock it. Al's only recent griping has been about the need to find us a reliable, affordable second car.

The roof of cloud disperses as I whizz through Dorset. Blue skies. A bright, wintry sun. When I reach Salisbury, even the blessed ring road is flowing as sweetly as a tap. The round-abouts, the signposts, the cathedral poking out over the city wall – sublime, surreal – the familiar landmarks nudge me, potential triggers all. On this luminous, fresh November morning, however, this suddenly feels like something to relish. I am near where Rob spent a decade breathing instead of being dead! Where he raised his two beautiful little girls. Where he found the security he craved, even if it was with a person who, having courted my friendship, then decided to keep me at arm's length.

The thought catapults me back to Rob and Joanne's actual wedding. A service in a square-towered little church a couple of miles from the Andover family home, for which, at my brother's request, I undertook the role of 'Best Woman'. The two of us had stood, in classic tradition, waiting at the front of the church for the white limo containing Joanne and her father to arrive, exchanging looks and smiles, while Al pulled faces at us from the pew. In his hired grey morning suit and blue silk waistcoat, a white rose standing proud in his buttonhole, my brother looked as radiant as I had ever seen him: hair and skin glowing, eyes like sapphires. The Joanne Effect, I had taken to calling it, the result of two years of healthy eating and a steady job, of loving and being loved by a partner. And of not drinking. Years of my pleadings and his broken oaths, but he had managed it for Joanne. The deep, despicable reflex of hurt about this never failed to fill me with shame. All that mattered was that Rob had, at last, found his equilibrium. As I had, with Al. We were the perfect four. I had handed my twin brother the gold ring for his vows that day without a fumble, my face streaming with tears of joy. Never once did it occur to me that I was actually giving him away, completely and for good.

At the last minute, I decide to approach the garden centre via Rob and Joanne's road. It will be such a minor detour – a matter of minutes – and sits easily in the new pattern of occasional fly-pasts in other locations to which I have continued to treat myself in recent weeks. One glance at the house – like one glance at either of the girls – and I shall *feel* Rob more, that's the point. To reach a stage of not wanting to do that would feel almost like betrayal. Like I'm beginning not to care.

As I draw parallel with the house, I slow down, taking in the usual orderliness of the front garden, the clods of earth in the beds looking freshly turned and the two neat piles of raked leaves sitting at either end of the lawn. It takes a second more to register that the garden man is half-inside the front door, his back to me, his body half-masking a person who is clearly Joanne. He has a hand on her arm, I'm pretty sure, but the impression doesn't have time to settle before he disappears inside, pulling the door shut behind him.

* * *

'That big floppy brim, the dark blue – it really suits you,' says the woman eagerly, having left her position behind the shop counter to join me by the little row of hats I've been pulling off pegs and putting on my head.

'Oh, no.' I whip the hat off, shaking out my hair. 'I mean, thank you, but I was thinking of it as a Christmas present for a friend. I like your shop. It's got everything.' I swing my arm around all the somewhat over-crammed displays, which include books, clothes, ornaments, games, toiletries, as well as a corner devoted entirely to Christmas-themed items which I have found myself avoiding. Ryan and Sadie will be their usual quirky, sweet selves, but the shop's little festive grotto has brought home the fact that I am soon to face my first Christmas as a twin-less twin. Not to mention my first twin-less birthday, two days before. Our forty-eighth. Or rather *mine*.

I bring the woman's weather-beaten but determinedly cheerful face back into focus. 'I'll take the hat, and this little chap too, please.' I pluck a doughty little black bear – on its hind legs and roaring – which had caught my eye among a sea of ornaments on a low shelf, and follow her to the till. Watching my gifts being fussily wrapped in tissue paper and fiddly, gold stickers, I allow my thoughts to travel back to what I had seen – or almost seen – that morning: Joanne, four months a widow, *with* the garden man. Outrage on Rob's behalf feels good somehow – something to hold on to. Better than Christmas jitters. A fleeting impression it may have been, but it feels like further proof that my sister-in-law is a woman with a strong private agenda and a ruthless heart. Maybe the two of them even had a thing before Rob died. Maybe it's been going on for years.

'The bear is for my partner,' I chatter, surfing this new tide of private excitement. 'He's been working such long hours lately – the two of us have been passing like ships in the night, you know? But I'm meeting him off the train this evening for a lovely night in. I'm cooking a curry – he'd eat one every night given half the chance – and now I've got a hello gift to go with it.'

'How super,' the woman says, handing me a large brown paper carrier bag containing my purchases, a tone of reserve in her voice. Because I have been needily oversharing, I realise with a jolt, hurrying out of the shop so fast she has to come after me with my bank card.

Tamsin is seated in the far corner of the gastropub she has chosen for us, two flutes of champagne already on the table, and her bright-yellow cagoule a neat parcel by her feet. She is studying the menu, which gives me a moment to register both how happy I am to see her and how sparse our encounters have grown recently, even our weekly meetings having become virtual. 'My treat, remember,' she cries, leaping up to give me a hug the moment she spots me. 'You look well – I mean you always do, dearest Cath, but given everything that you're still...'

'I am doing okay, Tam, truly,' I assure her quickly, 'and you look amazing – from all that fresh Irish air, I assume? But – wow – bubbles! What are we celebrating?'

'All sorts of things, and because *we're worth it*,' she jokes, as we settle into our chairs and clink glasses, me having to rein in the urge to launch straight into my new Joanne Theory, because of knowing how Tam will gasp and agree that my dear sister-in-law is, and always has been, a total nightmare. I surprise her with the hat instead, which she rips out of its meticulous paper layers and pulls onto her head with protestations at my generosity.

'I totally love it – stylish, comfy – thank you, Cath, darling.' She tugs the brim down to a roguish angle and swivels to make out what she can of her reflection in a framed picture of a dusty wine bottle on the wall by our table. 'Jules will nick it, though,' she says cheerily, doing her best to wrap it back into the calamitously shredded paper. 'She's mad about hats – she's got loads of them, mostly in baskets and boxes under beds, full of spiders and dead woodlice, the noodle.'

'I liked her so much, Tam,' I say, not for the first time, aware of how odd it still is to have Tam in this loved-up, loving state, while Al and I have got a little lost. Talk about tables turned. I touch my coat pocket where I have stowed the bear, a reminder of my lovely evening plans.

Once the waiter has taken our order, each of us going for the tuna starter and risotto main, Tam reaches across the table and seizes my hand. 'I've got some stuff to say, sweetie,' she announces solemnly, 'so, try not to interrupt – though we both know that's a big ask.' She flashes me a wolfish grin.

I pull a face back at her. 'A huge ask. Monumental.'

'The fact is, I've let you take on far too much too soon,' she says firmly. 'So, the new plan is that I shall be covering all the gigs we've got between now and Christmas. They're decently spaced out, so it will be fine. And then January is pretty quiet, as per, so I can handle that too.'

'Tam—'

'This is not something you are allowed to refuse, sweetie pie. You are doing so well, Cath – anyone can see that – but it's only right that you should have some time out – time *not* doing events, at the very least. I am a crap friend for not suggesting it sooner. Actually, it was Jules who set me right.'

For some reason, this makes her well-intentioned proposal a little harder to swallow. 'Tam, there really is no need. I'm on top of things. I'm doing okay.'

'I'm not saying don't get stuck in with a bit of the admin.'

'Oh, ta, very much.'

'Say yes, Cath. Please?'

I groan a yes as we tuck into the slivers of tuna, soy, ginger and spring onion that have been discreetly placed in front of us – so tasty and so petite that we both empty our plates in minutes.

'Denial, anger, depression, acceptance,' I go on merrily, eager to prove how completely all right I am, 'I honestly think I've done the lot now. Al might say there's some anger left, but – apart from the occasional snipe at him – it's really just towards Joanne, and for some mysterious reason, the excellent grief book he gave me doesn't seem to have a section on horrible sisters-in-law.' I am pleased with this, especially for how it tees up the chance to launch into my new Joanne speculations, but our mains arrive and Tam quickly moves onto another subject from what I am starting to suspect is a pre-rehearsed list.

'So have you thought any more about counselling?'

'God, you're as bad as Al.'

'Don't you want to talk to someone, then?'

'No, Tam, I do not.'

'Sorry, darling. All any of us want is for you to get back to your old self.'

Old self. The words jar for some reason. Oliver chooses the moment to enter my mind. I elbow him out, blinking at Tam, my head buzzing, but not in a good way now. The day began so well, and yet here I am, floundering again. It's baffling. Maddening. Dispiriting. I take another spoonful of risotto, not really tasting it. 'So tell me all about Dublin and Jules,' I urge, in a bid to regain control of myself and to see off the compassion still clouding her kind eyes. 'Did you have a good trip?'

'*So* good. Four days and it went in a second.' Tam beams at me, tapping her fingertips on the table like she's pretend-playing a mini keyboard. 'I mean, *really* good, Cath. Special.' The beam has become a grin that almost splits her face in two and she's going mad with her faux piano-playing, so mad that even I – dimmest and most unforgivably self-obsessed of best friends – notice the new ring sitting among all her other usual baubles: a ring that stands out for being so slim and classy – a gold band studded with tiny diamonds – circling the fourth finger of her left hand.

All the exuberance, the champagne – the reason for the lunch – fall into place. 'Oh, my God, Tam. Is that what I think it is?'

'It is!' she squeals, turning heads.

'Oh Tam.' I lift her hand up for a better look. 'But it's exquisite.'

'Isn't it,' she croons, cradling the finger as she gawps at its new adornment. 'It's actually an eternity ring. It belonged to Jules' gran.'

My innards are doing a strange ping-pong between joy and something like fear. On Tam's account, I tell myself, for gambling her bruised heart, even with someone as obviously extraordinary as Jules. In the middle of it all, Jules' remark about getting Tam to Ireland is flashing like a red light, together with relief and gratitude that I'd managed to keep my big mouth shut. Tam and Jules have every right to wedded bliss, in Ireland or wherever they choose.

'More details, please,' I command, having given her a proper congratulatory hug and sat back down.

Tam – a burst dam – launches into a minute-by-minute account of Jules dropping to her knees on the stage of her own theatre in order to recite a Neruda love poem, before whipping the ring out. I am about to ask who Neruda is when the waiter glides up to the table to clear our plates and Tam – with an apologetic glance at me – asks for the bill.

'Sorry, but I hate cycling in the dark and I was hoping we might squeeze in a quick stroll up the famous Gold Hill. It will give us a little more time – and peace – to talk.'

Outside, we do our respective coats up to our chins against the afternoon chill and set off at a brisk pace, Tam's hat bag banging against her leg. It's further than we expect so we decide to go just halfway, stopping to take in the famous view, ghostly that afternoon, the trees and undulations of the valley peeking through low, floating tablecloths of mist.

'So, have you got anywhere with wedding plans?' I ask as we head back, somewhat puzzled that Tam, despite her justification for the stroll, has been largely silent. 'Because I happen to know this great company called PartyParty that will give you the mother of all weddings, possibly at a knockdown—'

'Actually, Cath...' She has grabbed my arm and is staring at me with watery eyes. 'We've already done it,' she whispers.

'Done what?' I say stupidly.

'We got married, Cath. Jules and I – with this ring, I went and wedded her.' She is shrieking suddenly, waving her left hand in the air. 'On Tuesday. Can you believe it? *Tuesday*. After spending all Sunday going round in circles about where, when, who, how, we both suddenly thought – at the exact same moment – why make it complicated? So we did a super-quick, super-simple, in-and-out of the registry office job, followed by a nice meal with a few of Jules' lovely theatre friends afterwards. I can't tell you how amazing it was, Cath. I've been a married woman since

Tuesday,' she exclaims again, as if it is only by repetition that she can truly believe the fact herself. 'Isn't it totally insane?'

'Totally,' I cry, while my ever-treacherous thoughts ricochet between shock, delight and an unforgivable sadness. 'So long as you are happy, Tam, that's all that matters. Are you happy?'

'Completely. Madly. Deeply.' The glassiness in her eyes is spilling out as real tears, which she swipes away as we walk on. 'Oh, thank you, Cath. I wasn't sure how you would take it. It almost feels wrong, to be this on top of the world when you're still... but nothing's going to change, okay?' she gabbles. 'On the work front, I mean. I shall take over for the next couple of months, just like I said, and after that, Jules and I want to enjoy having two homes to shuttle between. I'm going to Ireland for two weeks over Christmas and for now, we're going to call that our honeymoon – her brother is coming, so it should be fun...'

I nod and smile as Tam continues talking, and when it comes to parting, we hug each other hard, rocking like wooden dancers, prolonging the moment.

'We'll speak soon, sweetie,' she says as we pull apart, 'and you are the best friend, ever. Nothing will change that.'

It is already changed, I think, watching her walk away, her neon-yellow anorak a beacon against the darkening afternoon sky.

13

CATHERINE

When I open my eyes the next morning, the bedroom is still dark. I am lying on my side, facing my bedside table and my phone, which shows me it is still only a few minutes past five. Outside, the oak that has outgrown the garden is tapping on the windowpane. I blink, trying to make out what the small black shape is, sitting on top of the grief book. Al's bear, I realise dreamily, retaining a clear image of the figurine as my eyelids fall back closed – standing on its little hind legs, arms wide, mouth open in its show of a roar. Or was it a yawn, Al had joked, examining it gently in the beam of the reading light in the station car park because – remembering it was in my pocket and desperate for an upbeat end to what had somehow morphed into a difficult day – I had handed the little gift straight over.

I let myself drift back into the moment, smelling the scents of the cumin and coriander still on my fingers from the curry I had put together before setting off. Al's train had been delayed by twenty minutes – *faulty signal*, he had messaged, followed by a fuming devil-face emoji. He had nonetheless emerged from the platform in a buoyant mood, so sweetly grateful to be met that he did one of the hugs that lift me off my feet. To be greeted in such a way – the happiness of it – after all our recent 'co-existing' – almost hurt. We interlaced fingers for the walk to the car, me lobbing out question after question about Southampton – partly as a way of shelving my own big news and partly because he was clearly relishing it. He was brimming with good things to report – about Building Regs approvals and the fact that Phil, as well as being a decent guy and the best site manager he had ever worked with, apparently knew someone with a second-hand runaround to sell.

'But why the gift?' he had chuckled, still cradling the little bear as we joined the main road, having refused my offer to let him drive. 'Is it our wedding anniversary? Oh no, hang on, we don't have one of those,' he pulled a goofy face, 'because you don't want to marry me – or anyone. Ever.' He said the last word under his breath, tenderly, reaching out to steer a swatch of stray hair behind my ear. 'Thank you for the bear, Cathy. He's cool.'

'It used to be a thing, Al, do you remember? Early on. You were my *bear*.'

'Of course, I remember. I liked it.'

'I bought it in Shaftesbury – I had a bit of spare time and he caught my fancy.'

'Did he now?' Al chuckled, as he carefully stowed the ornament in the work bag wedged between his feet. 'And Tamsin? How was she?'

'In top form, actually.' I go on to give a mini account of our lunch, including the insistence that I take some time out, before lobbing out the headline story.

'*Married*?'

Al being flabbergasted was such a relief – like we had truly, effortlessly, jumped back onto the same wavelength at last. My own jumbled reactions to the happy announcement no longer seemed quite so heinous. Within moments and without prompting – having taken care to say how happy he was for the pair of them – he was in full flow on all the dilemmas this development could pose for me and the business, between assurances that things would sort themselves out, because they always did.

At home, after a groan of delight at the alluring aromas of our supper, Al danced with the dogs, grabbing their big front paws as they leapt on him. While I stirred and warmed the curry, he laid the table – chutney, poppadoms, coconut – a beer for him, a glass of red for me. We know what we like. Every so often, he touched my shoulder, or my back, or my arm as he moved around, saying how spoiled he felt, how lucky.

I bring my bedside table back into focus. The bear is more sharply outlined thanks to the grey dawn light, now seeping in round the edges of the curtains. My mind, too, is waking up properly. Yes, the evening had begun so perfectly – like a scene out of a movie – everything and more that I had hoped for. Until I mentioned having seen Joanne and the gardener.

'Really, Cath? So what?' He lifted my feet – which he had been rubbing in the way I love – off his lap. 'What on earth were you doing there, anyway? I thought you said you were going to the garden place.'

'I was – I did. But on the way, there was a closed road, so—'

'So you *had* to go that way, did you?'

On the telly, a woman with hollow cheeks, an ashen face and wearing a bullet-proof vest was reporting about something from amidst a pile of rubble.

'No, Al, I *chose* to go that way. Because driving past where my dead brother used to live has meaning for me. Okay? And then I just saw what I saw. I'm sorry I said anything – it was probably nothing—'

'Correct. It was *nothing*. I expect the poor man needed the bathroom.' He had switched the television off and was standing in front of it, arms buckled across his cupboard of a chest. 'But that is not the point. What *is* the point is that what Joanne chooses to do is no business of yours. Just leave the poor woman alone.'

'Al, I meant no harm—'

'Didn't you?'

Bobby and Belle, attuned to us – the timbre of our voices, the atmosphere – were keeping their distance, heads slumped on their front paws, their big soulful eyes rolling between our faces as we took it in turns to speak.

'Of course I didn't. I just saw what I saw.'

'Look, Cath,' he went on wearily, 'your obsession with that woman—'

'I do not have an *obsession* with Joanne.'

'I beg to differ. It's got to stop.'

'What's got to stop?'

'Your *obsession*.'

'Or what?' I, too, had stood up, glaring, standing my ground, inwardly fighting the loathsome – and always dimly, darkly familiar – sensation of being treated like a child in need of castigation.

Al made a moaning sound, running his hands over his face. 'Or I am going to get seriously worried, that's what.' He snatched up our empty tea mugs and trudged out of the room.

The dogs, pushing themselves into sitting positions, glued their eyes on me, heads cocked, as if to say, *What the hell have you gone and done now*?

By the time I pushed open the bedroom door some ten minutes later, Al was fast asleep – with the lights still blazing – lying on his back, the covers up to his chin, breathing soundlessly despite his mouth being half-open.

And yet, here the little bear is, within ten inches of my nose. Heart pounding, I roll over to reach for Al, finding nothing but empty sheet. I see from my phone that it is still only half past five. The bedroom air is icy, the house silent. Gathering the duvet round me, I stumble out onto the landing. Al has gone. Of course, Al has gone. Parking my dumb, sentimental little gift by my face was his goodbye. He has left. Given up on me. Because who could blame him? And because people do leave you – that's just what happens. Again, and again. We push our way into the world alone and we leave it alone. Even twins.

On the stairs, I lose my footing among the big folds of the bedding, half-wrenching my shoulder as I manage to catch hold of the banister.

But Al has not left me. He is sitting at his computer in his blue towelling dressing gown, his head bent over the keyboard. As I enter, he looks up.

'Hello Cath. Okay?'

'Yup.' I can feel my shoulder throbbing slightly. I shuffle to the desk, careful not to knock over the plug-in heater, belting warmth from the corner of the room. 'I wondered where you were.'

'I am right here. I woke and couldn't get back to sleep. I left the bear to keep an eye. Didn't you see?'

'I did. Thanks, Al... and sorry.'

'For what?' There is challenge in his voice. He has tipped his desk chair back and interlaced his hands behind his head. The top of his dressing gown has parted enough to show a portion of the impossibly perfect shield of dark hair that covers his chest.

I look down at my toes, poking out under the duvet, and burrow them deeper into the soft pile of the carpet – a recent acquisition because moths got the old one, great islands of baldness appearing under the hoover out of nowhere. 'For the Joanne thing, for jumping to conclusions.'

'Stop thinking about that woman all the time, Cath,' he says heavily. 'It's not good for you. It's always held you back.'

'It was just something that crossed my mind, that's all.' I know I sound lame. I am lame.

'Promise me.' He lets the chair fall forward with a thump. 'Your sister-in-law, as we have long since agreed, can be tricky. You once felt obliged to try and deal with her, but now you don't have to.'

'But Stephanie and Lau—'

'Nothing is going to change there for a while. Give it time. Before you know it, they'll be old enough to make their own minds up about who they see. Promise me, Cath, that you are done with her.'

'I promise.' I move closer to him and slide a hand across the bare bit of his chest.

'I've got to work,' he growls.

'Really?' I start to stroke the shield of hair.

'Cath.'

'No?'

'No, love. Not now.' He draws the sides of the dressing gown more firmly together, tightening the cord at his waist. 'It's still so early. Why don't you try and get a bit more sleep and I'll bring up some tea when I'm done. I've got three windows to lose and a staircase to shift.'

'I'd like to come to Southampton and see the site,' I mumble, pulling the duvet more tightly round me as I turn for the door. 'If that's allowed.'

'Of course it's allowed. That would be nice.'

'It's not like I won't have the time, is it? Not now. Also, I'm no good at visualising things from drawings. I need to *see* them.'

'Great. See them you shall,' he mutters, his attention already back on his screen.

Upstairs, I lie on the bed and billow the duvet on top of me. As it lands, I feel a momentary comfort and then only its heaviness and the mounting heat of my body. *Rest.* It's what everyone keeps demanding of me. Like it can be done to order. As if contentment can come from relaxing, when it's so obviously the other way round. Al's hands yanking his dressing gown together flash across my brain. He has every right to say no to me, just as I do to him. But – until tonight – I cannot recall him ever having done so. Not once. The rejection stings. But far, far worse is the drip-drip fear that he is really pulling away from me, that I could lose him, on top of everything else.

14

OLIVER

Amelia's hair, wet from their swim in the hotel's rather poky, basement-level pool, was soaking the shoulders of her red top, Oliver noticed, going to fetch a dry hand towel from the bathroom. He did his best to rub the cute, wavy tresses dry, not wanting to disturb the game she was playing with the miniature set of animals Faith had bought her during their trip to the Seattle aquarium the previous day. The animals were plastic and came in a little see-through bag with a zipper: a seal, a seahorse, a starfish, a crab and – biggest of the group – a Giant Pacific octopus, all of them in bright, primary colours that had nothing to do with their real-life appearance. Amelia liked the octopus best – partly for its many legs and partly because of its name, which she used in full, religiously, whenever she said something to it, which was quite often.

'Ow, Daddy, you're hurting.'

'Sorry honey, but we've got to go soon and I want you looking nice for Gram and Gramps.'

'Will we have pizza again?' She had put the animals in a

circle on his and Faith's bed and was going round picking each one up in turn, making them dance.

'That's up to Gram and Gramps. We're here to give them a good time, because it is special for us all to hang out together.' Oliver was glad that his daughter did not yet have the where-withal to hear the hint of an edge in his voice. The previous evening's outing to the pizza parlour a couple of blocks from Fairview – frequented on many previous visits – had turned into a major undertaking. Getting both his parents buttoned up against the cold – scarves, hats, gloves, his father rejecting the fleece-lined boots that had been that year's expensive birthday gift, in favour of his flimsy, ancient trainers – had required more patience, Oliver decided, than Amelia's very brief tantrum phase of only ever wanting to wear her tutu. The thirty-yard walk had felt like thirty miles, the slow pace making him more than usually aware of the dull ache at times still lurking in his healed ankle. His mother, clinging to his arm in her finger-pinching way, moaning that the wind would fire up her sinuses, had needed constant cajoling and reassurance. His father, mean-while, had politely declined Faith's offer of the arm that was not busy holding onto Amelia, and tottered along in front, his neck stuck in the fixed angle that granted him a view of the sidewalk and little else.

They were in Seattle for three days, having left inconve-niently early on the morning after the Connecticut Thanks-giving in order to have some of Friday as well as the weekend for the visit. Yet already, Oliver was longing, guiltily, for the moment just twenty-four hours away, when they would be doing the journey in reverse, dropping back the rental and joining the queue to board their flight home. He *did* love his parents – or at least, he felt a deep-down loyalty to them, for bearing and raising him, no matter the manifold strains and difficulties along the way. But, dear Lord, he loved the life he had forged for himself far more. On top of which, the undisclosed fact of Robert's death was weighing a little heavy in his heart, adding to his tension. Indeed, without Faith's unfailing cheerfulness, sticking – in loyal, innocent compliance with his instructions – to bland, 'safe' topics in every one of her sterling efforts to make conversation – Oliver wasn't sure how he would have borne it.

It had been Faith's suggestion that he take Amelia down to the hotel pool for a mid-afternoon dip. His parents would be napping anyway, she had pointed out, and with his work back at full pace, he should grab the chance of some quality time with their daughter. She would see him at Fairview, she said, once she had picked up some farewell gifts from the mall – to soften the blow of their departure the following day.

Five weeks since the awkward conversation round Sue Ellen and Don's table, and Oliver was still pinching himself at the way his wife's naturally caring nature had gone into overdrive. Upstairs afterwards, he had found it impossible to hold back on the full extent of his discomfort at having had his most private territory tossed around so openly, without any warning or permission, and all on a day when he had been feeling a little low and left out anyway. His family was so small and dysfunctional compared to hers, he had conceded wretchedly. But it still needed respecting, and that was what he felt had gone out of the window.

Instead of firing back counterarguments, Faith had come to sit next to him, her eyes wide, her expression stricken. 'I am so sorry, Oliver. I respect you and your family with all my heart.' She had run her fingers down his cheek, forcing him to look at her. 'Please forgive me if sharing information with my folks about Robert caused you distress. How did your parents take it, by the way? Was it very terrible?'

Oliver had managed a shrug, having to avert his eyes as his mind skittered back to his decision to keep his promise to Catherine. Was he a liar or a coward? He had no idea. 'Oh, you know them,' he had muttered, 'with all their off-limit subjects and zero interest in the past. They said they never wanted to hear the matter spoken of again, which I guess also needs respect, from me as well as you.'

'Okay, honey, okay.' Faith had cupped his face with her palms, steering his gaze back to meet hers. 'I hear everything you say and will do my best. I just wish sometimes that you would share your feelings with me more, because then I could do a better job of understanding them... but that doesn't stop me loving you, dearest Oliver.' She had kissed him on the cheek. 'Let's go visit them just as soon as you're better. Maybe at the end of November, right after Thanksgiving? Also, I'm going to call the physiotherapist who worked miracles on Don's shoulder that time. You've been having a tough ride, sweetheart, but I'm going to fix everything.'

* * *

They set off for Fairview a little behind schedule, Amelia having asked for a hair-braiding which had taken Oliver several goes to get right, and which was now giving a funny lump to her bobble hat, Oliver noted fondly. Then there had been a to-do about having to go back for the pack of aquarium animals, Oliver – cursing himself for the oversight – first telling her she could wait to enjoy them later, and then relenting because this prospect caused so much distress. Luckily, there was no real rush, he reminded himself, since Faith, armed with a jigsaw of Seattle lit up at night, as well as a huge box of chocolate liquorice candy – pictures of both had been sent from the mall – had confirmed that she was on her way there.

'Is that a new dance?' Oliver asked jokily, as Amelia started hopping sideways instead of walking forwards. 'Or are you a jumping bean?'

'I am!' she cried gleefully. 'Jump! Jump! Jump! Look, Daddy!'

'I am looking, honey,' Oliver assured her, throwing an apologetic face at the hurrying man in a beanie and padded coat forced to swerve past the acrobatics.

'Can I have a shoulder-ride?' Amelia asked next, all the bounce suddenly going out of her. 'I'm *so* tired.'

'We're nearly there, honey,' Oliver pleaded. He would scoop her up if absolutely necessary, but was still a little uncertain of his upper-body strength, let alone the extra weight on his weaker leg. Sue Ellen's physio had indeed proved something of a miracle-worker, but not pushing a healing process beyond its own readiness to progress had been a recent mantra, delivered with such a penetrating gaze that Oliver had felt she was referring to something far more significant than his recovery programme.

'I want a snack. *Please*, Daddy?' Amelia groaned the request. Instead of actually moving in any direction, she was now hanging off his elbow, letting her legs fold under her.

'We finished the snacks after our—' Oliver did a double-take as his daughter – apparently not so tired after all – broke free of his hand-hold to race back to the store window they had just passed. A vintage charity store, by the look of the range of paraphernalia it contained: a wall clock, a tailor's dummy, a guitar, a cooler bag, a birdcage, as well as a whole stack of vinyl albums and several shelves of books.

'Honey, we don't have much time to hang around.'

'But look, Daddy, it's an octopus,' she squealed, pointing at a large book Oliver hadn't spotted, propped against an umbrella stand and sporting what was indeed an image of a cephalopod, under the title *Weirdly Human Aliens*. 'Can we buy it, Daddy?'

'No honey, because we don't have time.'

'But I want it,' Amelia wailed, exhausted by the intense half-hour in the pool, Oliver decided grimly, and the break to her routine, not to mention a night that had seen her wake no less than four times. Bad dreams, she had said, sobbing, but then falling quickly back to sleep each time, leaving him and Faith shaking their heads.

The book was hefty, and about lots of things other than octopuses, but at least it had some good photographs, Oliver consoled himself, stepping out of the shop some fifteen minutes later with it under his arm. The diversion had taken a while, because a woman in front of them had wanted to chat as well as purchase two greetings cards, and because there had been no persuading Amelia that the purchase could take place another time.

'Hi, sorry we're late, but we bought ourselves a great book, didn't we, Amelia?' Oliver declared, striding into his parents' shoebox of a main room with all the goodwill he had vowed to maintain for every minute of the remaining twenty-four hours of the trip. 'She wants to show it to you all, don't you, honey?' he said, crouching down to pull off his daughter's hat and unzip her coat, before removing his own. He carefully placed the book, which was heavy, into both of Amelia's hands, offering big smiles all round as he propelled her deeper into the room. His parents were side by side in their usual recliners, while Faith was perched on the edge of the small two-seater sofa, her legs tucked under the coffee table, where the jigsaw and chocolates sat, one box on top of the other, still in their cellophane wrappings.

It took Oliver a few long seconds to realise that there was an atmosphere. Faith had cooed a hello, smiling at Amelia, but remained sitting with her fingers interlocked in her lap, while his parents, too, after muted nods of greeting, fixed their gazes on their granddaughter, like she occupied the safest space in the room. Amelia, oblivious to atmospheres, aware only that she appeared to be the focus of everyone's attention, trotted proudly to her grandfather, placing the book on his lap as she started to spout all the octopus facts Oliver had relayed in a bid to speed up the final part of their walk.

'They have *three* hearts, Gramps, *eight* arms and *no* bones.' She patted the picture on the cover and then grandly folded her little arms in the manner of one deeply satisfied. 'And I have a *giant* one of my own.' She turned to Oliver, who quickly pulled the little pouch of animals out of his coat pocket and handed it over.

'So, all good here, I hope,' he ventured brightly, as Amelia shook out the plastic animals onto her grandfather's lap, on top of the book. 'Did you like the gifts that Faith picked out? We're so sorry it's a short trip, but we'll come again soon. Maybe I could fly up for those tests you said you're going to have, Dad, and then it will be Christmas before we know it.'

'The more we see of you, the better, Oliver, dear,' his mother said in her low, dry way, while his father, busy with Amelia, did a thumbs up sign.

'You too, Mom.' Oliver was about to sit down next to Faith, but his mother flung out an arm by way of an invitation for him to come closer, clicking her fingers as she liked to, just to make sure he got the message clearly. He tried to shoot Faith a look as he obeyed, but she kept her gaze on the jigsaw box, like it was the first time she had seen the famous Pin Needle skyscraper, sprouting like a giant mushroom out of the heart of the Seattle urban jungle.

'I need to take my meds, dear,' his mother told him. 'Could you help me out of this darn chair? I have such a head this afternoon.'

'Or I could fetch them, Mom. Just tell me where—'

'No, Oliver, I need to get out of here – to lie down.' She was scrabbling at his arms with a sort of desperation.

'Right, Mom, that's fine.' Oliver looked again at Faith, who met his eyes this time, widening hers in a don't-ask-me response.

'There was an incident,' his mother declared the moment he had closed the bedroom door. She sat on the bed with a weighty sigh, sticking out a foot and waggling it by way of a command for help in getting her slippers off. 'That is, I think I may have spoken sharply to Faith.'

Oliver, having quickly crouched down to perform the task, stood up abruptly, dropping the slippers. 'To Faith?' His insides were twisting. 'That is too bad, Mom. Faith tries so hard to—'

'If you must know, she took it upon herself to talk about Robert. About him passing. As if she thought we knew it. And I told her we did *not* know it, and that it was no business of hers.'

Oliver pressed his face into his hands and groaned softly.

'I told her,' his mother continued, 'that – like that sister of his – the boy was a creature poisoned with sin, who had treated you, your father – and *me* – with the utmost ingratitude and contempt, despite years of extreme forgiveness and kindness. I told her that I was offended by her choosing to utter his name under our roof and please could she not do so again. Actually, I told her to butt out,' she concluded, a hint of triumph in her tone.

'Mom, you shouldn't have done that. I wish you had *not* done that.' Oliver spoke through gritted teeth, mostly to prevent himself raising his voice. 'Faith meant well – Faith always means well – she has a large, very loving family and therefore finds it hard how we, in contrast, have one that is small and full of division—'

'Do *not* talk to me that way, Oliver. We have our own loving family. We are *not* full of *division*. Your grandma and grandpapa loved you dearly, just as your father and I have always done. Always, do you hear? Making countless sacrifices – for *you*.' Her voice was growing strident enough to carry into the sitting room.

'Mom, please, there is no need to speak so loudly—'

'There is every need – those two were *evil*, and after all that I did for them,' she bawled hoarsely, as if having to defend herself to a noisy crowd now, rather than just Oliver. 'They wanted to ruin our lives, but I would *not* let them.'

'Mom, for God's sake, stop shouting.'

'I will not have the Lord's name taken in vain, not in my house,' she cried, at even greater volume. 'Apologise to me this instant.'

Oliver froze for a moment as the room spun. 'No, Mom, I will not.' His hand found the corner post of the bed, and he gripped it hard. Her screeching was making his head hum. It was a long time since she had used such decibels, and after the twins, it was his father who had borne the brunt. His default role – apart from the occasional explosions during his student years – had been to watch, to feel afraid. Powerless. 'You have upset Faith and that upsets me,' Oliver said, summoning steadiness through sheer willpower. 'I warned her that you would not want to hear of Robert's passing, but Faith has higher ideals, and so she—'

'And what is that supposed to mean? *Higher* ideals?' his mother sneered. Two fingers had found their way to the sore patch above her left eyebrow.

'The belief that people should forgive each other, I guess...' Oliver faltered, gripping the bed post more tightly. 'Especially family members.'

'Robert and Catherine had their chances.'

'Did they, Mom? Really? Because it kind of hit me recently that they were just six years old when their own mom was taken. *Greta*.' He said the word with force because of it being forbidden. 'They were *six*. That's Amelia's age.'

'I need to rest. I want you to leave, Oliver. I do not know what has gotten into you.' Her voice had grown plaintive. Her free hand plucked at the counterpane, twisting it into little peaks.

'You raised your hand to them, Mom,' Oliver went on doggedly. 'I know those were different times, but you never once did that to me, that I can recall.'

She let out a throaty cackle of a laugh. 'Oh, but they deserved it. The things they did, Oliver, day in, day out – I was trying to protect you – protect all of us – I cannot believe that you do not remember.'

'Oh, I think I remember a fair bit,' Oliver said bitterly. Sadness was washing through him. His mother was a bad person, or maybe a damaged one, from whatever it was that she had been through back in her youth. Pregnant, jilted, the termination. Yet such traumas could have made a person more humble – more inclined to treat others well – instead of filling the heart with venom. But it was all too late now anyway. He would never know the whys and wherefores. 'I don't even know what she died of,' he said hoarsely. 'Greta, Robert and Catherine's mother, what was her illness?'

His mother hunched her shoulders, looking at the floor.

'Mom?'

'Oh, right from the birth, there were complications – damage that couldn't be fixed, infections. It was a stomach tumour in the end, but those two as good as killed her.'

'No.' It was Oliver's turn to raise his voice. He took a step towards her, his entire body trembling, a terrible urge to strike her coursing through him. 'That is an unacceptable thing to say. Please take it back.'

'I will not. The Lord has His ways and it is not our job to question them.'

Through the wall, Oliver was dimly aware of sounds of movement. He took a deep breath. A curious combination of defeat and calm was surfing through him, taking his fear with it – an old fear, Oliver realised, that had been crouching inside, scared even of itself, for his entire life. 'I haven't forgotten what Catherine and Robert were like, Mom,' he said dully. 'How could I? They bullied me pretty bad. It's something I've had to work through. But what I am ashamed to say I've only recently got my head around, is how bad they had it too – from you. Sure, they were ill-behaved – wild – but there are always reasons for that – in kids, anyway. Especially ones who have lost their mom. You never gave them a chance.'

He walked away from her, turning only when he reached the door. She was staring after him, looking dumbfounded, her fingers furiously stroking the raw patch above the eyebrow. 'I need to go check on Faith and talk to Dad. We'll come back tomorrow, when we've all settled down a bit.'

'You can send your father in here. I need him.'

To Oliver's dismay, only his father was in the living room. He was sitting on the sofa, bent over the jigsaw box, which had been opened.

'Faith said she would see you back at the hotel,' he said, not looking up from the pile of pieces he was sorting through.

'Okay. Thanks, Dad. And look, I'm sorry if Faith—'

'It was a shock, son, that's all I can tell you.' He concentrated on picking a piece from the pile and adding it to several already in front of him. Outside pieces, Oliver saw, a memory flashing of the two of them side by side at a table, his legs swinging in a too-high chair, being shown how to tackle a jigsaw of a battleship. An ancient memory. Catherine and Robert had been at the table too, with no histrionics that he could recall. Or maybe his mind was playing tricks. Why had he not thought of his father's enjoyment of jigsaws until now? Why had it had taken Faith's inspiration in the mall to bring it back to him?

'The fact is, Faith thought you knew about Robert because I—'

'It doesn't matter now, son.' He picked up another piece, holding it very near his eyes. 'No one can just change, Oliver, remember that. Not her,' he nodded in the direction of the bedroom, 'not me, not you, and certainly not those two. It is what it is. It was what it was.'

Oliver had no strength left to take issue. After dealing with his mother, the resignation – the absence of drama – in his father's manner was a relief. And the old man was in a pretty fragile state, what with the faint tinge of yellow in his complexion now fuelling talk of more tests, and the pitifully crooked neck – even if that was kind of an ideal angle for tackling a puzzle, Oliver noted wryly, crossing the room to place a hand on his father's bony back.

'Mom wants you, by the way.'

'I thought she might.' He connected two outside pieces together, giving the join a little tap of satisfaction.

'I don't know if Faith told you, Dad,' Oliver found himself adding, there being nothing left to fear, 'but Robert's death was from skin cancer that metastasised to his lungs.'

'Okay, son. Thank you.'

'Will you go to Mom, then?' Oliver ventured, when the old man hadn't moved.

'In a moment.'

'I'll come by tomorrow,' Oliver said, reaching for his coat.

'Sure, son.' He had stood up at last, tugging down the shapeless hem of the old, grey, home-knit sweater he was wearing – a survivor from the days when his wife had still wielded her knitting needles. 'One more thing. How did you know – about Robert?'

Oliver had started to answer when his mother's voice, shrill with outrage and impatience, cut through from the bedroom. His father, dropping his chin, set off towards it – as he always had, as he always would, Oliver despaired, because people didn't change, just like the old man said.

Out on the street, he took several gulps of the icy, November air before messaging Faith to say that he was on his way and would explain and make up for every single thing that had happened that afternoon.

Five o'clock, and between the street lamps, it was pitch dark. He felt drained. The ordeal of the visit was beyond words, and yet he felt lighter inside. To have stood up to his mother instead of tolerating her. To have spoken truth. All thanks to Faith. Oliver quickened his pace, thinking how very different his own life would have been if his parents had been able to talk freely, as Faith's family did, about every matter under the sun – microscopes held up by all of them to one another – no one escaped – as he had experienced all too keenly. His mom and dad were locked inside iron boxes in comparison, held to ransom by their own terrors.

In their spacious family room, the light was on and the beds not made, thanks to the *No Housekeeping* sign he'd forgotten to remove from the door. Faith must have gone out for food somewhere, Oliver guessed, no doubt because of Amelia being starving and not knowing how long he would be. Needing the bathroom, he went through to the ensuite, noticing in the course of relieving himself that it looked a little tidier. Barer. His shaver was there, his toothbrush, their shared toothpaste, but all of Faith's various pots of creams, serums and cosmetics had gone. Oliver did up his fly and whirled round, checking the bath. The wind-up plastic frog that swam, the bright-blue bottle of bath soap for Amelia's sensitive skin, had also vanished.

He ran back into the bedroom, fumbling for his phone which he had dropped onto the bed. Finding no messages from Faith, he was on the point of calling when his eye was caught by a piece of folded white hotel writing paper on the pillow on his side of the bed. White on white, it had not stood out.

Dear Oliver,

I have managed to get seats on a flight home this evening. Please do not cut short your visit to come after us.

You lied to me and I need to think about that.

I felt humiliated today in a way that I never want to experience again.

Faith

He tried to call her, but she didn't pick up. Instead, while he was leaving a garbled voicemail, a message pinged through.

> Pls give me some time. Laurie has said we can stay with her and Seth for a while. I'll get what we need from home first. You have issues to sort out with your parents, Oliver. I suggest you get right on with that. F

Laurie was Faith's second eldest and least favourite sister, who lived on the other side of the park. A senior partner in a law firm, while her husband, Seth, ran a hedge fund, the pair had more money than the rest of the family put together. Their two kids, Elise and Lance, were both at college, except that Elise wanted to give up her studies and pursue a career as an influencer instead. It had been one of the many family matters to get kicked around the long Thanksgiving table the previous week, along with the new Russian boyfriend apparently responsible for Elise's absence from the gathering.

Oliver texted back.

> Please, don't do this, Faith. We can work this out. I NEED to work this out – WITH you.

Oliver stared at the phone for a long time, but there was no reply. The thought of chasing after her made his heart flip with hope, and then crash. She had such a head start. And she had asked specifically for that not to happen. He had to begin by honouring that at least.

> I love you

he wrote instead, his thumbs moving feverishly as he blinked back his tears.

> My heart is breaking. I am nothing without you. Call me, any time, day or night. Oliver X

15

CATHERINE

'Thank you for coming today.'

'Don't be silly. The biggest project of your life, won against all odds – how could I not want to take a proper look. I also have my Christmas shopping plan, remember? You'd go mad if I hung around all day.'

'Maybe.' Al throws me a sheepish grin.

'I like this car.'

'Me too.' He gives the steering wheel of our new, second-hand, black Volkswagen Polo an appreciative thump. 'Good old Phil. It's a gem.'

This Southampton visit was a great idea, I congratulate myself, turning to gaze at the rolling grey-greens of the New Forest without quite seeing them. Putting effort into 'together-ness', showing interest in the work now gobbling up 90 per cent of Al's time and headspace – I really am doing my best. Me not working and being less frazzled has definitely helped too: no rows, occasional love-making, hearty meals, telly-watching... A blessed sense of stability has started to creep back into me – us – and I intend to hang onto it for dear life.

I keep my head averted as little Laura flickers in the corner of my mind: clambering out of the car last Saturday, the gauzy tent of her ballet dress poking out through her unzipped, pink anorak, performing on-the-spot hops to fill the time it took Joanne to get out of the driving seat and join her on the pavement. Laura, properly – at last. Though I have managed a couple of brief break-time glimpses of her as well as Stephanie now, this was my first satisfying sighting of my youngest niece. It had taken only a wee bit of the stealth Al had got so het up about when exacting the promise about Joanne – necessitating both waiting and following at a sensible distance to what turned out to be a church hall where the ballet club took place, a mere five-minute drive away from the house. A few other mini-dancers clutching the hands of grown-ups and similarly attired – a bobbing flock of baby flamingos – had been heading towards the same entrance.

Ballet, aged eight. The world as it should be. At that age, I would have been fearful of how a tutu might expose the come-and-go bruises on my upper legs. The mortification would have hurt far more than the flat of Diane's hand ever did, or the broom handle, or even the spikey hairbrush. I never cared about any of her punishments. Except for one. I don't want the memory, but in it barges. We had hidden Oliver's shoe – a shiny new black leather one, aggravatingly superior to our pinching, too-small, scuffed sandals – and the predictable ructions ensued, even after I had fished it out, unscathed, from the kitchen bin. Marched into our bedroom, we endured the usual threats of slaps for Rob and actual ones for me, because he only wept, while I stuck my tongue out. I knew how to rile her. But the scissors, plucked out of the baggy front pocket of the old yellow apron she was wearing – the one that had been our mother's – had caught me by surprise. As did the hissed instruction to stand in front of our little mirror and cut my own hair. When I refused, she savagely embarked on the job for me, cursing – because it was so thick – as she hacked. Something broke inside me then. My hair, it was a piece of my mother. It *was* my mother. But I didn't show it, and gave warning eyes to Rob that he wasn't to say a word. Even Oliver, invited to laugh at my supposed reckless idiocy, had gasped. And when my father got home, plainly too shocked to say anything except that hair always grew back, I proclaimed that I had done it because I *liked* it. Oh yes, there were many routes to victory over my stepmother.

I realise Al is saying something about Tamsin, how she will never leave me in the lurch because she is too decent and loyal. It takes effort to climb outside my head. During these recent, less busy days, it's happened a few times, my thoughts starting to pop more randomly, invariably taking me backwards. Almost as if a latch has come loose in my brain, turning it into an open window.

'The most important thing is Tam being happy,' I parrot, because this remains true, regardless of my knee-jerk selfish reservations about her wedded bliss. 'Oh, and by the way, I've been looking into options for doing an MBA,' I add, 'to sharpen my own skill set going forward, etcetera – whether or not Tam ends up deciding to make a new life in Dublin.'

'That's amazing, Cath,' Al exclaims, as I knew he would. 'Wow. Good for you.'

'Just trying to think ahead.' I am loving my breeziness, my air of motivation. In truth, barring one skim-reading of a Google search, I still barely know what an MBA even *is*, beyond something that sounds good and business-y. 'And I'm looking forward to meeting Phil,' I add quickly, wanting to see off any further interrogation on the matter.

'And he you. He's such a nice man, Cath – wife, three kids,

the coolest house – which he designed – overlooking the Solent. Mad keen on sailing, keeps his own boat – a real can-do person, which I admire so much.'

And that's what I am trying so hard to be, I think proudly. A *can-do* person. Like Phil.

A moment later, we pass a couple of ponies, shaggy as donkeys, nuzzling for grass in the hard December ground. Unperturbed, content, they barely glance up. They are so inside the immediacy of their own lives, and I know I must get the hang of that too – stay *present*, as the psychobabble goes.

* * *

The school, set in a residential area on the outskirts of Southampton, is grander than I have been expecting, entirely of red brick with Gothic overtones to its sloping roofs, and protected by tall, sharp-tipped, black railings. Al waves a card in front of a security barrier across a makeshift works access down one side, and we are soon bumping along a track towards the back of the campus, where his great project is underway. Modernising old buildings and creating new ones, including a music school and theatre, Al has taken to calling it a Rubik's cube of a design, despairingly on bad days, and proudly on good ones. Adding to the challenge is the fact that the school has to be kept open throughout the works, requiring the construction of temporary facilities along with everything else. With the Christmas holidays having just started, I know he has high hopes of what can be achieved with the entire place at the disposal of the construction team for three weeks, even though Phil is apparently due to disappear for ten days of it on a family ski trip.

As soon as we are out of the car, a stocky man in his late thirties with chin stubble, thick, fair hair and blue eyes bright enough to remind me very faintly of my brother, hops out of a door set into a big yellow container of an office.

'Hey, Al – and you must be Cath. Phil Evans – great to meet you.' He has a booming voice with a hint of an Aussie twang, and gives my hand a warm shake before slapping Al on the back. 'So, it's to be a guided tour, is it? We could grab a coffee first if you like? All amenities on offer, right, Al?' He sweeps his arm in a faux grand invitation for me to enter the container and then lands the arm back across Al's shoulders, saying something that makes them both laugh as they follow me inside.

Fifteen minutes later, pleasantries and coffee done with, we are standing in the foyer of the sports centre – an area not destined for demolition – staring into a glass cabinet containing a mini-model of how the finished buildings will look. It is an exquisite construction in itself, mesmerizingly complete, with tiny figures and illuminated rooms and path-ways. Studying it, I am filled with something like longing – such a perfect world! So orderly! So manageable! But both Al's and Phil's phones keep going off, and soon Phil rushes away, saying he'll catch us later. Al nobly continues with the promised tour, fielding all my ignoramus questions between making get-back-to-you-soon signals to various people who try to approach him as we go.

Saying goodbye at the car, I find myself tearing up, but in a good way – because, for once, it's about Al, instead of flaky old me. 'It's so much more mega than I imagined, Al. Unbelievable. I can't tell you how proud I am.'

'Ah, thanks, Cathy...' He's handing me the car key when his phone buzzes yet again, this time with something that causes him to freeze, saucer-eyed.

'Al? Everything okay?'

He lets out a wild laugh. 'Dear God, I did *not* see this coming... It's Ryan... Oh bloody hell... Take a look for yourself.'

He holds the phone out, revealing a blurry black and white x-ray-type image above the caption:

> Not planned, but whaaaaaaa! 8 weeeeks old. Hellooooo grandad!!!!!

'Can you believe it? I mean, the idiots. But also... bloody hell. *Bloody hell*, Cath.'

I am half-laughing too, half-aghast. The hapless pair – becoming parents. It feels impossible. Ryan might be twenty-four, but I still think of him as a teenager. I don't even know how old Sadie is, but she looks barely into her twenties and has a figure so boyishly skinny, it is hard to imagine it ever swelling sufficiently to carry a child. The two of them scratch a living between events. They busk in parks and at train stations. They live in a bedsit in Crouch End and drive a clapped-out camper van because of gigs and festivals.

'Granddad. Now, there's a crazy notion.'

'Grandma is crazier,' Al murmurs, gawping again at the scan. 'By which I mean very-*young*-still-not-quite-forty-eight-year-old partner of a grandfather,' he adds hastily – sweetly – pulling me close with such tenderness that I feel a rush of gratitude to Ryan and Sadie, simply for giving us the moment.

* * *

I look up the postcode of Southampton's main shopping centre and put it into the satnav, but then see a sign for the docks and Isle of Wight ferries and before I know it, I am taking that instead. I have most of the day after all and, with the sun high and the sky blue, the notion of a mini-stroll along the waterside takes hold. I head for Mayflower Park, guessing I'll easily find a slot for the car near there, which I do, buying an hour of parking time and then wondering what on earth to do with it, since there's only so much staring-at-water one can do, especially when the view across it is dominated by container vessels, cranes ten times the size of Al's school one, and scores of moored boats.

It takes a little while – the familiar sights, the glittering reach of water – an arm pointing south – to acknowledge that what I have really come for is Rob. To catch a little glimpse of him – of us – during our glory days. All the years of toing and froing on the ferry, the blissful Granny Jean summers, all that escaping. My eyes stream, but only because of the glare and the wind blowing off the water. For a moment, I see our grandmother, small and plump as a ball of wool, with her gruff way of loving and her foghorn voice, scolding us or Pip, but never for long. *Thank you,* I tell her in my head, *and well done – for being* yourself, *and for managing to look after us. To love us.* My heart swells but it is mostly with a sort of self-pride. My grief book may have been patchily consulted, but its messages about feelings have been clear enough: the importance of allowing them to arrive. And here I am, doing just that. *Bring it on, feelings!*

I head back to the car via the park – a significantly sprucer layout of grass and paths than I remember, though we only set foot in it twice that I can recall. Once, with our father because of some sort of delay with the ferry, and then many years later, when – at the grand age of fifteen – Rob and I had been deemed old enough to manage the return journey to London on our own. We had money for our tickets and reminder notes from Granny Jean on how to get to the train station – though we knew the way well enough. In our teenage wisdom however, we decided to spend the travel money on cans of cider and cigarettes instead, both newly discovered pleasures thanks to the coins that had been pressed into our palms all summer for doing chores. Chopping wood, mowing the slope of wiry grass that overlooked the beach, carrying heavy shopping bags – anything too physical that year and our grandmother's chest wheezed as noisily as the dusty set of bellows she pumped to make the logs in the fireplace flare. A hot summer, but she was always cold.

To Rob and me, the park seemed the ideal spot for discreet enjoyment of our illicit spoils. We had hunkered down away from the main path, using our rucksacks as back-rests, puffing and swigging, in love with our own audacity. Until I was sick. I was always sick, eventually. But Rob, as we had learnt that summer, could drink and drink. It made him so happy. Confident. So much more fun to be with, truth be told. Alcohol morphed the world into amazingness, Rob declared, like someone had reached into his head and switched the lights on.

We had no idea that our last holiday on the island was behind us. Not just because never going again was the immediate punishment meted out when – having hurdled ticket barriers – we finally got home, reeking of drink and smoke, but because six weeks later, Granny Jean went for one of her swims and then never made it back up to the little white house. Pip was given to a neighbour, which upset Rob and me almost as much as the thought of her being gone. A parental row then broke out over the funeral because our father was alone in thinking we should attend. For once, he took on our stepmother, holding his ground against a barrage of ludicrous arguments, including the importance of not missing a single day of our new O-level courses. Something deeper and darker than concern for our education was afoot, we knew, because with her, there always was. Power. Loyalty. Motherhood. Wifehood. As the rows raged, with Baby Oliver, a weedy nine-year-old, still skulking and scuttling between his room and his mother's skirts, Rob and I heard the first reference to the problems once caused by our mother being German: Granny Jean's intransigence, what that had put our father through. All of it came firing out of our stepmother's thin, spitting mouth, grist to her baffling mill. Physical punishment of us – of me – had ceased by then. Maybe because we had grown so large, so strong. Or maybe she already had desertion in her sights.

In the end, we went. Granite-faced and silent behind the wheel, our father drove us, via the ferry, to a tiny, local church, so packed that a crowd soon gathered outside. At the graveside, he released just one deep, dry cough of a sob as he stepped forward to cast in his handful of stony earth, which landed on the coffin with a clatter. For Rob and me, the gruesome knowledge that our grandmother's rotund, robust body was now to lie rotting in a box underground was superseded only by the sense of an era ending. That the best bits of our childhood were done.

I stop at the grey-brick tower erected in memory of the Pilgrim Fathers. I see my father standing in the exact same spot, Rob and me on either side of him, our small hands encased in his, our heads tipped back as he points out the little copper sailing ship perched on the cupola. The Mayflower, dainty as a feather against the blue December sky. I hear my father's voice as I stare up at it, telling us all the details of the ordeal of the journey to what became New England: the months it took, the hardship, the courage, how America was still the land of great opportunity for those brave and pioneering enough to venture there. As if – maybe – the seeds of his own big leap were already germinating.

* * *

The vast shopping centre is in exactly the state of infectious Christmas frenzy I know I need. All of life is here getting in the Christmas groove, spurred on by a gaudy stage set of baubles, angels, Santas, fairies and illuminated fir trees. Near the entrance, a large glittery reindeer sits on a bench, human-style – legs crossed, one arm stretched out – ready for cuddling up to as part of a photo. There is a long queue of people waiting to have a go.

Would Al worry about my state of mind more – or less – if I sent a selfie of me canoodling with a giant flashing reindeer, I wonder wryly, dodging the queue and plunging deeper into the mall, eager to lose myself in the mêlée and my task.

An hour later, I have several gifts for Al, including a leather rucksack-style briefcase that I know he will love. *I'm doing okay,* I tell Rob in my head, swinging my shopping bags as I walk, loving the sharper sense of him from all my recent skips down memory lane.

Swerving round a long line of parents and children queuing for a cavernous 'Santa's Grotto', I spot a mother and baby shop and sail straight in. My intention is to browse – even a non-mother like me knows an eight-week-old foetus cannot be counted on. Nevertheless, I am soon standing in a queue for the tills, clutching a stretchy, red dress that I know will look stunning on Sadie – making her feel sensational as well as pregnant – and a mind-bogglingly minuscule, yellow Babygro that I plan to hide in a bottom drawer. Hearing my phone ring and glimpsing a long and unfamiliar number, I ignore it, in no mood for a cold caller, let alone when I am fishing for my credit card.

Ten minutes later, I am ravenously tearing at a pasta salad with wooden cutlery – wishing it was a tad less flimsy – between sips of the ginger shot I have bought to be healthy and glugs of the Frappuccino I actually *want.* It's mouth-popping sweetness feels like a deserved celebration of what has turned into a rather wonderful day. And Sadie is expecting a *baby*. The news hits me again, in all its improbability and enormity. Parenting – the most important of human jobs, yet anyone can have a go. It should be taught, I reflect wryly, like spelling and addition, with hard and fast rules. Then no kids would get hurt and spend the rest of their lives trying to work out why.

Getting up to go, I manage to nudge my little paper napkin off the table. As I bend to retrieve it, my heart performs a double-somersault at the sight of Joanne, Stephanie and Laura, processing across the other side of the food court, carrying drinks and food boxes. I duck as they scan the busy tables, thankfully finding one – being vacated by a family of four – a good twenty yards away. Normal sisters-in-law, aunts and nieces would catch each other's eye, I think sadly. Wave. Pull up extra chairs. Chat about plans for Christmas – who's going to who, what the girls are hoping for from Santa, whether it was the gargantuan grotto that had lured them all the way to Southampton. But we are not normal. We are the opposite of normal, because Rob is dead and Joanne hates me, and because I have made a promise to Al.

I remain crouched on the floor like a woman who has lost her mind as well as her paper napkin, gathering together my things, waiting for a safe moment to scuttle away. Joanne has taken a chair which is side-on to me, and the three of them are talking animatedly – happily. Because they *are* happy and why not? It is the school holidays, after all. As well as having lots of presents to look forward to, they probably have the usual Christmas trip to the Algarve lined up. Grandparents and warm weather. The thought makes my heart hum a little with wistfulness for Rob, missing out. But mostly, I am glad, especially for my dear nieces, who deserve anything and everything that might help them mend their precious, shredded little hearts.

The last swig of my ginger shot – because it cost the earth – and I am walking away, only looking back once I have reached the safety of the main concourse. I then buy gifts for all three of them: party dresses for the girls – a floaty, green one for Stephanie, and a blue one with an embroidered yoke for Laura, because they are *not* clones and deserve the dignity of having that recognised – and an exquisite, grey, cashmere scarf for Joanne. I make sure to get tags, wrapping paper, tape and three big jiffy bags as well, and have posted everything before I leave the mall. It would be so much nicer to have dropped the presents round in person – a practice I have deployed in the past as a pretext for a visit. But space, as I have repeatedly been told, is what everyone needs, and space is what they shall continue to get.

The works barrier is up and the site quiet by the time I have navigated the rush-hour traffic and arrived back at the school. Al and Phil are in their yellow office crate, full of jollity and beer, to judge from the empties in the bin by the door and the cans clasped in their hands. I refuse one for myself, joking that I am clearly the designated driver, and answering their polite enquiries about the success of my afternoon. 'So, absolutely no peeking in the boot,' I tease Al as he hastily drains his can and says he's ready to go.

'I shop on Christmas Eve myself,' Phil laughs, quickly downing the last of his own drink and then giving Al an are-you-ready look before the two of them – in perfect unison – lob their cans neatly into the bin by the door.

I am witnessing the blossoming of a full-on bromance, I realise, laughing as the men high-five like schoolboys. For Al, a bit of a loner since Traitor Mark, I know this is huge.

'Those of us whose partners have birthdays on the eve of Christmas Eve have to be a little more organised, don't we, Cath?' Al quips, shooting me a grin as he gathers up his things, cramming them into a splitting rucksack that makes me even happier about my Christmas gift.

'You mean the Volkswagen Polo wasn't your birthday present, Cath?' Phil jokes, coming outside to see us off. 'Seriously though, it's been great to meet you, and – as I've already said to the boss here – you guys are welcome to make use of the house while Debs and I are away. Al knows the ropes for getting in and out from his sleepover that time. It will mean this workaholic can have an easier commute if he wants, but might also be nice if you both fancy a change of scene. Dogs welcome. Our three will be in kennels – saying goodbye to them is crap. We all bawl our heads off every time, but then they have a blast.'

'That's so kind, Phil. Thank you.'

'And I am really sorry for your recent loss,' he adds in a rush, puffing out his cheeks as if his naturally cheerful face doesn't know how to exhibit gloom. 'That must have been tough. But nice you've got a grandkid to look forward to now, right?'

'Really nice.' I catch Al's eye to show I mean it.

'What a guy,' I laugh once we are on our way home, 'if he was any nicer, he'd have a halo.'

'Yeah, Phil is a one-off.'

'Enough to make a girl jealous.'

'Hah, Cathy – no need for that... and thanks for driving. I'm bushed, I must say.' He adjusts the seat as he talks so he can stretch his legs out. 'But tell me properly about the rest of your day, anyway. I hope you got what you wanted?'

Al tips his head back against the headrest as I launch into an account of my exploits. As I move from the Mayflower Park stopover to the cheesy reindeer, to the maternity shop, I am aware of the near-encounter with Joanne and the girls looming ever closer. It must be referenced of course, but in the *right* way. With the right lightness of touch. The right tone. The bloody woman has become such a trigger, it is impossible not to be wary. I am nearly there – on the tuna salad and Frappuccino – when my phone, which is in my handbag, parked between Al's legs, starts ringing.

'Shall I get that?'

'Just tell me who it is. They can leave a message if it's urgent.'

'No one on your contact list,' mutters Al, fiddling and scrolling, the phone having fallen silent anyway after a couple of rings. 'Just a number – no message – but hey, they rang before and left a voicemail – at 2.38 this afternoon, to be exact. Shall I play it?'

'Sure,' I say, remembering the cold caller when I was in the mother and baby place.

Al has already pressed play and a stream of gibberish is filling the car. A man's stream of gibberish. An American man.

'*...sowhatthefuckandwhyiswhatiwannaknow...   nothingwrong... nothing...   andsheslikeineedtime...   hahyeahrightlikeweallneedtime... andallalong... itsliketryingtodotherightthingforfuckssake...*

'*butyouknowwhatthereisNOrightthing...   andsoiamsorrybecausesi- didmybestbutsheaskedandhowwasisupposedtolieforfucksake... andtheresthetruthbutallitsgottenmeCath...   isthebiggestfuckingnight- mareofmylifebecausewithoutthemivenothing...   dyahear...   nothing... soyouknow...*'

'What – *who* – the fuck is that?' says Al, having listened, clearly rivetted, to the end.

'I'm afraid it might be Oliver,' I admit grimly.

'Oliver? As in, *Oliver?* Blimey. He sounds... in a bad way. But, how come? I mean, I didn't know you two were in touch.'

'We are *not* in touch. He managed to wangle my number from Joanne's bloody father and sent a couple of messages ages ago – much more normal ones – to which I replied, but only to say that I wanted no further contact.'

'This is you *talking* to me, is it, Cath?' Al says after a pause. 'Opening up to me? Oliver – *Oliver* – communicating – and you don't even mention it.'

'Sorry, Al. It was my way of not making it into a big deal. It isn't a big deal.'

'If you say so, Cath. But please, don't shut me out, love. Try and share with me what you are going through. Or how can I help? And... Whoa... that truck is parked—'

'I know that truck is parked, thank you very much, Al.' I slow right down, performing an exaggerated check of the wing mirrors before pulling out and driving on. I hadn't realised the truck was parked. I had barely registered it.

'So, are you going to reply to him?'

'No way.'

Al has dropped the phone back into my bag and suddenly slumped lower into his seat. 'Actually, I'm not feeling too clever. Itchy throat. Thumping head.'

'Oh Al, I'm sorry.' I glance at him, noting that his face has indeed acquired a worryingly doughy, sheeny look. 'Nearly home now.'

As soon as we're in the house, he ignores Belle and Bobby's manic greetings and staggers upstairs. After releasing the dogs into the garden, I follow, finding him flopped on his back on our bed, arms and legs splayed, in the manner of a beached starfish.

'I cannot be ill,' he groans. 'I've got too much to do.'

'A good night's sleep – maybe a day in bed – might be wise,

though, Al. You're burning up.' I run my hand over his scalp, feeling the bristly patches that need shaving. Sympathy is flooding me – Al has never been in the man-flu brigade – but I am also aware of being glad that, for once, I am not the one causing concern. 'I'll get some paracetamol and make you a lemon and ginger tea.' I fuss around, pulling back the covers, putting his night T-shirt within reach, puffing up the pillows. 'Better to give into it, love, rather than ploughing on. You'll feel better quicker then.' I kiss the top of his head and trot downstairs.

In the kitchen, while the kettle boils, I can't resist playing the voicemail again, cursing Oliver and his phoney sign-off a few weeks before, as well as my own negligence in still not having taken the extra precaution of blocking the number. I shudder as I listen, irresistibly curious, but mostly creeped out. Wasted or demented, it's a version of my half-sibling I could never have imagined. As soon as the message stops, I press delete and then ban the number properly, before grating some lemon rind into Al's drink – to give it extra zing – and taking it upstairs.

16

OLIVER

'Thanks for this, Brad.'

'No problem, pal. I'm just real sorry for what's happened. I tell you, I did not see it coming. Not for one second.' Brad shook his big head, twirling his beer bottle by the neck.

'Well, it's just a temporary situation,' Oliver countered bleakly, taking a sip of his beer, ice-cold and good – exactly what he needed to see off the tail-end of the worst hangover he had inflicted on himself since his early, experimental college days. That he could allow himself to sink so low – become that sad guy who drank all night because his wife had left him – was terrifying in itself. The attempts to call Cath, both when he was still out of it and later to make a swiftly aborted attempt to apologise, sat like a lump in his gut. A lump of shame. A part of him had wanted to give vent to the fact of his whole miserable domestic situation being her fault – for exacting a promise that had precipitated the decision to lie to his wife. When in fact, the greater pain – deep down – was how naïve and misguided he had been to reach out to her in the first place. The woman had hardly made a secret of her antipathy towards him. Understandable antipathy. Yet, like a jerk, he had persisted in the reaching out. Not once, but several times now, even after he had gone to the bother of telling her he wouldn't. One of those jerks, therefore, who kept on getting to his feet asking for another face-punch. A jerk who had learnt nothing in all his forty-two years.

'How long's it been then? Since Faith moved out?' Brad prompted, when Oliver didn't answer.

'Four weeks.' Oliver, blinking Brad's meaty features back into focus, could hear the disbelief in his own voice. *Give me some time* had been Faith's exact words, not just in the first, shattering hand-written message on the hotel notepaper, but in all their subsequent encounters and calls. It wasn't just how he had lied to her – saying he had reported Robert's passing when he hadn't – and the position that had landed her in with his parents, Faith had explained in their most recent miserable phone conversation, the one that had preceded his drunken binge. It was that in recent months, something in him seemed to have changed. She wasn't sure who he was any more, she said. The way he came at things. How he saw the world. At times, she had felt like she was living with a stranger.

'Who are you, Oliver?' she had burst out at one point.

He was a man who loved and needed his wife and family, Oliver had croaked back at her, fighting down a panic that threatened to throttle him. Who was anybody, for fuck's sake? It was no kind of question.

And now, somehow, Christmas was just under two weeks away. An unimaginable prospect since, as things stood, he was destined to spend a meagre couple of hours of it with Amelia, playing the manic, tense, desperate, child-pleasing father that the rift with Faith had forced into being. After that, the two of them were rushing off to Connecticut, while he travelled to Seattle. Because, exiled from the paradise of his wife's family gathering, what else was he going to do?

'She's with Laurie and Seth, right?' Brad said, in his dogged way. 'Across the park.'

Oliver nodded grimly. Laurie and Seth's East Side apartment, which occupied three floors, had spare rooms galore – spare bedrooms, sitting rooms, bathrooms, even a spare kitchen. Once upon a time, he and Faith used to joke about the insanity of so much excess space, how you would surely tear yourself in many pieces trying to make use of it all, how it must be like living in a half-empty hotel. Oh, yes, there had been bags of gentle humour to be had behind the backs of his top-lawyer sister-in-law and her hedge-fund supremo of a partner; but now the joke was on him, because all the spaciousness of the accommodation meant that Faith and Amelia could live in the place in privacy, luxury, and zero pressure in terms of big decision-making. In consequence, as the days went by, Faith had gradually been taking more stuff from their own apartment. To the point now where Oliver's shirts and suits, hanging with painful freedom in their shared closet, jangled like forlorn windchimes every time he opened the door. Just as he could now take his pick of hooks for his big winter coat and drop his shoes anyhow on the empty rack below. Worse than anything, however, was the pristine state of Amelia's room: the bed, with its comforter cover of blue dinosaurs as smooth as an untouched block of paper, the shelves pock-marked with gaps from where favourite books, toys and games had been removed. He had taken her for pizza and to the park a few times. Mostly, he saw her when Faith brought her over, because it was a way of seeing Faith and because Oliver was doing his best to go with his wife's new terrible flow. The last thing he wanted was to start instigating systems of drop-offs and sleepovers and childcare arrangements, out of fear that they might become the norm. Far better, he had decided, to wake each morning, even when he had a pounding head, in the hope that this would be the day he persuaded Faith to come home.

'So do you wanna talk about it?' Brad ventured, swivelling on his stool to signal to the barista for two more beers. They were side by side at a grand, circular bar on the lower ground floor of a downtown hotel – a venue suggested by Brad when he messaged the idea of meeting up. The mere act of accepting the invitation felt to Oliver like a measure of his own despair – a beer with Brad! Yet he had also been touched and humbled. Faith was right, the man did not have an unkind sinew in his body, and yet for years, Oliver had secretly looked down his nose at him. The rest of the clan, meanwhile, were keeping their distance, letting things play out, tacitly supporting Faith, as of course they would. Oliver got that. But, without them all – without Faith, the lynchpin of every single thing he did outside his long working hours – Oliver's life echoed with emptiness. He had always recognised this dependence on her – but as something to cherish rather than fear, never once having entertained the notion of losing it.

At work, he hadn't yet mentioned the separation. His colleagues were good people and old friends, Harrison especially, but business was hectic, and after all the time he'd taken recovering from his accident – plus a recent midweek Seattle trip to honour the promise to his father to accompany him on the latest round of tests – Oliver was keen to prove he was back in the game and ready to pull his weight. There was talk of a European trip in the first quarter of the New Year, and he had already said yes. Harrison, perhaps knowing him well enough to glimpse signs of strain, had shot him the occasional enquiring look – implicit assurance that there was more support there if he needed it. But Oliver did not want to need it. Faith, as he kept reminding himself, was just taking *some time*. He hadn't said anything about the situation to his parents either. Every disclosure to any quarter would have felt too much like a step nearer defeat, making it more real, more permanent. Which could not happen. Ever.

'Oliver? Talking about it might help? That's why we're here, right?' Brad scooped a handful of the mixed nuts that had been delivered along with their beers, chewing vigorously.

'Sorry, Brad. I'm distracted.'

'I know, fella, I know.' He nudged Oliver's second, still untouched bottle of beer a little nearer. 'And it's okay. You don't have to say a word.'

'I allowed her to believe something that wasn't true,' Oliver admitted bitterly, taking a swig of the beer. 'I don't really want to go into it, Brad, to be honest, but trust me when I say that I was just trying to do the right thing. I had no idea how it would backfire.'

'Oh, I know all about that,' Brad cried, his small brown eyes lighting up. 'Women, they set bear traps, right? And as for those sisters, they are like their own members club. Even Petra says so. The best thing, pal – take it from me – is to go along with *every- thing* they say. Submit. Lie down. Roll over. They'll eat you for breakfast otherwise.' Brad whistled softly, swinging his big head from side to side. 'Not that they aren't great. They are great. The whole damn bunch of them. Strong women. Good women. But they're big on *truth*,' he added mournfully, like the concept was something reasonable people opted out of, 'and that can be like living in a force-ten gale. Best to submit, pal, is what I am saying. Whatever it takes. Own up. Eat the humble stuff.' He gave a little punch to Oliver's shoulder and picked up his beer. 'Petra is the same way inclined, but I can talk her round, if you know what I mean.' He winked as he tipped the bottle to his lips.

'For the record,' he went on, wiping his mouth with the back of his big hairy hand and waggling the empty nut dish at the barista, 'Petra has always had her doubts about you, but not me. I knew from the get-go that you were a *good* guy, Oliver. A cuckoo family, maybe, but that's hardly your fault. And you're kind of British, too, if you know what I mean, which I guess isn't so surprising,' Brad laughed, slapping Oliver lightly on the back, 'given that you're half and half. You've got that *reserve* of theirs, that's for sure. You hold your jokers and aces close. Which I respect. Totally. You value your *privacy*. Like finding Sue Ellen's dinner-table grilling tough that time. She can be the worst,' he went on, a rare shadow momentarily darkening his genial face at some distant, specific memory. 'A dog with a bone, but I just let it all wash over me. I'm pretty much an open-book kind of guy anyway, Petra says, and I think she's about right.'

The fresh bowl of nuts arrived, together with two more beers, which Oliver wasn't aware had been part of the order. He didn't want more beer. He wanted to leave – not to return to the apartment, but just to leave, so that he did not have to carry on making conversation while his heart was trying not to collapse in on itself.

'Talking of books,' Brad charged on, fortified by a gulp of his fresh drink, 'I meant to tell you that I've gotten back into reading – big time. That remark of yours when we dined at Akio's – the one that got the womenfolk upset?' He paused to chuckle. 'Well, it set me googling. I looked up the top twenty greatest books of all time – I mean, life is short, right? I've probably got no more than three decent decades left in me. So, I picked out a couple to be going on with. *War and Peace* – a tough one, I'm not going to lie, until I got the hang of all the names – such a crazy number for each character – but then it was like, kapow!' He slapped the bar top. 'What a story. And now I'm into *Moby Dick*, which we did back in high school, when my only interest was in getting a football scholarship...'

Oliver's gloom deepened as Brad chattered on. He was glad – touched and humbled all over again. Only someone of Brad's deep affability could have interpreted his horrible, and deeply regretted snipe in the sushi restaurant three months before as a spur to action. But he did not possess the wherewithal to discuss anything further with Brad, let alone the ins and out of his most treasured novel, Ishmael's account of the maniacal whale hunt being a nihilistic quest for meaning, as everybody knew. Once, in his student days, it had been thrilling to pore over the narrative, extracting new layers of existential angst and interpretation, swelling his own sense of cleverness in the process. But now, the whole story felt too raw, too damned close to the bone of real-life despair to ever want to pick over again.

'Excuse me?' interjected a woman who was sitting on the far side of Brad, stopping him mid-sentence with a tap on his shoulder. 'I couldn't help overhearing. Did you mention *War and Peace* just now? Because Tolstoy happens to be my favourite writer *ever*.'

'Well, how about that?' Brad countered eagerly. 'Did you hear that, Oliver?'

'I did.' Oliver smiled at the woman, who had scarlet nail varnish that matched her lipstick and a narrow, pale face framed by tumbling, silvery-blonde curls. Every bar stool was occupied now, the place having been steadily filling up in the hour or so since he and Brad had taken their own seats. Two more baristas had arrived to help with this later shift, and were in constant, graceful motion round the circle of the bar, refreshing glasses, shaking cocktails, fetching snacks, wiping spills. It was turning into something of a party, Oliver realised, and this wonderful new conversationalist on Brad's right had given him a ticket right out of it. 'But I've got to make a move, Brad, so forgive me, and you too...' Oliver threw a questioning look at the Tolstoy fan.

'Carol Ann.'

'I'm Brad and this is Oliver,' Brad cried, as delighted as a kid in a candy store.

'Nice to meet you, Carol Ann,' Oliver ploughed on, 'and sorry, Brad, but this is where I check out.'

'Oh no, can't we change your mind?' their new friend cooed. 'Fellow bibliophiles – it's such a treat.' She grinned in an expansive way that for one unnerving moment reminded Oliver of his mother, back in the day when she still bothered with making up her face.

Three minutes later, Brad having gallantly refused any contribution towards the check, Oliver was safely out in the street, shoulders hunched against an icy, tunnelling wind that had been keeping the temperature of the city below zero all week. A white Christmas was the word. A white Christmas – like such a thing could ever have mattered. Oliver had ordered a fake tree – white nylon and tinsel – just so there was something for when Amelia came round, and under which he would place her gifts. These so far comprised: a big, soft, orange octopus with bobbly eyes, as well as a wooden dollhouse – complete with sets of furniture for every room, a family of four figures, a garage, a car, fences for a field, grass matting, and a pony. A model family, full of his own longing, Oliver knew. A part of him was even hoping that Faith might pick up on the fact. Be melted by it. For her, he had picked out a bracelet – from the same jewellery store where she – star-struck, as was he – had chosen her engagement ring. The bracelet was delicate, of tiny gold links studded with diamonds, and he had had her name engraved on the clasp. It had cost him a month's pay. Oliver was so certain she would love it that he would have paid ten times the amount.

Faith. He had to hear her voice. Oliver pulled his hands out of his coat pockets and dug inside his jacket for his cell. Even her voicemail message would be nice, he thought feebly. But her cell was turned off. He kept his fingers clenched round the phone as he walked on. You never knew. Maybe she was already back at the apartment with Amelia, ready to shout, 'Surprise!' the moment he opened the door. Ready to hurl herself into his arms. Oliver increased his pace, aware of the faint ache that still lingered in his right ankle. In the emergency room, the pain before the meds kicked in had been intense – the worst of his life. Until now.

17

CATHERINE

'I like this one the best. Can we get it?' I poke my finger at the mobile of miniature silver angels, making them dance. It is one in a line of mobiles hanging along a slim rail encircling the stall – reindeer, stars, Christmas trees – all glinting in the fairy lights strung up around the Christmas market. Laid out underneath are tempting rows of handmade festive decorations – snow-crusted bells, rotund snowmen, beady-eyed doves, woolly donkeys, cross-eyed sheep – but our train leaves in an hour and our rucksacks are already at bursting point. Memento mugs, bottles of local beer, handmade truffles and chocolates, we have treated ourselves lavishly, as well as wanting to be armed with rewards for Ryan and Sadie, back in the UK looking after the house and dogs.

'Of course you can have that one. You can have all of them. This is your Surprise Birthday Treat, remember,' Al laughs, unhooking the little angels, before joining the queue for the till, manned by an elderly woman with ruddy cheeks, bundled up in a black quilt of an overcoat against the chill.

Late afternoon, and the Bruges sky is already inky black,

pricked with stars and a gold sliver of moon, perfectly reflected in the still, dark canal running alongside us – one branch of an intricate network that circles and criss-crosses the city. Across the water, the now-familiar slim, neat houses, pressed shoulder to shoulder, with their pointy roofs and white framed windows, seem to keep a sort of vigil, as if to remind us that we are visitors and the secrets of this world entirely theirs. A few yards from the square, one of the little stone bridges we have been trotting over all day has troughs of winter pansies hanging over its sides, their bright colours still glowing faintly in the dark. It all looks like a scene from a fairytale. It *is* a scene from a fairytale – the perfect tonic for my still yo-yoing spirits and extra Rob-sadness at this first un-shared birthday of my life.

My treat for the day was a trip to the cinema and then out for a slap-up dinner, Al had declared, by way of an explanation for Ryan and Sadie's camper van pulling into the drive the previous afternoon. They were coming for Christmas anyway, so it made perfect sense for them to arrive a day early and dog-sit, he pointed out, hurrying along the hall to greet them, Belle and Bobby bounding at his heels. I had trotted after him, protesting happily about having already been spoilt enough by the beautifully wrapped and perfectly fitting, fur-lined leather boots that had accompanied my morning mug of tea.

Instead of our usual local cinema, however, Ryan had driven us – squashed together on the lumpy front bench-seat of his van – all the way to Salisbury. And not to the cinema, but to the railway station. The film was a cult-hit masterpiece called *In Bruges*, currently showing only in London, Al had explained, his expression deadpan, and he had booked somewhere special for a bite afterwards. Only when Ryan – first out of the van and grinning impishly – produced our two hiking rucksacks from the back did it finally dawn on me that some seriously grand design was afoot.

'I can't thank you enough, Al,' I say, not for the first time, nestling against him once we are settled into our comfy Eurostar seats for the final leg of the journey home. 'To have organised all of this for me on top of everything else on your plate – including being under the weather. And I still don't know how you managed to pack and sneak the bags out of the house without me noticing, let alone thinking of *everything* I needed.'

'A rush-job – while you were talking babies with Sadie,' he laughs, 'and being brilliant with her, if I may say so.'

'You may.'

I close my eyes as his mouth brushes against my temple. We have been connecting, at last. Properly. Without me having to *try* – to be 'can-do', or anything else. Looking back, I am certain that the Southampton day was the turning point, not to mention having to nurse Al through what proved to be a truly gruesome bug – fierce enough to keep him off work for three days, and for us to dig out some old testing kits to rule out the obvious.

'I just hope all this racing across Europe hasn't set you back,' I murmur, as Al turns away to succumb to one of his still occasional bouts of coughing. 'You must take it easy through the Christmas break, though. I'll make sure of it.'

'Nice thought, love, but as soon as Boxing Day is done, I'm afraid it will be business as usual. You're the one who's still got to take it easy, remember?'

'How could I forget.' I pull a face designed to give no hint of the worry about impending realities: no work distractions to fill my busy head, Tam absent and hatching who knew what future plans, Al at full throttle.

A string of photos arriving from Ryan on Al's phone provides a welcome diversion: the dogs looking dismayed in party hats, a tray of lopsided, half-burst mince pies, a whisk in a bowl of butter beside a mini bottle of brandy, mistletoe and holly sprigs dangling from shelves and doorways. 'Looks like we'll both be able to put our feet up tomorrow at any rate,' Al chuckles.

'It sure does.'

As he settles back for a doze, I take a peek at the screensaver of Rob that I've had on my phone for twenty-four hours – an old favourite that's also in a frame back home, of him on a good day, stretched out on the lumpy, Shepherds Bush sofa, clear-eyed and grinning.

Happy forty-eighth birthday, my darling brother. Never forgotten. Always my twin.

* * *

'Okay, me first. Listen up.' Pleasantly woozy from the two glasses of wine that followed the Prosecco Al opened before lunch, I fish for the riddle in the cracker paper and pastry crumbs on my pudding plate.

'Hang on, I need to pee – don't start without me,' Sadie cries, jumping out of her chair.

I sit back, happily surveying the debris of our Christmas meal, while Al and Ryan pick up on a conversation they were having about guitars – always a favourite topic, Al having been in a band himself in his teens. Despite his comment on the train the day before, he has done the opposite of taking it easy, bois-terously assuming full charge of the kitchen, as he likes to for big occasions, and producing a moist, crispy-skinned turkey and trimmings so perfect that we have all agreed he could have a second career as a restaurateur. Ryan and Sadie's full-to-burst-ing, deliciously sticky mince-pies have also been lauded, along with the brandy butter, so clearly overladen with its key ingredient that Sadie, on alert about alcohol in general, virtuously declined to have any, even though she had apparently made it. My role all day has been as a very contented assistant and dogsbody, whose small private highlight was finding the time – and inspiration – to manage the fiddly job of fixing the mobile of my Bruges angels to the light over the kitchen table. All through our feasting, the little crew of five have been performing slow-motion twirls thanks to the heat of the bulb, casting shadows – and the sense of a little magic – as they go.

We have worked as a team, as someone said to someone at some point, a true observation and so unexpectedly pleasing that I find it has stirred in me a glimpse of how future festive milestones might go, with a baby in the mix. A simulacrum of a family, in a way I had never imagined. Aunthood may not have worked out as I had once hoped, but playing some sort of *young* grandmotherly role – and enjoying it – suddenly seems more within reach. Doable. Nice.

Sadie drops back into her seat with needless apologies for making us wait, and I make a deliberate to-do of clearing my throat and unfurling the little riddle paper before reading it aloud.

'*I'm always around the corner but never arrive. What am I?*'

Happiness. The thought – not the correct answer – arrives before I can stop it, on the back of a swooping sorrow. It is Christmas. And I am twin-less. Family-less. No new babe, however cute, could make up for that.

'*Tomorrow!*' Ryan and Sadie shriek, in unison, turning to each other to celebrate with a high five.

'Correct,' I say, sheer surprise helping me through the moment.

'How the hell did you know that?' Al booms.

'Everyone knows that,' they chorus happily. 'It was in a film.'

'Actually, I need to lie down for a bit,' Sadie announces, stretching as she stands up, lithe as a cat in the red dress I have given her, which she sweetly put on at once, and which looks as stunning as I had hoped. 'Sorry.' She blinks sleepily. 'I'm fine one minute, and then it's like, a wall...' She puts a hand over her mouth to succumb to an extravagant yawn.

Ryan, skinny and agile, his paper hat at a roguish angle on his bushy head, has leapt to his feet. 'You okay, Sades? Do you need anything? Like water? Or tea?' He pulls the party hat off as he talks, scrunching it into a ball and dropping it onto the table.

'No, babe, I'm good. I'll see you all in a bit. We're singing later, right? A concert of our latest – and maybe some carols.' She performs a half-shimmy as she heads off, pausing to bend down and give Belle – parked like a draught-excluder across the open doorway – a quick tummy-rub.

'It's so amazing that she doesn't feel sick,' Ryan declares proudly, sitting back down, 'and also super-lucky, because we've got a bunch of gigs coming up. In fact, since we got the news, it's all gone a bit mad.' For a moment, something like panic crosses his face.

'That's so often the way, and babies love music,' Al says kindly, going on to repeat a story we all know well, of Ryan, as a newborn, falling asleep to certain soundtracks – Stevie Wonder being especially effective, and how – equally familiar – he started requests for a guitar from the age of five. 'I might grab a lie-down too, if that's okay with you two?' he adds, draining his last mouthful of wine and getting to his feet. 'No touching the washing-up, mind. We can do all that together, before the home-gig and an action-packed night in front of the telly – at least that's as far as my plans for the evening go.' He pulls a comical face and gives us a wave as he heads off.

Ryan and I – without discussing the matter – set about

clearing up anyway. What with presents and dog-walking, lunch had got so late that it is already gone five o'clock. Getting busy helps contain my still-hovering sadness-wobble, as does Ryan, promptly taking charge at the sink, while I dry up and load the dishwasher. He whistles absently as he works – the threads of pure sound that he can conjure at will, either of his own composing, or riffs on tunes of others. I watch the back of his lean frame and the thickets of his mousy-brown hair, thinking how, for all such physical differences, there is so much about him that reminds me of Al – an innate grace and deftness, a person who knows what he is about and with the quiet determination to bring it into being.

'I think you'll be a great dad, by the way,' I tell him, knowing in my bones that this is true.

'Really?' He glances up, bashful and pleased. 'Thanks. I know Dad's worried about us needing money – he's given me this mad, fat cheque for Christmas – but we don't. We'll be fine. I've already upped my delivery-work hours – until the band goes properly viral – which *is* going to happen, I just know. Like I said, it's all been kicking off recently. There's this agent who's been sniffing around for a while, who wants to bring this, like, really big producer to one of our gigs. Soon, he says.'

'Wow, Ryan, that sounds really promising.' I have set to work carving and picking off what's left of the meat on the turkey. The sadness has contracted into a stone in my gullet – manageable, but impossible to swallow away. The heartbreaking optimism of this dear boy of Al's doesn't help. Life can be so brutal, even – especially – for those who least deserve it.

'Thanks for today, by the way, Cath. It's been cool.' He tosses the towel over the back of a chair.

'Thank *you*, Ryan – for holding the fort here while Dad and I were away, and being such a help today.'

'No worries.'

He heads off to settle in front of the television, and I tiptoe upstairs, in need of Al. As I reach the landing, Sadie appears out of the spare bathroom, wearing an old towelling dressing gown of Al's that lives on the hook on the back of the spare room door. It is laughingly huge, swamping her still-thin frame, and she looks slightly dazed, presumably from her nap. I smile as I press my finger to my lips, nodding in the direction of our bedroom door, which is sufficiently ajar to reveal that inside all is dark and quiet.

'Hey, Cath,' she whispers, half-retreating towards her room and then swinging back round. 'Just now, there was, like, this bit of blood... I mean, that's okay, right?'

I steer her gently into the spare room, so we can talk properly. 'A bit of blood?'

'Yeah – I've just googled it and it seems like it's something called spotting and is really common. I don't want to worry Ryan – he's really into what I should and shouldn't do. I mean, like the brandy butter, I'd have loved some, but I could feel him getting ready to say it would be bad for the baby...'

'Sadie, I really think you should tell Ryan – not to worry him, but just so that he knows.'

'It was literally, just this teeny bit.' Sadie emphasises her point by holding up her hand and squeezing her thumb and index fingertip together. 'I mean, hardly even worth changing my knickers for, if you get me.'

'Yes, totally. And er... no tummy ache, or anything?' I bluster, touched to be consulted, but totally out of my depth.

'No. I feel great.'

'Okay. Good. Well, perhaps stay lying down for a bit anyway? I'll fetch Ryan for you.'

'Aw, thanks, Cath – yeah, that would be great.' She puts her arms round me, just for a moment, and I feel the strength in her wiry body and smell the faint floral scent of her hair, which for this visit has had its natural glorious ebullience tamed into tight, exquisite braids threaded with gold.

A couple of minutes later, I am following Ryan back up the stairs. He goes ahead, taking two steps at a time, quickly disappearing into the spare room and closing the door. Across the landing, the shaft of darkness exposed by Al's and my room remains silent. I tiptoe inside. Al is a sound sleeper. With the right caution, I fancy my chances of sliding onto the bed without waking him. I hesitate, giving my eyes a moment to adjust to the pitch black, which comes from the moonless evening sky on display between the undrawn curtains. Al is on his back, on top of the covers, motionless, his phone on his chest, his hands interlinked on his belly. When he turns his head towards me, I jump.

'I thought you were asleep.'

'No, I am not asleep.'

'Sorry if I woke you.'

'You didn't wake me.' He rolls his head back into alignment with his spine, returning his eyeline to the ceiling.

For a moment, I wonder if there is some sort of atmosphere. A tension. But there can't be. We have had a beautiful day, a beautiful break. We are closer than we have been in a long while. 'Sadie has had a little scare,' I report quietly, closing the door and going to sit on the bed. 'A drop of blood. According to Google, it's really common and not necessarily anything to worry about.' As I talk, I unzip my treasured birthday boots, which I have been wearing pretty much non-stop, and settle into a cross-legged sitting position facing him, rubbing my toes because they are still getting used to the stylish narrow tips. 'I fetched Ryan for her. I mean...' I untangle my legs and turn onto

my side, punching my pillow into a shape that will provide a
satisfactory headrest, 'it's obviously not something I have a clue
about. But hey, you're the one with the wisdom – did Sandi have
anything like that early on?'

'I have no wisdom.'

'Yeah, right, mister uber-smart and ace father,' I say,
detecting a hollow note in his voice and wanting to counter it.
'Actually,' I continue, when he doesn't reply, 'downstairs just
now, talking with Ryan, I kept thinking how much like you he is,
always sensing a clear path to what he wants, not getting down
or distracted by—'

'Sadie should see a doctor. Get checked out.'

'Right. Yes.' The curtness in his voice is because the rigours
of the day are catching up with him, I tell myself. And why
would he be in the mood for my cute observations anyway, with
his own return to work looming and the annoying tail-end
chestiness almost certainly prolonged by having organised the
glorious hell out of my birthday. I shift nearer to him, cush-
ioning my cheek on my hands as well as the pillow. 'I'm sorry, Al,
if you're still feeling a bit rubbish. Maybe you should get
checked out too?'

'I'm fine.'

'Okay. Just so long as you're not feeling worse, or anything?'

'No, Cath, I am the same. Because nothing has changed.
Absolutely nothing.'

A coldness runs through me. I wish I could see his face
better. 'Al, what is it?' I reach for his arm, but he propels himself
off the bed – shaking me off, it feels like. Soundless in his socks,
he is out of the room in an instant. A knock on the spare
bedroom door is followed by the murmur of voices. By the time
I venture out onto the landing, it has been decided that Ryan
and Sadie should return to London there and then. They seem

keen for it, and Al eggs them on, saying they will be nearer their own doctor, as well as having a choice of several A&E departments – should the unlikely need of such drastic action arise. It seems a touch over-dramatic to me, given the details Sadie has shared, and when the obvious option of a virtual consultation could be deployed first. But no one – understandably – is asking for my opinion, so I go downstairs to do a bit more tidying up instead. Soon, Ryan and Sadie are trotting round me, gathering up their stuff, and Al is in the study, fiddling with something at his desk. He has clearly crossed some sort of new exhaustion threshold, I realise, and actually, the sooner we are on our own, the better.

'They'll have more peace of mind, at least,' I say, filling the kettle once all the goodbyes are done with and Al has come back inside from waving the little van safely out into the road. 'I've decided I need some tea to see me through that action-packed night on the sofa you mentioned. Would you like one?'

'No, thanks.'

Our glances meet and I see a new haggardness. He looks away quickly, crossing to the cupboard where we keep drinks and reaching for the whisky bottle and a glass into which he pours a generous inch. He tips it to his mouth at once, swilling the liquid round his teeth before swallowing. Instead of heading off to the sitting room, he then tugs out a kitchen chair – with such force that the Bruges angels flutter in protest – and turns it to face me before sitting down.

I stay where I am, leaning back against the kitchen counter, hugging my tea. I sense that I am to be told something serious – almost certainly to do with the school development. Maybe the contractors have gone bust, or Phil has walked out. Whatever it is, I know it is bad.

'While I was upstairs after the meal, I had a phone call –

from Joanne.' He drops his gaze to the glass, cradled in his lap between his big hands.

Not his beloved crystal tumbler, I note suddenly, but one of our oldest, most smeary glasses. I grip my tea mug, even though the subject of Joanne holds no new terrors. 'Was it a Christmas thing?'

'No, it wasn't.'

'I sent them all gifts – but then I've always—'

'It wasn't about Christmas, Cath. It was to tell me that you've been spying on them.'

'*Spying*?' I can't help laughing. But Al's expression remains deathly.

'She was pretty upset. As were the girls, apparently.'

'Look.' I carefully set my mug down. 'I know exactly what this must be about...'

'What this is *about,* Cath, is that now – thanks to Joanne – I know that you have been lying to me; that, for all our endless talking and agreements to be open, to share things – and to leave that poor, grieving woman and her children alone, as she *requested* – you have been doing the opposite. Repeated promises to me – all broken – not telling me *anything*.' There is disgust in Al's voice. 'But how could you? Sneaking around her and those little girls, scaring them...'

'*Scaring* them? What is this? What has she said?' My brain has catapulted me back to the Southampton day. They must have seen me – which is cruel as well as almost funny, given my efforts *not* to be seen or to intrude. Now Joanne has clearly gone and twisted it into some wild, vengeful story for her own purposes, I realise, rushing on to explain – about the fluke of the encounter and trying to stay out of sight. 'I didn't lie to you, love, I just decided not to mention it, precisely because I was afraid of this.' I fling my arms out, to indicate the horribleness of the conversation we are having.

'But you're *still* lying,' Al groans, rolling his eyes at the ceiling. 'Because we're not just talking about your ingeniously engineered Christmas-shopping expedition, are we?'

'*Engineered*? I told you—'

But Al is an avalanche.

'Or that supposedly necessary peeping Tom *detour* of yours on the way to the garden centre. No, there's been so much more, hasn't there, Cath? Joanne told me – months of it. Hanging around Stephanie and Laura's school like some kind of stalker. It all came out this afternoon, she says, almost wrecking their Christmas Day. The girls hadn't seen you in Southampton, but Joanne did, and outside Laura's ballet class too, apparently...' Al pauses to groan again. 'She was telling her mother about it when Stephanie chipped in to say she'd also seen you, several times. Joanne said that if it happens once more, she'll consider calling the police. She was pretty distraught – and it's not hard to understand why.' He takes a vicious swig of his drink and slumps back in his chair, fixing me with his new, ruthless eyes.

'I have been mad with grief,' I say in a small voice. The phrase floats in, a white feather of surrender and rescue, from Tamsin's use of it, months before, in this very kitchen, when I was hanging by the tips of my fingernails in the days after the funeral. Dear Tam. Who is leaving me. Pulling away. As everyone seems to. In the end. 'Yes, Al, I did go to places where I could catch glimpses of the girls a few times,' I confess hoarsely, sickened by the notion that such behaviour could be deemed to have a dubious side, when it had come from a place of pure love. 'It... helped me, just to see them, that's all. I never meant any harm... She didn't have to go and threaten the police... dear God, Al, those two girls are all I've got left, of... *everything.*' The word comes out as a wail, along with thick, streaming tears, as the suppressed thread of sadness that has been running through the day catches up with me. 'And I'll write to Joanne, of course,' I babble on, wiping my face on my sleeves. 'Anything to make this right, Al.'

Al merely shrugs. 'It's up to you Cath. You always do what you want anyway. And thanks for saying that the girls are *all* you've got left. It explains – or should I say *confirms* – a lot.'

'Al, of course that's not what I... what do you mean, confirms?'

'The *truth*, Cath: that is what you have confirmed.' He has gone all matter-of-fact and for some reason, it's worse than anything.

'I don't understand, Al.'

'The truth that I've never been enough for you, Cath. Because no one could be. No one, except... Rob.'

'Don't bring Rob into this.' The words – cold and hard – fly out of my mouth before I can stop them.

Al flinches, but ploughs on. 'How can we *not* bring your brother into this? It's always been about you and your brother,' he adds softly, leaning forwards, resting his elbows on his knees. 'Never me.'

I know I need to get on top of how the conversation is unravelling. The coldness in me has already given way to terror. My brain is spaghetti. Al is my one forgiving, endlessly compassionate constant. He alone knows what I can bear, how I need to be handled. He does not talk to me like this. Or about Rob like this.

'Al. Please.' I have to gulp air between the words.

Al blinks at me slowly. When he starts to talk, it is with the steady fluency of one releasing thoughts long held in. 'Twenty years ago, I believed I knew what I was taking on. I thought I had the measure of it. Your brother, he was a nice guy. You were upfront about the bond between you – what had brought it into being – and I got it. Twins, going through hell, with only each other. I understood. That Rob drank himself stupid made terrible sense too. You were the more resilient one, Cath. Always. And boy, did that brother of yours know it. Living in the shadow of that knowledge, it can't have been easy.'

'Shadow?' My mouth sticks round the word.

A trickle of sweat is sliding down Al's temple and he stops it with his index finger. 'Joanne was the best thing that ever happened to him – and to us, I thought. Because of how she got him clean, took him off *your* hands. Freed you up – freed *us* up – or so I carried on hoping, despite how you sobbed through that wedding of theirs, like it was a life sentence instead of a marriage. Because you couldn't let even a piece of him go, could you? So we had to move nearer – push for more contact – even though they made clear, repeatedly, that they weren't keen on it. I had my doubts, but went along with things because of you loving him and me loving you. We *did* see them from time to time. But still you weren't happy, Cath. You were never happy.'

'Yes, I was, Al. Please stop – you're trying to make all of this into something it isn't.'

But Al isn't even listening now.

'God forgive me, but I actually enjoyed those early lockdowns. Just you and me and Belle, hanging out, footling around. And then getting Bobby, all those fun, wasted hours when he was a puppy, trying to teach him tricks...' He gulps, briefly masking his face in his hands. I have slid to the floor, leaning back against the counter, not knowing how to bear another word, or how to stop them arriving.

'But then Rob's illness,' Al grinds on, 'the way it all went... Christ, no one deserves what happened to your poor brother.

And watching you go through it – how you flailed – made me feel even more helpless than usual. Useless. Sidelined. *Irrelevant.* Trying to get inside that damned locked-up head of yours... but I've been out of my depth, then and ever since, with all your rages, all the pushing me away, or grabbing me – nothing I've tried works; everything makes you angry. Because you're always angry. Not just this year but always. In fact, I've realised that you *like* it. The world versus Cath – yeah, that's what lights you up. Just like your brother's *need* of you lit you up. Being his protector. You loved it. You couldn't let it go.'

'That's a fucking lie.'

I have shouted, and afterwards, there is a long silence.

Al moves first, taking his empty glass to the sink and rinsing it out. I watch him, waiting. In this new quiet, if I can bear to maintain it, Al, surely, will find remorse for his despicable accusations. He will come to me and extend one of his big comforting hands to pull me up off the floor. He will say that it isn't true, that he went too far, that he is sorry and can we now try to get some sleep. But after carefully placing the glass upside down in the drainer, he walks past me, not pausing until he reaches the door.

'I'm sorry, Cath, but...'

Here it is, thank God. The apology. The mending. I do not look up for fear of showing the rawness of my need for the climb-down. Instead, he says that everyone has a tether and that he seems to have reached the end of his. That competing with Rob was hard enough when he was alive, but no one can compete with the dead. That he will sleep in the spare room.

As the tread of his heavy footsteps recedes upstairs, I slither down until I am lying on my back on the hard tiles. The dogs shuffle in, sniffing at me, drifting to their beds when I ignore them. I watch the angels circling over the table, envying their weightlessness and effortless shine. I tell myself that Al has a right to his feelings, as I have to mine. If he thinks he's now in too deep to apologise, then all I have to do, just as soon as he has calmed down, is to reassure him that his central, sickening accusation is groundless. That he is, and always has been, more than enough for me. That there is no *competing* and never has been. Rob just took – takes – headspace, as how could he not?

The angels stir, as if they would speak if they could. And somehow, I am glad they can't.

A sense of total aloneness creeps over me. Forty-eight years and two days, and here it is, the thing most dreaded without my realising it: having no one, except myself. An abyss has opened up under me and I am falling. Its blackness contains not just Al, falling next to me, but the stench of the past. I see a woman brushing her long red hair. I see her blue-blue eyes, fixed on me. I see love. *Mummy*.

* * *

At some point in the small hours, I go upstairs. I am so stiff, each step hurts. I ache for Al, and the big radiator of his beautiful body. I gently try the spare-room door, but it is locked. I crawl, fully clothed, into our icy, empty bed and curl up in the foetal position, clutching my phone like a lifeline. But there is no one to call. *Mummy*. I wish the word, and its yearning, would leave me alone.

Hastily, I start and delete message after message to Al. Nothing sounds right, because there is too much to say. But we shall sort this out, because it is Al, and because we always do. Blearily, I swipe through emails, but they are all from retailers with seasonal offers. It takes a while to spot the presence of what will be the usual electronic festive brag from Oliver deep in their midst. *Happy Holidays from Mr & Mrs Smug!* The prospect of the customary hit of derision stirs something akin to consolation. To hate someone other than myself, yeah, that will feel good. Maybe I could even forward it to Al, I think wildly, underline how much of an open book I truly am about my estranged half-sibling and everything else – add some funny, wry comment – start the long haul back to peace through finding some common ground.

Was Rob in my shadow? The thought pulses, momentarily distracting me. Can anyone *be* in the shadow of someone whose love for them is beyond words, who wants only for them to be happy? No. Not possible. Al has poured poison in my ear, just as Joanne has poured poison in his. If only Al would see it. He *shall* see it. I must make sure of that.

My brain is throbbing. Oliver's Christmas round-robin email is still sitting on my screen. I open it, bracing myself for schmaltzy music and cartwheeling Christmas icons heralding the usual list of banal achievements. But this time, there's just one line, without so much as a sprig of holly to accompany it.

Wishing you all happy festive holidays, best wishes, Oliver

* * *

I wake with no idea how much time has passed. The sun is on my face and I am still fully dressed, my hand half-curled round my phone. Throwing back the covers, I stagger out onto the landing, coming to a halt at the sight of the open spare-room door and the bed neatly made. I tumble downstairs to find all is quiet. Belle lumbers over to greet me, an air of bewilderment in her big toffee-brown face, and then retreats to the doormat, whining.

'It's all right, sweetie,' I tell her, hearing the panic in my own voice as I open the door and see – as I had somehow known I would – that the black car has gone. To Southampton, of course. Work. Al's default refuge. I check my phone, only for it to dawn on me that the blank screen is because of a dead battery. Rubbing the sleep from my eyes, telling myself that Bobby must have sneaked upstairs, I walk steadily into the kitchen. Belle pads forlornly in my wake, her big feathery tail trailing on the ground like a lowered flag. A charger lives by the toaster. I ram the plug into my phone and wait. As soon as I have put in my code, the screen lights up with a message from Al.

> I think we both need time. And radio silence. I have gone to Phil's. Forgive me taking Bob, I just couldn't bear to leave them both. You are stronger than you know, Cath. Too strong for me.

18

OLIVER

The snow squeaked under the ridged soles of Oliver's shoes – his most heavy-duty pair – as he set off towards the park, the plastic tray-sled he had dug out of the coat closet pinned under one arm, the ear coverings of his winter hat flapping like little wings. Compared to Seattle, which had received such a dump of snow before Christmas that it had looked at one point as if he might not make it up there, this was lightweight. But still, pretty as a Christmas card, and with temperatures forecast to stay cold enough for at least a day before the inevitable, speedy conversion into grey slush. Best of all, the snowfall had meant the chance to suggest sledging with Amelia that morning, instead of her coming round to do their usual indoor things, or him braving a playground and trying to keep her warm on a swing.

She could drop her off or meet him there, Faith had said, in the new, carefree tone that hurt on top of all the other hurt, because of its suggestion of her own indifference as to how he answered. Oliver, being the opposite of indifferent, as well as newly determined never to be the buttoned-up Brit that Brad had detected, said no, he wanted her there too, because he loved her and missed her and any chance to spend time with her was something he would seize with all his heart. To which Faith had said, sure, and she'd see him at the Cedar Hill slope at eleven.

Bad drips were gathering on his nose, but Oliver performed a snorty sniff-and-swallow instead of going through the rigma-role of tugging his gloves off and digging under his long fat winter anorak for the handkerchief that he had stuffed, inconve-niently, into his front trouser pocket. On top of round-the-clock heartache, such myriad minor inconveniences seemed to be the outstanding feature of his new, solo life. Not so much because he had allowed physical chaos to overtake him – if anything, he had done the opposite, finding it eased his stress levels to stay on top of what he *could* control – laundry, dishes, tidiness – but because his brain was in a state of constant distraction. He would swing open the freezer compartment, or walk into a room, or tug out a kitchen drawer and then stand and stare, his brain empty. He had noticed his mother doing the same thing on recent visits, standing so long and looking so vacant that he wondered if it helped her to pass the time. Or whether she was frozen in the memory of their recent hellish conversation, which continued to haunt Oliver too, mainly for the fact that it hadn't happened sooner. All the years it had taken for him to stand up to her – to call her out, to burst the bubble of her power over him.

As the park came into sight, Oliver abandoned the snorty sniffs and gave his nose a thorough wiping on the backs of his gloves. How Faith would hate that, he thought with dark satis-faction, observing the snail-trails this left across the smooth, state-of-the-art wool-synthetic and black leather gloves she had gifted him on some occasion or other – anniversary, birthday, Christmas, there were so many pretexts for her invariably exquisite presents, they all merged into one. Faith loathed any sort of boorish mannerisms, Oliver remembered wistfully, already feeling bad about the gloves. It was just that now, *not* being with her, it was harder to care. About anything.

'Daddy! We're here!'

Oliver spun round at the familiar voice of his daughter, dropping the sled onto the snowy path and spreading his arms wide as he crouched down, so that she could run – or rather skid – between them.

'We were calling and you didn't know.'

'I'm sorry, Princess. It must be my big new deaf ears.' He pulled a dorky face and jerked his head from side to side to make the flaps of his hat dance.

'They're not ears, they're your hat, silly Daddy,' she shouted, laughing.

'Hello, Oliver,' Faith said, as he got to his feet.

'Hello, Faith.'

'How are you doing?'

'Great, thanks. Though all the better for seeing you guys, of course.' Not to moan, that was a new resolution, talked through with Brad, who seemed to have become his self-appointed wingman in the situation, calling every couple of days to see how he was doing, as well as to talk about his latest read from the Top Ten download on his kindle. He had gone from Melville's masterpiece, which he had declared, aptly, to be 'one hell of a ride,' to George Eliot's *Middlemarch*. A hundred pages in, and he was struggling with Dorothea, he had confessed. 'She's so up herself, Oliver, that I keep thinking the woman deserves everything that's coming to her.' Oliver had replied that he couldn't agree more, but from what he could recall, that was kind of the point, because at the start of the story, she's still young and full of self-righteous ideals and what the book goes on to show is how life – reality – whittles away at such stuff, leaving people in better – or worse – shape, depending mostly on their moral courage. Brad had said he just loved the things Oliver came out with, joking that maybe they should start some sort of guys' book club. At least, Oliver was pretty sure he'd been joking.

'I'm hoping we can get a coffee afterwards?' he said brightly now, giving Faith his best grin. 'And maybe a brownie?' He winked at Amelia, looking up at him with her pretending-to-be-mad face from the sled, in which she had already settled herself, arms crossed, impatient for a tow.

'Or I could go and get us something,' Faith said, 'while you and Amelia play. I passed a wagon selling hot drinks and cookies a little way back.'

She wasn't wearing any make-up, not even round her eyes, Oliver noticed, loving how fresh-faced it made her look, her skin bare and sparkling like a teen.

'Giddy up!' Amelia shouted, jigging the loop of twine that Oliver had threaded into the front of the sled the previous winter, in the end having to purchase a hand-drill to make the hole because the plastic was so thick and hard.

'Whatever you prefer.' Oliver managed another expansive smile. 'You look beautiful, by the way. Is that a new hat?'

'Thanks. Actually, it was a Christmas present.' Faith touched the woollen hat, which was white and glittery with a big soft fur pompom. Her mittens were white and glittery too. A gift set then. Perhaps from a relative. Perhaps from some new admirer. Laurie and Seth were always hosting grand parties, especially through the holiday season. Who knew whose paths Faith had crossed, the conversations she had had, all while wearing one of the clinging-style cocktail dresses which, even after all their years together, made Oliver want to rip the zipper down the moment she asked him to pull it up. At least she was wearing a coat he had given her, he consoled himself, a long, padded, electric-blue one, selected via a string of links she'd sent as a helpful steer. 'I'll get the coffees and some snacks and see you soon.'

'I want a brownie!' Amelia yelled, at breaking point from being ignored.

'A brownie, *please*, Mommy,' Faith chided, but without enough conviction to get a response.

'Say please to your mother,' Oliver interjected quickly, spurred on by a sudden horrible insight into the possible damage being wreaked on the most precious element in the entire hateful situation: kids messed up by parents, unhappy mothers holding you too close – he had all too much experience of where that could lead.

The hill, a few bald patches already showing through the snow, was swarming with families, out in the park making the most of the weather. Oliver, pulling Amelia along on the sled behind him, made his way to the least hectic spot he could see, under a tree, halfway down the gentlest side of the incline. Faith had set off on her coffee mission, but then paused to watch them, he noticed, a blue smudge on the white path. Should he wave? Oliver couldn't make up his mind. She hadn't had to ask what sort of coffee he wanted, he remembered suddenly, because she already knew. He swung his arm at her like a madman, feeling wildly reassured. Such straws to clutch at, but they were better than no straws at all.

'There's Mommy!' Amelia cried, spotting Faith's return wave, just as they set off.

'Hang on tight, honey,' Oliver ordered, experiencing a jolt of fear about how to keep her little body safe, despite the cradle of his knees, bent almost up to his chin on either side of her, and his hands and big boots ready to help with braking and any necessary changes of direction. Thanks to his weight, and the powdery snow on their bit of the slope, they flew, and for a few long seconds, there was only the bliss of the whooshing sled and Amelia's high-pitched screams of joy. She'll be watching, Oliver thought exultantly. She'll be watching and she will see how good this father-daughter togetherness is, how formative, how restorative, how necessary.

Twenty minutes later, when they had just completed their fastest, riskiest descent of all, ending up in a gentle tumble that Amelia seemed to enjoy as much as being securely inside the tray, Faith reappeared on the path, carrying a paper bag in one hand and two coffees in a cardboard holder in the other.

'Sorry, they must have gotten pretty cold.'

'They're great. It's all great,' Oliver panted, exhilarated, looking round for – and failing to locate – an empty bench. 'It would be nice to sit for a while.'

'I'm afraid we haven't got long.'

'We're going *skiing*,' Amelia piped up, through a mouth crammed with brownie, 'with Aunty Laurie and Uncle Seth, and lots of other people.' She crouched down to dig out a twig half-buried in the snow and then started drawing patterns with it.

'Skiing. Wow. That's sounds nice.' Oliver took little sips of his latte, even though it was indeed, barely warm. The sky had closed in and the temperature was dropping fast. Soon, Amelia would be cold anyway, and with the coffee gone, they would no doubt embark on the long trek back across the park. Upper East and Upper West, a little over a mile apart, but they might as well have been parallel galaxies.

'Well, it came up at Christmas and everybody was keen, and Grandma said she was happy to see in the New Year on her own, so... so we're going to try Hunter Mountain, because it's close, and Amelia is the ideal age. Look, I'm sorry I didn't mention it before – it's been kind of a last-minute thing and I really wasn't sure, until Laurie and Seth persuaded me.'

'Look, Daddy, I did an octopus.'

'That's beautiful, honey. Maybe draw another, bigger one.' Oliver threw an encouraging glance at his daughter's scrawl in the snow. He had taken off his right glove and was feeling in his coat pocket for the bracelet box. It wasn't an ideal moment. But there were no ideal moments, not any more. 'I got you this.' He plucked out the box, wrapped in sparkling red paper that had looked nice enough in its roll, but which shed its red flecks like dry skin. 'Sorry, it's kind of messy.'

'But we said no gifts,' Faith said, staring at his present instead of taking it.

'I know, but I wanted to give you this, okay? It's no big deal. I mean, you don't have to open it now. Just take the damn thing, please?' Oliver shoved the box at her and knelt down to pretend to help Amelia with her second octopus when all he wanted was a few more seconds of having her close.

'Okay. Thanks. It's just that we had agreed... but thanks,' Faith muttered, dropping the box into the paper bag that had contained Amelia's brownie – among the chocolate crumbs and grease, Oliver noted – before stuffing it into the roomy, zipped pocket of her coat.

'What will you do for New Year's, do you think?' she ventured, in a voice that had the grace to sound sheepish.

'Seattle.'

'How are they both?'

Oliver swallowed down his self-pity. 'Not too bad. Dad is having more tests because it turns out he has jaundice, and Mom is her usual cranky self, so nothing new, I guess. I've said you wanted to spend Christmas with your folks – nothing else – and also made clear that how you were made to feel that day, about Robert, was totally unacceptable—' He stopped because Faith was widening her eyes at him and nodding towards Amelia.

'Thank you again for picking out the Seattle jigsaw,' he went on quickly instead. 'Dad averages about one piece an hour, but it makes him happy. Mom is less keen, to put it mildly.' He pulled a comical face that did little justice to the barbs and vibes of aggravation being fired between his mother's TV chair and the little sofa and coffee table in his parents' box of a living room. The way they ground on, such a sad, damaged, mismatched pair – within Oliver's despair and abhorrence, there gleamed something like compassion. At least, when he was away from them. Being in their company was a different story.

'I'm glad you had a happy Christmas, Oliver,' Faith declared – for Amelia's sake, Oliver very much hoped, since the words sounded so stiff and forced. 'And now, we best be going. Come on, Amelia honey, hold Mommy's hand.'

'Can I cross the park with you both?'

'Sure.'

Without needing instruction, Amelia did what she always did, which was to walk between them, one tiny hand in each of theirs. The small, vital link in their chain, Oliver reflected, wondering if a heart could break with love. Predictably, she was soon asking to be swung. So they did that too, gingerly, for fear of falling, but still managing to elicit the old, familiar squeals of delight as they counted one, two, three before letting her fly. Then Amelia asked could she *please* be carried, so Oliver scooped her up – handing the sled leash to Faith and carrying her until his arms ached, before suggesting she let him pull her along in the sled instead.

'How much more thinking time will you need?' he blurted, unable to contain himself when Central Park West was almost upon them.

'Let's get into the New Year, shall we,' Faith said evenly. 'I'm glad you're spending time with your parents, Oliver, and using the chance to talk properly. That's really good.' She picked Amelia up as she spoke – to thwart the possibility of an embrace, Oliver decided wretchedly, getting in a last kiss to the back of his daughter's head before they walked away. He turned on his heel, needing to have his back to them in order to deal with the onrush of misery at yet another separation. So many now, and each one a blade twisting in his gut. Faith was so calm, and what could that mean except that she didn't care? The one who cared the least had all the power, he decided wretchedly. But then, applying pressure wouldn't work either, as he and Brad had agreed when talking through his hopes for the encounter.

To say his had been a 'happy' Christmas was a joke, Oliver reflected, trudging back the way they had come, pulling the empty sled like some sad dad who'd mislaid his kid. But he had also done his dutiful best, with his gifts – another jigsaw for his father – an old map of Manhattan this time – and a lilac cashmere cardigan for his mother, which she said wasn't her colour, but which she wore nonetheless, for every moment of his three-day visit. He had taken them out by taxi to a top restaurant for Christmas lunch and then stayed with them each evening until their heads were nodding – despite longing to scuttle back to the luxury hotel to which he was treating himself for his own sanity. Hardest – but best – of all, Oliver had made a point of freely sharing any thoughts that came to mind about their London days and his half-siblings, each time ignoring his father's warning glances and his mother turning up the volume on the television. If nothing else, it had been a way of getting stuff off his chest. Robert and Catherine had deserved more tolerance, he had told them one afternoon, planting himself in front of the TV screen, because they had lost their mom and no kid was born bad. Emboldened – with only facial tics and head-shakes from his mother, and head-hung silence from his father – he had even mentioned attending Robert's funeral, saying Catherine was clearly struggling with the loss, but not going into details, since his half-sister's wine-hurling and hostility didn't exactly serve his cause. Only when he produced his recent photograph of Ackland Court did they sit up.

'It hasn't changed,' his mother had declared with a scowl, peering at the image for a few seconds from under the hoods of her eyes. His father had looked for longer, staring and staring, absently scratching the new patches of flaking skin on his fore-arms that he was supposed to leave alone.

'The past is the past,' he had growled at length, shoving the cell back into Oliver's hands and returning his attention to his beloved jigsaw, grabbing an obviously too-large piece and trying to press it into a tiny slot.

Oliver, in his new shout-to-be-heard-over-the-TV voice, had said he no longer believed that to be true, that what formed us never left us behind. When neither parent so much as twitched, he turned the television off and stood in front of it again, saying he didn't blame Faith for choosing to spend the holiday break with her family instead of his – in accordance with his explana-tion for her absence – because they at least *tried* to communicate with one another. And if either of them ever made Faith feel less than welcome again, he would cancel his payments to Fairview and let the state take over their care. That this was completely untrue – he would never stop funding all their needs – and that Faith appeared to have left him for good anyway, felt, in the heat of the moment, to be neither here nor there.

'Faith's a good woman,' his father had said solemnly, 'and we miss little Amelia, don't we, Di.'

'Yes, we do, Ian. Faith is over-sensitive, but she means well.'

And Oliver had felt heartened, even if it had taken scaring the hell out of them to get a hint of a thaw.

19

CATHERINE

I am sitting on the river bank, along from the bend where bits of the old wrecked bridge stick out of the water. The manor house shimmers like a film set in the distance, more in evidence through the leafless trees than on my first visit. Beside me are my trainers and Al's once for best, now slightly moth-eaten, old black overcoat from our London days, which he never wears but still keeps, because he doesn't give up on things, only on people, apparently. Belle, in her baffled, Al-less, Bobby-less, clingy state, is lying close but not touching, because not even the most devoted hound would want to rub up against a shivering, drenched creature – no matter how adored – on a cold, blowy, late-December morning. My legs, in my sodden jeans and socks, hang a few inches above the water, which is deep and dark, and moving fast, frilled with the crests of little waves being stirred up by the wind. Its breathtaking iciness made me cry out, as did my failure to surrender to it.

Leaving the house, I had got into the car alone before going back for Belle. She would come in with me, I decided in the despairing, dawn madness of exhaustion. We would succumb together, if only because she would try – and fail – to rescue me. But two days and two nights without sleep now, and it turns out my brain has stopped making correct judgements. It did not, for instance, factor in Belle's own animal instinct for comfort and self-preservation, nor mine. After I jumped in, she had stayed on dry land, watching and emitting the occasional yelp. While I, instead of sinking, swam immediately and with mad violence, hollering, as I fought the cold and the rushing current for the long minutes it took my feet to somehow rediscover the sludgy bottom along the reedy edge and haul myself out.

'Were you *swimming*?'

It is a little girl who has asked the question. She is standing on the opposite bank and has straggly hair and a chalky face. A scruffy brown anorak dangles half off her shoulders, revealing a loose-knit green jumper. She comes in and out of focus as I blink the water from my eyes, not seeming to mind when I don't answer.

The time without Al – all forty-eight hours of it – has passed in a sluggish blur, broken only by seeing to Belle's needs. Food. Walk. Food. Bed – upstairs for both of us, because I cannot be alone. Instead of bounding up to the landing as I had expected, however, Belle had required cajoling, as if breaking house rules was part of some anarchic doggy fun and nothing that could be connected to this alien, solitary, zombie pushover of an owner. When I patted the mattress for her to jump onto the bed, she took several moments to obey and then promptly jumped off again, retreating to do her draft-excluder act along the door. On the first night, I crawled on my knees in my dressing gown to join her, wounded further by her apparent indifference to my efforts to clasp her big warm body for comfort, until the first threads of true despair – and sheer cold – drove me back under the duvet, where I clung to Al's pillow instead.

The little girl is still there. She is wearing mud-caked black wellingtons that look too big. 'What's your dog called?' Her voice is small but clear as a wind chime.

My freezing body has started jerking. I try to say the word Belle, but my teeth get in the way.

'What were you swimming *for*?'

This seems a fair question, but I don't know how to answer, not to this painfully young, slip of a child. She looks six, maybe seven years old. All my powers of concentration are focused on tensing my body against the shakes, but they fight back.

'Did you lose something?' She peers at the water.

I sit up at that, following her gaze and thinking of the little urn, perhaps caught on the riverbed, perhaps long gone, like the dissolved shreds of Rob. So, yes, I have lost things all right. Or rather, people, because the loss, as I have lately been realising, goes beyond Rob. To the time long before. But I cannot say that to the little girl either, such a waif of a thing, thin as an autumn leaf, out alone on this dank morning. Children need protection from hurt, I know that much. I grope for Al's coat, clenching it round my shoulders as I struggle to my feet.

'Mummy says this place is not for swimming.'

Mummy. The word tolls in my head, as it keeps on doing. A beautiful word. But hard to hear. It has played its part, I know, in bringing me here – to try to do what it turns out I couldn't. The word makes me unable to continue looking at the girl, with all her vulnerability, all her innocence. Like Ryan doing the dishes, too sweet to be afraid of fatherhood, or life. I concentrate instead on trying to persuade my sodden feet into my trainers, wondering why I even bothered to take them off. When they won't co-operate, I ram them half-on, flattening the backs under my heels. Glancing up again, there is no sign of the child. I scan the manor house field beyond, squinting because of the brightening sky – blue nudging out the grey – but nothing moves except the clumps of nettles fringing its near side, swaying in the wind.

Belle does one of her woofs and starts the half-lollops that mean *are we doing this walk or not?* We are not and she doesn't take it well, slouching behind me as I stumble back to the car. I managed to park it sensibly this time, some part of my wired state relishing the focus required to manoeuvre it in the clearing so that it was facing back down the narrow tunnel of the lane. A tidy exit option, I had thought, for whoever found it.

'Change of plan,' I tell Belle, as a new, unexpected resolve starts to swell inside. 'First stop, home. Then it's London.'

By the time we rejoin the main road, the car heating has seen off my shakes and I am in a state of glorious hyper alertness, as if my brain has been rebooted by the shock of the freezing water. Like the last time, I think, spurring myself on with the recollection of the joy that had followed my wild-swim scattering of Rob's ashes back in the summer. The speedometer needle bobs past seventy as I bomb along the country lanes. I glance to my right and left, savouring the beauty of the gauzy, morning sun, now free of cloud, feeding light into the drab browns of the fields and woods. I have a project for the day and it feels fantastic. Something to aim for. Something to accomplish. It will be quite a round trip, but my gut is pumping with new, wild certainty.

As soon as we get home, I drape Al's coat over two kitchen chairs – pushing them up against the radiator for the quickest possible dry – and peel off my clothes, stuffing them straight into the washing machine. Aware of my nakedness, my cold skin tingling, still – wondrously – alive, I scamper upstairs and force myself under an icy shower, instead of the hot bath I crave, fearing how that might send me crawling under the duvet to close my eyes.

Back downstairs in comfy clothes – old cords and T-shirt, a big jumper, my beloved birthday boots – I make a mug of strong tea and carve off two fat chunks of an only slightly stale sourdough loaf, which I smother in butter and hefty wedges of leftover Christmas cheese. I eat standing up, ravenously, between slurping my tea and picking out other bits from the fridge – a couple of truffles from a Bruges box, bits of turkey, a cold roast potato, two sprouts still dotted with delicious flecks of the bacon Al had served them with. Spotting the bowl of bones and gristly bits of the bird on the bottom shelf – stripped by me and kept for Al to make the annual stock he's always so mad about – I take it to the bin to throw away, but then find myself cramming it all into our biggest saucepan instead. Roughly chopping a carrot, a potato, and an onion, I toss them in too, along with pepper, salt, a bay leaf and lots of water, before putting it on the big back hob ring to simmer. Al's stock. It feels almost like an act of reparation. Of love.

My phone is still on the table where I had left it – part of the intention to leave the world behind. I check it eagerly, fighting plummeting spirits when there's still only the usual festive nonsense. Radio silence, like Al said, and boy is he sticking to it. Because Al is not someone who says anything lightly, I remind myself bleakly. He follows through. He speaks his mind... I grip the mobile as the cruelties that fell from his mouth – sitting almost in this exact spot two and half days ago – surge back at me. They made me angry as well as despairing, and a part of me yearns to have that rage back, the protection of it, but it's like clutching at air. I miss him, that's the bigger truth. I *miss* him. And no, I am not strong, Al, I am *not*... Somehow, my phone slips from my hands onto the hard stone floor. I scramble to retrieve it, thankful to find nothing more than a hairline crack across the screen. Still on my knees, I message him.

> Silence imposs. U ARE enough. Always have been. Sorry if I hurt you. Never meant to. Rob was not in shadow. He had his own light. Am making turkey stock. I love you.

Received or not, the act of writing – of expressing myself – is instantly steadying. The words have gone, and Al, eventually, will read them. In search of similar peace of mind, I go into the study to find paper for writing to Joanne. The too-tidy desk, stripped of so much Al-stuff, nearly derails me, but I push on through, snatching a biro out of the mug pot and a piece of paper from the printer tray.

Dear Joanne. I am sorry. I meant no harm. Please make sure the girls know that.

My grip on the pen falters as one of the recurring aches to call Tam assails me. She may be in the thick of her honeymoon of a festive break, except Tam – being Tam – would pick up. But then, one tender enquiry and I'd be in pieces. Again. I have forged a plan for this third day of hell and must manage it alone. I look down at what I have written, feeling it needs more.

I hope you – and they – can forgive me. Cath

I fold up the page anyway and seal it in one of the envelopes that live in Al's top desk drawer, adding a stamp from the stock he also keeps there, before writing the address. I pause before closing the drawer, seeing Al's ordered mind there as everywhere – his command over life instead of being at its mercy like

me. Like the coherence in the arrangement of the room itself –
the walls of bookshelves, the little armchair positioned in a
corner under a standard lamp, the big central carpeted space –
where I too, could have a desk, as Al kept saying when we first
moved in. But no, the less fixed, more chaotic base of the kitchen
table has always been my preference, because why the hell
would I, Cath Reynolds, ever want to make life easy?

At the front door in Al's still-damp coat and eating another
truffle – the box under my arm by way of snacks for the car – I
do a sweeping mental checklist: phone, letter for posting, dog
lead, poo bags, keys, and a destination entirely unconnected to
the desire for self-eradication – yes, the day has swerved onto a
new track, and I shall keep it there. The truffles, a box of twelve –
champagne flavoured, half white chocolate, half dark – were a
great idea. Three eaten, and I am buzzing.

It is only as I'm about to close the front door that I register
the faint whiff of boiling turkey bones. Racing back inside to
turn the hob off, I realise that I'd somehow also managed to
forget Belle. *Step by step, Cath*, I warn myself, coaxing my dog off
her bed and into the car, and then taking extra care over nosing
my way out into the road.

* * *

The journey takes so much longer than I envisaged. Manic, post-
Christmas traffic – when did that become a thing? By the end of
the painful stop-start snail-crawl at the end of the A3, where
three lanes merge into one for the approach to Wandsworth, I
have consumed all of the remaining nine chocolates. Then it's
new speed limits, speed bumps, queues for temporary lights,
road-hogging buses and roundabout after roundabout after
roundabout. Bloody London. There were many reasons to leave

the place – quite apart from seeking relative geographic proximity to my brother. But soon old landmarks are leaping out at me like ghosts from the past: *Welcome to Wandsworth Borough*, the pub signs, the road names, the genteel houses that get less genteel as I near the still-gritty grid of my home patch. Before I know it, I am turning into the road that leads to Ackland Court itself – not part of my game plan for the day, but the temptation is too strong.

Twenty yards, and there is the bus stop, now with a fancy shelter, but the low wall behind it hasn't changed. For a moment, I can feel the cold hard stone under my backside, trying to keep myself upright while Rob, boozy-breathed and carefree, flops against me, as we gather our wits after a night out. His trust in me – to get us home, to handle consequences – never wavered, then, or later, during all the years of similar trials living on our own. And yes, Al, there *was* something about that which I liked – the sense of being needed – useful – in a world of so much else that I couldn't control.

Nosing on round the bend, I brace myself for Ackland Court, only to see a wall of hoardings, the lower panels sprayed with lavish, psychedelic graffiti. I pull over to take a hurried photo through my window and accelerate away, thinking, good riddance, but not quite feeling it. Somehow, I then manage to lose my bearings and have to criss-cross Garratt Lane several times before finding the road I am looking for – the one containing the entrance to the cemetery. By then, it is mid-afternoon, with the wintry brightness of the day already palling. End-of-year darkness. How have I not factored that in?

Finding a legal parking space hoovers up yet more precious time. Jogging through the gates at last, tugging a bemused, reluctant dog behind me, anxiety tips into panic. I thought I would remember, but all I see is a bewildering, deserted metropolis of intersecting walkways and gravestones. From the handful of early visits with our father – before they petered out – I know there was a large stone angel near the grave, but everywhere I look, there are angels of all shapes and sizes. And now my father's voice is booming in my head, reading out the gravestone inscription as he grips Rob's and my hands. *Forever in our hearts.* While all I could think was, *liar, liar, pants on fire.* Because our mother was not in his heart; Diane was. Diane, who hated and punished me, while he did nothing.

'Excuse me, Madam.'

Madam. Oh God. I jerk round to see an officious-looking, elderly man approaching, clutching a large weathered briefcase. It will be about closing time. Or no dogs.

'Yes?'

'I don't mean to intrude, but I was wondering if you needed any assistance.'

'Assistance?'

He glances pointedly at his watch. 'Were you, perhaps, looking for a particular grave?'

'Oh, I was just, you know, getting my bearings...' I drop my gaze to Belle, slumped now half across my feet in what feels like a show of support over the interrogation. 'It's been a while since I was here, that's all.'

While I talk, the man has unbuckled his baggy leather case and extracted an iPad.

'There's a map, you see. And a find-the-grave option. If that would help.' His fingers fly. 'So long as you have a name and the dates.' He peers at me over the top of the small wire spectacles that have slid halfway down his nose. 'If you are interested.'

'Oh thanks, but I'm sure I'll be able to...' I stammer, having no desire – no ability – to spell out my mother's name and dates of birth and death to a stranger, no matter how amenable. 'It's almost dark, so I'd better get on.'

'Oh, there's some light left yet. You could put in the details yourself, if you like. Here.' He holds out the iPad for me to take. 'It might be quicker in the end. Then I could help you make sense of the map.'

'Goodness... er... thanks.' He has placed the tablet in my hands. The form is easy – three boxes to fill in.

'A cuppa?' He offers me the lid of the thermos he has been fiddling with as I pass the iPad back. 'I've not touched it – scouts honour – and only a grain or two of sugar.' The eyes behind the glasses shine with such goodwill that a refusal feels churlish.

I take a polite sip. Finding it sweet, delicious, and not too hot, I down the rest in one go. The warmth of the liquid spreads through me like a sort of happiness. And to think, I might not have been here, I reflect suddenly, murmuring thanks as I give the empty lid back. To think I could have drowned.

'There, found it... Not far at all, but let me point you in the right direction.' He sets off at a brisk pace before I can answer, pausing only when I do to let Belle have a pee. A couple, appearing out of the maze of gravestones ahead, drift past us, arm in arm, expressions glazed. A young couple, and my heart tightens at the thought of what they might be mourning. But when the old man gives them a nod, they tip their heads in return, their expressions softening, as if he is an old friend.

'It's my mother's grave,' I blurt, my heart performing a violent flip at the sight of the angel a few yards ahead of us – instantly recognisable with her arms spread wide and wings as big as clouds. 'I haven't come for so long. I don't know why.'

'Oh, we all come when we are ready,' he replies breezily. 'In some cases, it's learning *not* to come that's hard. I was on all day every day with my Dot for a while. But now I'm down to once a week. To tell her my news and so forth. Your mother is eighth on the left along this path here. I'll leave you to it.'

The gravestone, plain and grey, only slightly mottled with age, stands erect in grass that is shaggy, but – like all the graves – clearly tended regularly to keep it from serious overgrowth. Her name is big and clear, the indents deep. I let go of Belle's lead and kneel in front of it, tracing the letters with my fingers.

GRETA AGNES REYNOLDS

1940–1982

Forever in our hearts.

I am aware of watching myself. Waiting to see what I will feel. Here it is: the earliest, biggest, worst loss. The first abandonment before all the others that seem to have followed. The first loss, so rarely thought about – shut out – because it hurt too much. A shrink, it occurs to me – Al's answer to everything – would have a field-day:

So, Catherine, you lost your mother when you were six. How did that make you feel?

Like crap. Thanks for asking.

And acquiring a stepmother who hated you, and a father who did nothing about it. What was that like?

Oh, that was a blast too, thanks. And don't forget my twin, the one who's now dead.

I've always known my bad stuff. It's just living with it that's suddenly got so hard.

Greta Reynolds. *Mummy.* I stare and stare at the slab of stone, feeling empty. I no longer know why I have come, or what I thought it would solve. There is no torrent of emotion. No sudden easing of hurt. No seismic insights. No new perspective about anything. To cry would feel like *something*, but I can't even do that.

I am about to leave, when a gust of wind blows at my back. Another follows, stirring my hair, chilling my neck. I shiver, closing my eyes. And in the same instant, a memory moves through me, of cool, loving fingers sliding over my scalp and combing down through the thick strands of my long hair, left always to grow and grow. The sensation repeats, again and again; the fingers combing, stroking, soothing. A soft mouth at my ear whispers, *Your crowning glory, Liebling, like mine.*

When I open my eyes, Belle is sniffing at something in the gravel by my feet. 'Forever in my heart, Mum,' I say aloud, enjoying a sudden notion that – in the unlikely event of there being an actual, proper 'afterlife' – she and Rob will at least be cavorting round the damn place together. Before I know it, I am sobbing. Howling. I can't stop myself and have no desire to. There is no one to be brave for any more.

When the worst has passed, fearful of the fading light, I force myself – and Belle – to run back towards the entrance, regretfully ignoring a toilet sign at the back of the chapel as we go. The sight of the gates – still open – and the old man there too, swamps me with relief.

'All well?' he asks cheerfully.

'Yes. Thank you so much for your help. I wanted to stop to use the Ladies, actually,' I find myself confessing, as my full bladder pulses again, 'but I was afraid of getting locked in.'

'You won't get locked in.'

'How do you know?'

'Because I'm the one closing the gates tonight. Filling in for the usual person. I could hold your dog for you, if you like. While you go?' He looks at Belle, who looks at me.

'That's very kind. I'd have to command her to stay, or she might howl.'

'Well, we wouldn't want that now, would we?' He gives Belle a little pat.

I tell Belle to stay. I go to the toilets. I give my nose a good blasting into a long trail of too-thin loo roll. I wash the dirt out from under my fingernails. I even run my handbag comb through my hair.

When I emerge, it is almost dark. But within seconds of rejoining the main path, I can see the outline of the old man and Belle, waiting patiently by the open gate.

20

OLIVER

'Hey, Oliver, have you tried an *empanada* yet? From what Harrison tells me about your game this morning, you guys have sure earned the right to burn some calories.' Katarina, Harrison's petite, raven-haired Argentinian wife, smiled warmly as she held out the platter of fat pastry parcels.

'Don't believe everything that husband of yours tells you,' Oliver quipped, taking one gratefully. He had been loitering on the edge of the party, painfully aware both of his new 'single' status and of the charity of having been invited at all. It was a cocktail-style lunch party, with eighty or so guests, mostly local, Harrison had said, which probably explained why Oliver had not yet recognised a single one of them. Zipping in and out of the clusters of guests were various children, including Harrison and Katarina's two boys, who had turned from chunky toddlers into lean youngsters since he had last seen them. They made his heart lurch for Amelia, currently on the ski slopes with Faith's family. His beloved child. She was still so small compared to these kids, and yet now in the thick of something she had no hope of understanding and which – Oliver feared more and more – could scar her for life.

'It was a tough match, yes,' Oliver went on, forcing himself to make conversation – holding back on trying the canapé because it was so large and clearly going to be a challenge to eat. 'Your super-fit husband ran me ragged for three straight sets, the reason being he's a great squash player, whereas I've always been pretty lousy. I guess it suits me better to run in straight lines, although – as I guess you heard – I can make a mess of that too.' Oliver pulled a rueful face at the reference to his accident back in the autumn.

'Oh, that was too bad – but you've made a full recovery, right?'

'Oh yes, I'm doing great now, thanks.'

Katarina launched into a story about something similar happening to a friend and Oliver seized the chance to take a bite of the pastry, which was delicious – stuffed with soft cheese, spinach and serrano ham by the look of things. He was aware in the same moment of a brief, faint vibration from his cell in his pocket. Or maybe he had imagined it. He had been doing a lot of that lately, each time hoping Faith had sent another snap from the slopes. There had been two so far, both of Amelia: in one she was doing a goofy squint at the camera, her goggles pushed up onto the rim of the pink helmet that matched her pink ski boots, and in the other she was in action on a nursery slope, wearing an orange reflector vest like all her little classmates and adopting the pose of a slalom racer despite the near-flat gradient of the course. Imagining notifications arriving on your phone was actually a thing, Oliver had read recently. It even had a name: Phantom Vibration Syndrome. So, he wasn't totally losing his sanity. Although, to be part of a tribe of souls either lonely enough – or sufficiently device-addicted – to imagine such efforts at contact did feel kind of tragic.

'It was really great of you and Harrison to invite me,' he said shyly, once Katarina's story had ended, aware he was venturing into the only recently revealed, still agonisingly tender territory of the situation between himself and Faith. The sorry truth had spilled out when Harrison had called to suggest the squash game, the invitation to the party coming on the back of it. Oliver had known at once that, for his own mental wellbeing if nothing else, it was an offer he had to accept. Brad was good. Brad was amazing. But he wasn't enough.

'Not at all, Oliver, it's been far too long anyway,' Katarina replied kindly.

Over her shoulder, Oliver caught a look from Harrison, standing in the thick of a circle of guests, his dark, curly head towering over everyone by several inches as usual. The man had rowed at Harvard, as well as being a force to reckon with on the squash court and making millions long before the founding of their own company. To have managed all that while remaining an all-round nice guy seemed increasingly to Oliver, in his own newly floundering state, to be the most monumental achievement. This house of theirs was palatial, like every other residence in their salubrious patch of Brooklyn. And yet Harrison was his same old easy self, in a T-shirt and loafers, still looking more like a student than a businessman.

Katarina had stepped closer, turning her tray so that Oliver – now chewing down the last of the empanada – could help himself to one of the small red paper serviettes piled on that side of it. 'I was so very sorry to hear of what you and Faith are going through,' she murmured. 'Now is not the time, of course, but please know, Oliver, that I have the details of the *best* relationship therapist in town, okay?' She fixed her dark soulful eyes on his. 'A *magician* of a guy, if you get me?'

Oliver muttered his thanks, for a moment wondering what exactly he was being told. Harrison and Katarina were rock-solid, weren't they? But then who really knew anything about anyone, he mused, dejection threatening, as he hastily used the napkin to dab his mouth before excusing himself to find the bathroom.

He didn't need to relieve himself, but it would offer the chance of some time out. Without Faith at his side, the room of people made him feel raw and fearful, like he had lost an outer layer of skin. On top of which, his cell had buzzed again, he was sure of it this time and itching to check. The obvious bathroom to use – in the hall – had a couple of people already waiting at the door, so Oliver swivelled quickly and headed down the polished wooden staircase to the lower ground floor. There, he knew, was another handsome toilet, serving what Harrison and Katarina blithely referred to as the 'gym', a mirror-walled empo-rium of training equipment that sat between a snooker room and a den the size of a small cinema. Oliver pulled the phone out as soon as he was off the bottom step, thrilled to see at one glance that there was indeed a new WhatsApp notification, and one with a photograph. Not from Faith – that, too, he could see at a glance – but maybe a considerate member of the family ski party had decided to send him a snap. He slipped into the bath-room, bolting the door and closing the toilet lid so he could sit in relative comfort to take a proper look.

Finding himself staring at some bright, ugly squirls of graffiti across the perimeter fencing of a building site – rather than rela-tives posing in jazzy ski-wear on a mountain – Oliver's first fear was that it might be a scam. It took a moment or two more to register the *FYI* under the picture and the fact that the sender was Catherine. Catherine. Oliver swore softly. That he was staring at the piece of South London occupied by Ackland Court took another few instants to dawn. Indeed, he was still absorbing the fact when his cell – on silent for the party – began to vibrate with the very un-phantom-like persistence of an actual call. From Catherine.

Oliver raked his fingers through his hair. He blew out his cheeks. His half-sibling's inevitable vitriol, he couldn't deal with it. He was too fragile, too weakened. Not to mention decidedly ashamed of the profoundly misguided drunken rant of a message he had been insane enough to leave her. Two unanswered attempts to apologise – the second not even getting a ringtone – had caused him to believe she had blocked his number. Email had crossed his mind, but anticipating a wall of silence – or worse – there too, he hadn't been able to face it. He had enough of his own demons to deal with.

Oliver continued to watch his cell, feeling bad for letting it ring out, but also mad at himself for being so. Placing it carefully on top of the cistern, he peed and washed his hands. For all the newfound perspectives he had been endeavouring to impress upon his parents, the woman trying to call him had contributed to making his childhood hellish, he reminded himself. Catherine was a destructive force. Bad karma. There were people like that in the world. People who were the opposite of Harrison and Katarina. People who, without being able to help themselves, wreaked havoc and unhappiness wherever they went, infecting everyone else's attempts to lead normal, decent lives.

As Oliver was drying his hands in the soft white folds of a large hand towel, the cell sprang into life once more. Catherine. Again. Oliver groaned, raised his eyes to the ceiling, and then took the call.

'Catherine?' He held his cell at a little distance from his ear, out of some instinctive hope of self-protection from what might be about to pour forth. 'Thanks for sending the photograph,' he said at once, eager to delay any eruptions for as long as possible, 'though it's hard to make out exactly what's going on.' When still she did not speak, his misgivings surged. He owed her nothing, he reflected bitterly. In fact, she *owed* him, for all the rudeness at his efforts to reach out in the past and now for this sick new game, whatever it turned out to be – still trying to play him, still trying to call the shots.

'I'd blocked you. I unblocked you to send the picture.'

'Yeah, I kind of worked that out,' he muttered, having been on the verge of hanging up, 'and if this is about the voicemail that I left the other week, then I'm sorry, okay? I wasn't – for various reasons – in great shape that day. I tried to apologise but—'

'They're knocking it all down. Did you see?'

'Ackland Court? Or maybe it's a refurb?' Oliver found himself suggesting, because she actually sounded kind of forlorn – the opposite of someone calling the shots. 'I mean, from your picture, it's hard to tell. Not that the place would ever have won a beauty pageant...' He let the sentence hang, having no idea how or where he wanted the conversation to go.

'They are knocking it down,' she repeated dully. 'Because in the end, everything gets knocked down, doesn't it? Buildings. Hopes. Dreams. Illusions. Literally... everything.'

'Hey, Catherine, are you okay?' He spoke cautiously, still bracing himself for her to flip out.

There was a long pause. 'It's been a hard day, actually... Lots of... downs and ups... trying to work stuff out... I'm bone-tired, to be honest. Hard to think straight, you know?'

Oliver lowered the toilet seat and sat back down, torn between wanting to care and not. 'Sure – at least, I think I do.'

'I am sorry if Rob and I were foul to you, Oliver. I mean, I *know* we were foul to you and I *am* sorry.'

'Well, thank you, Catherine.' Oliver held his cell at arm's length for a second, giving it a stare of astonishment. 'That means a lot.'

'You were our enemy. At least, we thought you were.'

'You guys sure gave me a hard time, but then you—'

'Why did she hate me, Oliver? Your mother... I mean she literally *hated* me.'

'Wow, Catherine... er... I guess she found you guys hard work sometimes, and – don't take this wrong – but the way you two acted out all the—'

'No,' she cut in. 'It started *before* – while my mother was still alive and she visited to help out. She *always* hated me. Could she have been jealous, do you think? *Can* a grown woman be jealous of a child? And why, anyway? Was I too cocky? Too pretty?'

'Hey... I think we'd need a professional to answer those questions,' Oliver flannelled, adding into the silence that followed, 'but I guess anything is possible.' He had thrown himself forward, resting his elbows on his knees, shock at what he was being told spurring him on in his desire to be honest and to think clearly. 'She's never gotten the hang of being happy in herself, that's for sure. Dad once told me there were some bad experiences before he knew her – pregnancy and a termination, because of the guy responsible walking away. There was a huge amount of shame back in those days, I guess, but he wouldn't say more and there was no way I could ever ask *her* about it...' Oliver had to stop himself elaborating on all the off-limits subjects that had raged throughout his upbringing and beyond, including Catherine herself. 'Whatever happened,' he continued, 'I guess it can't have helped her mental health... but look, all I can say is sorry on her behalf, for whatever she put you through – you and Robert—'

'I'm doing the apologising here, Oliver,' she snapped, sounding much more like the person he was used to, 'and, for the record, Rob only ever got the occasional little slap. It was me she focused on – making sure to pick places where any serious marks wouldn't show. She even hacked all my hair off once – you probably don't remember... like I say, she couldn't stand the sight of me.'

'I do remember,' Oliver said hollowly, seeing his new school shoe, sporting a bit of egg shell and a few wet tea leaves. 'Jesus, Catherine, I had no idea... I mean... the hair... I just thought you'd found a new way to make her pissed. I mean, of course I knew you guys got smacked for misbehaving... but not the extent of it... What can I say – I was just a kid, I—'

'And why the fuck did Dad just let it *happen*, anyway?' she interjected furiously.

'I know,' Oliver cried, something like pleasure pushing through at the fact of them having stumbled on genuinely common ground. 'Dad was – *is* – so darn passive. It's always driven me crazy. A peace-lover, I guess, but also – maybe – just plain afraid of her. Like I was too, once upon a time.' Oliver could hear the pride in his own voice, and would have talked on, but Catherine had begun saying her goodbyes, sounding dazed suddenly rather than fired up.

'...only rang to set the record straight and to apologise. None of the bad stuff was your fault, I can see that now... I wish you well, Oliver. But it's very late here and I've got to get back on the road...'

'The road? Are you still in London then?'

'No. I've left London. I'm on the hard shoulder of the M3...'

'A highway?' Oliver's mind was whirling, in up to his neck with caring now, whether he liked it or not. 'It doesn't sound like you should be driving anywhere at this moment, Catherine, if you don't mind my saying. Like you said yourself, you are bone-tired. So maybe give your husband, Alastair, a call? See if he could come and fetch you—'

'Al's left me. And he wasn't – isn't – my husband. Also, he took Bobby.'

'Oh dear.' Oliver squeezed his temples between the thumb and third finger of his free hand at these fresh horrors, while a dim part of him found a moment to marvel that she too, had been left by her partner. As for who the hell Bobby was, he had no idea – since he was pretty sure they didn't have kids – but dared not trigger anything further by asking.

'There must be someone else you could call, Catherine,' he went on, anxious at the image of her – even if she was a touchy nightmare of a person – having a major meltdown on a highway pull-off. On top of which, he could see from his phone that he had now been incarcerated in Harrison's lower ground floor bathroom for almost fifteen minutes.

'To request collection from the side of a motorway?' she sneered. 'I don't think so. And anyway, my only proper friend is on her honeymoon in Ireland – where she'll soon be living permanently. So actually, no, I haven't got *someone else*, Oliver. I'm the proverbial sinking ship, you see, with everyone jumping safely clear. And do you know what? I honestly don't blame them. I mean, the way I've been, the way I am, I'd have left me too, if you see what I mean. Long ago.'

'Well, right now, you've got me, haven't you,' Oliver pointed out stoically, finding the new false jollity in her tone more concerning than anything, and because it felt good to prove to himself that – despite his own difficult childhood memories and current woes – he had not lost the capacity to be kind. 'Hey, Catherine,' he exclaimed, as inspiration struck, 'how about you share with me your exact location and home zip code, so I can sort you out an Uber? You could collect your car tomorrow.'

'Oh, my God, Oliver – thank you, but *no*.'

She sounded not far off amused, which was good in a way, but also not good.

'Catherine, I am not sure you are up to driving,' he repeated doggedly.

'I have to be,' she cried, over a roar of sound that suggested she had started her car or wound her window down, or both. 'Earlier today – this morning – I didn't think I could go on, but what doesn't kill you, etcetera etcetera...'

'Catherine, wait...' There was definite hysteria in her voice and the background noise was growing worse – like she was driving through a wind tunnel with her phone on her lap. 'Right, well let's keep talking then,' he shouted.

'Low battery. No charger. Bye, Oliver.'

'Message me when you get home safe then, okay? Catherine? Will you do that?'

But she had gone and someone was rapping on the bathroom door and trying the handle.

'Just one moment,' Oliver called, flushing the toilet, even though it wasn't technically necessary, before opening the door and stepping straight into Harrison.

'All good?' His friend eyed him quizzically, his handsome face crinkled with concern.

'Yes, all good. Sorry, I had to take a call...'

'Yeah, I couldn't help hearing.' Harrison slung an arm across Oliver's shoulders as they headed back towards the staircase. 'It sounded like a tough one, fella.'

'It was. A story for another time.' Oliver shook his head, still preoccupied, but also aware of being sort of pepped up. Catherine had told him terrible things and was a mess. But she had said sorry. It was kind of momentous.

Harrison was silent, but as they reached the top of the stairs, he tightened his grip across Oliver's back, bringing him to a halt. 'Are you seeing someone else, Oliver? This Catherine you were just talking to – I couldn't help hearing – is that what this whole thing between you and Faith is about?'

Oliver started to laugh at so ludicrous a suggestion, but quickly checked himself. 'No way, I would never... Jesus, Harrison. Catherine is my half-sister. Remember, I told you about her way back.'

'Oh, okay. The one you hadn't seen in years whose brother died, back in the summer?'

'Exactly,' Oliver cried, irked to hear a note of scepticism in his old friend's voice. Like he thought a fudge was going on. 'Like I say, it's a long story, which I will go into properly one day. For now, I'd best be getting home. Thank you so much for the party – for inviting me – it means a lot.'

'He's been hiding in the downstairs bathroom and now he says he's gotta go,' Harrison told Katarina as she emerged from the central reception room, exclaiming that she had been looking for them both. 'But come for New Year's, pal, okay?' he went on, turning back to Oliver. 'Just family, but you're always welcome.'

'Oh yes,' Katarina exclaimed, giving Oliver a farewell hug, 'We are always here for you, Oliver.'

Oliver, swallowing a throat lump of gratitude, said they were both beyond kind, but that duty required him to get himself together for a flight to Seattle early the following morning, where he would be seeing in the new year with his parents.

Fifteen minutes later, he was sitting on the subway

surrounded by a noisy family of six, shout-talking and laughing at one another over the clatter of the train as it sped back towards Manhattan. Oliver put in his AirPods and tuned into a true-crime podcast that Brad had recommended, but his thoughts kept skittering. He scrolled and re-scrolled to Catherine's graffiti photograph, marvelling at their phone conversation, hoping she would get safely home, and quelling stabs of guilty dread at the prospect of seeing out the end of the year with his folks – a prospect all the harder given what he now knew.

Worse than anything, however, as he watched the chattering family, was his deepening longing for Faith and Amelia. They were due back from skiing early on Sunday morning – New Year's Day – well before him, and so might be able to make a late-afternoon visit, Faith had said, when he messaged her with the request, as long as Amelia wasn't too exhausted. Oliver allowed himself to savour the idea. A reward after the ordeal of Seattle. That was at least something wonderful on which to set his sights.

He got off the subway a couple of stops early, wanting the walk. Every trace of pre-Christmas snow had long since melted, and the streets were thronged with people bargain-hunting and getting ready for the turn of the year. Oliver willed himself to feel a part of it, popping into a couple of his favourite delis to buy food he could call his dinner. He would have a glass or two of wine in front of the TV, and then read himself to sleep, he decided, leaving his packing for Seattle until the morning. He made himself walk for another hour, delaying having to return to his empty home, stopping in a bar for a beer, because that too, surely, was the sign of someone engaging with the world instead of being overwhelmed by it.

Phantom Vibration Syndrome, he warned himself, feeling his phone stir in his pocket when he was back in the flat and attending to his packing after all, knowing he would be grateful for it come the morning. But it wasn't a phantom; it was Catherine sending the message he had asked for.

> Home. Thank you. Over and out.

Oliver messaged back at once, experiencing something like relief at the tone of finality in the exchange:

> Thanks. Take care and good luck

They had made their apologies and their peace – and that was something to be grateful for. Now she had to get on with working her own life out, as did he.

21

CATHERINE

The young woman at the checkout picks out the towering, purple orchid sitting amid the jumble of my shopping on the conveyor belt. 'Ooh, isn't this lovely. What a colour, eh?'

'I know. I love orchids.' The white one I gave Joanne back in August flutters to mind. I wonder if she threw it straight in the bin, and whether – if they are home from Portugal yet – my posted scribble of an apology will have suffered the same fate. 'The challenge for me will be keeping it alive,' I tell the girl, pulling an I'm-hopeless face, despite knowing she is only making conversation, no doubt as per her training on 'how to BE with customers', especially wild-eyed ones clearly doing a last-minute shop on the morning of New Year's Eve.

'But orchids are a doddle,' she says, not sounding remotely like she is complying with a training script and expertly deploying her long, immaculately painted nails to tease out the price tag and bar code for the scanner. She starts firing out detailed orchid-care watering instructions as she checks through the rest of my stuff, while I absorb, with some amazement, my own extravagance: wild boar pât, black grapes, a wedge of camembert, four conference pears, half of a fat, home-made pork pie, fresh scallops, gleaming sprigs of purple-sprouting broccoli, chorizo sausage, a seeded, wholemeal, sour-dough baguette and a bottle of champagne. I have, in short, gone mad, I acknowledge cheerfully, carefully stowing each item in the tote bag I have actually remembered to bring for the purpose, instead of thinking I should bring it and leaving it on the kitchen table.

'One root-soaking a week for guaranteed results – or your money back,' the girl laughs, handing me my receipt.

The automated doors release me into the full-on beam of winter sunshine. Two full days of it now, albeit short ones, but each one a little lighter... I check myself, aware that my new, upbeat mood is starting to feel perilously close to a steady state, and therefore highly likely to skedaddle.

Sleep, I know, is partly responsible: two nine-hour stretches of oblivion now, wrapped inside the cocoon of Al's and my double duvet, with my phone off and Belle back in her old kitchen night-time routine of curling up on her kitchen bed with a doggy biscuit. It has wrought a dizzy lucidity that would have been unimaginable in the exhausted daze in which I arrived back from South London, two days ago. Indeed, having made it safely into the drive, I could have slept slumped over the steering wheel. For a few moments, I had.

But there had been Belle to feed, and Oliver to message, along with the realisation that I was starving. With the first two chores seen to, I had heated up the turkey stock – rejoicing that I hadn't left it to burn the place down – lobbing in every leftover I could find, including a dash of red wine. The result was a soup so tasty that I closed my eyes and groaned with sheer pleasure at every swallow. Made with 'Al's stock', it was like Al was nour-ishing me, I had decided dopily, leaping across the kitchen when my charging phone trilled, to find a message from Al himself. The first to break his hideous 'radio silence'.

> Cathy, thank you for the words in your message and for the time out. I hope you are doing okay. More soon.

I had longed for much more, but it was a start. A notable absence of kisses, but – on the plus side – Al only ever called me 'Cathy' when he was being loving. I had tapped back at once:

> I am doing so well apart from missing you. The world is starting to make sense again and I need you in it, Al. I have always needed you in it.

I had waited but he didn't come back online. *More soon* was still brilliant, I consoled myself, and New Year's Eve had to be what he had in mind. It was no night for anyone to be alone, and what better moment in the year could there be for a reunion? However late he left to confirm it, I had two whole days to ensure I would be ready.

Upstairs, basking in the blanketing warmth of a scented, sudsy bath, I had let the events of the day float and settle, before deliberately forcing myself to look back at the state of black despair in which it had begun. The icy river in full winter spate. The instant, knee-jerk desire to fight it – to live. The little girl, helping to bring me to my senses. A veil lifting. It felt almost as if I was looking back at another person. So much so, that I had managed to doze off, only to wake, spluttering and terrified, as bath water flooded my nose. It brought the desperation of the morning back to me and I wept a little afterwards, huddling in Al's big towel. The madness of grief – Tam had got that right from the beginning, bless her, without knowing how old the madness was, or how deep.

In bed at last, catatonic with fatigue, my brother had drifted
to mind, along with a yearning to hear his voice. How wonderful
it would have been to be able to call Rob and share all that had
happened – the kindness of the old man in the cemetery, the
otherworldly sense of our mother's touch as I stood by the grave,
Oliver's decency when, in my wired state, the urge to ring him
had become overwhelming, despite the inconvenience of being
on a motorway hard shoulder at the time. And to talk over snippets of our potted past – good and bad – what a joy that would
have been.

Except that Rob almost certainly wouldn't have picked up
the phone, let alone co-operated in the conversation, a dry voice
inside my sleepy head had pointed out. Because my dear brother
had been consistently lousy at answering calls – even before
Joanne – and there was nothing he had resisted more than being
invited to look back or to discuss emotive subjects of any kind. In
fact, my darling twin brother had been an emotional ostrich,
happy for me – or anyone else in his life – to do the empathetic
heavy lifting.

Oliver had answered my call, though. It had taken two goes,
but he had answered and then been gracious in the face of all I
had to say. Kind. We had managed an okay conversation. All of
which raised the extraordinary possibility that my monstrous
stepmother and feeble father had managed to produce a decent
human being. *Wonders never cease.* The phrase had played in my
head as the waves of sleep at last pulled me under. There had
been no one else to call. And Oliver had answered. Thirty years,
and we had wrought a sort of peace.

* * *

With the results of my New Year's Eve shopping spree stowed in the car and half an hour of parking time left, I set off down the high street, simply to enjoy more of the brightness of the day. *More soon.* This morning, there were blue ticks on the reply I'd sent, together with a thumbs up. A thumbs up! Which means Al will call today – I can feel it in my happy bones – probably when he's setting off. Not bombarding him, giving him time, has paid off and I will stick it out as long as I can bear.

As I walk, my hair – long and loose, and treated that morning to one of my rarely used expensive moisture masks, in addition to shampoo and conditioner – bounces on my shoulders. I can almost feel it shining in the sun. My choice of clothes – an old weathered leather jacket over a white polo, black stretch jeans and my beloved boots, so worn in now, they are as comfy as slippers – feels good too. Self-care – everyone knows how vital that is, but I am fully aware of having also dressed for Al. Just as I have shopped for him. Every delicacy I picked are among his favourites. His big face will crumple with delight. And the make-up sex, oh God.

Passing an outdoor gear shop, I pause to check out the sale prices, spotting a dark-green cagoule that I know Al would love. In the corner of the window are a few flyers, including one offering a beginner's yoga class. I get out my phone to take a picture of the contact details. It's the sort of thing I have been meaning to do for years and could be fun as well as good for me. I might even make a couple of new friends... The thought catapults me straight to Tamsin with such force that I FaceTime her on the spot.

'Cath, how lovely!' she shrieks, bobbing into view at once, still in a dressing gown and looking endearingly dishevelled and sleepy-eyed.

'Happy New Year!' I shriek back. 'I thought I'd get in early, before the airwaves get overloaded.'

'Cath, how are you? You look amazing. A bit of rest was clearly the right call. How was your birthday, and Christmas? How is Al?'

'He whisked me off to Bruges for a twenty-four-hour birthday bonanza. Ryan and Sadie looked after the dogs – she's accidentally expecting a baby, but it's only eight weeks so no one's counting chickens – or foetuses,' I gabble, quelling a pulse of dismay at how old all the information feels, a fresh reminder of how our paths have swerved apart. 'As for Christmas, it began well but then somehow ended up with Al and me having a bit of *thing*, though it's all getting sorted now...'

'What sort of thing?' she asks at once, in her cut-to-the-chase way.

'Oh God, it's too much to go into now, Tam. I'm out shopping – or rather loitering outside a shop...'

'Go into it,' Tam commands, the background behind her shifting as she clearly moves to another room – out of earshot of Jules, I rather hope – folding herself into an armchair.

'Honestly, Tam, it was just...' I have backed into a gap between the camping shop and the pub next door. 'Like I say, it's all *much* better now, but it did get a touch... dire for a while.' I go on to give a very swift summary of Al's Christmas Day explosion and all that had prompted it, including my own clumsy, stealthy efforts to see my nieces. Tam widens her eyes throughout, shaking her head, but not interrupting because one of her many outstanding qualities is knowing how to listen. 'Also,' I rush on, performing a mental leap over my riverside plunge – still unable to imagine being able to share that with Tam or anyone – 'I've visited Mum's grave – for the first time in forty years – apologised *again* to Joanne, and I've even said sorry to Oliver, for how shitty Rob and I were, back in the day.'

Tam's eyes are bulging. 'Oh Cath, but this is all massive,' she gasps. 'I'm so proud of you. I only wish we could have... you know... talked about some of it sooner.'

'Tam, you're in Ireland, on your honeymoon,' I remind her gently, slightly surprised to hear the hint of hurt in her voice.

'That doesn't mean I don't miss you, okay?' she retorts, dabbing at a rogue tear with her dressing-gown sleeve. 'Marrying a person should *not* mean having to give up your *best* friend, okay?' She glances over her shoulder, adding in a much quieter voice, 'Jules and I had a bit of a Christmas blip too... I still love her to death, but she is more... well... insecure than I thought.'

'And have you tried to talk to me about that?' I point out.

She sticks her tongue out. 'I was *going* to. It's not exactly been easy to get time alone,' she hisses, 'and we're still in the thick of trying to see how everything is going to work. The blip was because I said I just didn't think I could live over here full-time... I'd miss everything too much... including you...' Her voice has shrunk to such a whisper, it's taking all my lip-reading skills to follow.

'I miss you too,' I say, with deliberate force and volume.

'And now,' Tam cries in a loud, completely different voice, leaping out of the chair, 'I must jump under the shower and pack some things because we're off to see Jules' brother who's renting a swanky place in Bray. But say hi to Jules first,' she commands, swivelling the phone towards her wife who, as I had already guessed, had stepped into the room.

'Hi, Jules.'

'Hey, Cath. Happy New Year.'

'And to both of you,' I call, just before the screen goes blank.

I head back to the car park, enjoying pondering my own dumbness in not having imagined that Tam could be missing me a little bit too. And if the super-charismatic Jules ever tries to keep my dear, smart, super-kind gem of a friend on too tight a rein, I'll be onto it like a shot, I vow. Having the backs of the people I love is at least something I know how to do – second nature, in fact.

I have begun to edge out of my parking space when a man, who turns out to be Isaac, the marquee man from the Lathbury party, jumps down from a white van that has just pulled up alongside.

'Hey Cath, how are you doing?' he exclaims, presenting a gleeful, newly bearded face in the frame of my window as I wind it down. The beard suits him, I have to concede, being thick, closely trimmed and dark, giving handsome emphasis to his blue eyes and square jaw.

'Hello Isaac. Happy New Year. Sorry, but I can't stop – I'm out of time and the effing cameras will get me.'

'I don't think they're working, actually, Cath. Anyway, all well? Good Christmas?'

'Not too bad, thanks. You?'

'So-so. There's just so much one can take of one's parents and siblings, right? *Family.*' He rolls his eyes and I chide myself for the temptation to take offence when the notion of causing any has not even half-entered a person's mind. 'I heard you were taking some time off. How's that going? You look really well, by the way, if blokes are allowed to say such things these days.'

'They are. Thanks, Isaac.'

'And if you and your other half want something a bit more than Jules Holland tonight, I can vouch for a do at The Cricketers – it's just a couple of miles down—'

'I know The Cricketers, thanks. We've got other plans, but I promise to bear it in mind.' I give him a wave and accelerate away.

At home, after making a fuss of Belle – who goes madder than usual at our reunions these days because of not having Bobby – I unload my purchases straight onto the kitchen table, arranging them in an attractive tableau style, with the orchid and the champagne centre stage. I then take several pictures and send the best one to Al – jazzed up with a non-stop shower of balloons and the message:

> Catherine Reynolds cordially invites Alastair Boland to a New Year's Eve party at 'ours'.

> Or Isaac (marquee man) has recommended The Cricketers, if you prefer… or we could do both!?

> My NY resolution is to show you how much I love you. Cathy X

'Because loving someone should have nothing to do with trying to be *tactical*,' I explain to Belle, reaching for her lead once I have found a windowsill for the orchid and put all the food away. 'Just like you, sweetie – you wouldn't know a tactic if it hit you over the head, would you?' I give the underside of her chin a good scratch, enjoying the usual glaze of pleasure it brings to her soft brown eyes, and thinking how the essence of my beloved pet's power over me is that she has no knowledge of it. 'And now,' I tell her, grabbing my coat, 'since you are a good girl, as well as my only current companion, and because I have some of that long-forgotten stuff called *energy*, we are going to the clifftops to swallow up the rest of the day with a big blowy walk.'

For the drive, I place my phone between my thighs, so as not to miss a single thrum. Arriving at the hillside car park, not visited since Al's and my row after Tamsin's birthday lunch, feels

like a welcome reminder of how far I have come. Sadness never
evaporates, but it dawns on me that I am starting to learn how to
live with it. Opening the passenger door for Belle, I laugh out
loud – at myself – for being such a slave and chauffeur – to an
animal. She leaps out – a hefty gazelle – and I stride after her
along the path towards the coast.

* * *

'The next one's on me,' says the man who is called Hal, or
possibly Paul – there have been a lot of names – who is of strik-
ingly small stature and who stands too close, in the manner of
one fearful of being overlooked. Given that the pub is packed,
and that our little group is already in a tight huddle, this means
he is standing very close indeed.

'No, it's my round,' Isaac declares, stepping between us,
relieving me of my empty wine glass and asking what everyone
else wants. Having begun in the middle of the room, our ring
has been shunted, gradually, into a corner space between the
dartboard and a somewhat weary-looking, over-decorated
Christmas tree, standing on a thick carpet of its own shed pine
needles. 'Cath, another Sauvignon Blanc?'

'Yes, thanks, just a small one. And a glass of water, please.
But let me give you a hand and we can go halves.' I follow him
through the crowd that needs some elbowing for the purposes of
reaching the bar. I am keen to pay my way and be helpful, but in
truth, I am also eager to have a break not just from the warm,
slightly acrid breath of Hal-Paul, wafting into my face with every
word, but also from the string of well-intentioned yoga tips that
have been coming from a woman called Daphne – a self-
proclaimed afficionado – on my other side. Most of all, I am glad
not to have to watch the person who introduced himself as Peter,

a lively city commuter in his thirties with blue eyes and strawberry-blond hair, now standing in the lee of the Christmas tree, swaying with increasing extravagance as he drains pint after pint, to the accompaniment of whisky chasers.

Rob and New Year's Eve – it was always a wild ride during our just-the-two-of-us years, sometimes fun, sometimes not so much. The Peter guy, with his short, gingery hair and commitment to getting wasted, keeps spinning me back to the worst one of all, when Rob managed to vanish from whichever bar we had ended up in. No one had seen him leave. No one cared. I ran around asking – shouting – and no one listened. I checked alleyways near the bar, phoned hospitals from call boxes and hollered his name racing up and down streets. We had just turned twenty-one, without so much as a peep from across the Atlantic. I was deep into my Jed phase and Rob's friends were drinkers, pouring their wages down their throats instead of worrying about bills. Oblivion was his goal, and yet, as I had been trying, with increasing desperation to point out to him, he never found it. The night had ended with me almost tripping over his body, spreadeagled on the pavement at the top of our basement flat steps, blood and vomit on his shirt, his handsome cheekbones swollen with bruises, his cherubic mouth crusted with cuts. He was on his back and I thought he was dead. But as I cradled his head, he started to cry and say sorry, burying his face in my lap, telling me I was the only reason he wanted to stay alive.

Isaac has finished putting the order in and is talking to me, raising his voice over the throng, 'I'm really glad you decided to come, Cath, but sorry, of course, that your partner couldn't make it.'

'Me too – thanks again for giving us the heads-up on this place – and do, please, let me help with the round.' I talk at speed, not wanting to get into any sort of discussion about Al, whose latest message – an email, sent during my clifftop walk with Belle – had not contained one single thing I wanted to hear.

Really glad you have the pub invite, Cath. You should go. To be honest, I've been torn about whether meeting up tonight would be a good idea – such pressure on both of us – but now it turns out I'm heading up to Crouch End anyway. Sadie has had another blood scare – worse than before apparently – and Ryan is all over the place. Will write again properly when I know more and have got my head straight. Sorry. I can see you went to a lot of trouble. In haste, Ax

'Sensible girl, drinking water as well as wine,' Isaac says, once we are back among the group by the tree, all my efforts to contribute having been refused. 'Cheers.'

'Yeah, well there's the drive home to consider, isn't there,' I say lightly, as we tap glasses, Isaac putting his pint of beer against both my wine and my water.

'Too true,' he laughs. 'Although – full disclosure – I cadged a lift here, and intend to get a taxi home.'

'My twin brother had a serious drink problem, so I'm pretty careful,' I find myself saying, before downing my water in one go. His expression falls so quickly, I feel almost guilty.

'Hell, I'm sorry to hear that, Cath. He got on top of it, though?'

'Oh yes, eventually. When he met his wife. The power of love, eh?' I pull a funny face, thinking yeah, the power of love, and feeling a surge of terror about whether Al really is done with me.

'And what does he do, your brother?'

I start to talk, in the past tense, about the Andover job, but then find myself telling Isaac instead about Rob having died, and the key painful circumstances.

'Jeez, I'm so sorry, Cath. That sounds really grim.'

'Grim is the word. But hey, I'm sorry too – I didn't mean to kill the mood. Though, I must also say thank you, because it actually feels good to be able to talk about him. It's taken a while,' I confess shyly, feeling a stab of something like pride in myself, despite Isaac's still stricken expression.

'Christ, you are not to apologise, Cath. On the contrary, I am honoured. Hey, why don't we head into the back bar where it will be quieter and easier to talk?' He has to shout in the direction of my ear in order to be sure of me hearing the suggestion, thanks to a party of new arrivals surging in through the entrance, adding to the crush. 'It's a bit of a dungeon,' he yells, as we start to move, 'but we'll get more peace.'

I let him pull me by the arm through the crush, and then along a narrow passageway past a sign to the toilets. At the end of the passage there is a room which is indeed much emptier, albeit darker and less festive too. A pool table, evidently the usual focus of the space, has been covered with a blanket and pushed to one side, and a few people are sitting on the benches lining the walls as well as the few chairs, scattered here and there.

'What a bloody relief,' Isaac cries, heading straight to the far corner, where an old-fashioned jukebox is parked, next to a section of empty bench. 'Nice to be able to hear ourselves think. But someone will start producing coins for this baby soon enough,' he laughs, giving the jukebox a fond pat, 'and then all merry hell will break loose.'

22

OLIVER

Wasn't that just typical, Oliver reflected gloomily, to race to the airport only to find his flight delayed. By twenty minutes, the board said when he first looked, although on his return from the restroom it had notched up to forty. With it being New Year's Day, the concourse was teeming with travellers, and just moving around with his carry-on was like playing dodgems. Oliver headed off to seek consolation in the Premium Flagship lounge, which was overcrowded too. There was still plenty of good coffee, though, and snacks, and ten minutes in, clutching a second cup and a Danish, he managed to bag himself a chair by a window, swooping in just as an elderly man vacated it.

He sipped the coffee and wolfed the sweet, doughy snack, grateful that the delay wasn't bad enough to jeopardise Faith and Amelia's planned afternoon visit. And his filial duties were done with for a while, Oliver congratulated himself. Big-time. Spending the entire New Year period on his own with his parents hadn't happened for as long as he could recall. It shouldn't have felt like a loser thing to do, but somehow, in the context of everything else going on in his life, it sort of did. It had also been more of an endurance test even than Christmas, with all that Catherine had said coiled inside his head and heart. Sometimes, he had found it difficult even to look at his mother. And when she'd done her finger-clicking thing at his father a couple of times – warier now of Oliver and not trying to boss *him* around – he had found himself snapping that no person on the planet was her slave and could she at the very least ask for help nicely. Like she was Amelia. Or rather some other kid, because his daughter would never in a million years behave so imperiously. Difficult formative years or not, Oliver had found himself confronting the sore, undeniable truth that his mother's nature harboured real tyranny. That he had tolerated – maybe even enabled – that tyranny to any degree, was something with which he was still struggling to reconcile himself. The only consolation was that no amount of hindsight could ever undo the past. He had been a shy, confused, bullied kid, as much doted on as exploited. With a passive, downtrodden dad and an authoritarian grandfather as his only role models, what options had there been, except to put up with it and then make a life for himself as far away as possible?

His version of atonement over the New Year visit had been to focus on his father, sitting with him at the jigsaw, providing a physical as well as a verbal buffer when required. Once or twice, when his mother was out of the room, the old man had even mumbled a few questions about Catherine – what she did, whether she had family – clamming up the moment there was a danger of Diane being back within earshot.

When the flight departure time had held firm for half an hour, Oliver reported the delay to Faith, saying that he should still be home by mid-afternoon, so the proposed Amelia visit – between four and five o'clock – shouldn't be affected. Seconds later, the delay time clicked forwards by a further forty minutes.

Like some malicious deity had it in for him, Oliver brooded, fetching himself more coffee and another pastry – an apple cinnamon croissant, this time – which he could call breakfast, he reasoned, having skipped what was on offer at his hotel so as to be in good time for the flight.

With yet more time to kill, his thoughts drifted back to Catherine. Eight hours ahead, she was already a lot further into the new year than him. He reached for his laptop, settling deeper into the chair. A New Year greeting. What could be the harm? But no. He scrolled to his work inbox instead. *Over and out.* There had been a finality to Catherine's text message and it was important to show her he could respect that.

* * *

It was nearly six o'clock by the time Oliver pushed open the entrance door to their apartment block. The concierge said Happy New Year's and, in keeping with the man's inability – or unwillingness – to pick up on the demeanour or mood of other people, was then keen to make the most of every single second of Oliver's journey to the elevator for the purpose of sharing his views on the world.

Street crime and global warming were indeed terrible, Oliver agreed, during the interminable time it took for their block's sole, measly, sluggish, elevator to arrive and open its doors. Safely sealed inside at last, and riding upwards nose to nose with his own pallid, baggy-eyed reflection in the elevator mirror, his spirits sank to what felt like a new low. He had got home too late for Amelia. All that now stretched ahead was a long, empty Sunday evening, followed by an even longer working week and then another, through January, and the next month, and the one after that. He had been trying so hard – to get on with life, to do the right thing – and yet still it felt like his fortunes, in the one area that mattered the most – his beloved wife and child – were bent on disintegrating.

Oliver put his hands over his face. To run out of luck, that was how it felt. A three-hour flight delay because of a no-show by a pilot. What were the chances? And if Faith was done with him, they'd have to sell their beautiful home, Oliver reflected miserably, stepping out of the lift shaft and into the small lobby that housed their front door – to let some other young couple full of hope and ideals take their turn. Distracted, he fought with door keys before it dawned on him that it wasn't double-locked. To have forgotten to perform such a basic task did nothing to lift his mood. Nor did tripping over something parked right in his path, until he saw that it was Amelia's miniature pull-along suitcase, newly covered with stickers of unicorns.

'You came!' he cried, dropping his bag and crouching down to receive his daughter, already hurtling out of the living room, shrieking, 'Surprise, Daddy, because I am *not* tired!'

'You sure don't seem tired,' Oliver laughed, having to brush away a couple of tears as he held her close. 'Did you have a great time skiing?'

'So great, Daddy. I got a certificate,' she added, self-consciously getting her mouth round all the syllables in the word, and pulling back enough for Oliver to note the strong white circle of protected skin the huge pink ski goggles had left round her eyes, as well as the emergence of a new firm white ridge in the middle of the section of the gum that had once hosted her two front baby teeth.

'Hey, Oliver,' said Faith, appearing in the living room doorway behind her.

'Hey, Faith. Thank you so much. For bringing her. You said

you wouldn't, if it got later than five...' He was so close to choking up, it was hard to get the words out.

'Like Amelia said, we decided to surprise you, didn't we, sweetheart?'

She stayed leaning against the jamb as she spoke, arms folded, weight on one leg, the other tucked behind, her feet shoeless and in soft grey socks he didn't recognise. She had something of a face tan as well, although the white area round her eyes was a lot smaller and fainter, simply making their greenness look endearingly startled. That said, Oliver could tell she was tired from the violet shadows under her lower lids and from how her hair looked raked rather than brushed. It wasn't surprising, he knew, given the amount of après-ski activity there would have been during the week, not to mention a New Year's Eve apparently so wild and hectic that she hadn't sent him a single line.

'So, no journey delays for you guys, anyway,' he said, summoning a breeziness he didn't feel and ruffling Amelia's hair as he stood up.

'No. It all went like clockwork. We were back across the park by lunch. I hope you don't mind us letting ourselves in.'

'It's still your place too – of course I don't mind,' he cried, exasperated, but quickly reining it in because of how Amelia was looking at him. 'Like I told you,' he rushed on, 'I'm just so very happy – so grateful – that you guys came. I only wish I had some food to offer Amelia – I was intending to have time to go to the grocery store – but we can get takeout, if you like?' As he made the suggestion, he bent down to give Amelia's head another stroke, not wanting to see Faith's face when she said no.

'I brought some pizza. It's warming up.'

'You did?' Oliver glanced at her. 'Clever Mommy, huh?' He grinned at Amelia. 'Are you hungry now, honey? Or would you like to do something with Daddy first? We could read a book, or play a game, or—'

'I wanna watch *teevee*,' she yelped, squirming free of his touch and running into the living room.

'Well, I guess that's okay,' Oliver murmured, as Faith followed. 'I'll be right back,' he called. 'I'm just going to freshen up.' He picked up his bag and went along the passageway to their bedroom, adjusting a couple of wall-hung pictures that had somehow gotten lopsided in his absence. When he tried to open the bedroom door, he had to push hard as something appeared to be in the way. It was another bag – a suitcase, on the floor by the bed. From the ski trip – of course. Faith wouldn't want all the gear with her at Seth and Laurie's. Oliver dropped his own bag on the bed before heading into the bathroom to wash his hands. He turned the faucet on and then spun on his heel and went back into the bedroom, needing to check something else that had half-registered in his frame of vision. An open wardrobe door, yes there it was, with several of the empty hangers now occupied. She was swapping things in and out, of course. Faith had lots of clothes and believed that how you dressed each day was an important component part of self-esteem. Wearing any item for two days in a row was not her thing. Oliver trudged back to the basin, where the tap was still running, and the jetting water so hot that he snatched his hand away with a gasp.

Easy, pal, he warned himself, slowly turning the water off. *Easy.* He leant on the basin, gripping its sides with both hands. He was dizzy from the stresses of the day, and from eating unwisely. Returning to the bedroom, he took off his heavy brown leather shoes, which he should have done at the door – it being a family rule – and took them back along the hall, to the rack that lived under the coats. He took his time, still inwardly steadying himself, carefully placing his shoes, one by one, alongside Amelia's mini blue outdoor lace-ups and Faith's chic tan ankle boots. He then stood staring down at the little array of footwear for a few seconds, marvelling how he had never fully appreciated the beauty of the sight before, each pair so different, yet side by side.

In the living room, Amelia was sitting on her own, cross-legged right in front of the TV, elbows on her knees, supporting her hands, which were in turn supporting either side of her face. She too – for all her sweet protestations – was exhausted, Oliver realised, and yet still they had come. On the screen, Olaf the snowman was in full throttle on a song. Amelia was barely blinking as she watched, like a part of her had already closed down.

'Move back a little, honey,' he said softly, 'it's bad for your eyes to be so close.' When Amelia didn't so much as acknowledge the comment, Oliver gently lifted her a few feet further back, to which she submitted without protest, settling back down into the exact same position.

Rounding the wall that screened off the kitchen, designed to keep it a part of the living space, he found Faith with her back to him, peering in through the microwave door at the pizza. On the counter beside her, the big wooden salad bowl which he hadn't used in months was full of leaves as well as its matching serving forks. There was rocket, spinach and avocado in there, by the look of it. And basil and radicchio peeking out too. Oliver went closer, picking out a spinach leaf and pulling a comedic uh-oh-caught-red-handed face when Faith turned round.

'I'm glad you had a good time on the slopes – the photos looked great. You did have a good time, right?' he muttered, when she didn't so much as blink.

'Yeah, we did. And you? How was Seattle? With your mom

and dad?' She picked up one of the salad servers and prodded the greenery, avoiding eye contact, it felt like.

'Okay, I guess. As in, they are dysfunctional and depressing, but I survived. Turns out Dad has a touch of jaundice, and as for Mom...' Oliver hesitated, not wanting to use up these precious moments by going into it all. 'She knows she messed up with you – badly. I've made sure of that.' He folded his arms to help contain the urge to reach for her. She was hanging her head and looking not far off miserable. 'A late night, huh?' he said, experiencing another pang of hurt that she hadn't judged him worth a New Year greeting.

'I didn't message you last night, Oliver,' Faith burst out, like he'd complained out loud, 'because I didn't know what to say at such a juncture – where to begin – on top of which, Amelia was pooped but couldn't settle, so I lay with her for hours. In fact, I think she might be going down with something – Laurie had these friends who joined us, with kids who were both, clearly, *so* ill – I mean, have people learnt *nothing* about germ-spreading in the last three years?'

'Oh dear, I'm sorry to hear that,' Oliver murmured, when she paused to breathe, 'though Amelia seems okay now – I mean, tired, but—'

'And actually, they all drive me totally fucking nuts,' Faith swept on, ignoring him. 'All of them. Especially Laurie. She has no concept of reality. All that money of theirs, it has warped their brains. I mean I truly do *not* blame Elise for wanting to get the hell out with her social media promotions and the boyfriend, who is called Ivan, by the way, and who seems a genuinely nice guy – ohmyGod and some of his snowboarding stunts, I just couldn't look... but Laurie is like, so *judgemental*, bitching behind their backs at every opportunity, instead of letting them work it out for themselves... like she understands anything any better than anyone, when she doesn't... and of course Sue Ellen takes her side, because when doesn't she?'

'Hey, come here a moment,' Oliver said, because she had started crying. He held open his arms and she shuffled into them, head down, allowing herself to be held, but keeping her own arms limp at her sides. 'Families, huh?' He cupped the back of her head with one hand, rocking her very gently.

'I'm so scared of coming back to you, Oliver,' she groaned, tugging her body back, but keeping her forehead pressed against his chest so that she was, through the chokes of her tears, addressing the kitchen floor. 'In case it doesn't work out. In case you carry on going into yourself instead of reaching out to me. In case you lie to me again. Why did you lie anyway?' she asked viciously, raising her face to scowl at him. 'Saying you had told them about Robert when you hadn't? Why would you even do that?'

'I guess I was afraid,' Oliver admitted bleakly, 'of their reaction... of all that it might unleash. Old, bad stuff. Also, because of Catherine having told me specifically not to tell them. Cowardice then, or maybe trying to do the right thing. Take your pick. But it was wrong of me, honey – I see that now, so clearly. In fact, it's been really good that they know – broken some ice – in me, anyway. Mom... well, I'm afraid she's never going to change, but she's quietened down some. And there's been a small shift in Dad too, like he's a little more open, more ready to stand up for himself. So, thank you, sweetheart, for that and so much else.'

Faith's gaze had softened. 'I find your folks really hard, Oliver. I mean, even before your mother said terrible things to me. I literally dread going to see them. I know that makes me a bad person.'

'No, it doesn't. I dread it too, more and more. I've always

dreaded it,' Oliver confessed, wondering if love could explode his heart. 'But you don't have to worry about my parents, I can handle them.'

'I know. You *have* been handling them.' She thumped his chest with the palm of one hand. 'I've so admired – and hated – you for it: how you've just got on with what needs to be done, *accepting* me not being here. I mean, a part of me has been, like, *why* isn't he *fighting* for me – that's what Laurie said too. But then, whenever we have seen each other, you've been so sweet, and undemanding, and going along with all my suggestions, not pushing to discuss all the things I've said I don't want to discuss, to the point where I got this sudden terror that maybe it was actually because you wanted to find someone else and didn't care, and that made me just... I mean, the thought of that is just... but then you go and give me... ohmyGod Oliver, that bracelet... so, so beautiful, but all I could think was how cheap it would seem to you if it looked like a piece of jewellery had persuaded me back... like I'd let myself be *bought*...'

'Faith... honey.' Oliver placed his hands on her shoulders. 'I would buy ten – twenty – a hundred – more bracelets – take out a life-loan – and throw them all in the Hudson, if it meant you agreeing to come back to me. Now – don't move, while I check on Amelia.' He tore off a piece of kitchen roll, pressing it into her hands for her tear-streaked face, before jogging round to the dividing wall. Finding their daughter fast asleep on the carpet in front of the TV, he carefully scooped her up, nuzzling the scent of her jumbled hair, before tucking her into her bed, pulling the dinosaur comforter down a few inches so she wouldn't wake too hot in her clothes.

Back in the kitchen, Faith, sniffing, but composed, was dividing their pizza into neat triangles with the roller-cutter.

There were two, a margherita and a pepperoni, their respective favourites.

'Are you moving back in?' Oliver asked quietly.

'I thought you might not have noticed.' She put the cutter down and turned to face him. 'Because you didn't say anything.'

'I didn't dare say anything, in case I was wrong. Dear Lord, Faith,' he gasped, 'I have been utterly lost without you. But I also needed you to *want* to come back because – deep down – I've always known I am not truly worthy of you—'

'Hush now, that's nonsense talk.' She put her fingers over his mouth and then traced them over the contours of his face, like she was re-acquainting herself with it.

Oliver's eyes closed at her touch, the relief of it, the physical longing it was unlocking. It was an effort to summon the room back into focus. 'You should know that Catherine and I have had some... exchanges... not just at the funeral, but since then as well.'

She pulled back at once. 'Exchanges with Catherine? Really? But why? The woman is a nightmare, Oliver. Isn't she?'

'She's been through so much, Faith,' Oliver pressed on, knowing he had to tell her everything if they were to have any chance together. 'She and Robert, they were Amelia's age when their mom passed. Imagine that.' He saw her shudder. 'And my mother was brutal with them – with Catherine especially – more than I had realised. Which makes better sense of why the poor woman has spent her whole life being mad. Losing Robert clearly broke her. Also, her own relationship recently folded – all of which is a heck of a lot for one person to deal with, you've got to admit.'

'It is.' There was guardedness in her voice.

'She's made a proper apology to me, Faith – I've been so desperate to share it all with you, honey.'

'I felt I had lost you, Oliver,' she whispered, stepping closer again, threading a hand in his.

'I thought I had lost myself,' Oliver confessed hoarsely. 'All the years of *talking* about my issues, it was like I had made them someone else's story rather than my own. Robert's passing – going to London – Catherine – I think it has helped me get back inside myself. Made me braver.' Oliver lifted a swatch of the raggedy hair off her face. 'We can take this as slow as you like, darling. I can sleep in the guest room until...'

Faith's mouth arriving on his prevented him from completing the sentence. They kissed tenderly and tentatively, like two people starting something new, Oliver reflected joyfully, closing his eyes to savour every moment.

23

CATHERINE

I am balancing on the solid little curvy-legged desk that had belonged to Al's mother, rubbing a duster across the top of the spare room windowpane, when I spot the post van. As the man gets out – a much younger one than our regular, with a topknot and tattoos on his neck, and carrying the usual clutch of junk mail – Belle starts barking from the hall, as she does for any first-time visitor to the doorstep. One hello, and she never does it again. I see the poor chap falter before finding his courage and striding on, disappearing beneath the windowsill. Service on the second morning of the new year – impressive. A few moments later, he reappears, swinging his arms, clearly happy to be free of his load with ankles and fingers intact.

Early spring cleaning. Getting on top of things in an area that mercifully can't fight back. I have been at it since a hearty breakfast, dragging the hoover, mop and bucket out of the jumble of our understairs cupboard, working methodically round the ground floor until coming to a halt, heart cantering, at the doorway to the study. Almost two weeks without use now, and the place, despite – or perhaps because of – its orderliness, is starting to exude the faint aura not just of neglect, but of abandonment. It chimes with my own feelings – triggered by Al's latest cool cucumber of a New Year missive.

Dear Cath,

Happy New Year. I do hope the pub party proved enjoyable.

Yes, all is well with Sadie, thank goodness. The doctor says it is hormonal bleeding, and has advised lots of rest. If it persists or gets worse, they may prescribe progesterone.

I am heading back to Southampton now. Phil and Deb aren't back for another week, and say they are grateful for the house-sitting, which is kind.

As for us, Cath, thank you again for your messages and all that they have said. I must ask you, however, to please bear with me. I have a clear head, for what feels like the first time in a very long while. I need it for work, which is at a critical juncture, and also for myself. The moment we talk, I know everything will start to get complicated, which is why I am being cautious.

What I would like to propose – if you agree – is for us to meet face to face, somewhere neutral and equidistant, for a proper conversation about everything. I would also like to say that I have deeply regretted some of the things I said to you. I spoke too harshly – far more harshly than you deserve. You are an extraordinary woman, as I knew from the first moment I set eyes on you.

Please tell Belle that Bobby misses her too.

Al x

The email had landed in my inbox the previous afternoon, when I was curled up on the sofa with a book and a cup of tea, still more preoccupied with the events of the previous evening than the words on the pages I was turning. The truly startling fact, to which my brain kept spinning me, was that I had not only braved a huge, noisy New Year party on my own, but that I had actually *enjoyed* it. Because of Isaac – to whom, side by side in the back bar of The Cricketers, I had talked with unprecedented openness and ease about my brother, in all his technicolour glory, good and bad. The dear man had listened patiently, asking occasional, thoughtful questions, all with an intensity in his gaze that suggested there could be more than sympathy on offer if I wanted it. He had talked openly in return, of his recent painful divorce, how he never saw enough of his three kids. We were still in the thick of it when – just as Isaac had predicted – someone bounded over and started up the jukebox. Elvis, 'Rock Around the Clock'. In moments, the room was a dance floor and we had launched ourselves into the heart of it, roaring out the familiar words along with the rest of the crowd. 'Best New Year party ever,' Isaac had shouted at one point, unspooling me and pulling me back, so close that I felt the bristle of his beard against my temple.

The ten-second countdown to midnight had caught everyone by surprise. There was a scramble to get into a circle for arm-crossing and 'Auld Lang Syne'. Afterwards, Isaac and I hugged each other and everyone else, before I quickly peeled off to fetch my coat. I had just tugged the zip up when Isaac had appeared at my side, sheepishly reporting that there wasn't a free taxi in the county, and might there be a chance of a lift home. Or at least to somewhere near his home, so he didn't have such a long walk.

Al's email the following day had made me burst into tears – for the depressing caution of it and the whole sorry situation. Meeting *somewhere neutral and equidistant* – dear God, the sentences could have been conjured by a bot. Maybe they had been. Only the final line – and the kiss – indicated the still-beating heart of the man I know and love, I seethe now, first closing the study door and then pushing it open again, ploughing on in with the hoover because, in the end, all things must be faced, including the Al-shaped hole in this, his most used and beloved space.

Thirty minutes later, for all my clumsiness, the study looks so restored – so inviting, indeed – that I tramp back upstairs to fetch the doughty little desk from the spare room. It is surprisingly heavy and its rangy legs want to catch on every corner, doorway and banister, not to mention Belle, criss-crossing my path, suspicious of this non-routine activity and my panting curses. I manhandle it into the middle of the now fluffy blue and gold rug, shift the armchair nearer the bookcases and wheel over Al's super-duper desk chair, to see how it looks – because why the hell not. I put a kitchen chair at Al's big desk by way of a temporary substitute and then fetch my laptop and the pile of papers that passes as my in-box – stowed for weeks now in a corner by the fridge. I place them side by side on the little desk and then retreat to the doorway to admire my handiwork: two work-stations, one study – the room looks as if it was never meant to be any other way. The sight is so comforting that Isaac flies back into my head, along with a rush of relief at how our evening had ended: the lift home, the exchange of brief, affectionate cheek pecks, followed by only the slightest tug of what I knew was mutual *what-if* curiosity when he gave me a final wave from his front door.

Parking the hoover back into the understairs cupboard, I notice that the postie has left the box under our letter flap full to bursting with Christmas junk mail. Rifling through the flyers and catalogues as I head for our paper recycling box along the hall, I almost miss the one small conventional envelope among all the nonsense – a late pigeon-post Christmas card, by the look of it, covered in wonky foreign stamps, and with my name and address written in tall, spindly capital letters. Al and I haven't bothered with cards for several years, getting fewer and fewer in return, though there are always a couple. I lean against the wall as I run my finger under the flap, my mind still only half on the task.

The envelope turns out not to contain a Christmas card however, but a few lines on a page, in a spidery, faltering, distantly familiar hand.

Dear Catherine, I am sorry Robert passed before his time. I hope things are not too bad for you. I never meant for it all to turn out as it did. Your mother was a good woman and deserved more than she got. You and Robert too. From your father.

24

OLIVER

Faith only realised that Oliver had left for work without his cell when it rang from the habitual jumble of clothes on his bedside chair a few minutes after he had gone. She answered it because she didn't want to wake Amelia and because she happened to be standing only inches away, staring at the clothes, lost in fond puzzlement over the joy of reconnecting with all the things that had driven her mad about her husband as well as those she adored. Two days since returning from skiing and making the decision to come home, and her six-week sojourn at Laurie and Seth's place was starting to feel like a surreal dream. Her sister's apartment, so vast and pristine, with priceless objects everywhere, had at first felt like a cross between an exquisite art gallery and a luxury hotel. During the initial weeks, it was precisely this immaculate orderliness which Faith had found so comforting, for how it allowed her to rest her unhappy, fizzing heart and head.

As time went by, however, and her own emotions started to settle, bringing perspective and tendrils of hope about wanting to reconnect with her indisputably dear, well-inten-

tioned, somewhat messed-up husband, the place had
started to feel as cold, irksome and misguided as Laurie
herself, riding ever higher on her already high horse of
What Faith Should Do rather than allowing her younger
sister the space in which to decide for herself. Even before
the skiing holiday, which Laurie and Seth both attempted
to take over completely with their know-it-all bossing –
which slopes, which lunch stops, what food, what drink –
Faith had known – quite apart from missing Oliver – that
her time as a house guest of her sister and brother-in-law
was done.

Seeing the name by the number on the cell, Faith hesitated,
but only for a split second, curiosity more than anything getting
the better of her. There was to be no more contact, Oliver had
said, and yet here she was.

'Hello, Catherine, this is Oliver's wife, Faith, speaking. I'm
afraid he's managed to set off for work without his cell, but I
know he would be real sorry to miss your call.' She was barely at
the end of the sentence when Oliver appeared round the door,
still in the dark winter coat that looked so handsome against the
sweep of his fair hair, his cheeks pink from the outside January
cold. Faith would have handed the phone right over, but
Catherine was already talking, very fast, about a letter, sounding
upset in a way that chimed exactly with the volatility that Oliver
had done his best to describe and account for in the frank, in-
depth conversations they had continued to have since their
reunion.

'Catherine,' Faith interjected, the moment there was a pause,
'Oliver has just walked in so I am going to hand you over now,
okay? I know that he will be very happy to speak with you.' She
pulled a face at Oliver, who had been making his own faces at
her the whole time, beckoning for the cell, which he now took,

having hurriedly pulled off his coat and tossed it onto the chair on top of all his other clutter.

'Hi Catherine, it's Oliver, I'm so... Really? Oh, my word. He did? That must have been... Yes, of course.' He sat down on the bed as he spoke, undoing a second button on his white work shirt, like he needed more room to breathe, and widening his eyes at Faith. When she made a questioning signal as to whether she should leave, he shook his head, patting the space beside him and putting the phone onto speaker, bringing the so very English voice of his half-sibling into the room: a voice that sounded both even-toned and ready to explode.

'He wrote that he was sorry about Rob, which means you must have told him, when I explicitly asked you not to. And the fact that he has my *address* – bloody hell, Oliver, I thought I could trust you. I did not want this door opened. I did not want, ever, to hear from either of them again. But now, thanks to you, I have this *letter*...' She broke off, so abruptly that Oliver and Faith glanced at each other, both wondering if she had hung up.

'Catherine, are you still there?' Oliver spoke cautiously, tenderly, it seemed to Faith, who was wringing her hands in her lap, grateful to be there, but also feeling like a snoop.

'Yup. I am here and waiting to hear how the hell you thought you had the right to tell him anything about me, let alone where I live... Jesus, I cannot begin to... I've apologised to you, haven't I? I thought we had reached an understanding...' The sentence dissolved into what sounded like a moan of pain.

'We had, Catherine. I did not give him your address. I couldn't because I don't know it. And I swear, if Dad had asked me for it, I would have said you didn't wish to hear from him in any way, shape or form.'

Oliver's continuing gentleness, his comforting, steady tone, was filling Faith with love and pride. She had been forgetting to breathe, she realised suddenly, allowing herself a big quiet inhalation and exhalation of air while not taking her eyes off her husband, who, even with the speaker on, was holding the phone just a few inches from his mouth.

'Yes, I told him about Robert,' Oliver went on in the same kind, respectful voice – making no mention of her own role in the disclosure, Faith noted, her heart bursting, and having to remind herself to inhale again as he went on to explain to Catherine that he had done so simply because it had felt like the *right* thing to do. He would have owned up to it when she called him from her car that time, he went on, had she not sounded so wrung out. 'Please forgive me,' he pleaded gravely. 'It was a judgement call. Never once did it occur to me that Dad would reach out to you, by letter or in any other way. He never hinted to me that he would. Also, as you might guess, he kind of lives under the thumb of my mother, who, I fear, with her harder heart, wouldn't have countenanced contact anyway. And Catherine, since we're talking, I want to thank you again for your apology and your candour when we last spoke. It meant – it means – more than I can say. And in return, I cannot apologise enough for whatever my mother put you through. Like I said, we were all of us just kids, with no real clue what was going on or why.'

Faith kept her eyes on Oliver's face, wanting him to turn so that he would see and feel the love she had for him, beaming out of her like heat. But his gaze remained fixed on the shelving unit opposite their bed, somewhere between the books and a small silver frame containing a beautiful black and white photo of him cradling Amelia as a newborn.

'So how did he find me then?' Catherine's voice burst back into the room, clearly unappeased, though Faith could not for the life of her think why. Oliver was trying so hard. He was such a *dear* man. So peace-loving. Such a wonderful father. She wanted to weep from the luck of being married to him. She also wanted to hold his hand, but knew now was not the time. This was Catherine's moment. His moment. She was a bystander, already reaping untold benefits because of his courage in confronting all the mess she had lately realised she'd been complicit in wanting him to leave behind.

'Dad has asked a little bit about you recently,' Oliver was admitting, 'that is, since hearing of Robert's pass... er... his death. Sorry, I didn't mean to...' Faith frowned, not understanding the sudden stumbling over his choice of words, but the phone remained silent, waiting, it felt like. 'So, yes, I have given him some answers,' Oliver said.

'What answers?' Catherine shot back, in her clipped, British way.

Oliver hesitated for the first time and Faith put a hand on his back, willing him on.

'That you live in the south west of England. What your line of work is. I may also have mentioned the name of your company, which was something your sister-in-law's father had referenced. I am so sorry, Catherine, I guess that could be how Dad found you – though he's never really mastered search engines, let alone anything more complicated. But look, I'll find out, okay? I'll ask him straight and get back to you. If that's what you would like.' Oliver had lost some of his cool, and was talking fast. From down the corridor, Faith heard a noise that could be Amelia stirring, but then all went quiet. She didn't want to go before the conversation was done. She didn't want to miss a single word.

'I had no notion he might reach out,' Oliver stumbled on. 'I hope he didn't write anything hurtful, and of course, there is nothing you need do in response anyway.'

'Of course there is a *response*,' Catherine countered, giving Faith a jolt because of the croak of distress in her voice. 'Now – here – me – opening, holding, reading the bloody thing, is forcing a *response*. Do you see, Oliver? It cannot be *un*-read, can it? I cannot stop myself *responding*.'

'Yes, I see that now,' he said humbly. 'Sorry, Catherine, it was a dumb thing to say. Forgive me.'

'The letter is very brief,' she continued, after a pause, her voice deflated suddenly, all the high dudgeon gone. 'And no, nothing remotely hurtful. It's just a few lines. It's nothing. Actually, I'm not sure I feel anything at all. I mean, a few written words after thirty years, it doesn't change a thing, does it?'

'No. It doesn't.'

Down the corridor, Amelia was definitely out of her room, and watching one of her kids TV channels, to judge from the faint hum of happy voices and music. Faith stood up, pressing a hand to her heart as an I'm-with-you gesture to Oliver before tiptoeing away, soundlessly closing the door behind her.

Alone, Oliver immediately turned off the speaker mode and pressed the cell to his ear. 'I am so sorry for the shock it must have been, hearing from him, Catherine.' He spoke with urgency now because of the certainty that she was about to hang up, 'but I am still so glad that you called. I hope you're doing okay. I totally respect how you want to stay inside your world – keep the past where it belongs, even if that is actually impossible. I mean, it kind of rushes back at you, doesn't it, usually when you least want it to. At least that's my experience. But what I've also come to see,' Oliver galloped on, 'is that the tearing apart of a family is the saddest thing on earth. Becoming a parent myself opened my eyes to that, as well as to the magnitude of the loss endured by you and Robert.' He had to clear his throat. 'Trying to understand stuff, that's all we can do in the end, right? Also,' he ventured, 'not to get personal, but I have been very much hoping that you and Alastair might have found a way back to each other since we last communicated.'

'Not yet.' Her voice had shrunk so much, he could hardly hear her. 'He wants us to meet, somewhere neutral, to talk.'

'But that's good,' Oliver cried. 'I mean, really. A non-judgemental conversation in a place with no associations – the guy clearly wants it to work. I didn't say before,' he gabbled, so happy she was still speaking to him – answering him – 'but when you called that time, Faith and I were also separated. Her call and my fault. I won't go into the whys and wherefores, but we're back together now and everything is so much better – like the separation forced us to work through our issues. I am full of hope that you and Alastair can have the same happy outcome.'

'Thanks, Oliver. I'm pleased for you. But Al's borne the brunt of a lot of things. My troubles. Not his. I can't really think why he would want to come back to me.'

'Don't be too hard on yourself. He'll have had troubles too, because all of us do. And anyway, from what I saw back in August, I would say he's clearly crazy about you.'

'Hah, I'll try to bear that in mind.'

'Might you let me know how it goes?'

A long silence followed, while Oliver held his breath.

'I highly doubt it,' she muttered at last. 'But I guess there's a chance.'

'Great,' Oliver exclaimed, despite knowing he was being too exuberant. 'And in the meantime, I'll find a quiet moment to speak to Dad about how he got your address – and by quiet, I mean out of earshot of my mother,' he clarified quickly, 'given that she is not your biggest fan.'

'Nor I hers.'

'I promise I'll get to the bottom of it,' he began, but she had already gone.

Oliver remained where he was, letting the adrenalin subside. To be talking to Catherine – it was never a straightforward ride – but somehow, it felt *so* good. Too good simply to head straight back out into the cold and then down into the fuggy heat of the subway to jump back into the groove of work. His first day in the office after the holidays – it would be a shock immersion. And besides, there was Amelia to say hi to first. He could hear her along the passageway, calling to Faith about something, and Faith calling back. His wife, his daughter and now – Oliver lowered his gaze to his phone, still sitting in the palm of his hand – his half-sister. It was a sweet feeling, like a long, deep hunger sated.

25

CATHERINE

Being alone is an art that I'm actually getting the hang of, I decide, padding to my desk with a coffee on the first Friday of the new year to continue with the assault on admin at which I have been throwing myself all week. Quotes from suppliers, client queries, venue possibilities, including the still-unvisited river manor house – as well as all of Tamsin's spreadsheets and tax-return documents needing a final sign-off – there has been a lot to catch up on. It is a little sooner than I was supposed to get stuck back in, but Tam had teased that admin was okay. And with so much else buzzing round my head, including the 'equidistant' meeting with Al – finally arranged for 6 p.m. tomorrow in a pub I remember from our early Dorset days – I have relished the absorption required.

As yet, there has been no follow-up from Oliver, but most of the outrage that prompted me to leap on the phone to him has subsided anyway. Why need I fear an old man deciding to write three lines from halfway across the world? And the conversation with my half-sibling had been soothing in itself, with that calm, lilting voice of his, so compassionate and apologetic, promising to do what he could, as well as sharing the disarmingly personal confession about the difficulties between him and Faith. I knew throughout the call that I was being artfully 'defused', and yet for some mysterious reason, the knowledge had done nothing to spoil the effect of the strategy.

I go to the tabs I have open on Open University MBAs – a further running project of the week – and have another read, continuing to make a few proper notes, because this time, I am researching in earnest instead of faking it. The summary says:

Gain a better understanding of general business management functions; 8-12 hours a week for ten weeks of self-paced learning.

How could that not be a good thing to do, irrespective of whether Tam changes her mind and jumps ship to Ireland? The price tag is daunting, but Al and I have some joint savings, and he was pretty keen on the idea... Al... my screen blurs. One more day, and it will all be done with. Us. Our future. It almost makes me want to postpone the meeting.

If I know what I am going to wear, I shall be able to relax a little bit, I tell myself, abandoning the study and racing upstairs. Yet, staring into the wardrobe, my brain turns to mush. What clothes are right for a date that isn't a *date*, with nothing riding on it except the terror of a shattered heart and the direction of the rest of one's life? Dungarees? A ball gown? A mini skirt? The dirty jeans and jumper in which I have recently completed a spring-clean of our entire, jointly owned house?

Outside, it starts to rain suddenly, not in the old-fashioned, English, pre-climate-panic way, but with the force of a biblical plague, pounding the roof and the bedroom windows with such violence, I half-wonder they don't shatter. I yank out a close-fitting black dress studded with bright flowers and a longer looser woolly green one. Holding them against me for comparing in the wardrobe mirror, I freeze as the morning of Rob's funeral hurtles back, five months and five hundred years before. The despicable part of me wanting to out-dress Joanne. To outshine her – at Rob's *funeral*. Spilling the wine over her at the wake...

I shove the dresses back onto the rail as the shame pumps. No grieving woman, no matter how prickly or possessive, could ever deserve such disrespect. Mad with grief, I might well have been, but I was also an insane jealous angry nightmare of a giant cow, I reflect grimly. And Al can have me in a T-shirt, jumper, trousers and the increasingly scuffed birthday boots. As I *am,* in other words. He wouldn't be fooled by any flirty nonsense anyway.

I feel behind me for the bed and sit down, breathing hard. I can sense a dip coming. I lie back, letting the tears trickle out of the corners of my eyes and down my temples into my ears and hair. Not quite such a master of being on my own then. Not yet. Crying though – I'm definitely getting better at that. Hah. I raise my legs in the air, waggling my toes, which are in thick, dog-decorated house socks that Al gave me years ago, complete with little dangly ears at the ankles. Such silly socks, but so warm and comfy.

Outside, the rain has thickened into a full-blown storm, crouched directly over the house by the sound of it. At a long, explosive crack of thunder, I sit up with a start to see Belle creeping in through the open door, her big body quivering with the terror invariably triggered by fireworks or any other ear-splitting noise.

'It's all right, sweetie.' I lower myself onto the floor and try to sit with her, but she cowers under the dressing table – prefer-

ring, for impressively logical reasons, to have a roof over her
head. I retreat back to the bed with my phone and am staring at
a weather forecast of globular raindrops and lightening forks,
when a text notification arrives, from Oliver.

> I've written you. An email. No pressure, truly.

It is a long letter, I see, having clicked to it at once, my heart
sinking even before I begin to read.

Hey Catherine,

You know what? One of these days, I shall communicate
with you about something feel-good and trivial. All this heavy
stuff coming your way is not what you need or deserve. So
just hang on in there, okay? And though you will have a
'response' (as you so aptly corrected me when we last talked)
to the information I am about to impart, there is nothing –
from my point of view anyway – that you need to do as a
result of it.

In the meantime, it's bad news straight. I'm going bullet
points for brevity and clarity.

- The day after we spoke Dad had a fall when he was in the
  bathroom (we think he slipped on the tiles after
  showering), which is partly why it's taken so long to get
  back to you. No broken bones, but he's bruised himself
  pretty bad. He's in a wheelchair now – for good, it looks
  like, since it turns out he has other health issues, namely
  cancer of the pancreas, for which he is so far refusing
  treatment.

Faith and I flew straight to Seattle and are still here. (Amelia, our daughter, is staying with close friends and neighbors back in NY)

- Catherine, Dad says he wants to 'see you'. On Zoom. I have promised to set this up and send you a link, but have made it absolutely plain to him that you won't show up, which he says he understands and can we try it anyway. I am going for tomorrow morning (Saturday) at eleven, which will be seven in the evening your time. The timing is kind of key because he doesn't want Mom to know or to be there and she has a hairdressing appointment which Faith is taking her to.

Turns out he got your address thanks to a young helper here called Isidro, who, as I have ascertained, went down a ton of rabbit holes, using your company name (which I believe I told you I had mentioned) and then tracing your address through where it was registered for tax purposes – not quite the dark web, but these youngsters can do almost anything. I am sorry, Catherine. Entirely my fault. My loose tongue. It was the first time Dad had brought you into a conversation in so long, and I guess I got carried away. Truth be told, that is how it has been for me right from the start of all this reconnecting. Getting carried away, I mean.

Sorry, the bullet points have gone to hell. I am finding it a little hard to think straight.

The fact is, Catherine, Faith has enough close family in and around Manhattan to populate a new planet. They are like, all over each other, at every opportunity. It's great and I love them, but at times, I suppose it has kind of rubbed in how, in contrast – for all their failings – I only have Mom and

Dad (both only children themselves, as you may recall), and not for much longer, as has been brought home to me even more this week. Still trying to get my head around it.

All I'm really trying to say, Catherine, is that having you, a half-sister, means a heck of a lot. No matter how this plays out and whether you click the darn Zoom link tomorrow evening (7 p.m. your time) or not.

Oliver

An hour later, with the storm having abated to heavy rain, Belle and I are labouring through the muddy gullies on the far side of the field opposite the house, heads down, blinking the thick drizzle out of our eyes. I curse as I slide around the sludge in my wellies, my feet bare because the dog socks aren't designed for footwear and I couldn't be bothered to go upstairs for another pair. While Belle, getting the scent of something that turns her trudge into a trot, makes a better fist of enjoying herself.

Even so, the fresh air – which I have been making a big do of sucking in and blowing out – has been helping to pump out the effects of Oliver's email. My half-sibling is clearly naïve as well as kind. Writing back to him at once – to extinguish any uncertainty – I resisted saying as much, confining myself to a straight *no* to the suggestion of hooking up with my *erstwhile* father on Zoom – tomorrow evening or any other time. What I also thought and refrained from mentioning, was that, given the clash of timings, I would choose my make-or-break meeting with Al a trillion times over. It was no decision at all, in other words.

By the time we cross back over the road and into the drive, it is completely dark. Our soaked, mud-spattered state means heading round to the rear of the house, via the outside tap and the hose, and into our small godsend of a utility room. Belle endures the dousing with her usual stoicism – head hung, tail limp – and then transforms into a ball of puppyish playfulness once it comes to drying her off with the big old towel, kept on a hook next to the washing machine for the purpose.

'Silly mutt,' I croon, as the drying rapidly morphs into the usual tug of war with the towel. It feels like a blessing to be inside, especially with the rain-drizzle suddenly ratcheting up again to a thunderous, thwacking assault on the flat utility room roof. In the kitchen, the noise is less intrusive and the storm feels a world away, but Belle, much to my surprise, heads straight to the front door instead of starting her customary jump-up dance for her dinner.

'What?' I ask, following her.

She cocks her head and big scruffy ears, emitting her *I-am-excited* whimpering, while casting longing looks at the door.

'I don't care what it is. Fox, squirrel, deer, sheep, horse – alien – you are not going back out. At least, not till the morning.'

I leave her to her mewling and go into the study to close the curtains. I've grabbed one side when I see exactly why my dog has started a vigil on the doormat. A car, engine still running, is parked in the lee of the hedge. A modest-sized, black car. I screw up my eyes to see through the streaming rain, trying to be sure it means what I think it means. A moment later, I'm calling Al's name before I've even started my sprint to the front door. I grab the first coat my hand finds on the row of hooks – my smart camel wool and cashmere, as it turns out – and deploy it as a mini-tent for the race across the drive. Belle, barking her own excitement, overtakes me in the charge.

Only when I am within a few feet do I realise it is not Al's car. Or Al.

'Joanne?'

'Hello, Cath.' She has turned the engine off and wound the window down, projecting her voice through it because of the deluge. She is lightly tanned and stoney-faced, and her hair is in a new style, cut into a thick wedge up her neck, exposing her small ears and falling in a heavy line across the centre of her forehead, giving greater prominence to the neat dark arches of her eyebrows. Belle, having determined after a couple of leaps that it is not Al, starts sniffing at something by the back tyre.

'I can't do the dogs,' Joanne shouts, the revulsion in her voice unmistakeable, even with the water drumming around us – off the car, the gravel, and the thick green leaves of the laurel hedge separating the drive from the main road. 'Would you mind shutting them away somewhere first – I was about to text you to ask.'

And I am not sure I can *do* a face-to-face dressing-down, I think darkly, still completely off balance with disappointment as well as sheer surprise. 'You know I am sorry,' I stammer, swiping water off my face as my lovely coat starts to leak. 'I wrote to you – it was all a misunderstanding; I never meant to alarm the girls or—'

'I am not here about that,' she says crisply, 'and by the way, thank you for your Christmas presents – they were generous and much appreciated.' As she speaks, she reaches for a brown leather handbag and an umbrella from the passenger-side footwell. 'You're getting drenched. The dogs – really, Cath, is it too much to ask?'

Dog not dogs, I think, swinging round to look for Belle, who is no longer by the tyre, or anywhere that I can make out in the drive. Blinking the rain out of my eyes, I squint at the house, where the front door is still slightly ajar, casting a slit of light onto the front step.

'There's only Belle here at the moment anyway,' I shout, 'and I think she's gone back inside. Did you see?'

'No, I did not,' Joanne replies, still with the brusqueness that reminds me – for all my recent shame and contrition – of how very difficult this woman is. At least with regard to me.

'I'll go and check then, shall I?' I holler through the still-thunderous rain, not caring how much I betray of my exasperation at her request. I have taken a couple of steps towards the door when a car horn sounds in the road – a protracted, whining shriek that stops me in my tracks. A moment later, the roar of an engine – accelerating away – cuts through the pounding slap of rain, but I am already running, flinging the coat off so I can go faster. I arrive in the gap in the hedge that constitutes the entrance to our drive just in time to see tail lights – two devil eyes – disappearing into the dark.

'Belle!' I yell with a force that feels like I'm ripping my throat out. 'Belle! Where are you?' I scrabble for my phone – desperate for its light – from the back pocket of my trousers, but my fingers are still fumbling uselessly when I spot the dark lump of an animal on the far verge. *A deer*, I tell myself, in the seconds it takes me to reach it. But it is not a deer, it is Belle, on her side, one back leg twisted. As I fall to my knees, she raises half her body to look at me, her soft, gold-brown eyes full of puzzlement, before her head flops back down onto the muddy verge. Across the road in the drive, I turn and see Joanne, standing under her brolly, watching.

* * *

'Thanks again, for driving.'

I am parked in the middle of my sofa. Joanne has taken the armchair – keeping her distance is my sense, and I am glad. It is a struggle to speak, or even to bring her into focus. All I can see is the grave face of the young vet, with the too-early bags under her eyes and the swing of her high ponytail, its tips dyed crimson, as she reports that though Belle is alive, I might want to consider putting her out of her pain.

Mostly, I am fighting the hard, horrible logic that this always-feared, dreaded moment has been brought into being because of my sister-in-law – arriving, uninvited, at my house, choosing not to ring the bell and then diverting me from my usual vigilance over my beloved hound with her needless, daft insistence about *locking her up*. Lurking unhelpfully too, are the sporadic conversations Al and I have had over the years about dog-proof automated gates, both of us always dismissing them on account of the expense, the faff and our own faith in the obedience of our pets. Bobby, being younger, can still be wilder, but with Belle, it takes just one shout from me to stop her in her tracks, no matter the nature of the temptation crossing her field of vision. But today, I could not shout because I did not see her bolt. I was too busy listening to Joanne. My nemesis. My nightmare, now it seems, finding yet another, unimaginable, unspeakable way to undo me.

'Anyone would have done the same,' Joanne replies, in a flat tone, giving no hint of recognition of her share of responsibility for the calamity, let alone any obligation to be regretful about it. It occurs to me in the same instant how impossible it is to like someone who has made a decision not to like you in return. But I am too drained to summon any sort of comeback. On top of which, one wrong move and my sister-in-law might – according to her bombshell Christmas Day call to Al – officially report me for 'stalking' her children.

I check my phone – balanced face-up, on my left knee – but there are no new messages. The urge to ring Al pulses for the umpteenth time. If I called about Belle, he would come from North London or Timbuktu, wouldn't he? It was the doubt that had been holding me back. For Al not to come would be the worst thing – far, far worse than me not having asked. On my other leg, I am resting Al's treasured crystal tumbler, in which there is half an inch of whisky. With each sip, it is not the heat of the alcohol that has been soothing me, so much as the thought of Al's big solid hand round the glass, his mouth on the rim, the small throaty sigh of pleasure he makes after his first swallow. He only used the tumbler when he was happy, I realise miserably, recalling the smeary old glass he had reached for during the ugly, end-of-the-world conversation heralding his decision to leave.

On our return from the emergency vet, Joanne had followed me into the house unbidden, hanging up her big padded, hooded coat, while I stumbled into the downstairs toilet to throw water on my face and do some private weeping. As I fumbled with fixing my drink in the kitchen, she had briefly disappeared and then thrust a pair of jeans and jumper at me, extracted – I realised – from the shameful heap on the floor by my bed. 'You'll catch a chill otherwise,' she had remarked, adding that she'd rescued my coat from the drive and hung it in the utility room. I had moved out of her eyeline to put the clothes on, while she busied herself at the sink, rinsing out an already washed glass and filling it from the tap.

'Have something stronger, if you'd like,' I had mumbled. 'I've got wine. Or whisky.'

'Water is all I want, thanks, Cath. Actually, I haven't had alcohol for a long time.'

Through my dazed state, I sensed an import behind the disclosure – a desire for congratulation or further enquiry, perhaps, which I had felt in no state to give. I half-hoped she would drink the water and go, but she had headed into the sitting room with it, clearly assuming I'd follow.

'Look, Joanne,' I blurt now, plucking up my courage, 'thanks for all your help, but if whatever you came for could wait, I'd actually prefer to be on my own.'

'I'll stay till Al gets back,' she says stoutly, appraising me with her clear grey eyes, more exposed thanks to the new haircut. I notice too, that she has lost weight, the blue jumper she's wearing looking decidedly chic for being tucked inside the top of her loose dark trousers. *Moving on, then.*

'Al...? But he'll be very late,' I stammer, there being no question of disclosing the rubble of my own moving-backwards private life. 'And he'll have Bobby,' I add, jumping on anything to put her off.

'An Alsatian chased me when I was five,' she announces quietly, pausing to take a sip of her water. 'At a birthday party. We were all in the garden, playing tag, and it came from nowhere, at full pelt. Big teeth, big mouth, strings of saliva dangling...' She shivers visibly. 'I started to run – everyone did – but it picked me to chase. In the end, it did nothing but knock me over – or maybe I tripped – but it's the fear you remember, not just of being chased, but of what *could* have happened. Rob was always sweet about it. I knew of course how much he loved dogs, because of that one of your grandmother's, what was it called?'

'Pip.'

'Pip, that's it.'

'But why did you never say before,' I exclaim, bafflement getting the better of me, 'about the Alsatian?'

She shrugs, flicking at something invisible on her trousers. 'I was embarrassed. It sounded so lame – it *felt* lame, with the two of you so mad keen. And then with the girls... Well, as a parent, you don't want to make a big deal of such things. Not wanting your kids to see you afraid – of anything – it's a deep instinct. Hard to explain.'

'To a childless dog-lover, you mean.'

'No, I—'

'I know a dog is not a child, Joanne, but that does not mean the love is any less.'

'I never said—'

'In fact, I don't think you can measure love. It just *is*. Anyway,' I speed on, because I know I have been too sharp and because talk of love makes me feel wobbly – on so many counts – when I need to be strong. 'That Alsatian – all these years – you should have said. I mean, it would have helped me understand why you never...' I run out of steam, defeated by the unedifying prospect of igniting a row about the past. All the years of this woman stonewalling my efforts to reach out, what did any of it matter now? That my brother never saw fit to mention the dog-chasing story gives me a pang, but that doesn't matter either. Rob's first loyalty was to his wife, I had learnt that much.

Joanne remains poker-straight in her armchair, staring across the room. For an instant, the rigidity of the pose casts me back to my glimpse of her when our vehicles passed on the school road back in November: a woman enduring a heavy load, a woman prepared to deal with whatever life throws her way.

'No news is good news, I suppose,' she ventures.

The platitude is offered with all the emotion of a newsreader, but I find hope flooding me. 'Yes,' I gasp. I had indeed been promised a call if things took a turn for the worse. A fractured pelvis and a leg so badly broken it would take pins and plates to fix – it was going to be touch and go at every stage, the young vet had warned, before I had made the decision to sign the paper-work for the surgery and handed over my credit card details. 'And obviously, I'll pay to have your car cleaned,' I tell Joanne in a rush, my brain leaping to the mess Belle had made of the back seat of her car.

'Don't be silly. I just hope she pulls through.'

'Thanks, Joanne.' I meet my sister-in-law's gaze, privately acknowledging that, for all my grand declarations about love, Belle's death could never be weighed against the loss of a husband. It couldn't begin to measure up to losing a twin brother either, I reflect bleakly, although, coming so soon after that loss – with Al still hanging in the balance and the contents of Oliver's email crouching in the corner of my mind like a demon – it also sort of feels as if it does. Because all sorrows are interconnected, it dawns on me, as my mother slides to mind. Gathering in the depths of us, they are always there, ready to surge with each new suffering.

'About the girls, Joanne, I—'

'It did my head in a bit, that's all, Cath, landing on top of everything else. We were just trying to keep to ourselves – carry on – you know.' She is talking at speed, as if something inside her has given way. 'I know I probably over-reacted – ringing Al – I just needed it to stop, and I couldn't face... well, *you*, I suppose. The girls are fine about it. They understand that you miss their dad. We miss him too. Every minute. It's been hell, actually. It *is* hell. I don't know how I shall ever get used to it – though they say one gets used to anything in the *end*, don't they...' She has got to her feet and is peering round the chair, lifting its cushion, looking for something as she talks. 'For the record, Robert and I were good – very good – but there were... that is, he had... lapses over the years... You don't know the half of it, and he never wanted you to.'

'Lapses?'

'The biggest joke...' She has stopped moving and is staring at me with wide, sad eyes, clutching the chair's tatty back cushion to her chest like a comforter. 'The biggest joke, Cath, is that when he went and got sick, he was actually really *well* – in himself, I mean – the best he'd been in years. All those weeks of us all being forced to stay at home – no work pressure, no need to socialise, or be tempted, just our little family routines and me not drinking either – it was like a miracle cure. We both thought he'd turned a corner – a real, lasting one. And when the cough came, we never imagined... *Where* is my bloody handbag?' She flings the cushion back into the chair, swiping savagely at a few tears spilling down her face.

'Joanne...' I stand up, but she swings an arm between us like a closing gate.

'This happens. I shall be better in a moment. I must have left it in the kitchen. And Cath, I have spoken of things I vowed never to speak of. Please put them from your mind.'

I lower myself back onto the sofa, dumbly watching her retreating back. *Lapses*. How could I not have known?

When Joanne reappears a couple of minutes later, she has her coat on and the brown handbag over her shoulder. Her bobbed hair looks freshly brushed and her mouth gleams with a coating of fuchsia lipstick.

'I'll leave you in peace then, as that's clearly what you want. Here, this is why I came...' She plucks a small brown jiffy envelope out of her handbag and places it on the table. 'Actually, Cath...' She shifts her weight from leg to leg, fiddling with the buckle on her handbag. 'There are a couple more things I need to say first, despite how Rob would hate me for it... I've started so I'll finish, sort of thing. Sorry, love.' She raises her eyes to the ceiling and crosses herself.

'About the lapses?' I say weakly, still absorbing the shock of what I've just been told. Rob still drinking. Not cured.

'He was so ashamed of them, Cath. He couldn't bear for

anyone to know, least of all you. It was our secret – a challenge – that we bore together.' There is pride in her voice.

'Least of all me?' I cry, before I can stop myself. 'But why? I would have helped, I would have...' But I can't go on, because she is right, there was nothing I could have done. Trying to save my brother from himself, I had long since learnt the impossibility of that.

'To be honest...' Joanne is twisting her mouth in the manner of one on the verge of disclosing something they would rather not. 'You sort of made things worse.'

'Worse? How so?' I am caught off-guard yet again, all the old outrage coursing through me.

'Oh Cath...' An insulting, where-to-start weariness has entered her voice. 'Because you were always so sure of yourself, so certain and strong-willed – like you thought you could make Rob that way too, when all it did was make him feel inadequate. You sort of dwarfed him, actually.'

'*Dwarfed* him?' I have to laugh, despite the outrage. But Joanne is on a roll.

'Cath, come *on* – when I first met Robert, he literally hardly dared breathe without your say-so. You were *everything*. He hadn't a single drop of confidence in himself. It all came from you. With me, he at least had the chance to try and find himself. As did I, frankly. Because the truth is, you made me feel inadequate too, Cath – always so quick to judge, to voice those opinions of yours, like you couldn't bear to let us make our own choices, or for Rob to...'

'To what?'

'Love me.'

I laugh again, freely and scornfully this time, a part of me relishing the certainty of this blatant untruth amid all her other loathsome claims. 'Joanne, no one – *no one* – could have been happier than me when you and Rob got together. Especially as I was already lucky enough to have found…' But it turns out my throat is too constricted to release even the solitary syllable of Al's name.

'Maybe.' She hangs her head, as if the fight has gone out of her. 'But you still wanted full *access* to him,' she continues quietly, 'to us and *our* marriage – a swing door for you to push through whenever you chose. Neither of us wanted it. Seeing you always churned him up. Held him back.'

'If Rob had felt that way, he would have told me,' I counter feebly, trying to press away echoes of Al's soul-shattering words on Christmas Day, 'because we always told each other everything – we had a pact…' The sentence dies on my lips, because of something childish in it, something long done with.

Joanne slowly shakes her head. Her face has reddened with emotion, heightened no doubt from still being in her thick coat. 'I am sorry to have added to your distress, Cath. Rob would be so angry with me. He never could bear to see you upset. He couldn't deal with any sort of confrontation either. I always had to be the Bad Cop – with the girls, with life, with you. It allowed him to hide, I suppose. It infuriated me at times, but… *Christ,* I adored him…' Her voice breaks and she pulls a balled-up tissue out of her bag, dabbing at her eyes with it. 'Shit. Shit. Shit. I swore I wouldn't do any of this, God help me.'

I have belted my arms around my ribs, as a way of staying upright, it feels like. The room is swaying a little. The whisky on an empty stomach, I tell myself, knowing it is nothing of the kind.

'Dear Cath…' Somehow, she has come to stand behind me. 'Sorry, but I couldn't hold back any longer. Rob loved you so very—'

'Do not speak to me of my own brother's love.'

'That's fair. Forgive me.'

I feel her hand arrive on my shoulder. I want to shake it off, but the strength – the necessary movement – doesn't come. The hand feels sure. Firm. Kind. She says some things in a soft voice, about keeping her fingers crossed for Belle and how Stephanie would like me to come to her eleventh birthday tea in a few weeks' time, if I feel up to it. How there's no rush to decide. How she'll see herself out.

'Also, there is so much of him in you, Cath,' she adds gently, pausing in the doorway. 'Your eyes, your colouring, the shape of your head, the set of your mouth... I have found that hard.'

'Okay.' I keep my eyes on Al's tumbler, noting how the cuts in the crystal catch the light.

When, at last, the front door thumps shut, I turn my head to locate Belle, for comfort, only to remember that she is not there. I reach instead for Joanne's little padded envelope, tearing it open with needless violence. A charger lead and an iPhone tumble out, neatly wrapped in a piece of A4, on which there is a hand-written message.

Cath,

The passcode is 122375 – your birthday, but with the day and month done the American way – Rob always used it like that for everything. I was thinking you might like the photos (we did Google Share so I have them all). But then I found something else too, on an app called Movieclip – it's the very last icon – the most recent – for reasons that I guess will become obvious. You won't find much of interest in his emails. He never was one for the written word, was he?

FYI: I started to watch the clip and then stopped. You'll see why. I am not the bitch you think I am.

Joanne x

I take both my phone and Rob's upstairs, one in each hand, for balance, it feels like. Placing them carefully on the duvet, side by side, I get ready for bed, taking my time, checking for vet messages before getting under the covers.

My fingers tremble putting in the code: our birthday, *American* style. Had he meant something by that, or was it just a bid for extra security? The screensaver is another gut-punch: four sunny smiles on a blowy day before any sickness, the girls with younger, rounder faces, sitting on my brother's lap, squirming at being tickled – by him, from the look of it; Joanne crouched behind, her chin resting on his shoulder, her arms round all three of them. Rob's face beams out from the middle, the sunniest of all.

Resisting the photos – a treasure trove in store – I search at once for the app Joanne mentioned, easy to find, as she said, for being the very last. It only contains one clip. One touch, and oh God, there he is, moving and alive before my very eyes, his soft, slightly wheezy, sick person's voice, talking only to me. My brother. Never dwarfed. Or in my shadow. Always beautiful.

'Hey, Sis. How are you doing?'

He flutters his fingers in a wry wave, his eyes – just visible beneath the brim of a soft blue baseball cap – full of merriment, despite the hollows of the sockets containing them. Behind him, the green sofa and the window onto the garden, tell me he is in the small downstairs room he liked so much and made his own towards the end.

'You'll only be watching this if I have the courage to send it before... my DEMISE.' He pulls a ghoulish face. 'Cue violins.'

Behind him, a cluster of roses bob in and out of view on a sudden gust of wind. I hold the phone a little closer. To hear him, to see him, just the two of us, together in this moment, it feels like cheating time.

'Oh God, what to say. I should have written a script, shouldn't I, Cath? You would have, Ms Organised, Ms Never-let-the-buggers – whoever they might be – get-you-down. But I'm on my own, and I haven't got long – ha ha – inappropriate joke alert. But no, I mean Jo and the girls are out, which doesn't happen often these days. Though Jo knows I need my own space too. Jo is good like that. Jo is good, full stop. If there is a heaven, she'll get a first-class, one-way ticket – and then have to meet someone else, because I'm bloody sure I won't be there, ha ha – not. Because if there are some pearly gates, I'd actually quite like to make it through the damn things.

'Look, I always knew you weren't mad about her, Cath, but be kind, okay? She admires you hugely and is good at putting on a bit of a show when she's down. Not unlike someone else I could name.'

He pulls another stupid face and then reaches for a glass of water, taking several small sips before hanging onto it, his knuckles bulging white stones in his big thin hands.

'Sorry for being a bit of a crap brother. Not making enough of an effort. We took different paths and that sort of felt right – for me, anyway. Looking forwards, not backwards. But, we were always a part of each other, right, Cath? And thank you for how you've tried – I know how you've tried – to be there for me and so on. You never give up, Cath, it's one of your many giant superpowers as well as being annoying as hell. And if I could, I'd...'

A bout of coughing overwhelms him, and it is so hard to watch, I cover my face. Eventually, he stops for long enough to sip more water, and his chest quietens. If it is water. It would be water. By now. Surely. I get a glimpse – both remembered and imagined, on my sister-in-law's behalf – of the vigilance of life with an alcoholic: the drip-drip attrition of hope and energy, the Sisyphean labour of restart after restart, dragging the object of your hope and love up the hill, only to turn your back for an instant and find they have tumbled to the bottom again. Joanne took that on – took the baton from me – hanging on with that endurance of hers, out of loyalty, out of love. The woman had deserved a medal, not my infantile resentment.

Rob seems to have trouble swallowing a second sip – because he is trying to swallow another cough at the same time, by the look of it, containing the monster rather than succumbing to it. When he starts talking again, it is in a raspy rush, between shallow breaths, like a swimmer taking gulps between strokes.

'Look, this is a goodbye, Cath. That's the horrible point of this little film. The thing is, I can't have you there, when the grand finale comes. I just can't. Joanne understands. It would make the letting go so much harder – do you see? To have to leave you, on top of my own life. Your determination for me not to give up – that last time you came – telling me to fight – so excited about that new treatment trial I mentioned – it was – fucking hard to take – not peaceful, not peaceful at all, Cath. And I need peace, because I can't do it any more. Cancer is not a fight. It's a fucking disease and often, it kills you. That's why – forgive me, Sis – but I've always made it clear to Jo how difficult I find your visits, and how, when the crunch comes, I want it just to be her and... oh God – that's the car.'

His eyes widen with panic and he swivels his head towards the door, but with an old-man slowness that shows the extent of his frailty, the nearness of the final chasm.

'I'll get back to this – finish properly – no need for those violins just yet. Also want to talk to you about the old bastard. I keep thinking of him, much as I try not to. But he must be long gone, don't you think? Maybe he'll be waiting for me on the other side. Hah. Or more likely, one glimpse and he'll do another runner. Do ghosts see each other, do you think? I plan to haunt the fuck out of you, by the way, Sis. In the birds and the breezes, I'll be there. Gotta go now – love that man of yours – Al – you picked a winner there – more soon.'

I sink deeper into the chair, already pressing rewind.

26

CATHERINE

The almost-empty car park of Al's pub tightens the knots inside my stomach, as does the fact that neither of the two vehicles there – a blue van and an old Ford Escort – belong to Al. But it's not quite six o'clock and a dank, windy January Saturday night, so little wonder the place isn't exactly buzzing. I stay in the car for a few minutes, daunted by the prospect of a lonely wait at a table. Somewhere, a church bell strikes the hour and my brain leaps to the Seattle Zoom invitation sitting in my inbox, just an hour away. I have not wavered in my resolve, but even so, it is impossible not to be *aware* of it.

The prospect of seeing Al keeps jumping in and out of focus. With so much having happened since he left, I have no idea how – where – to begin to go into it all, let alone how he will react. My only plan is total honesty. There has been no last-minute costume change this time, no pre-departure dithering in front of the wardrobe mirror. I have washed my hair because it needed washing. I started to put on some make-up and then scrubbed it off, settling on moisturiser and lipsalve – the taste-free kind for which

Al has expressed a preference in the past, back in the days when he wanted to put his mouth on mine. I feel pared back, exposed, vulnerable, but completely myself. I want Al to want me, but I understand now, better than ever, that he is not 'mine'. Because no person 'belongs' to another person, not even a beloved twin.

For twenty-four hours, Joanne's words have continued to whirl and settle, merging with the indescribable mulch of sadness and elation wrought by my brother's 'little film'. Self-effacing, brave, funny, candid, diffident – so *himself* – each viewing makes me long to reach into the screen for the final hug he did not feel able to give. But in place of that – thanks to what I am beginning to recognise as the most astonishing of sisters-in-law – his words have given me peace of heart: a far greater gift. My darling brother. He wanted his own life – his own family, his own privacy – for his failings as well as his successes. He wanted not to have to be stuck in the trench of our beginnings, which is where I always took him. It hurts, but I get it. I have been the weaker twin, the one unable to let go.

Five-past six and the pub sign – an orange-red coat of arms under the words *Kings Arms* – is rocking precariously in the wind gusts. It is the place I remember from a few years back – it came up on the satnav as soon as I put in the name – but Al's and my last visit was on a sunny day, sitting out at the back in the beer garden. Now, I have to pull up my anorak hood and hunch my shoulders against the cold, glad of my sensible clothes. When, at ten-past six, a silver car sporting a taxi sign swings into the car park, pulling up by the entrance, I jog towards it. The Polo must have broken down. Or maybe Al decided to come by train and grabbed a cab at the station. But when the rear passenger door opens, a man in a leather jacket with a bushy ponytail hops out, followed by a woman in towering black boots and a padded beige coat. Moments later, the cab has swept off and the couple have disappeared inside.

With stiff, icy fingers, I tap at my phone, but there are no new messages since the vet's latest, heartening update that Belle is holding her own. I could write to Al – or call him – but I dare not. I have got so much wrong. He must come freely. He must *feel* free. He *is* free. *As am I*, I remind myself fiercely. Taking a deep breath, I plunge into the pub, only to find myself looking round a near-empty bar. Al is decent, I remind myself. He would never just stand me up. Something is delaying him – maybe another SOS from Ryan about Sadie and the baby. He will tell me, when he can.

I buy myself a ginger ale and take up a position at the furthest corner table, facing the door. The couple who arrived by cab are settled on bar stools, knees interlocked, laughing as they swig pints. Two men, sitting with the ease and weathered demeanour of regulars on a bench at a table under the window, barely glance up.

It has to be traffic, I tell myself, as the minutes grind on. It is traffic and I mustn't hassle him. I seek solace and diversion in the picture gallery on Rob's phone. There are thousands of photos, and I have been devouring each new sighting of my brother. Mostly, the images are of Joanne and the girls, steadily growing, altering, blossoming, while Rob – appearing less and less frequently – starts to do the opposite, turning thinner, greyer, frailer as, through the brutality of the metastasising tumours, his body starts to shrink from the world.

'Excuse me, Miss? Can I get you anything else?'

I drop Rob's phone back into my bag. 'No thanks, not right now.' Somehow, it is twenty-past six. Al, despite being a decent man, has not kept his word. Which means he has either lost his decency, or something terrible has happened. I grope for my phone.

> Al, sorry if you're driving, just wondering where you...

I am still typing when a message arrives.

> Jesus, Cath. Where ARE U?

I type back madly, my fingers missing letters.

> Me? I am HERE – and have been since well before 6. We agreed 6, right?

An instant later, my phone rings and Al's voice is booming in my ear.

'Cath, is this a wind-up? I've been sitting on my hands trying not to call. Are you hiding out the back or something?'

'No, Al, I am at a table in the front bar.'

'No, you are not. Because I am in the front bar – and I've checked the rest of the place, including the toilets... Cath, you have gone to the right place, haven't you?'

'Yes, Al. I am at The Kings Arms in Wareham, just like you—'

'The Kings *Head* in *Wimborne* is what I said.'

'Oh God, Al...' I feel sick as well as mortified. Al has started to laugh, but I don't know if it is from anger or incredulity. Fury or upset? Not to be able to tell makes me panicky because it's like I don't know him any more, like I've already lost him for good. I start gabbling about misremembering the pub name – about being a bit frazzled – before giving up and bursting out with the news about Belle instead, the easiest by far of the many reasons why my brain has been haywire.

'Run over? What? When?'

'Last night – Joanne came and—'

'Joanne?'

'It looks like she's pulling through – Belle – but it's still very—'

'You should have called me. Why didn't you call me?'

'I wasn't sure – I was trying to give you space – I—'

'Look, stay where you are. I'm on my way, okay? Fifteen minutes tops.'

'I should drive to you. I'm the one who's fucked up...'

'Do not move. I thought you weren't coming, Cath.' There is croak in his voice. 'I'm setting off now. Stay where you are. Do *not* move. Promise?'

'Promise.'

The waitress approaches and then quietly retreats. I stare at my phone screen till it goes fuzzy. This was not what I had envisaged. Nothing, it seems, is ever as I envisage. I pay for the ginger ale and go outside to wait, reasoning that it's only a few yards and therefore not breaking my promise. The wind has dropped and somewhere in the darkness, an owl hoots. A soft whoo-hoo, repeating like a heartbeat. As the church bell strikes the half-hour, I find the thing I have been endeavouring not to think about coming into focus: Oliver and Faith in Seattle. Faith, ushering Diane to the hairdressers, Oliver helping his father to set up the computer.

27

OLIVER & CATHERINE

Oliver flicked an eye to the wall clock, but it had only moved by a minute since his last glance. Across the room, with his back to it – almost on purpose, he decided – his father had parked his wheelchair at the jigsaw, which was progressing in its slow, painful way, a chunk or two more completed on each of Oliver's visits. He was working on the Pin Needle skyscraper now, still only at the base, building it up, piece by piece – actual brick by brick it felt like, given the length of time it was taking. Did he have his own demise in mind as the deadline? Oliver wondered, his mouth going dry at the thought of what staring down that narrowing tunnel must *really* feel like. His half-brother had gone through it, and one day – Lord help him – it would be his turn, and Faith's and... dear God, Amelia's. Death – it was always there. A fact of living. The deal struck. And yet all anyone could do – for their own sanity – was to try not to think about it. Oliver looked at that near-bald, mottled, now pitifully scabrous head bent over the puzzle. Somewhere inside, he had to be staring at the end head-on. Didn't he?

'Would you like a herb tea, Dad?'

'No thanks, son.'

'Or some water, for your pain medication?'

'I have taken my meds, thank you.'

At the sound of the front door opening, they exchanged looks, his father, with his poor locked neck, having to rock back in his chair to manage it. When Faith and his mother's voices broke the silence, his father's eyes widened. The two women had left a good ten minutes before. For the appointment at the salon. If it was cancelled, or his mom had changed her mind, then the whole Zoom scheme was off.

Oliver threw a look at his laptop, ready on the dining table in the corner. He would have to message Catherine and explain. Even if she was sticking to the decision not to show, which, from the silence since her speedy, firm refusal, Oliver was guessing she had.

Why should she oblige anyway? he had asked himself, his eyes blinking wide open at five o'clock that morning, despite the thick brocade curtains of his and Faith's luxury hotel room. The poor woman was fighting to save her relationship, quite apart from being in the depths of grief and a life-reconfiguration which it took no shrink-wisdom to realise would be churning for a good while yet. Her childhood traumas had been far worse than his: the physical and mental hurt, the *abandonment*. No, he would never blame Catherine for staying away.

'It's only us,' Faith chirruped, all fake joviality as they stepped into the room. 'We forgot our glasses, didn't we, Diane?'

'My *reading* glasses,' said his mother bitterly, 'and now I'm so worn out with all the up and down of the elevators and going back and forth through the parking lot, that I really don't know if I can *face* doing it over.'

'Your glasses are right here, dear.' His father had already steered his chair to the table, where the slim blue leather spectacles case sat right alongside the laptop via which – Oliver checked the clock – in exactly eight minutes – they would be logging in. 'You know you hate the bother of having to go get your hair seen to, Di,' his father went on, in his new, increasingly raspy voice, 'but then remember how good you feel afterwards.' He handed the case over. 'And now you'll be able to have a nice browse through all those magazines you love so well.'

Oliver didn't dare catch his eye, or Faith's, hovering in the doorway clutching the key to their rental and doing her best rendition of being-calm-against-the-clock. 'Okay, Diane?' she said brightly.

'Well, I guess I still have my coat on, don't I. Oliver, try and make him do *something* other than that darned puzzle, can you? It is so very bad for his eyes, but he won't listen to me.'

'Sure, Mom.' Oliver put his arm across her back and accompanied her to the door, his gut twisting at her inability – or refusal – to engage with the reality of his father's condition. Wheelchair-bound. Two months of life left – tops – at the last assessment. Eye-strain was hardly going to be high on the priority list. Who knew what mattered to his father now, except the jigsaw, and being comfortable, and making peace with Catherine – if indeed, that was what he wanted. The old man kept most of his thoughts to himself. Like he always had. Not unlike Robert, in fact, it struck Oliver suddenly, his thoughts jumping to how quiet his half-brother had been, how Catherine had always led the charge.

Please, Catherine, be there, he pleaded silently, once Faith and his mother had gone. Except who knew what she would bring to the encounter either? It could turn into a bloodbath of vitriol and recriminations. *So, if that's the plan, Catherine, please stay away*, he told her in his head, sick at the mere thought of having to bear witness to such demolition. The old man was so frail, and the truth remained that his half-sister possessed the capacity to be blunt to the point of cruelty. She had thrown wine over her brother's widow, for Christ's sake.

But the woman had a good heart too, deep down, Oliver assured himself, his eyes flicking yet again to the wall clock, where the second hand was ticking on, suddenly too fast for his liking. Only two and a half minutes left. It was time to get his father settled at the table.

* * *

I am glad I am in the car park, seeing Al before he sees me, his wide face pale and fixed behind the wheel as he swings into a space under the front lights of the pub. I glimpse Bobby, on the back seat, his Scooby-Doo face pressed against the window, sensing – because both the dogs always do – when a journey is about to end. As I step out of the shadows, he seems to sense me too, cocking his big, sticky-up ears in my direction.

'Al, I'm over here,' I call, because, having slammed the car door, Al is running towards the pub entrance. He stops, doing an almost comical cartoon of a double-take before cantering towards me instead. 'I am so sorry,' I say, when he is still several yards away. 'I am an idiot.'

'No, you are not.' He has come to a sudden halt, leaving some distance, breathing hard. He looks bigger than I remember somehow, more solidly built, more splendid. 'Wareham, Wimborne, kings with heads and arms – all of it so easily muddled.'

'Oh, Al.'

'Cathy.'

'This is just a date, I know.'

'Yes, it is...'

'But I need to make a sort of speech.'

'Uh-oh.' He takes a little skip-jump back – comedic again. At least I think so. I am finding it hard to think straight. 'Tell me quickly how Belle is first,' he growls.

'Broken leg, fractured pelvis, but they've been putting her back together with pins and a plate, and so far, so good, the vet says.'

He whistles softly, shaking his head.

'And Sadie?'

'All well for now. She's on folic acid and iron tablets; Ryan's a nervous wreck but in an okay way – more of a grown-up every time I look at him... Do you need to be somewhere else or something?'

His voice is sharp with hurt and disapproval, because I have – in some sort of spasm – tugged up my anorak sleeve to check my watch. It has gone seven o'clock. By five minutes. Awareness of the waiting now taking place four and a half thousand miles away has been building in my head like white noise.

'Al, I'm sorry, but the speech is going to have to wait.' I am fumbling with my phone, scrolling clumsily to find Oliver's link. 'The gist of it – so you know – is that I am sorry – for my obsessions, my ingratitude, for driving you away, for being blind, self-centred, selfish... I've been getting my head around so much... but I can't give up on us, Al... I'll try anything – grief counselling, couples counselling, Jungian dream analysis, ice baths – if you'd just give me another chance—'

'Cathy—'

'Please don't answer – bad news would be hard to take at this exact moment, because, yes, I *am* supposed to *be* somewhere else

– in the virtual sense...' I have found Oliver's email at last. 'My father is dying and he wants to speak to me, Al,' I gabble as I start, repeatedly, to tap the link, which won't open. 'Oliver has set up this Zoom call – with his she-devil mother out of the way. It was due to start five minutes ago. I said I didn't care and wouldn't be there... but now... now this bloody link won't work.'

'Send it to me,' Al says at once, 'and I'll get it up on my laptop. In your car would be best,' he shouts, already back at the Polo, withstanding a Bobby-bombardment in order to fish his computer out of a pile of stuff occupying the rest of the seat.

A couple of minutes later, I am on the back seat of my car with Al's laptop on my knees and Al outside, about to close the door. 'Al, stay with me – please?' I don't look up as I press the necessary buttons. How long would they wait? Two minutes? Ten? 'And why is your car so full?' I mutter, keeping my eyes fixed on Al's screen as he bundles himself in beside me and slams the door. On the laptop, the Zoom page keeps saying it's loading, but to no effect.

'Because, if you agree, I want to come home.'

'I do agree, Al. And this thing isn't working either.'

'Here, let me,' he says calmly, taking the laptop. 'I'll go back to the link and start again.'

I peer over his shoulder, making sure not to grab him – not yet – but close enough to feel the heat of him, the energy, the warmth, the capability. He remains concentrated on his task – deftly, speedily, moving the cursor from box to box, breathing in the slightly heavier way he always does when fully applying himself to anything. Through my churning apprehensions – I have no clue why I am doing this, or what I might say if the link eventually opens – I am overwhelmed too by a sense of Al – of us – coming back into focus.

'Rob had moved on,' I whisper, 'and I couldn't see it.'

'I know, Cathy. It's okay. Please forgive the cruel things I said. I was so strung out, so beyond having any answers. But you know what,' he shoots me a swift, sweet look, 'these last two weeks, you've not left my thoughts for one single second. I've been holding back so hard, trying to hang onto the space I said I wanted us to have. New Year's Eve – the thought of you having fun at the pub – it was unspeakable.'

'For me too,' I murmur, because it is no moment to go into anything, least of all Isaac.

'Ah, here we are – all systems go, darling.' He speaks softly, placing the computer back on my lap and shifting a little further away. 'Sure you want me to stay?'

I nod, as terrified as I have ever been, but also lost to a strange, mounting certainty that every step and misstep in my life has been leading to this moment, on the cold back seat of the car, with Al by my side, and my father about to flicker into view before my eyes. Except that it is Oliver's head that fills the screen, looking somewhat fuller of face, but otherwise exactly as I remember him from the funeral almost half a year before: kempt, smooth, the hint of a bulge to the light-green eyes, the longish hair brushed backwards, giving greater prominence to the strong jawline. 'Hey, Catherine, thanks for this; I really appreciate it.'

'Hello, Oliver. I nearly didn't come.'

'It's great that you have. He's just in the bathroom. He'll be right here. And for the record, I've no idea what he's going to say or how this will go.'

'That makes two of us. I have Al with me.'

'I am so pleased to hear that, Catherine. Can I say hi?'

I swivel the screen and Al raises a hand. 'Good evening, Oliver. We're in the car.'

'I can see that. I'm glad you could make it too, Alastair. It's

morning here – a big morning, I guess. Oh, here he comes now.'
Oliver continues talking as he stands up, replacing the screen
image of his face with a close-up of shirt buttons, a leather belt
and chinos. 'You okay there, Dad? Do you need some help? No?
Okay. Catherine is online and waiting right here for you.'

I reach for Al's hand, squeezing it hard enough to stop the
blood flow. The screen empties, leaving a stage set – a table-top,
a small green pot plant, half a window – and then a wheelchair
slowly slides into the frame. I see a brown lap blanket, papery,
liver-spotted hands, scaley with small sores, and then a grey,
home-knit jumper, shapeless with age and use, and finally, a
bowed head covered by a few baby strands of grey hair. The
head is too stiff to raise, I realise, as Oliver continues to adjust
the position of the chair and the angle of the laptop screen,
disappearing and returning with a lap tray to which he transfers
the computer, granting me my first view of two watery but
instantly familiar dark-brown eyes.

'Oh, Catherine, but it's good to see you.' The voice is low and
crumbly, and so strongly American that I would not, in a million
years, have recognised it. 'Oliver said you received my letter. How
are you, my dear?'

'I'm not sure.'

'I am sorry Robert has gone.'

'Me too.' There is spittle in the corners of a mouth I wouldn't
have recognised either, for how thin it has got – the lips shrunk
to a line. I feel nothing but numbness. 'Will you say hi if you see
him on the other side, do you think?' The words tumble out,
prompted by what I now know of Rob's own final thoughts –
how preoccupied he seemed to have been by this father of ours.
I can hear the wavering in my voice, the threat of something that
could become hysteria if I let it. 'Turns out he was wondering
about that, you see – he told me so, in a farewell message he

recorded before he...' I sense Al gawping at me as he gives a return squeeze to my hand. 'You know, before he went and died.'

'To see Robert again in the next world would be nice, Catherine. I never meant for things to turn out as they did for you two. I loved your mother very much. It was the worst thing when she passed. We were so happy with you both, our twins... but life takes you places you don't expect...' His voice, crackly from the start, disintegrates. Tears have begun spilling over the big red lower edges of his eyes and running from his nostrils, which are wide and hairless. Oliver's hand appears, attempting to deliver a large clean blue handkerchief, and then performing some clumsy mopping of the old man's face when the attempt is ignored.

'Yes, life can be unexpected, you're right about that...' The word *Dad* sits in my gullet. I try to conjure something to add – a platitude – anything – but all I can think is how awful he looks, how close to being dead.

'Is that enough for now? Do you want to say goodbye, Dad?' Oliver prompts after a few moments of us both being silent.

'We loved Mum too,' I blurt, 'Rob and I. And Granny Jean. And Pip. And you. We loved what we all used to have, okay, Dad?'

'Okay, Catherine,' he rasps. 'Thank you, dear. I loved you and Robert too. Losing touch... it has been my greatest sorrow. I should never have let it happen. Forgive me. Goodbye, my dear... Sorry, but I'm a little tired now...'

Oliver's face appears, mouthing, *Thank you,* and deploying the blue handkerchief to wipe off his own damp cheeks. Then the screen goes blank and we are done.

Al moves closer, putting his arm round me and rubbing my shoulder. He tells me everything will be all right, and I believe him.

A few moments later, my phone lights up with a notification from Oliver.

> Thank you, Catherine. You are one remarkable woman. One day, I'd like for us to meet up again. If – when – you are ready. No pressure, ever. Your brother, Oliver x

EPILOGUE

It is an early May morning, bright and hot enough to feel like high summer, when a stop-start email correspondence leads at last to a date for visiting the manor house. I would be arriving across the fields, on foot, if that was all right, I had explained on the phone, and the woman had said fine, she would leave the padlock on the lower garden gate open so that I could find my way to the front door, and to be sure to check for ticks because the grass was long and it was that time of year.

I park in the clearing by the river bend so that I am facing back down the lane, like I did the last time. My clearing – my lane – it feels like now, with a dead-end sign that had been too buried in undergrowth for me to notice it before. My river bend. I have left the dogs with Al and brought my wellies, in case I need them for crossing, but the water level, thanks to a dry spring, is low and the chunks of broken bridge stick out like giant ill-arranged teeth, offering themselves as easy stepping stones. Staying in my summer sandals, I stroll along the bank first, making myself remember my two swims, one exultant, one full of near-deadly despair. Stones in my pockets and the job would have been done. Virginia Woolf style. But that idea had never occurred to me, I muse, recalling instead, with grateful wonderment, how, on plunging in, nothing had entered my head except the immediate, urgent need to surface. To breathe. To live. Even in a Rob-less, mother-less world. And then there was the little girl, of course, with her disarming questions, easing the journey back from the brink.

I have brought a few flowers from Al's and my small tangle of a garden. Poppies, daisies, buttercups and forget-me-nots, somewhat weather-beaten, but their colours – yellow, red, blue, white and the bright green of their delicate stems – make quite a palette. I lob them, one by one, into the water, taking my time, thinking of Rob – because that is why I am here. But myriad other things spool through my mind too. Like my father, dying in his sleep within twelve hours of our Zoom back in January – because I gave him peace, Oliver claimed kindly (because Oliver *is*, unrelentingly, kind). And Tam, still happily shuttling between Dublin and the bungalow, open about needing her own life as well as Jules. And Sadie and Ryan, in talks with a music producer, while still trying to process the prospect of becoming parents to twins, one baby having managed to hide behind the other for the first scan. *Twins!* Every time Al says the word, he dances me round, going mad, asking how I feel and whether I am *okay* with it, which I am. Beside myself, in fact. Life, you just couldn't make it up.

Feeling observed, I swivel round, half-expecting to see the little girl in her too-big wellies, but there is only a robin, hopping bravely close, cocking its head from side to side as if pondering a conundrum, or a wise comment for him to know and me to guess. As I set off towards the stepping stones, it hops after me, keeping a weather eye, and I smile, remembering the words in my brother's farewell and thinking *surely not.*

The lumps of stone are solid and inviting. Glancing to my right when I am halfway across, I notice a perfectly sturdy wooden footbridge a little further round the river bend, weathered enough to have been there quite some time. A safe bridge all along! It seems like such a perfect manifestation of my own blindness – excelling at not seeing beyond my own nose, picking the hard route when there was an easier one within reach – that I emit a hoot of a laugh, causing the robin to whizz off to the safety of a high branch.

Ahead, the handsome terracotta brick walls, white framed windows and tall chimneys of the manor house rise out of its big green oasis of a garden like a scene from a fairytale. Hotels in old buildings can make fine, photogenic venues for every sort of event, but there is nothing like the authenticity of a real home. The owners' photos have not done the place justice, I decide, pausing – as soon as I am safely on the far bank – to take a couple of snaps for Tam, before striking out across the field, deciding not to worry about ticks because the brush of grass against my bare legs feels so good. Tam, I know already, will take no persuading – we'll soon have clients queueing up for bookings this year and beyond. But suddenly, it's not clients I am picturing, but Al and me, on a glorious summer day exactly like this one. I have gone full pre-Raphaelite, with a long floaty floral dress and a garland of flowers on my head. Al is towering beside me, nailing a yellow silk waistcoat and a pale-grey linen suit, with a huge white rose sticking out of the top buttonhole.

A *non*-wedding, I tell myself, giving my imagination permission to run riot: with rings and personal vows, exchanged in front of friends and family and the dogs, both sporting white neckerchiefs in honour of the occasion and causing mayhem as they bomb around – Belle's still-improving limp having done nothing to impede her energy for charging after rabbits, squir-

rels and an unguarded cocktail sausage or three. I see my
nieces, Stephanie and Laura, in their own floaty dresses and
daisy-chain coronets, dancing shyly to whatever Sadie – a
sinuous S-shape with her gloriously full womb – and Ryan are
playing and singing behind their mics on a little stage under a
gazebo on the edge of the main lawn. Joanne will be looking
on – of course – but also holding the hand of the gardener who
has recently been announced as a 'close friend'. Most clearly of
all, I picture Oliver, schmoozing in his easy American way,
keeping an arm round Faith and a hand held out for Amelia,
his attention and ready smile always there for me if I seek
them out. He would make a good speech, if asked. *I am the lost
brother who got found*, he might say. And when it came to my
turn, before eulogising about Al, I would say that Oliver did
the finding, and that having lost one brother, I was lucky
enough to discover another, and that I know Rob would have
agreed.

Oh yes, there is a lot to think about as I cross the field – not
just dreams for the future, but all the unexamined days, weeks,
months, years which have gone before, now scuttling out from
their dank, dark places thanks to the counsellor who is helping
me dare to examine them. No judgments, no directions, no
anything except what I want to say and need to feel. A 'safe
space' and all that *blah*, I report after each session to Al, who
nods and grins, never saying I told you so or asking questions,
because he is wise and loving and knows that *blah* doesn't begin
to cover it.

The padlock has been left open as promised, and the garden
– ebullient in its early-summer glory from any angle – could win
awards.

'Welcome,' says a woman, when I have barely placed one
foot on the lawn, emerging from a blue tunnel of wisteria that

matches the blue scarf-hairband keeping her long grey hair off her face.

'What an absolutely stunning place, and so secluded,' I say once we have shaken hands and introduced ourselves. 'Thank you for letting me come from the river – it's a spot I've visited a couple of times and really love.'

'Yes. The children used to enjoy themselves down there, back in the day, gosh, forty years ago now.' She seems to hesitate. 'We do still love it – all the more so, actually, because it's where our youngest died.'

'Oh, my goodness, I am *so* sorry – I didn't mean to—'

'It's okay. I like to talk about her. She was our surprise – the last of our four. A good little swimmer, but it was winter and she was wearing wellingtons, so... Forgive me. I spent years *not* mentioning her, and now I grab every opportunity. But that's not what you have come for. So now,' she dusts her palms briskly, 'let me give you a guided tour, and then maybe you would like a cup of tea? We shall be good at making ourselves scarce when required, I assure you,' she chatters on, 'being lucky enough to have a house in London. Wimbledon, not far from the park. I have a smaller garden there of course, which I can manage without help...'

I let her words drift around me as we walk. There could be rational explanations, but I find that I do not want to seek them, nor to ask if the wellingtons of her little girl were black and a little too large. I think of the wry, friendly robin, and of my index finger deciding to include Oliver in the short list of addressees to be notified of Rob's death; and of Tam at a bus stop in the rain meeting Jules, and of Al, who was both not my type and exactly what I needed. I think of how mystery and serendipity surround us – shape us – and whether there is even a difference between the two.

You would have loved this place, I tell Rob, as I smile and nod at my host. In the same instant, a sense of my brother engulfs me, from the tips of my toes to every follicle on my scalp, filling me with joy and light and warmth, dissolving all my grief to love.

* * *

MORE FROM AMANDA BROOKFIELD

Another emotional, page-turning read from Amanda Brookfield, *Life Begins*, is available to order now here: https://mybook.to/LifeBeginsBackAd

ACKNOWLEDGEMENTS

Huge thanks to thank my extraordinary, pioneering publishers, Boldwood Books, for their unfailing support and know-how in getting this, my nineteenth novel, into the best shape possible and onto a global radar of readers that expands with each book. The world of publishing has become the fiercest of jungles, and Boldwood navigates every avenue of it fearlessly and expertly, while this lucky author can only look on in grateful wonder.

Behind every novelist there are longsuffering loved ones, especially if that novelist happens to spend much of her creative process racked with doubts, and eager to off-load each and every one of them... I cannot thank my two sons, Ben and Ali, and their dear partners, Georgie and Grace, enough for their steadfast patience and encouragement in the face of this. Their belief in me never falters and remains vital to my ability to believe in myself.

Finally, unquantifiable gratitude goes to my partner, David Langslow, for being all that a writer dreams of – loving supporter and indefatigable sounding-board, as well as a supremely accomplished reader-editor of final drafts. Cath, Rob and Oliver's story is all the sharper for his gentle eagle-eye.

Amanda Brookfield

April 2025

ALSO BY AMANDA BROOKFIELD

Alice Alone

A Cast of Smiles

The Wrong Man

A Summer Affair

The Godmother

Marriage Games

A Family Man

Single Lives

The Lover

Sisters and Husbands

Relative Love

The Simple Rules of Love

Life Begins

Before I Knew You

The Love Child

For the Love of a Dog

Good Girls

The Other Woman

The Split

The Twin

ABOUT THE AUTHOR

Amanda Brookfield is the bestselling author of many novels including *Good Girls*, *Relative Love*, *The Split*, and a memoir, *For the Love of a Dog* starring her Golden Doodle Mabel. She lives in London and has recently finished a year as Visiting Creative Fellow at University College Oxford.

Sign up to Amanda Brookfield's mailing list for news, competitions and updates on future books.

Visit Amanda's website: www.amandabrookfield.co.uk

Follow Amanda on social media:

facebook.com/amandabrookfield100
x.com/ABrookfield1
instagram.com/amanda_and_mabel_brookfield
bookbub.com/authors/amanda-brookfield

BECOME A MEMBER OF
THE
SHELF
CARE
CLUB

The home of Boldwood's
book club reads.

Find uplifting reads,
sunny escapes, cosy romances,
family dramas and more!

Sign up to the newsletter
https://bit.ly/theshelfcareclub

Boldwood

Boldwood Books is an award-winning fiction publishing company seeking out the best stories from around the world.

Find out more at www.boldwoodbooks.com

Join our reader community for brilliant books, competitions and offers!

Follow us
@BoldwoodBooks
@TheBoldBookClub

Sign up to our weekly deals newsletter

https://bit.ly/BoldwoodBNewsletter

Printed in Dunstable, United Kingdom

72095593R00193